THE
TIGERCLAW
TREE

P.A. KRISHNAN

TRANQUEBAR PRESS
An imprint of westland ltd

61, II Floor, Silverline Building, Alapakkam Main Road, Maduravoyal, Chennai 600095
93, I Floor, Sham Lal Road, Daryaganj, New Delhi 110002

First published in India by Penguin Books India Pvt Ltd, 1998

This edition published in India in TRANQUEBAR by westland ltd

10 9 8 7 6 5 4 3 2 1

ISBN: 978-93-80658-62-9

Typset in Garamond by Arun Bisht

Contents

Acknowledgements

I am grateful to T. Nambi Krishnan, my nephew, who goaded me into writing this book and who was my first reader; Dominic Goodall, that gentle friend, who went through the manuscript with a magnifying glass; P.R. Rengaramanujum, R.S. Ramaswamy, Ashok Malik, Venkata Swaminathan and Sundara Ramaswamy who read the manuscript with interest and gave several useful suggestions; and Ian Mitchell, my literary agent. I am also indebted to Revathi, my wife, without whose selfless support this book would not have been possible and Siddharth, my son, whose table and chair I usurped while typing the manuscript.

I am thankful to Vidwan N.S. Krishna Iyengar for giving me useful information on Nanguneri and its Matam.

I consulted a selection of books for historical material: *Va-Ve-Su Iyer* by R.A. Padmanabhan; *Bharathi—Kalamum Karuthum* by T.M.C. Raghunathan in Tamil; *Peasant History in South India* by David Ludden; *Kasturi Renga Iyengar* by V.K. Narasimhan; *Bal Gangadhar Tilak* by T.V. Parvate; *The Tinnelveli District Gazetteer, 1917; South Indian Rebellion* by Rajayyan and *The Nationalist Movement in Tamil Nadu 1905-14* by N. Rajendran.

I am indebted to A.K. Ramanujan for his splendid translation of Nammalwar and the Sangam poetry.

The Descendants of Raman and Ponna

Raman – Ponna
(b.1865)(b.1871)

Nammalwar – Lakshmi
(b.1887)   (b.1895)

Andal
(b.1891)

Pakshi – Veda
(b.1889)(b.1897)

Madhurakavi – Kamala
(b.1911)   (b. 1916)

Tirumalai – Renganayaki
(b. 1914)   (b.1920)

Nambi – Rosa
(b.1941)(b.1937)

Kannan
(b.1947)

Radha
(b.1954)

Indu
(b.1972)

The Tigerclaw Tree

What she said

Friend, listen.

I'll not think any more
of that man on whose sandy shore
   birds occupy the tigerclaw tree
   and play havoc
   with the low flowering branches,
and my eyes will get some sleep

Ammuvanar
Ainkurunuru 142
Translated from one of the eight
anthologies of classical Tamil literature
by A.K. Ramanujan

The tigerclaw tree is *pulinakakonrai* in Tamil and *Cassia sophera* in Latin. The botanical name is *caesalpinia mimosoides Lam.* Its flowers look like tiger's claws.

Prologue 1970

*P*ERIA PATTI'S BED WAS AT LEAST A FOOT AWAY from the nearest wall and its legs were inside round stainless-steel bowls of water. The white ceiling was smooth and gleaming. The sheets and pillow covers were clean and they retained the comforting warmth of freshly-ironed linen. Even the harmless lizards scurrying all over the walls till a few days ago had been chased away by the servant. Ants were the problem. Irritating ants that had destroyed her sleep. They were thick on the last road of her life's journey, a journey she started almost a century ago.

She did not want to open her eyes but if she had she would have made out the lovely silhouette of her great-granddaughter sitting on a stool nearby. Her hearing was still sharp and the pleasant rustle of pages being turned told her that Radha was reading a book. At Radha's age she did not have a moment to sit at this time of the day. She would probably have been in the kitchen helping her mother-in-law. Books were sacred commodities for girls then, worshipped every year on Saraswathi Puja but rarely opened. Like her weary, goo-filled eyes.

At Radha's age she was suckling Nammalwar. He came running to her for milk whenever the mood took him till he was four; she had at times to give suck from both breasts to Nammalwar and to his younger brother, Pakshi. Though she was still full of milk when Andal came, the child did not relish her milk. It was cow's milk that gave Andal the plumpness which she never lost until her death. Nammalwar, even when he was a child, did not have one ounce of extra flesh. Great-grandmother's mind, which had swiftly effaced the episodes of the recent past to retain those of distant years, had imprinted on it several montages of her first son, Nammalwar. She did not see him going out of the house on that rain-washed day sixty years ago but she remembered his face when she had spoken to him harshly the night before. That was the last time she spoke to him.

The pulley screeched. The rope must be rushing through Shenbagam's palms, mildly scratching them. Presently she heard the sound of the vessel breaking the surface and water gushing into it. How many times have I heard this tireless sound? This is the sound of my existence. The dreary days when the well was dry – did I live those days?

The screech started again, noisier now, with the vessel coming up. There was no one in this house to tell that half-wit of a maid to oil the pulley. She wanted to murmur a command but changed her mind. She had been with the screech for so long its absence would be unbearable. Its return might take months and she did not have months. She suddenly realised that the other familiar sound was missing. Radha must have switched off the ceiling fan to keep her flowing hair tidy. Where is my hair? Her thin translucent hand touched her head. The prickly stubble hurt her. Why did I touch my head? The nest of these infernal ants is there. Her right leg, swollen, dark red, about to explode, demanded to be shifted. Should I shift it? The very thought exerted her and she opened her eyes to exorcise the ants.

It was a glorious late evening. The door leading to the courtyard and the well was ajar. The sun had nearly set but the room still appeared bright. I shall walk. I shall walk very slowly to the well. The smooth cement tub must be full of water. Shenbagam must have freshly filled it. I shall have a hundred-mug bath. Will these tenacious ants be washed away? Water may not cleanse minds. The light, so gentle and diffuse, had begun to irritate her. Why am I angry with light? Once I was very friendly with her and did everything in her presence, she thought. On that night too there was an earthen lamp. Its dying light shone upon the snake-bite boy, his capacious chest and his frightened face. That terrible night, into which the boy had dissolved, remains with me all these years, stubbornly refusing to go. She closed her eyes again. Sleep overtook her temporarily, freeing her from the ants.

Radha closed the book she was reading. She was going on eighteen, radiant and still untouched by the harshness of life. She knew she was reading a great book, but its greatness had not overwhelmed her. The dark brooding characters of *Crime and Punishment* did nothing to dampen her spirits. The epic human conflicts of the novel seemed far away in a never-to-be-visited land. Hers were routine, immediate and usually enjoyable. What a strange brother I have, she thought. Why was Kannan insistent that I should read this book? He is peculiar, but is he so weird that he imagines himself to be Rodia? Am I Dunia? I must finish this book and ask Kannan. On an impulse, Radha checked the year of publication. 1866. This old woman was not yet born when the book first came out, but just five years separate them. The lady is ancient and stubbornly refusing to go. Why should she?

Great-grandmother is saying something. 'What is it, peria paati?'

She stood up and bent closely over her great-grandmother to unravel her words but without success. She saw a fine dew of sweat glistening in the crevices of the old woman's forehead. I should switch on the fan. She walked away from the bed towards the wall, but stopped midway. Three days ago a mindless sparrow, intent on building a safe nest, came flying in and was struck dead by the rotating blades. Its soft little carcass fell on the old lady's chest and remained there till Radha came. The old woman was aware of what fell on her but she was deep within herself and did not brush the sparrow away. When Radha saw her, tears were streaking down her cheeks and her eyes pleaded that the fan should never run.

The great-granddaughter looked around and saw the palmyra-leaf fan wedged between the big wooden chest and the wall. She pulled out the sickly yellow kidney-shaped fan and began waving it over her face.

The fan seemed to infuse life into the objects on the bed. The limp threads – green, red, white and ochre – sticking out from the corners of the pillow cover started swaying gently and the thin cotton bed sheet puffed up in places, breathing. The lady was still. Her wispy stubble was too short to come to life. It still had abundant specks of black.

Radha found something new every time she observed her great-grandmother's room closely. This time it was a thick black walking stick standing in one corner. How did I miss it? The casing at the top is definitely silver. It must have been hiding behind the reed mat that had been there. Its elephant finial has become rounded due to use, and smooth probably due to age. This is definitely a man's stick; why, it must be heavier than peria paati. Probably *peria thatha*'s. No, great-grandfather died in his thirties.

She remembered that her grandfather toyed with the idea of getting a wheelchair for the old woman which he thought, strangely, would not impair her dignity, but did not have the courage to persuade her to use it. Now she is just too frail. Old age plunders dignity in a relentless, cruel way. This woman, though, must have secret, minuscule packets of it.

The ants were at work again. Why am I not thinking of the Lord? The *Prabandham* has deserted me. I could recite all four thousand of them but today I don't remember even one hymn. The debris that I had thrown out of my mind long ago has centre stage. These ants, they have dragged it back. The hymns have flown away but the taste of that infernal liquid is still with me after all these years.

Radha realised that the old woman was murmuring again. She leaned close.

'*Kallu venum.*'

Radha did not understand. 'Stone, paati? You mean the diamond ring?'

One of peria paati's ancestors had been a Sanskrit scholar of repute. He accompanied the sixteenth *Jiyar* of the Great Srivaishnava *Matam* of Nanguneri on his visit to Trivandrum to worship at the Padamanabha Temple. The Maharaja of Travancore came to receive him. Unlike other kings, he was a person of infinite curiosity and he wanted from the Jiyar an exposition of Srivaishnava philosophy. The Jiyar commanded the scholar, who gave such a lucid exposition that the Maharaja was immensely pleased and gave the scholar a ring set with a big diamond. This heirloom was the pride of the family and every child of the family born after that momentous event had worn it for a moment on its first birthday. The ring must be with grandfather.

The old woman shook her head. Her eyes were still closed.

'Kallu. Kallu.'

She was not sure what the old woman wanted. Did she want toddy? Or liquor? Great-grandmother's strange requests were usually familiar to Radha. The old woman plucked things from memory at unexpected moments and demanded to see them in their physical form. They were mostly eatables or objects she had once used. When an eatable was brought she took a tiny bit of it and kept it in her mouth until it dissolved or was swallowed. When it was an object she peered at it and felt it and smelt it or listened to it – once she demanded an ormolu clock which had lost its golden glint and long stopped ticking, and Pakshi had to find a clock-repairer to make it tick again before it was brought to her. Only rarely did she ask for things that were unintelligible to others and even if they had been so initially, Pakshi generally unravelled her demands. She never asked for persons except for Pakshi. She then demanded to see Nammalwar.

Radha gently shook her but the old lady had again lapsed into sleep. The girl tiptoed across the room, bolted the door to the courtyard from inside and went out of the other door to the corridor that ran alongside the dying woman's room. A flight of five rough-hewn stone steps led up to the main house. She stood on the third step for a moment, and through the shafts of evening light suffused with drunken dust, could see Shenbagam at the entrance of the house gathering water in her cupped hand from a bucket and spattering it to dampen the earth. Radha remembered that the Lord of the Temple would be in procession shortly. She reached the threshold in a few leaps.

Her grandfather Pakshi, a shrivelled-up old lawyer, was in his rocking chair on the veranda and squatting at his feet was his hapless client, silent and head bowed in supplication. He had stopped practicing long ago to return to his village, Nanguneri, for a restful life, but old faithfuls still came to him for advice. In a voice at once grating and surprisingly youthful, the lawyer was berating the client for his sins and his forefathers for having brought him forth. He halted his tirade when he saw his granddaughter.

'How is she?'

'She asks for kallu. I don't know what she means by that. Do you have any idea, thatha?'

'Kallu? Is she by any chance asking for the ring?'

'No. I asked her. She just shook her head.'

'I must ask Nambi, the great doctor, Mr Know-all, if that idiot condescends to return to this house.'

Nambi was Radha's cousin. He was Nammalwar's grandson.

'What is going on between you and Nambi, thatha?'

'Don't expect me to discuss these matters in front of this nincompoop,' thatha said in English.

Radha realised that her grandfather's anger had turned back upon the poor client. She quietly went behind the old man and took a tin container of rice flour from a niche in the wall. She had recently learnt a few intricate *kolam* patterns from her friend and she would draw one of them today to please the Lord in procession, the Lord perched on the majestic Garuda, Pakshiraja, the raja of birds, after whom her grandfather was named.

The Departure

One

I

PERIA PAATI HAD A NAME TOO when she was young. It was not an orotund Sanskrit name. It was an appealing Tamil one, common among Iyengars of the Tenkalai – the Southern sect. She was Ponnamma, the golden lady, which shrank to Ponna almost immediately after her birth. Ponna was normal and emaciated like other Brahmin children until she was eleven. Her catarrhal nose always had dried flakes of blood at the nostrils and she kept picking at them all the time. The catarrh stopped miraculously when she reached the threshold of puberty. She shot up and overtook her father. Her inexorable blooming, which was unlike that of other ordinary Brahmin girls of her age, and the spellbinding sheen she unconsciously radiated alarmed everyone in the house.

Her mother, who wore a permanent ring of resignation round her head and rarely stirred out of the fuliginous kitchen of her seedy house, was now worried about her child's blossoming but she had never learnt to complain noticeably. Ponna's grandmother was different. Normally a dull and practical windbag, now despairing of Ponna's progress, she found herself filled with an uncommon imagination. That girl could not have been sired by my son, she thought, looking at the lanky girl whose lemon breasts had begun to hop about. She had an irrational faith in her son's non-existent talents but even faith had its limits. 'The girl is definitely of different seed. She does not have any of our features,' the old woman cried aloud and listed out in her singsong wail a litany of her son's acts of incompetence right from the day of his marriage. Ponna's father did not answer his mother because he was conscious that most of what she said was true. Yet he did know that her main complaint was not true and that it was perhaps his only act of competence.

During those early days of sexual bliss he never let his wife out of sight. The Jiyar for whom he was cooking had had a serious stomach ailment then and he had no other work. He was always hovering around her with intent and her mild protests were rightly taken as invitations or violently brushed aside. Even during the days of her monthly bleeding when she was banished to a dark, dank, dirty room at the end of the house he insisted on sleeping in the corridor next to the room, though it was often enveloped in a sort of menstrual miasma. He kept an unswerving eye on his wife until she was heavy with Ponna. The bliss petered out after her birth, though copulation became a function to be performed regularly like other chores. Ponna's mother carried the burdens of that function year after year, which dried her up completely. None of those burdens, so assiduously borne and painfully delivered by her after unvarying brushes with death, grew to be anything substantial. Two survived for a while, only to give up the unequal struggle. Most of them were parcelled up, on arrival, in dirty rags and quietly buried. Such events were ablutionary and they rarely invoked tears or remembrance. Ponna's father could understand them. But he could never comprehend his daughter's efflorescence amidst the ruins of his existence. He too was sorry that he had an extraordinary daughter.

'She is long past the age of marriage. Who will marry her now? Her bleeding is going to start any moment. If a Brahmin girl is unmarried at the time of her puberty, the rain god will not come anywhere near the place she lives. And I don't see the signs of rain this year. The whole community is gossiping about her and about you and your husband's incompetence,' lamented the mother-in-law. She paused for breath and wailed suddenly in a shrill voice, 'Why don't you drown in the tank? And take that devil too with you.'

Ponna's mother had inured herself long ago to these barbs. She calmly said, 'The tank doesn't have enough water even to wash our feet. Where am I to drown? I don't have the strength either to drag that girl with me.'

She brought her mother-in-law a tumbler of buttermilk that she knew would mollify her and said, 'These are testing times for us. The Lord's ways are inscrutable.'

She saw that her mother-in-law's ire had subsided and she continued, 'Why don't you ask your son to request the Jiyar to find a groom for Ponna? I have been telling him every day, but I don't know why he is hesitant. They say the Jiyar raves about his *puliyodarai* and will do anything to please your son. More than that, he was your husband's best friend.'

II

The cook had been serving the Jiyar for more than twenty-five years but had never spoken to him at a stretch for more than a minute or two. He wanted to escape from Nanguneri and start a small eating place for Iyengars in Tirunelveli, the big town about twenty miles from the village, but had never managed to ask the Jiyar to lend him the capital required, a sum of one hundred rupees. He slogged quietly in the kitchen dreaming about the life he would have led if his father's successes had not been ephemeral.

The eighteenth Jiyar himself was worried about the impending failure of the rains that year. He walked slowly from his Matam, the monastery that squatted next to the splendid temple of Lord Vanamamalai, towards the massive irrigation tank whose southern embankment almost touched the walls of the temple and the Matam. He climbed up the steps leading to the canopied bathing ghat and looked around. This tank is one of the most glorious gifts of the Lord when it is full, thought the Jiyar. Now, its floor is visible and has the mushy consistency of jaggery syrup. The rivulets that bring water into it from the Western Ghats have all run dry. In a few days, as the sun relentlessly saps its moisture, the tank floor will crack into a massive, crooked chessboard with millions of crazy squares. The rice fields beyond its banks will be decimated slowly and the peasants will wring their hands and roundly curse the Lord. Our tradition is that the Lord has personally chosen Nanguneri as one of his abodes on earth. Why he has done so is not given to us to know. Perhaps it is his way of showing that he too can rough it out when he wants to, like most of his children. In the distance, he could see people bathing in the Jiyar's spring right at the centre of the tank. Narayana, the Jiyar prayed, at least don't let the spring go dry.

The temple of the Lord to whom the Jiyar had addressed his prayers was once under the control of the Namboodiri Brahmins from Travancore. The aridity of the Nanguneri landscape perhaps made the Namboodiris long for the undying verdure of their homeland. When an ascetic of the Tenkalai sect of the Iyengars who came to worship in the temple in the year 1447 showed an interest in taking over its administration, the Namboodiris gave him the temple keys and quietly retired to their rainy Travancore. The ascetic was the first Jiyar of the Matam and an unbroken line of Jiyars succeeded him right into the twentieth century.

The Jiyar was the lone ascetic of his monastery and it was he who nominated his successor when he sensed that his end was near. He had absolute control over the Matam and its wealth. As the foremost religious arbiter of the Tenkalai school of

Srivaishnavas, the Jiyar had disciples among both Iyengar Brahmins and Vishnu-worshipping non-Brahmins. But the Jiyar was a resident of Nanguneri and his relationship with its Iyengars, many of whom were his employees and from among whom he was usually nominated, had always been special. They ran to him with their problems and he usually found solutions for them.

The cook's father came to Nanguneri from another village to study in the Sanskrit school run by the Matam, like his forefathers before him, since it provided free education and board for Srivaishnava pupils. The Jiyar – this was before his becoming an ascetic – was his classmate and though they were close friends, the Jiyar was as nondescript as the cook's father was brilliant. At the tender age of sixteen, when the others were struggling with their Kalidasa and Magha, the cook's father could recite verse after verse of *Kumara Sambhava* and mastered the poems of *Sisupalavadha*. He could have become a great teacher of Sanskrit and Srivaishnava theology had he not chanced upon a hoard of palm-leaf manuscripts that remained unread for centuries in the Matam's library.

The manuscripts, he claimed, were Nature's infinite book of secrecy and they could convey to him everything: all that existed and would ever exist. No one disputed this because no one could decipher the manuscripts. Before he attained the age of twenty the cook's father became the most sought-after astrologer in the many villages and towns of the Tirunelveli region. His prophetic powers became legendary, and as his fame spread, every noteworthy event of the region was rumoured to have been forecast by him. His forecasts of floods, famines and epidemics and once of a construction of a great bridge across the river Tamraparani proved to be uncannily correct. His enemies pointed out that one need not be an astrologer to predict these occurrences, but his enemies were not many. People whose future had been correctly foretold by him spread the message of his skills and those who were disappointed were not chatty enough. There was even talk that he was once considered for the special appointment of Government Astrologer by Sir Thomas Munro, the Governor of Madras Presidency, and that it was the missionaries who persuaded the Governor to drop the idea as it would have seriously impaired their conversion plans. In any case he would have refused the offer had he received one, so the astrologer said, as he had been invited by the Zamindar of Chokkampatti to be his Court Astrologer. He left his village on a grand day when the stellar arrangements according to the manuscripts were identical to those of the days when ancient monarchs set off on conquests. He never returned to his village again.

Valangai Puli Thevar, the Zamindar of Chokkampatti, was one of those repulsive characters whose name local mothers used to frighten their children to sleep. His pastime was brigandage and his victims were the neighbouring zamindars. Whenever he was short of money, which he frequently was, he replenished himself by raiding the treasury of a nearby zamindar. The British, who were usually severe with such robber-zamindars, tolerated him, probably for reasons political.

The astrologer was familiar with these depredations, for the Zamindar's partners in crime comprised, almost wholly, the Nanguneri Maravas, who were expert brigands and who always consulted the astrologer before embarking on a mission. The Zamindar treated his chattles harshly, but the astrologer had thought, naïvely as it transpired later, that he would be treated differently because of the Zamindar's abiding faith in astrology. His initial days in Chokkampatti were good, as luck was in his favour. With the passage of years however his ineffectiveness became embarrassingly evident. Some said his precious manuscripts had mysteriously disappeared. Others said his nocturnal activities dissipated him so much that he had lost the skill of reading them. The increasing number of Chokkampatti widows began to blame him and his faulty matching of horoscopes for the premature departures of their husbands, but the crunch came when he fixed an auspicious date for the Zamindar, after innumerable calculations, to go on a great tiger hunt. The jungles around Chokkampatti abounded in tigers and the Zamindar's seconds were competent enough. Still the hunt, as some enemies of the Zamindar had claimed to have expected, reversed itself and the principal hunter barely escaped being mauled to death by an irate tiger. Though the astrologer desperately claimed it was the zodiac arrangements of the day that deprived the tiger of its dinner, His Highness was not impressed. He darkly hinted that there could be other ways of feeding the famished tiger. The astrologer left Chokkampatti hurriedly that night.

The next few years, which saw the arrivals of a daughter and a son, were spent in faraway Indore. He discovered that the people of Indore had an irrational reverence for South Indian Brahmins and that the thicker the *tiruman,* which marked his status as a Tenkalai Iyengar, on his forehead, the larger was the crowd that thronged to consult him. His language, a hotchpotch of Sanskrit, Brahmin Tamil and a few basic Hindustani verbs, was sufficiently nebulous to convince his clients that he said what they had wanted him to say and they all were greatly satisfied. Indore however had its noxious winters and they brought him near his death. The wood smoke aggravated his asthma and the freezing cold always succeeded in piercing his thick swathe of shawls and benumbing him. His agony made him long for the green bananas and *keerai* of the Tamraparani plains, miles away from Indore. Though he plodded on for a number of winters, he had to give up eventually and retreat to the south.

It was after a perilous journey of six months that the astrologer appeared in Sankarankoil, a small town about thirty miles north of Tirunelveli. It was a hot, dirty, dry and pestilential town, but the cold-shocked soothsayer found it heavenly. He could go bare-chested and the heat was even strangely healing for a while before the realisation came to him that he was sinking. It took him two years and a great deal of money to recuperate from the fever that he thought would never leave him. When it did, it scrubbed away the last remnants of luck that were sticking to him. His income ran dry and his savings evaporated, but the biggest blow was the loss of his daughter. On a cool July day, when the usually dry Sankarankoil was enjoying the showers brought in by a wayward monsoon, she departed without warning, picked off by the dreaded cholera.

The astrologer was a resilient man but his wife used up a few more years to gather the bits and pieces of her shattered life. Thirty years separated his departure and his reappearance in Nanguneri and the only fruits of his conquests appeared to be his grumpy wife and a none-too-bright son. He sought an audience with the Jiyar immediately on arrival.

The interview between the astrologer and his childhood friend, the eighteenth Jiyar of the Great Srivaishnava Matam, took place in an inner room where the holy man received visitors. It was a simple room devoid of any furniture except a silver seat with an ornate back that had as finials the sacred emblems of the conch and the discus and the tiruman of the Southern Sect and a stool in front of it, which bore a few silver ablutionary vessels. The Jiyar was sitting cross-legged, holding in his hand the long wooden staff – in fact three similar staves tied together – that symbolised a Vaishnava *sanyasi*. The astrologer brought with him a tray of bananas with a big silver coin on top. Placing the tray at his feet, he prostrated himself before the ascetic.

'Swami's lotus feet are the last refuge of all Srivaishnavas. Where shall we go if he does not bestow his grace on us?'

'My blessings are always with you but it is His writ that matters and not that of this miserable worm.'

'Your servant salutes Swami's humility. We all know the Lord, whenever He wills, speaks through Swami.'

'You are being unduly generous. Narayana has better vehicles at His command.'

'Such vehicles may be visible to an evolved soul like the Swami, but I am an ignoramus and to me you are His only approachable vehicle.'

'Don't shame me, my friend. I stand nowhere before your scholarship. It is to this saffron robe your salutations go and I am acutely aware of it.'

At length both grew tired of these preliminaries and the astrologer said, 'Swami does not have an astrologer for the Matam. It appears as though the Lord himself has sent me to set right this deficiency.'

The Swami had personal knowledge of the alarming astrological skills of his old friend. It was he who had compared the horoscopes for the Swami's marriage. The girl, Padma, appeared healthy and beautiful and the astrologer predicted that the pair would be the most envied in the village. Indeed they were for a period of five years before Padma died during childbirth. The Swami, after years of aimless wandering, became a close disciple of the preceding Jiyar, who duly nominated him as his successor.

'As you know, our Matam does not have this tradition. I am the eighteenth in the line and none of my great predecessors had an astrologer to predict his future for him. They did not need one, for they had intuitive knowledge of the past, present and future. I am not as gifted as they were, and you will be of great help, but it is difficult to change the traditions of the Matam.'

The astrologer was not happy. He said to the Swami, 'Your disciple is now a pauper. I have wandered enough and now I have come to you. I leave it to the Swami to find a way.'

The Swami said, 'I never desert a disciple and you are not only my disciple but my childhood friend. I have work for you in a place with which you are very familiar.'

The Matam library, where the astrologer's long journey began, had a huge collection of theological manuscripts, most of which were mouldering and in an advanced state of disintegration. Of the few that were well-preserved was a commentary on the *Sri Vachana Bhushanam,* a fundamental Srivaishnava work written from the Tenkalai point of view by Pillai Lokacharya, a great Vaishnava theologian. The Swami wanted his friend to edit it and print it at Tirunelveli.

III

The library was a narrow wedge between the Matam's kitchen and the lumber-room. It was packed with manuscripts in Sanskrit, Tamil, Manipravalam and Telugu. Most were moth-eaten and crumbled to musty powder at the first touch. The commentary however was in good condition and the astrologer was thrilled that his old friend had come to his rescue and given him a task worthy of his scholarship.

He knew as he turned the leaves of the manuscript that he was reading an unparalleled masterpiece in Manipravalam, a combination of Sanskrit and Tamil specially devised for writing commentaries on religious works. From now on, he thought, it will be my life's work to bring this commentary out in print. He took leave of his friend and engaged a cart to go to Tirunelveli for preliminary discussions with a printer.

The palmyra and acacia gradually gave way to bright green fields as his cart crossed the garrison town of Palayamkottai and reached the majestic bridge across the river Tamraparani. The river, the southern-most of the sacred rivers, famed in Sanskrit poetry for its fresh-water pearls, swerved north here. The astrologer asked the cart man to stop right in the middle of the bridge. He alighted and stood facing south. The blue-black hills of Podikai were visible at a distance and he could clearly see the Krishnan temple a few hundred yards away on the eastern bank. He folded his hands in salutation in the direction of the temple and prayed with his eyes closed. Krishna, you have come to my rescue many times in my life. Let this be the last time. This time, for the first time, I am doing something that should please you immensely.

His cart moved slowly through the avenue of *marudu* trees that connected the Tirunelveli Bridge and the ancient town, and reached the Matam's rest house. After a bath, the astrologer sat down to copy the commentary on paper with a reed pen.

'*Adiyen* Ramanujam, Swami,' blared someone into his ear and the astrologer started and shivered.

'I am sorry, Ramanujam. I was busy copying. I have to give these sample pages to the printing press today. If this fellow is unable to do a through job I will have to go to Madurai. How are you? How is your health?'

Ramanujam was a clerk in a jewellery shop nearby and when he heard that the astrologer was at the Matam's rest house he had come to greet him.

'Swami, I shall be happy if you could visit my house and bless us.'

I know why he is inviting me. He has a daughter of marriageable age and he wants to show me her horoscope.

'I will be busy for a few days with this work, Ramanujam. When it is over I will certainly visit your house.'

'Swami, don't you know? The printing press is not likely to be open today.'

The sleepy town had been shaken wide awake by a *Palla* who chose to die in the wrong place and at the wrong time.

The old town of Tirunelveli was perched on a slice of high ground, sandwiched between paddy fields that stretched out and licked the horizon. The magnificent temple complex at its centre, dedicated to Shiva and Parvati, was its pride. It was boxed in by markets, high streets, lanes and alleys that crisscrossed maddeningly, trying to elbow each other out. This bedlam housed the high-caste Hindus, a variety of shops, printing presses, minor places of worship, a few government offices and a hospital.

The untouchables did not inhabit this cramped universe. They lived on the fringes of the town or in clearings amidst the fields. The trouble started when a decrepit old Palla came to the *taluk* office on a futile search for some land records. The endless wait, the unspeaking clerks who occasionally opened their mouths to shout at their victims to silence them, the heat and the ubiquitous cholera all conspired to hasten the old man to his death, which came at the hospital in the town. The Palla's body was to be taken out of the hospital and his hovel was at the Palayamkottai end of the town. The segregation practised by the community extended to funeral processions too and the caste-Hindus were aghast that the Palla's funeral bier would pass through their streets, polluting them beyond repair. They could suffer a supplicant Palla on his legs, but a Palla dead, who would be carried like a lord by four other Pallas, with loud music accompanying the procession, was beyond tolerance. They decided to oppose the procession violently.

The year was 1858 and though the Great Mutiny was miles away, its reverberations had travelled this far and made the rulers jumpy. The acting Collector, Mayne, decided to be tough and dispatched a posse of sepoys from the Palayamkottai Garrison to accompany the funeral procession.

The astrologer was not worried. 'I have seen many such commotions, Ramanujam. I am not going to waste time here. The press can still function with its doors closed.'

The printing press was on the high road to Palayamkottai. Its doors were indeed closed but a knock was sufficient to gain entry. After an hour of satisfactory discussions the astrologer came out of the press. He could see that one end of the road was blocked by a mass of agitated people armed with staves, knives, sickles, axes, hammers and anything that came to hand. There were many more pouring out from the alleys into the high road. In the distance he could see a column of sepoys advancing slowly from the temple-end of the road. He had never seen so many weapons in his life. He was still deciding whether to seek shelter in the printing press or to disappear down one of the alleys when a bullet smashed his skull.

His body was picked up – one of the ten killed – from a gutter, along with his thick black silver-cased walking stick. That was his only possession. The commentary was probably trampled to dust in the battlefield.

The Jiyar wanted the astrologer's son to work in the library but when he found him to be dull, he offered him a job in the kitchen. He proved to be a reasonably good cook and as he gained experience, he became an authority on tamarind rice. Unlike his father's, his reputation was built on palpable foundations and the Iyengars who came to seek the blessings of the Lord and the Jiyar sat patiently in long rows to receive his delicious puliyodarai after it had first been offered to the Lord. They were not disappointed. His puliyodarai was always fit to be on God's menu.

IV

Goaded by the unremitting lamentations of his mother, the cook met the Jiyar. The failure of the rains unnerved him too and he too suspected that his daughter's unmarried status was responsible for the failure. The Jiyar's spring has survived this year but another waterless year will turn it dry. His worry gave him courage and he was determined to extend the conversation beyond the normal minute or two.

'Swami, your disciples come first to you with their problems, for they are sure you have answers for them. I am your humble servant and if Swami desires so, I shall make bold to present the problem that is slowly destroying my family and me.'

Without waiting for the Swami to indicate his desire he continued, 'My daughter is now twelve and she will be a woman any day now. The village is after me to get her married off and I have neither the money nor a suitable boy in view.'

The Swami said, 'Don't worry. The Lord is merciful. He shall indicate a way. Come to me next week.'

That evening the Jiyar led the Lord in procession. The *Panguni* festival was on and the Brahmins came out to prostrate before him as he walked through their streets. He blessed them and moved on. The cook's house was a narrow train of dark boxes hemmed in by big houses on both sides, but the gigantic kolam of a lotus in front of his house, which Ponna had spent her afternoon over, seemed to cover the entire street and dwarf the less splendid ones at its sides. The Swami was admiring it when Ponna touched his feet. It was the ninth day of the festival and the moon, just three days away from her fullness, was bright and lovely. The girl was in a dark red full skirt and a blue blouse. Castor oil torches accompanying the holy man lit up her face, and her soft cheeks glistened in the heady concoction of light from the torches and the distant moon. She was magical.

The Swami was wide awake that night. His past, dormant for long, had broken free and filled his mind, chasing sleep away. I have seen this girl as a child and she did not remind me of anyone. Now she is a print of Padma, he thought. Do I really remember what Padma was like after fifty years? Beauty perhaps touches off acquisitiveness even in an ascetic and makes him long for what he once had. No, he said to himself. I have seen many young girls and not one has so much as made me remember her name. This girl is surely Padma reborn. She is precious and shouldn't be allowed to wither away.

The next day he sent word to one of his disciples and when he called on him, the Swami did not waste any time.

'I understand you have a son studying in the Tirunelveli Hindu School. I have found a bride for him and if you approve, the marriage could be celebrated this *Chithirai*.'

Krishna Iyengar, the big moneylender of the village was not a desirable man, but his one blind spot was the Swami whom he obeyed without protest.

'It is indeed the good luck of my son that his bride has been chosen by the Swami. May I ask who the girl is?'

The Swami told him and added, 'Don't be upset. She is the granddaughter of a great scholar to whom fate was not very kind. I will take care of the marriage expenses and as her dowry I shall make over my family jewellery to you.'

The moneylender was satisfied. The Swami's family jewellery was already with him for safe keeping and the collection was worth more than two hundred sovereigns in gold.

When the cook brought home the glad tidings his wife was relieved. Strangely, the old woman grumbled. 'That old fox has not done you a favour. The moneylender boys die young. The villagers hesitate to give their daughters in marriage to that family.'

The cook said, 'You are foul-mouthed and it is impossible to satisfy you. Krishna Iyengar is at least ten years older than me and he shows no sign of dying. You think up ancient tales and flaunt them to scare us. If you speak one word against this marriage, I will be a very angry man.' That was the first time the cook had spoken in such a tone to his mother, which effectively silenced her. Nobody asked the bride about the choice, but Ponna was pleased that she was going to the biggest house in her village.

Krishna Iyengar was easily the most prosperous man of the village and his family history, told and retold through generations of inventive grandmothers who seemed to outlive grandfathers effortlessly and without exception, had an unbroken tradition of orthodoxy that lost its way only in the mist of pre-Matam days. The family was always of the true faith, holding aloft the banner of the Tenkalai in times of significance. It financed, strategically and with full fanfare, the sect's innumerable duels in law courts with its cousins of the Vadakalai – the Northern sect. If faith gave it standing, it was usury that made the family wealthy and gave it the biggest house in Nanguneri. The origin of its uncommon prosperity however brought the opprobrium – never publicly mentioned, only whispered among its impecunious rivals who made sure that only the whisper and not the details of its source, would reach the ears of the moneylender family—of betrayal. They were no doubt rich earlier, the rivals said, but they became enviously rich only after Dalavai Pillai was betrayed to the British. The story of betrayal was not fully true but it embarrassed the family with its persistence through generations.

According to family lore the greatest of its sons was Krishna Iyengar's grandfather, Kesavan Iyengar. He was canny, courteous and without a trace of sympathy – qualities that made him a thoroughbred moneylender. Like most moneylenders of the Tirunelveli region he had managed to carve out a comfortable alcove of profit even as incessant wars ravaged the Tirunelveli country.

It was Kesavan's grandfather who advised him to follow the stars of the British keenly. He happily lent them money even when they were nobodies, just a laughable segment of the Arcot Nawab's army. 'They have a knack with money. We must cultivate them,' the old man used to say.

Now they were in the ascendant and the *Poligars* their meek supplicants. The British military power intimidated every ruler. Well, except for one mad Poligar, Kattabomman, who refused to be intimidated. Kesavan Iyengar reflected: he considers the Company his implacable enemy.

Kesavan Iyengar knew a *kanakku pillai*, an account-keeper of the British garrison, who fed him with juicy information.

'Iyengar, you know Kattabomman killed Adjutant Clarke right under the nose of that Collector Jackson and the Company couldn't do a thing. That was in 1797, just two years ago. Now they have had their vengeance. They have reduced his Panchalamkurichi fort to rubble with their twelve-pounders. The Poligar has managed to escape.'

'He shall return, pillai. This is not the first time the fort has been stormed. Colonel Fullarton did it sixteen years ago, but the Poligar regained it in no time.'

'But that was before the Company's treaty with the Nawab. It will be different this time. Their firepower is awesome. The redcoats will surely win, Iyengar.'

It was the same kanakku pillai who brought to the moneylender the news of Kattabomman's capture and execution.

'He died like a great warrior though he was hanged like a common criminal. Major Bannerman says he was dauntingly supercilious. He looked at the Ettaiyapuram and Sivagiri Poligars who were at the hanging with a scorn that would have driven even buffaloes to suicide. His only regret was that he had left his fort instead of defending it to the death. His brother Oomaithurai is now in Palayamkottai prison.'

Iyengar knew that resistance was doubtless heroic but it also cost money. And for money the heroes had to come to moneylenders. True to his profession, Kesavan Iyengar joined a group of financiers who collectively lent money at a hefty rate of interest to a representative of Oomaithurai, Kattabomman's dumb brother, who was now regrouping after his daring escape from the Palayamkottai prison during a smallpox epidemic. It was with this money that the mute prince rebuilt the Panchalamkurichi fort within a matter of days. When the British returned in two months with reinforcements the fort was impregnable. It was only after the arrival of powerful siege guns that the fort was taken. The British razed the fort to the ground, ploughed it over and sowed the site with castor seed. Panchalamkurichi was expunged from the district records. The mute prince joined the neighbouring forces of Sivaganga where the Marudu brothers had risen in rebellion, but theirs was a lost cause. One by one they were hunted down and put to death, barring a few who were banished to Penang.

Lushington, the Collector of Tirunelveli, called a meeting of the financiers after these skirmishes. He could now speak with authority as the Arcot Nawab had just given away the Tirunelveli region to the Company in perpetuity. While thanking them for the help they had rendered to the Company, he hinted that lending money to rebel Poligars and their deputies would no longer be a profitable exercise.

Hardly had Iyengar heaved a sigh of relief that his funding of the dumb prince had not been viewed seriously by the Company when the news came that one of the chief supporters of Kattabomman, Dalavai Pillai, had joined hands with the Nanguneri Maravas. The Maravas have probably joined Dalavai Pillai, Iyengar thought, because they are afraid that the British will usurp what has hitherto been their monopoly – the right to protect the Nanguneri temple, the Matam and their extensive wealth. He knew the rebels would approach him.

Rama Thevar, the chief of the Maravas who had allied themselves with Dalavai Pillai, was a soldier of rare courage but strangely innocent of matters concerning finance. He was confident that he could persuade Kesavan Iyengar, from whom he had earlier borrowed, to part with cash for what seemed to him an unassailable cause. He brought Dalavai Pillai, at great danger, to Kesavan Iyengar to make him personally plead his cause.

Dalavai Pillai was not a voluble man. He gave the Iyengar a copy of the Rebel Proclamation of Trichinopoly, issued under the name of Marudu Pandian, the leader of the Sivaganga group.

Wherever you find any of the low wretches, destroy them and continue to do so until they are extirpated. Whoever serves the low wretches will never enjoy eternal bliss after death. I know this. Consider and deliberate on it. And he who does not subscribe to this, may his whiskers be like the hair of my secret parts and his food be tasteless and without nourishment and may his wife and children belong to another and be considered as the offspring of the low wretches to whom he had prostituted her. Therefore all but whose blood is contaminated by Europeans will begin to unite.

Whoever reads this or hears of its contents, let him make it as public as possible by the writing of it to his friends, who in like manner must publish it to theirs. Everyone who shall not write it and circulate it as before mentioned, let him be guilty of the enormous crime of killing a black cow on the banks of the Ganga and suffer all the various punishments of hell. The Musselmen who do not conform to this, let them be considered as having drunk the blood of a pig.

Kesavan Iyengar's blood ran cold when he read the proclamation, but he simply exclaimed, 'Narayana, why are you testing your children?'

Dalavai kept quiet but Thevar said, 'Swami, we need money immediately and we depend on you. We shall return it within six months and as a pledge I shall bring sufficient jewellery. It is too dangerous to sell them in Tirunelveli and you are the only dependable person who can give us the money we want without much effort.'

Iyengar seemed to go into a trance, staring at the huge diamond on his left ring-finger for a long time. He finally said, 'Rama Thevar, the amount is big and I don't have it now. Give me ten days' time. You need not bring the jewellery. I shall be in touch with you as soon as the money is arranged.'

Iyengar did not have to lend them anything. Within a few days of their meeting, Dalavai Pillai and Rama Thevar were captured and sent to Madras for deportation. The rumour was that Iyengar had given some indication to the British about the duo's whereabouts which made their capture easier. No one asked Iyengar whether it was true. The Maravas, whose ears the rumour reached, were dispirited by the loss of their leader and other able bodied men. Moreover, they needed Iyengar's money to buy seed. Some said Iyengar called on Lushington after the dust had settled and returned from the interview with a bag of gold sovereigns.

Iyengar's wife entertained no doubts. She was sure that her husband had had a hand in the betrayal of Dalavai. She did not worry about the Maravas, as she had faith in her husband's skill in buying peace. She was afraid of divine retribution. She donated a set of jewels to the Nanguneri temple. To clinch the issue, she went on a pilgrimage to distant Tirupati and pleaded with God to save her family from disaster.

The disaster struck ten years later with great severity. It had rained heavily in August and September that year – an occurrence unknown in the memory of the village – and it foreboded darker things to come. December had its minor floods and then the skies ruptured in January. The rains came in thick unrelieved sheets and it looked as though the sea had taken wings to invade the Tirunelveli country. Lakes that had never been full overflowed and merged through giant breaches. Rivers, uncommonly furious, effortlessly demolished their banks. Water reigned everywhere. The country surrounding Nanguneri, the *teri* country, whose dunes remained dry even during the wettest of monsoons, was one big expanse of water.

The rains left reluctantly in May, but the water stayed. Hardy dry-weather palmyras began to rot. The winds stood still and from the trapped water which could find no way to sea, a strange fever rose. With the gods choosing not to intercede, it embraced everyone, only leaving alone a few who were lucky. Villages putrefied without people to bury or burn the corpses. Revenue Collectors bewailed that the villages held no persons left to pay their dues. Though the dead were not many in Nanguneri, they included Kesavan Iyengar, his wife and two of their sons. The third son survived and he was Krishna Iyengar's father.

Two

I

THE ANNOUNCEMENT OF HIS MARRIAGE CAME as a surprise to Raman, the moneylender's son. He was happy spending his days in Tirunelveli where he had a troop of friends mooching off him. The school was a pretext to be away from the village. He would have liked to remain a bachelor a few more years, but his father's writ was inviolable. He wanted to sulk against it but then he realised that Ponna was not a bad choice at all. She had regularly figured in his wet dreams and those of most of the young men of the village. The poverty of her family did not worry him, for he knew that in endogamous communities such as his, the financial status of the bride's family did not count for anything except for the dowry, and his father had informed him that the Jiyar had taken care of that. He could hardly wait for his marriage.

The Jiyar ensured a magnificent marriage for Ponna.

Life then was not very long and the villagers had many opportunities to mourn. The memories of a few splendorous events that came their way were thus treasured by them for years. The marriage of Ponna was one such event. It was their measuring-rod to assess other marriages that followed hers. They found none of them measuring up to it. For years, the ultimate compliment for any grand marriage that took place in the village was this: it was almost as good as the one organised by our eighteenth Jiyar for the astrologer's granddaughter.

It was a four-day affair. The saris, specially woven for the marriage and finely brocaded, came from Kanchipuram. One, a red-and-gold marvel, was still with Radha's grandmother, looking crisp and unfaded after ninety years. The ceremonial reed mats were from Pattamadai, a village not far from Tirunelveli. They were interlaced by its Muslim artisans who were unbelievably good. The mats were intricate, with 120 threads used for a span's width of the wrap, and so soft and in such lovely colours that nobody sat on them after the marriage. They were among the few valuable things taken away by the torch-light robbers, when they raided the moneylender's house. The jewels were the Jiyar's family heirlooms, heavy and dazzling.

Ponna, though befuddled most times, was surprisingly lucid when she narrated to Radha – this was before her final illness – titbits about her marriage. 'Banana leaves disappeared from the market as every leaf available was procured for the wedding. Potatoes and tomatoes were served for the first time in an Iyengar marriage in Nanguneri. The locals did not partake of them. They were served only to your peria-thatha's friends from Tirunelveli. But the locals talked about the feast given to them for years. The Maravas and our own peasants were given separate feasts and they were all praise for the Jiyar. Even the *Kuravas* were happy. They said they had never eaten tastier leftovers.'

Raman was impatient but he had to wait for two years before he went anywhere near the nuptial bed. Compared to the rituals of marriage, the defloration ceremony was not elaborate.

He invoked the sun: 'Oh Pushan, make this girl desirous of me, make her spread her thighs for me so that my lingam can plant my seed in her.'

Ponna was in her prime and she was more than willing. She had been given hints about what sex would be like by her married friends, but she had never expected to be devoured by it. Unlike her house, which was a small single-storey affair, Raman's house had a first floor with a spacious room. Her days were spent in the kitchen with her mother-in-law who, in contrast to her grandmother, was very kind. Her desire mounted as evening approached and even her chores, like serving her father-in-law and husband their food and washing the used utensils, had a feverish air about them. She was impatient for the routine to be over and when it was she bid a hurried good night to her mother-in-law and rushed upstairs, untying the knots of her blouse on the way. She would stand before Raman, her healthy hay-like odour filling the room and her nipples erect and inviting. Raman's friends had told him that Brahmin girls never displayed an overt inclination for sex and they had to be cajoled or coerced into bed. Ponna did not need any such persuasion. She had a natural flair and she was too young to smother it, though she never allowed him to disrobe her fully and her sari always remained bunched around her waist. She shielded her eyes with her left arm from the light thrown by a small earthen lamp that flickered in a corner of the room. His face buried in her exposed armpit, Raman was unhurried. She did not want him to hurry and guided him without restraint.

II

It was when she was away with her parents expecting her first child that the *Thivatti Kollaikarars* struck at her husband's house. The Iyengars knew that the Marava village of Marukalkurichi adjoining Nanguneri had at least eighty families that survived on plunder. But as a rule they never operated in Nanguneri because it was a village that they were supposed to protect. Their domain was elsewhere. The band that came to Nanguneri must have come from outside the district. They chose a new-moon day to attack the Brahmin street, when the able-bodied Maravas of Marukalkurichi had themselves gone on their mission. The Matam had more wealth than the entire street, but the thieves left it alone, perhaps fearing God's intervention.

The robbers never moved surreptitiously. They came down upon the street with terrifying yells around midnight and the docile Brahmins locked themselves in. There was nothing worthy in their houses to be robbed and they all knew Krishna Iyengar's house was marked down.

The robbers first burnt a wooden cart right in front of the moneylender's house to light their work. They hurled stones at his house ordering him in loud voices to open the door. There was no response.

The door, made by the artisans of Kerala, was a masterpiece in teak. They used heavy crowbars to break it open. Inside the house they found Krishna Iyengar's wife and a maidservant cowering in a corner of the hall. The servant was dragged out by her hair and flung in the street.

'Where are the jewels?' asked the chief, a short man with a bushy moustache.

'I don't know.'

'Listen, amma. We normally do not touch Brahmin women. Don't force us to do so. Where are the jewels?'

'I don't know. My husband is away and he never tells me where he keeps the jewels. Take mine,' she said, removing her heavy gold bangles and the chain around her neck.

The Chief laughed. 'I know your husband has hundreds of such ornaments. Where are they?'

'I told you. I don't know.'

In one swift move she was stripped of her sari. She was a middle-aged woman, still sexually attractive, but sex was far from their minds. They bound her feet with rope and hung her upside down from a wooden beam. Her hands were tied behind her back. One of them stuffed a dirty cloth into her mouth, removed her diamond earrings and held her firmly.

Another held a thick lighted wick between her thighs.

Her cries were choked and there was a faint smell of singeing hair.

They removed the gag after a few minutes.

'Where are the jewels?'

'I don't know. Please believe me,' she said clenching her teeth in agony.

They gagged her again.

It took them more than thirty minutes to realise that the woman hanging upside down was speaking the truth. They brought her down, untied her feet and hands and threw a sari at her. She was barely alive when they left the house after ransacking it thoroughly. They did not get the jewels they came for. They only had a measly pile of silver vessels, silk clothes, reed mats and some ornaments to show for all their hard work. They were a disappointed lot.

The Brahmins came out at dawn, shaking their heads and cursing the Maravas who they said had deserted the village when it was desperate for their assistance. They were not ashamed of their own cowardice because they were not supposed to be brave. Their wives trooped into the ravaged house. They did not expect Krishna Iyengar's wife to live.

Death struck Nanguneri with such tiresome monotony, it was only a temporary inconvenience to the living, – unless it capriciously took away the one who brought them sustenance. But Krishna Iyengar grieved for his wife until his death, which took a long time to arrive. On that fateful night, he was away in the house of a Tirunelveli courtesan whom he found irresistible. His wife was aware of his preference for comely prostitutes but not once did she question him about it. The thought that he was probably sleeping with his whore when his wife was being disrobed by the robbers was too much for him. His sleep vanished and he spent his nights in an easy chair remembering his wife who had never raised her voice when she was living. Now whenever he closed his eyes he could hear her howling horribly for help. She was born in a house only a few yards away from his and she had remained tethered to Nanguneri, not even venturing to Tirunelveli. Now she was wandering with the wind. What sins had she committed in her previous birth that she had to go in this gruesome way? It did not occur to Krishna Iyengar that she would not have died if he had not been secretive.

The jewels were safe. They came to Ponna's rescue when her children needed sustenance.

Ponna's grief was naturally transient. She had dutifully wanted to name her firstborn after her mother-in-law but since it turned out to be a boy she called him Nammalwar – the Jiyar's name before he became an ascetic. The birth of a son to Ponna was the last news he heard and it made his journey to the Lord's abode much happier.

The Jiyar's body was sat in an ornate chair in the *padmasana* posture and was bathed ritually. After a series of rites, he was taken in procession in an ivory palanquin round the Brahmin streets and on to the Sacred Row, three miles away from the village, where all his predecessors were interred. He was then lowered into the burial pit, which was covered with salt, and coconuts were broken on his head to release his soul for its final journey to the feet of the Lord. The new Jiyar, now occupying the ivory palanquin, proceeded to the tank for a bath and entered the Matam as its new chief.

III

Ponna was as fecund as her mother and three children came in quick succession. Unlike her mother's, all her offspring survived infancy. The death of her mother-in-law gave her a position of authority in the house and the keys of the domestic kingdom were handed over to her. The business of usury no doubt ran to seed after Krishna Iyengar's lapse into vapidity, but the family still had large tracts of land to be managed and Raman, who came back to Nanguneri after a couple of ineffectual attempts to cross the barrier of graduation, was singularly unequal to the task. He thought his family's wealth was everlasting and waited for it to multiply fast on its own without any human intervention. Despite the fact that Krishna Iyengar was a pitiless employer, the family's tenants were loyal. They worked on the old impetus and on normal expectations that the son would take after his father. All they needed was an assurance from someone from the family that their actions would not be questioned later.

Raman's indolence baffled them. This was the first time they were seeing an Iyengar from the old moneylender's family not interested in the minutiae of rice cultivation and its financial aspects.

The only thing he did satisfactorily in those days was to sleep with Ponna regularly. It was this that defined life for her. There was no variation in their lovemaking. Ponna did not demand any. She savoured what was offered day after day in the way she savoured her plate of rice and curd. She forgave all his faults and took over the reins of managing the land. The tenants liked her. She was gentle and considerate and at the same time it was difficult to deceive her and tell her believable lies. It was during her two subsequent confinements that they were at a loss. After Nammalwar came Pakshi and finally Andal, who marked another phase of Ponna's long life.

Raman lost interest in sleeping with her after Andal was born. It was not that he was plowing elsewhere as his father had been doing. He was far too lazy to go in search of feminine flesh. The life of a gourmand, he discovered, lent purpose to his spinelessness and a pretext to be ecstatic from one sumptuous meal to another – if the snacks he continuously demanded in between were not counted. He ordered tins of imported biscuits at great cost from Madras. Lakshmi Vilas of Tirunelveli dispatched every second day, two pounds of halwa for him. He sent his local friends who visited him for tasty titbits to Nagercoil, at his expense, to buy English vegetables and pestered Ponna to cook them for him. Ponna did not refuse him, though most of what he ate did not appeal to her. When it took his mood, which happened frequently, he visited his father-in-law at his place of work. That was perhaps his only exercise.

The kitchen of the Matam was a fragrant place, as God and the Jiyar were always served food made of the purest ingredients. The cook, though not very pleased to see his son-in-law, had to maintain a veneer of respect and said, 'Come, come, your visits are becoming rare.'

'I was here only on Wednesday and you gave me that delicious *sakkarai pongal.*'

'Yes, yes. I should be pardoned for my forgetfulness. The wood smoke dulls one's brain.'

'Today is Saturday. It's your puliyodarai day . . .'

The cook had no other option but to give his son-in-law two big balls of his famous puliyodarai. He asked him in passing, 'What has Ponna cooked today?'

'Oh it is wonderful, She has made *paruppu, uppuchchar,* tomato *satramudu, vazhaikkai karatamudu* and *avial.* And yes, cabbage for me.'

Though he appreciated good food himself, the cook realised that the puliyodarai was merely a pre-lunch snack for his son-in-law and that he could never hope to match Raman's keenness.

He visited his daughter one night after serving the Jiyar his supper. The children were fast asleep in the hall. His son-in-law was not to be seen. He must have retired to the first floor. Ponna was awake and reading what looked like the *Prabandham* in the dim light of a hurricane lamp. She closed the book when she saw her father and tried to stand up.

'Sit down, sit down. No need to rise. You must be tired, looking after the children, managing the tenants and, above all, cooking every day whatever he demands. It's truly the Lord's grace. Without it, it is impossible for one frail woman to manage all these.'

'You need not worry, *appa*. I am perfectly all right. My mother's fate was probably worse,' said Ponna having a mild dig at her father.

'My son-in-law visits me regularly nowadays. No doubt it is my duty to serve him. But I think he has started to eat much more than what is good for him. You must consult a doctor. Not our *vaithiyar*, but a doctor of English medicine. You have enough money to pay for him. I attempted to strike up a conversation with Krishna Iyengar on the subject but he just stares at you and doesn't speak.'

'Appa, you know well the condition of my father-in-law. What is the use of talking to him? I don't think there is anything wrong with my husband. It is only a passing phase. A day will come when we will all beg him to eat and he won't touch a morsel. Oh yes, his visit to your kitchen. I will request him not to enter that place any more.'

The cook was startled. His intentions were genuine and he did not expect such a reaction from his daughter. He said, 'I am sorry Ponna. I thought I should inform you. If everything is all right, who could be happier than I am? He can visit me as many times as he likes. You know the purpose of my calling on you is not to stop Raman from visiting me.'

Ponna appeared to be mollified. She said, 'It is I who should be sorry, appa. Perhaps I was tired. I should not have spoken to you like this. It is getting late, appa. Amma will be alone.'

After the cook had left, Ponna slowly walked to the small open courtyard beside the kitchen and washed her face and hands. She came back and stood before a long mirror, carefully applying Yardley's powder on her face with a soft puff. When she was satisfied that her face had attained the requisite smoothness, she pressed the soft side of the puff to her nose and inhaled deeply. She came to the front door and locked it securely with a giant padlock. Adjusting the folds of her sari, she climbed up the stairs.

Raman was asleep with his mouth open on the floor next to an ornate bed, drooling and staining the pillow cover. His *veshti* was not in place and his hirsute thighs looked like black pythons in the dim light. His stomach that had been flat at the time of his marriage had ballooned up and looked distinctly obscene. His sacred thread – six thin cotton threads entwined – had left his chest to encircle his substantial neck. Ponna called him softly. He merely moaned in reply. She lay next to him, placed her left thigh on his and hugged him, her breasts pressing his ample back, her left hand roaming over his crotch. There was no response. After a minute or two, when Ponna felt a ponderous stirring, he extricated his thigh from under hers and held her left hand tightly. Ponna pulled her hand out of his grip and turned away from him.

She lay quietly on her back. Her eyes wandered caressing the objects that took their fancy – the beautiful brass lamp lit every day when her mother-in-law was alive, the rope coiling around one of the stout legs of their bed, which must be the same one she had used to tie around the waist of the child Pakshi to restrict his crawling when she was lost in lovemaking, and the black teak wood beam that ran the breath of the ceiling. Her eyes now stopped at the alcove formed by the beam and the joists above her. She sprang up and took out the object nestling in it. It was a labelled bottle with a dark liquid. She could not read English but she knew what it was. She opened it and smelled the liquid. It was strange, the heady whiff pleasant. She stood there inhaling the vapour for a few seconds, her foot unconsciously nudging Raman. She tilted the bottle slowly, until a few drops fell on her palm. She licked it and found the taste agreeable.

Plugging back the cork in a measured way and unbothered by the darkness, Ponna went down the familiar steps and came to the hall. Picking up the small night-lamp blinking there, she reached the backyard. The door leading to the garden had a flat iron bar hooked to one side of its vertical frame and securely padlocked to the other. Placing the lamp in an alcove, she unlocked the door and stood at the door. The air was still and the dying rhythm of croaking frogs was soothing to her ears. A weak moon behind its leafy branches, the mango tree loomed large and was threatening like Tataka, her arms akimbo, confronting the young princes of Ayodhya. She invoked Hanuman. Muttering 'Anjaneya, Anjaneya, Anjaneya,' she hurried past the demon tree and reached the steps leading to the brook. It was nearly dry, except for a thin glimmering ribbon of water. Now it looks silvery and inviting, she thought. Morning, it will turn odious, cleansing bottom after gluey bottom. My husband's will be the first. He wakes up early. There was a squat brown rock at the edge of the brook. Ponna threw the bottle at the rock and the sound of its smashing startled the frogs to silence. The aroma of alcohol began to fill the air, but she did not waste time. She ran back to the house, reached the hall locking the door behind her, and lay next to Andal, involuntarily cuddling her. The night lamp remained in the alcove and it shed light dutifully till the wick died.

Raman came to the kitchen exactly at six in the morning and Ponna handed him his silver tumbler of coffee. 'I broke that bottle last night.'

'I know. One of its broken pieces pierced me.' He lifted his left leg and showed her the heel and its scarlet spot. 'It was what the Tirunelveli doctor ordered. I am suffering from a bout of indigestion these days.'

You haven't stirred out of the house for more than a month except for your raids on my father's kitchen, she thought.

'Don't look at me like that. Yesterday was the first time I had tasted it. It will also be the last one. It tastes bitter! I don't know how Sarangan polishes off the whole bottle in no time. It smells awful.'

Sarangan was one of the many sponges supported by Raman.

She never saw alcohol again in her life. Its likeable flavour lodged itself in the folds of her mind, irritating her at inopportune moments like a sliver of coconut stuck between molars. She could not find a pick to ease it out until the end.

IV

Bitten perhaps by conscience, Raman took upon himself the task of making Nammalwar proficient in the *Prabandham*. They began auspiciously and the boy learnt the majestic *Pallandu* quickly, but he became bored with the scriptures soon and took to devising ploys to avoid the sessions with his tenacious father.

Ponna sang the hymns of the *Prabandham* whenever she prayed and they sounded extraordinarily melodious, for these unrivalled devotional poems were probably written for singing. But the Srivaishnava males never sang them. Instead, in their anxiety to mirror the Vedic traditions, they devised a system of learning the hymns by rote which destroyed their fine musical quality. They became gibberish to many of those who memorised and recited them mostly for ritual purposes. Proficiency in the Tamil scriptures gave many impecunious Iyengars a livelihood – the Matam employed them – but it did not make them lovers of Tamil poetry or its hoary musical traditions. Raman had an additional handicap. His voice had the tenor of a donkey in agony and the *Prabandham* sounded insufferable when he recited it.

Raman's son was too young to understand the philosophical and poetic nuances of the saint Nammalwar whose name he carried and whose *Tiruvaimoli* he was now being forced to memorise. His mind refused to subject itself to the regimen of learning by rote. The scripture sessions became cat-and-mouse games between father and son.

Raman was ritually pure when he tried to teach the *Prabandham* to his reluctant son. He bathed, donned a thick tiruman on his forehead, wore his veshti the orthodox way and howled for his absent son.

'Alwar, Alwar. Where has he gone? I told him to be here at seven o'clock sharp and he is not to be seen. I shall skin him today. Send someone to fetch him.'

When Nammalwar appeared on the scene, Raman jumped up and tweaked his ears before dragging him to the centre of the hall and giving him a quick slap on the cheek.

'Is this the time to arrive? Wash your hands and feet quickly and come back running. I have been waiting for half-an-hour.'

Tears welled up and blurred Nammalwar's vision. He did what his father told him. Both sat cross-legged in the small Perumal room where Raman had installed the family *salagram* and small idols of Vishnu in his various aspects.

'*Uyarvara uyar nalam udayavan evan avan.*'

'*Uyarvara uyar nalam udayavan even avan. Uyarvara uyar nalam udayavan evan avan,*' the boy repeated.

He stared at the heaving globes on his father's chest. He carries a mattress beneath his skin and . . . a fat bandicoot resides in his belly. He looked at the cobwebs hanging from the corner above his father. I want a giant spider to emerge out of them and fall on this fatso and bite him. He should not die. The bandicoot should. He should suffer long bouts of sleep like Kumbhakarna. I shall use a heavy pestle to wake him up whenever I feel like pardoning him. He will wake up without the bandicoot. I shall extract a promise from him, on pain of sending him again to sleep, that he will recite the *Tiruvaimoli* alone and without my help. He can keep the mattress.

The chant went on until Nammalwar stopped it.

'Yes, what do you want?' Nammalwar did not speak but raised his right index finger.

'Do it fast and come back quickly.'

The boy ran to the garden and stood silently under the mango tree. He was not afraid of either the darkness or Tataka.

He was terrified of his father. He waited there until Raman's yells were loud enough to reach him.

'Does it take this long to pass water? Have you washed your mouth?'

I am done for. 'Yes.'

'Come near me. Let me check.' Raman found that the corners of his son's mouth were dry. So was the cloth around his waist.

'You are a liar. You are here to chant God's names and pray to Him for good habits. Yet for a silly thing like this you don't hesitate to lie. Are you a Brahmin boy? How could you recite the *Prabandham* with an unclean mouth?'

He slapped him hard again. 'Ponna, Ponna,' he bawled.

'Don't give him any dinner tonight. Let him starve. It is too much food that makes him obstinate.'

Pretty rich, this coming from you. 'He is a child. You can't expect him to chant the Lord's names all the time and not play. If you starve a child, it will only stunt his growth. I hope you do realise that. As it is he hardly eats during the day. From tomorrow he will not give you cause for complaint.'

'That tomorrow will never come.'

Raman was right. It was impossible for him to tie Nammalwar down and convert him into a scripture-fiend. Things came to such a pass that one day in frustration Raman tied a rope around his son's waist and tried to lower him into the well. Ponna had had enough. She took both Nammalwar and Pakshi to Tirunelveli and got them admitted into the Hindu High School. She hired a house in Perumal West Car Street and asked her mother to stay with the children and cook for them. Raman did not say anything. His passion for the scriptures vanished with his son's departure. He spent his evenings in the newly opened Rao's Hotel that served crisp and delicious dosas.

V

Andal was not as tall as her mother and had none of her features. She was good-looking in a plump way. As then

Nanguneri was full of elfin girls, she received favourable notice. As soon as she reached the age of nine Raman began to feel restless and he told Ponna that they were delaying her marriage.

'She has already crossed the safe period for marriage and is now entering into the dangerous period. If we don't get a good bridegroom for her now, it may prove to be a difficult task later.' Ponna had her own experience before her and she did not want to delay her daughter's marriage either.

They called home the family pundit, a venerable old man from Alwar Tirunagari, and gave him Andal's horoscope. He pored over it for a long time and asked for Andal. When she came before him, he took her left hand in his right one and brought it very near his myopic eyes. When his appraisal was over, he said, 'Run along, girl, your friends are waiting.'

He turned to the anxious couple and said, 'Don't worry. Your daughter has all the attributes of a fine girl. She has the rare and lucky lotus mark on her palm, the mark Sita had on hers. This is the right time for her marriage.'

They paid him twenty silver rupees and he invoked all the gods he worshipped to give the family long life and undiminishing prosperity. He returned to his village to inform the other Iyengars of the generosity of the moneylender family.

Ponna told the elders of her village of her intention and word went round the Iyengar world of the Tirunelveli region that the Nanguneri moneylender family had a girl available for marriage. Finally, after months of searching, they found a suitable boy, twelve years of age, from one of the good Tenkalai families of Tirukkurunkudi. The boy was tall and fair and had shiny black hair, so long that he could sit on it. He was in the fifth class and Raman learnt to his satisfaction that unlike Nammalwar, the bridegroom could effortlessly recite the *Tiruvaimoli*.

The marriage was again a grand four-day affair and since both the families were wealthy, there was a surfeit of silk saris, gold and diamonds.

Dance parties arrived from Tanjore and the dancers' nights were booked for weeks after the marriage. The landlords from the nearby villages fell over one another to sleep with the Tanjore beauties. 'What breasts!' they exclaimed. 'Like hemispheres of jaggery. They will make even a limp rice-noodle stand erect.'

The marrying children had no concern with sex or the mantras the assembled pundits chanted on their behalf. They were thrilled by the glitter of the occasion and that they were at the centre of it.

The boy sat on a plank amidst cacophonous pundits who intoned Vedic mantras, smiling at each other and taking deep breaths between pauses. Raman proclaimed that he intended giving his daughter in marriage to the boy. The boy, giving his assent, went inside the house to make himself ritually competent for the purpose. A barber who got a silver rupee for his labour shaved him, and his uncles dressed him up in silk. He came back and sat on the marriage dais and was lost in a deluge of ceremonies. Andal frequently recalled one of them with amusement. She and her boy husband were both taken up on the shoulders of their maternal uncles. The boy's mother had a brother and Sarangan, temporarily free of alcohol, officiated as Andal's uncle. Both pranced about with their burdens, making mock thrusts and swift parries to the delight of the guests. Andal was steady but the boy went groggy and begged his uncle to release him. The elders remarked that it was Andal who would be in charge of the household. Like her mother.

On the fourth day, after their shoulders were smeared with reddened turmeric paste, they were made to sit facing each other and a coconut was given to them. They rolled it to and fro between them, while the boy's aunts sang the hymns about the other Andal – the Vaishnava poet who married the Lord.

'I dreamt of the Lord walking the festooned streets of the town, a thousand elephants surrounding him . . .'

The ladies sang the dream songs with their eyes closed and their voices trembling. They forgot the boy and the girl rolling a coconut. They forgot their husbands and their quarrels with them and the simpering reconciliations at night. The dream songs took them back to their personal dreams which Andal, the poet, had made wonderfully real for them.

The Nanguneri tank was full that year. Its waves overshot the protective wall and drenched the road beside it. Bathers were careful and they did not attempt swimming. They stood on the second step of the bathing ghat which lay immersed in knee-deep water. They either poured the water over themselves with narrow-necked brass vessels or, holding their neighbours' hands firmly, took a few quick dips in the muddy water, which turned their off-white veshtis dirty brown. They admonished the boys who wanted to be brave and usually kept a hawk's eye on them.

At times even hawks go to sleep.

When the boy did not return home after his bath, his parents, who had been accommodated in a house a few yards away from Raman's, were not unduly worried. Their son was fond of water and there were days when he bathed for a full three hours, returning red-eyed and wet-haired. His mother then used a big towel to dry his long hair, a chore she performed lovingly, though with feigned annoyance. When it was noon they sent someone to Raman's house to find out whether the boy had gone there. They then ran to the bathing ghat and made enquiries about their son. Nobody remembered having seen him. He had no friends in Nanguneri and a few boys had a faint memory of his bathing early in the morning. Raman joined the boy's parents now and they made a vow to visit the Lord's shrine in Srirangam if he returned safely. They sent a person to Tirukkurunkudi and another to Tirunelveli – one of his aunts lived there – to find out whether the boy, in a fit of madness, had decided to play a practical joke on them. His father secretly promised to himself that he would thrash his son within an inch of his life when he saw him next. The boy did not return. After a few days when the waters receded, the body of a boy, bloated and beyond recognition, was found tucked in a gap between the eleventh and twelfth steps.

The boys of Nanguneri frequently played a game when the tank was full and its waters were not angry. A boy would go down the steps under water, holding his breath and touching them one by one with his hand. Another boy sitting on the top of the steps would count, 'one, two, three . . .' till the boy surfaced. Although the count did not match with the number of steps touched by the boy underwater, it certainly gave an idea of how long he could hold his breath. Moreover, when the water was not too muddy, one could see at least the shadow of the boy going methodically down the steps. The boy whose count was the highest was declared the winner. Nobody played the game on that day. It was hardly possible as the water was thick like curd and its colour that of a brick. The waves crashed with such force that it was difficult to stand steady even on the second step.

The parents protested that the body was not their son's, but they knew it was.

VI

As long as he was alive, the embers of this tragedy kept smouldering in Raman's heart. His appetite did not leave him, but now he ate in silence. He rarely talked to Ponna who did not want to invade his mourning.

Ponna did not wail in public like other Brahmin women. The only request she made to the boy's parents, to which they readily agreed, was that Andal be allowed to live with her. To those who came to commiserate, she said, 'This is the will of the Lord, and we are just his playthings.' Why he chose to play with the life of a vivacious, plump little girl, she never understood.

Andal did not know the boy at all and his death did not affect her, at least initially. She, like her father, loved the dosas of Rao's Hotel, and waited every evening for her father to bring home a delicious parcel of them. Her playmates did not avoid her, though they became annoyingly considerate. Her world collapsed so very slowly that she failed to notice it. In a way it was good that she did not, for she would have never been able to prevent it.

After the obsequies were over, Nammalwar came to his father. Since he began living in Tirunelveli, he had learnt to speak to Raman boldly without fear of being hit. He was now as tall as his father. He was going to be fourteen and it was only because Ponna wanted him to concentrate on his studies that a marriage was not forced upon him.

'Father, are you reading *Swadesamitran*?'

'Yes, how does it concern you?'

'Its editor, G. Subramania Iyer, suffered a similar tragedy. You must surely be aware of it.'

Raman understood what his son was hinting at. 'Nonsense. Subramania Iyer is a big man. And he had to face the fury of his community. He ran away from Madras and performed his daughter's wedding in Bombay. I can't hope to leave Nanguneri and we need the support of our community.'

'Why don't you to talk to our Jiyar? Andal is still a child. She didn't even know the boy.'

'You should stop meddling in matters concerning your elders. Andal is my daughter and it is my responsibility to find a way out for her.'

The next day Raman went to Tirukkurankudi and met the boy's father.

'I am sorry, the Lord has ordained that I should make this request of you.'

'I don't follow, Raman Iyengar.'

'I . . . I am thinking . . . just thinking of finding a bridegroom for Andal. I though I should seek your permission first, since she has become the property of your house.'

'Oh, I have no objection at all. What objection can I have? If you are able to find a suitable boy, please tell me and I shall come with my wife to bless the child. She is our child and her happiness is important to us.'

Raman fell like a log at his feet. Recovering, he said, 'Swami, you are indeed rare. It is my daughter's misfortune that she could not live in your house to receive your blessing every day.'

Raman returned to Nanguneri and immediately asked his father-in-law to take him to the Jiyar. In stark contrast to Raman, the Jiyar was an emaciated man who looked as though he might depart the material world at any moment. He spoke in a hoarse whisper that made any conversation with him seem conspiratorial. They said he was indeed a conspiring man before he became the Jiyar.

'Swami, I am a helpless man and I have come to a person who all Srivaishavas know is a saviour of the destitute.'

'Raman Iyengar, if you are helpless the world is helpless. Do tell me your problem.'

'Swami, you know that my daughter has been widowed recently. She is still a child and I thought . . .'

'Yes, Raman Iyengar?'

'I thought I should find another groom for her. I need your support in this venture and without it, it will be impossible for me to go further.'

'Raman Iyengar, what are you saying? Your daughter is not the first child-widow of Nanguneri, neither is she going to be the last. If all such parents decide on their daughters' remarriage, how will our community remain pure? I am the head of this Matam and I can never be a party to a sinful deed which is against our ancient shastras.'

'Swami, we have made many changes with the time. This could also be one such change.'

'I will never permit a change that is against our shastras. Sandilya says, "Widows should avoid, even when in affliction or danger – please note, even when in affliction or danger – eating of sweets, betel nut, flowers, sexual intercourse, conversation with men and jewels." Clearly the shastras do not recognise remarriage. A widow who violates these injunctions will go to Rauravam, one of the cruelest hells imaginable. Do you want your daughter to suffer in hell?'

That is what she will do on earth if she does not remarry, thought Raman.

'Raman Iyengar, the Vadakalai's grouse against our community is that our widows don't shave their heads. If they hear that we have started the remarriage of our widows, they will use this as yet another proof of our inferiority. Tragedies are transitory and you will recover from the shock. Meanwhile, don't anything foolish that will bring a bad name to your great family and the Tenkalais.'

Raman returned a broken man.

Three

THE BUS STATION WAS THROBBING WITH PEOPLE and growling bus engines. Most of the buses were near superannuation, but their horns blared vigorously in unison. Glass-fronted shops inside the station had put on view mounds of brightly coloured sweets and savouries. Their mixers whisked frothy concoctions of fruit pulp laced with exotic syrups. Kiosks displayed an absorbing confusion of dailies, weeklies, monthlies, mysteries, romances, girlies, astrological books and religious tracts.

The bus to Nanguneri was surprisingly not crowded and Kannan managed a window seat without much effort. The April sun, white and searing, kept pace with the accelerating bus. It did not trouble him. He had grown up bathing in its heat. He had a Wodehouse on his lap to impress the girls, but there was hardly anyone in the bus who might be impressed.

Does Uma indulge in such silly infidelities? She has written that I am the centre of her existence, but what about the peripheries? Are they constantly nibbled at, as they are in my case?

Sitting beside Kannan was an old man whose cheeks ballooned with tobacco. The trapped juice bubbled at the corners of his mouth and flowed down his chin in irregular, vile streaks. Kannan opened the window and turned his face away from his neighbour.

The bus was crossing the bridge. The river was lean and ugly and its bed strewn with rocks that stuck out like pustules. The city's drain joined the river here, poisoning and blackening it. A group of unconcerned women lay immersed in the water, their wet heads bobbing slowly in rhythm with the flow and their saris billowing behind them in trails of brilliant colours.

The stink of tobacco had ceased to bother him now. He looked around, twisting his torso at odd angles, to survey the bus. Nothing interested him except the heads of a young couple a few seats in front. The strings of jasmine entwined in the girl's long plaited hair looked plump and fresh. The boy's black, bouncy curls brushed the collar of his shirt, staining it with hair-oil. He was saying something and the girl's hoop earring swayed in agreement. Though Kannan could not see their faces fully, their unhurried movements suggested that they were happy to be together.

The bus had just passed the Trinity Church and was now entering Palayamkottai town. There were some neat houses on the right side of the road and in one of them lived Chandran, Kannan's principal.

II

Kannan was able to secure the appointment of demonstrator in physics at the D.D.T. College (Dhanapakkiamammal, Draupatiammal and Tayammal College – the institution was given a hefty donation by a local benefactor and it carried in gratitude the names of his wife, mother and grandmother) even before his postgraduation results were out. His physics was wobbly but he was probably the best candidate interviewed by the college management. In any case there was no one from the Physics department on the interview board.

The college which had earlier been on the high road between Tirunelveli town and Palayamkottai was now located in a waterless wilderness beyond the town. It had had its glorious days – the college was more than a century old – but when Kannan joined it, it was mostly those that could not get admission in the other two colleges, St Xavier's and St John's of Palayamkottai, who came wearily to it. Some good students preferred the D.D.T. because the other two were too distant and expensive. Such boys were so hugely outnumbered that they were of little consequence.

Kannan could thus pass off as a not-too-incompetent teacher initially, but he was conscious of his lack of knowledge and of the need to learn more physics in order to teach it without sounding woolly. He had had the bitter experience of his own teachers who had steered him through his degree and postgraduation without a mishap. They were efficient – and mechanical, like clockwork. Physics to them was a gigantic set of equations, statements and formulae to be solved and stored in the mind for the singular purpose of satisfying eccentric examiners. Kannan was very successful at this sport and he emerged with numerous first classes. He nevertheless felt empty and did not want his students to suffer a similar fate.

Fortunately he had a friend in Muthu, a colleague who gently took Kannan through the seemingly arcane world of physics. He was soon aware of what he had missed and he began to teach physics in a language and style that his students could understand. The number of students who missed his classes decreased sharply.

It was more than twenty years since India had won her independence, but the college had a dress code that was absurd and amusing. Every male teacher was enjoined to come to classes either in jacket and tie or in dhoti, coat and turban. The latter, once a favourite of nationalist Brahmin teachers, had gone out of vogue probably the very next year after Independence, but the jacket and tie continued with a perseverance that the British had never had. The classrooms had no ceiling fans and heat, like God, reigned always and everywhere. It was even uncomfortable for one to wear a shirt, let alone a jacket, in these rooms. The students were sometimes down to their vests. The hapless teachers who were condemned to observe this senseless ritual routinely shared jackets and ties. These were never washed until some students obliquely reminded the teachers of the ripe aroma they were exuding. The charade was enacted only when the teachers were walking to their classes. They discarded the ensemble immediately on entry and it lay crumpled on a chair until the class was over.

Chandran's sartorial elegance was unmatched in Tirunelveli. He had a rather learned look, emphasised by his thin spectacles. When he spoke he was heard, depending on the occasion, either in reverential silence or sullen stillness. A devout follower of Rajaji, the arch-conservative, he sniffed at the Communists who seemed to have infested the college. As the principal, he was set on strictly enforcing the dress code which he thought would show the Communists where they stood. He ordered the teachers not to remove their jackets and ties while they were teaching.

There was an effete teachers' association in the college. When it met, which was not often, it was usually to greet a teacher on his marriage or to bid farewell to him on retirement or to condole about his final passage. This meeting was different. It breathed acid. A professor sternly warned that Mother Tamil would impale imitators of imperialism if they so much as raised their heads. Another said that no son who had been suckled by a Tamil mother would ever wear the contemptible livery of slavery. A resolution demanding the immediate abolition of the dress code was proposed by a myopic mathematics lecturer. He was plagued summer after summer by prickly heat and he naturally loathed the code. It was seconded by another whose asthmatic spasms steeply increased if a jacket-donning teacher passed him by.

The resolution was promptly delivered to Chandran who, the teachers thought, would be fazed by their uncommon unity. They were disappointed. He threatened those who violated the code with suspension.

When the association met again to consider this caveat, the original fire-eaters were nowhere to be seen. The few who attended the meeting decided that a delegation of two teachers, Kannan and Muthu, would go to Chandran personally to explain the teachers' case.

This was the first time Kannan was entering the principal's room. Minions like him were usually handled by the vice-principal. Chandran's room was airy and spacious and it was no wonder he was comfortable in his lounge suit. Being the principal he did not have to stoop to teaching. He looked fresh and exuded eau-de-cologne.

He glowered at the delegation and did not offer them seats. Muthu quietly occupied one of the vacant chairs and motioned his friend to sit on another.

'Sir, we have come to you . . .'

'I know why you have come. The answer is no. Please don't waste my time.'

'We can't be brushed aside like this, sir. We are not your domestic servants. You have to respect us and listen to us. The dress code is an imperialist relic and it can't be . . .'

'Have you come here to make speeches? This is not a Communist platform. A dress is a dress. It has a price tag, not an ideological one. And that is all that can be said of it.'

Muthu tried to be conciliatory.

'I am sorry, sir. We are not against every dress code, sir. We are only against this code. It is very uncomfortable to wear jackets and ties in this climate. We are not against trousers and shirts. You could suggest a uniform . . .'

'And make you all look like petrol-pump attendants? The present code gives you dignity and sets you apart from the riffraff. You are strange. You insist on either veshti and shirt, that crumple in no time, or tight-fitting trousers that bulge obscenely at the crotch.'

'You have completely misunderstood us, sir. We never said we would wear tight-fitting trousers to class. Or veshti. We . . .'

'Would you like to go to classes with nothing on at all?'

Muthu's eyes narrowed in anger.

'Mr Chandran, you are provoking us. We shall wear what we choose to wear. You can't compel us to follow your pet code.'

'Get out of the room. How dare you address me by name? I shall have you dismissed. You must be Tirumalai's son,' said Chandran addressing Kannan. 'You should be ashamed that you have made common cause with this Communist instigator. Your father shall hear of this.' Kannan did not reply and walked out of the room with his friend.

The delegation's failure to convince the Principal could have resulted in a victory for him, since many teachers were reconciled to suffocation in jackets and ties. But Chandran, who felt insulted that one of his lowly demonstrators could dare to address him by name, suspended Muthu within half an hour of the meeting. This was a tactical error for which he paid dearly. Now the students took over the agitation.

The students, athirst for action which they thought was long overdue, grabbed this gratuitous offer and went on strike. They launched a spectacular poster campaign. One poster called Chandran a Jinnah Minor (Jinnah was famous for his immaculate attire) and a blot on the fair land of Gandhi, who, as everyone knew, did not set much store by correct dress. Another lampooned him as a moffusil Hitler who had invented a slow and brutal method for the strangulation of good teachers. Chandran kept making terse appeals to students in local newspapers to withdraw the strike but his appeals invited only derision. After a month, the management intervened and revoked the suspension of Muthu. The jacket struggle was decisively won by the teachers and the dress code, though not formally withdrawn, was never enforced. Chandran, apart from grumbling at the billiards table of the District Club about the alarming decline of discipline among the teachers, took his defeat gracefully but he himself remained as tidily dressed as ever.

III

The sun was turning tangerine when the bus entered at Nanguneri bus stop. The girl was probably asleep, her head resting on the shoulder of the boy, who himself was recovering from a doze. The heat had killed off the flowers in her hair and only a few withered ones remained on the fibrous strings. They looked mean and tattered. The couple must be traveling on to Nagercoil. While getting down Kannan had a fleeting glimpse of her face. It was plain and disappointing.

Kannan did not speak to his grandfather who was still in his rocking chair. His client must have slunk off, and the War Book of Kamban Ramayanam, a tome probably heavier than many of his law books, was perched unsteadily on his knees. The old man did not display any desire to speak to him either; he simply snorted and stared into his Kamban. Kannan went straight to the kitchen to greet his grandmother.

Kannan's grandmother was delighted to see him. She was a ripe fruit of a woman whose lovely features had shed their sharpness and assumed an elegance that Kannan thought came unfailingly to Iyengar women of substance. No longer taut but heavy with diamonds, her earlobes quivered as she walked about, scattering light in dazzling colours.

'Kannan, I thought you had forgotten this old woman. I will fight with you later. You must now be famished. I have some idlis for you.'

'Idlis can wait, paati. I am looking for Nambi. Where is he?'

Her eyes clouded. Though Nambi was not her own grandson – he was the grandson of her husband's brother, Nammalwar – it was she who brought him up after his parents' death. She knew him better than she knew her own grandchildren and was now anxious that she would lose him.

'Don't ask me. He doesn't listen to me any more. He is a big doctor. Why should he seek my permission to leave the house?'

Nambi would never leave the house without informing paati. Kannan could smell the pungency of friction but he did not want to take issue with his grandmother.

'Leave him, paati. Tell me at least where Radha is. Is she returning to Tirunelveli or is she staying back?'

'Let her spend her vacations here. She is of great help to me and what is more, your peria paati has taken to her so much that she does not even like my presence in her room.'

'God, I have forgotten peria paati. I should run.'

Kannan rushed out of the kitchen and presently he was at side of his great-grandmother's bed.

'Peria paati, peria paati. Open your eyes. Look, it's me, Kannan.'

There was no response from the old lady and Kannan gently took her left hand and clasped it with both his hands. He could feel the faint regular throb of life. He was contented.

This boy has taken after my husband, thought the lady, her eyes closed. Kannan is as nervous as he was. May the Lord grant him long life, which He did not deign to grant to my husband.

Radha quietly entered the room. It was feeding time for Ponna and the young girl loved the chore.

'Who do I see here? Have you lost your way?' She stopped for a moment, and said, 'Yes, you must have made up with grandpa.'

'Nothing of that sort. He still glares at me. Considers me unspeakable. Like Oscar Wilde's English country gentleman galloping after a fox – the unspeakable chasing the uneatable.'

Radha broke into laughter, her teeth dazzling, her gums pink with health.

'I must say that was very funny. Why didn't you give me Oscar Wilde to read? Instead you gave me that gloomy classic.'

'Don't you like Dostoevsky?'

'I am not sure I do. I am now happy and I want to stay happy as long as possible. I wouldn't like to borrow contrived sorrow like you seem to do, though a fine girl has foolishly fallen for you. Have you asked Uma to read this genius of gloom?'

'Her feet are firmly on the ground. She says she will live life rather than read it.'

'I don't fancy floating about either. We already have two very buoyant persons in the family. You and Nambi. By the way, Uma asked me to coax you to try at the civil service examinations. Has she spoken to you about it?'

'She has. It is our standard love-talk nowadays,' said Kannan bitterly.

'Well, considering that she is saddled with a dreamy never-do-well, she has to chalk out plans for both of you. I hope you do realise that.'

Kannan was turning hot under his collar and it was with difficulty that he controlled his temper. He was fond of his sister but her unrelenting logic had upset him.

'I haven't come here to discuss this. Where is Nambi?'

'Didn't you know? Nambi has left the house. He had a quarrel with thatha.'

'What?' exclaimed Kannan. It was unthinkable that Nambi would desert paati. 'He hardly raises his voice before thatha. How could he quarrel with him?'

'I don't know. Paati wouldn't utter a word. The old man says airily that he does not like Nambi distributing free medicines to all and sundry. I don't believe him. Nambi has been doing it all these years and it could hardly be the cause of his departure. There is more to this than meets the eye.'

'I shall unravel the mystery,' said Kannan.

The old woman moaned softly. Radha waved him away. 'Get lost, Inspector Clouseau. It is feeding time for peria paati. Tell amma that I shall spend a few more days here.'

IV

Kannan came out of Ponna's room and reached the backyard. Paati was gathering flowers for the evening puja, slowly muttering to herself. Kannan crept up behind her and touched her softly on her shoulder. She was not alarmed, for she was familiar with this prank of her grandson's. She lightly brushed away his hand, turned around and took his right hand in hers.

'You haven't changed much, Kannan. Earlier I used to pretend I was scared, to delight you. You have no use for such simple games now. I shouldn't be speaking to you. It is more than six months since you visited Nanguneri last.'

'I am sorry, paati, but the college kept me busy. I am hungry now. Where are those idlis?'

'Idlis don't grow on plants. You have to come to the kitchen to get them.'

Grandmother was happy that Kannan had consented to eat in her house. The old man, though not on talking terms with his grandson, had asked his wife before leaving for the temple to ensure that Kannan did not leave the house before eating. 'I have no fight with his stomach,' was what he said.

Grandmother's idlis were as soft as the flowers she was gathering. She glowed with contentment at her grandson tucking into the idlis.

'Now you can tell me paati. What has happened to Nambi?'

'Are you spying for your sister? She has failed to extract the news out of me and she has sent you instead.'

'At least tell me where he has gone.'

'Tell me first why you are so adamantine and not speaking to your thatha. You shouldn't be this rigid. He is an old man and he is entitled to his idiosyncrasies.'

Kannan had no convincing answer. Paati is right. Why had I wantonly hurt his pride? He is entitled to it. Nambi would never have done it. There must have been weightier reasons for his quarrel with thatha.

Sankara Iyer, Pakshi's senior, used to say, 'Our Pakshi is a splendid fellow but these Iyengars are a curious people. They have among them people from every station – judges, cooks, ministers, bearers, scholars, illiterates, lawyers, clerks, ascetics, lechers and even lepers. And every one of them considers himself the most superior person on earth. In their pecking order, other Brahmins come low and figure somewhere close to the other lesser breeds, like the non-Brahmins.' Sankara Iyer was a Smartha Brahmin and the Smarthas are the most numerous of the Tamil Brahmins. They were the object of the Iyengars' collective and secret hatred. Iyengars did have close friends among the Iyers, but they customarily made snide remarks about them behind their backs.

Pakshi, for instance, maintained that it was a well-planned conspiracy of the Iyers to project to the world that the main pillar of Indian philosophical tradition was the Advaita Vedanta of Sankara. He used to tell his other approving Iyengar friends in Nanguneri, 'It was that Andhra Smartha, Dr Radhakrishnan who gave undue publicity to Sankara's false Vedanta in his books. He suppressed the true Vedanta of the incomparable Ramanuja.'

Kannan had initially been cavalier about his sect so passionately defended by his thatha, until Nambi gave him an idea of it.

'Sankara's Advaita Vedanta says that the entire universe is illusory and the lone reality that pervades everywhere is Brahman. Ramanuja says that matter, the souls and God, who is Narayana, are all real and distinct, though they stand in a close, inseparable relation to one another. Of the three, Narayana exists for himself and the other two exist for his sake and they attain salvation through his grace. It is the duty of every soul to surrender to him completely and await his grace.'

'I can understand the difference between Sankara's stand and Ramanuja's, but why are we at daggers drawn with our cousins, the Vadakalais?' said Kannan.

'The theologians quote eighteen differences between the Vadakalais and Tenkalais, but the division is primarily due to a schism on the interpretation of how the Lord will bestow his grace on the soul. We hold that the Lord's grace will be spontaneous and no special effort will be needed by the soul. Its surrender to the Lord will be its very nature. The Vadakalais say, on the other hand, that some effort will still be needed from the soul and surrender will be an occasion for the Lord to open the floodgates of his grace. The soul is as helpless as a kitten, we say, and all it has to do is to wait and it is for the Lord, the mother-cat, to seek it out and to shower it with affection. The soul has to cling to the Lord, the Vadakalais say, like a baby-monkey holds on to its mother. The other major difference is that while the Vadakalais regard the Sanskrit Vedas and the Tamil *Prabandham* as equally important, we of course hold the *Prabandham* superior even to the Sanskrit Vedas.'

'You know that the fight is not purely philosophical,' continued Nambi. 'The philosophical fight is for the scholarly and Srivaishnava scholars these days are as rare as cashew nuts in the temple puliyodarai. The real fight is for the control of rich temples. We have our set of rituals and the Vadakalais have theirs. Even an ignorant Iyengar who cannot tell the Tiruvaimoli from the *Peria Tirumoli* thinks he is an unrivalled authority when it comes to rituals. And he fights till the bitter end to legitimise his version.'

Kannan knew how acrimonious and prolonged these fights were. Some issues that to the uninitiated appeared laughable reached even the Privy Council in England. One famous case was about the tiruman, the caste mark the Iyengars don on their foreheads. The Tenkalai tiruman is like a trident with a short stem. The trident starts just above the brows and runs right into the top of the forehead with a central red streak that parallels the two white ones. A horizontal white streak forms the base of the trident just above the bridge of the nose and the stem, also white, runs down about an inch on the nose. The Vadakalai tiruman is similar, except that it is without the stem and is parabola-shaped. A dispute arose between these two factions as to which mark the elephant of one of the prominent temples should don. The Tenkalai Iyengars finally won the right, after years of see-saw battles in various courts, to parade the elephant with their mark, though there was no elephant to parade, the beast having reached in the meantime the lotus feet of the Lord. For my thatha who took a leading part in the case, Kannan thought, the principle was important. Death's irony was lost on him.

'Our thatha says the Vadakalais are scheming, money-crazy defenders of Sanskrit and Brahminical orthodoxy. He is no mean defender of the same orthodoxy but he wouldn't like to be reminded of it. The Vadakalais, not to be outdone, regard us as bogus Brahmins who are only fit to be cooks and whose overemphasis on the Tamil scriptures is just to hide our inability to master Sanskrit,' said Nambi.

'The problem is that thatha has been fighting with our Matam too,' said Kannan.

Nambi laughed and said, 'He is indefatigable. His war of the balls is well into its thirtieth year and he has shown no signs of giving up.'

Not only did Pakshi not give up but he eventually won the war as well, which uncannily resembled his earlier war of the elephant in some respects.

Every day without fail, a few Iyengars of Nanguneri, called Adhyabakas, chanted the hymns of the *Prabandham* ceremoniously in front of the Lord. The Jiyar gave them for their efforts a nominal chanting allowance, called the *adhyabaka padi*, which was usually a big ball of one of those many-flavoured versions of rice that had ritually been offered to the Lord. The Jiyar had an overseer to supervise the chanting group. He sat through the chanting and distributed the rice-balls to those whom he thought had chanted the hymns sincerely without dozing off. This arrangement was working well, till one day the overseer refused the quotidian rice-ball to one of the adhyabakas who chanted diligently but had had a tiff with the overseer earlier that day. The spurned Iyengar threatened in anger to spit on the container in which the balls were kept. He was physically expelled from the temple for this act of defiance.

The adhyabaka was one of Pakshi's admirers and Pakshi took it upon himself to defend him. He went to the Jiyar to plead his case.

'Swami, I thought I should bring to your notice the injustice meted out to one of your disciples right under your auspicious nose.'

The Swami had already been briefed by the overseer and he had made up his mind to stand by his servant.

'Pakshi, how can there be injustice in the presence of the Lord? I am sure there is some mistake.'

'Your overseer has denied the chanting allowance to one of the most sincere Srivaishnavas. This is against the dharma of the Matam.'

'Pakshi, I determine the dharma of the Matam. The adhyabaka, I understand, threatened to pollute the *prasadam* by spitting on it. I can't tolerate such acts of defilement within the precincts of the temple.'

'But that was after your overseer had unjustly refused him the adhyabaka padi. I shall ask him to apologise to you for his lapse. But he should not be banished from the chanting group.'

'I am not inclined to interfere with the decision of the overseer. After all if his authority is questioned today even on valid grounds, it may be questioned tomorrow on invalid ones.'

'Swami, you are forcing me to seek legal redress.'

'You are a lawyer, Pakshi. Can I prevent you?'

Pakshi left the Matam in a huff and never set foot inside it again while the Jiyar was alive. He first sat on a hunger strike in front of the Matam. It did not move the Jiyar at all though the local Iyengar women shed a tear or two. He then took the matter before the court. He won the case in the lower court but lost it in the high court. Undaunted, he went on appeal to the Supreme Court which took a full twenty years to decide the case in favour of Pakshi. The case that started seven years before Independence came to its weary end twenty-three years after that momentous event. Pakshi claimed that the victory, though delayed, was a deeply moral one. He arranged for a family feast to celebrate it.

Kannan as was his wont tried to needle his grandfather.

'This is a pyrrhic victory, thatha. You have wasted thousands of rupees over a non-issue.'

'Nonsense. It is my money and I will spend it the way I like.'

'That is hardly the stand a professed Gandhian would take.'

Pakshi was angry because his grandson had caught him on a vulnerable point. 'Are you doubting my principles?'

'Yes, I am. If you were a genuine Gandhian you would not have taken up such a hopelessly sectarian dispute and fought over it for thirty years. Who has benefited from this victory, except your tribe of lawyers?'

Kannan was substantially right. The adhyabaka, the Jiyar and the overseer did not wait for the judgment; they had passed on. Many of the Brahmins of the village having moved on to better stations, the chanting crowd had by now dwindled alarmingly. Being unable to tempt them with rice-balls, the Matam paid cash to the few chanters they could collect.

Kannan could have left it at that, but he pressed on. 'To you, what is important is your Tenkalai pride. No, not even that, it is your personal pride that appears to be more important than larger issues.'

Pakshi was livid. 'I won't talk to you again, Kannan, unless you apologise to me for what you have just said.'

'I haven't said anything wrong, thatha.'

Pakshi had stopped speaking to Kannan after that quarrel.

Both Kannan and his grandmother were so caught up in their conversation that they failed to notice the flurry in the hall. They were startled by Radha's shriek, 'Paati, see who has come.'

Grandmother rushed out of the kitchen and Kannan followed her with the empty plate in his hand.

Ponna had always maintained that her lost son Nammalwar was the most handsome in the family. She would have nodded in approval of Nambi. Though he was tall and rugged, his features had an unmistakable resemblance to Ponna's, barely diluted through three generations. He stood on the step leading to the hall, left hand in his pocket and the right holding on to one of the shiny brass knobs of the heavy wooden door. When he saw paati he hurried towards her and prostrated, his long hands touching her feet peeking out from the folds of her nine-yard sari. She bent down to lift him up. When he was on his legs with his head still bowed, she placed her right hand on his shock of hair to bless him.

'You will live to be a hundred. We were just talking about you and here you are.'

'I came here to see you paati. I knew thatha would be in the temple. I didn't want a scene.'

'Is he your enemy? You are not going anywhere today. Go upstairs and change.'

Nambi hesitated. 'She is alone in the house. I have to get back tonight.'

Kannan jumped. 'She? Who is "she"? What is going on, Nambi?'

'Keep quiet Kannan. Nambi, you are not living with her. Are you?'

'She is now my wife, paati.'

Grandmother was speechless and gaped at Nambi. Kannan and Radha looked at each other. It took some time for them to allow what Nambi had said to sink in. Grandmother reacted first. She went inside the dark room where the family valuables were kept and returned with a fine leather pouch.

'Here are your mother's jewels, Nambi. Now they belong to your wife. I shall come to your home with thatha to bless you both, whenever he agrees.'

'Wait, wait. This is not a movie. You are seeing too many of these Tamil films, paati. I am sure whoever he is married to is not in a tearing hurry to decorate herself with these precious jewels. The problem is that thatha does not approve of Nambi's choice. Right?'

'There was a big row the other day and Nambi went away in a huff. But I never expected him to marry without even telling me. I agree with you. I am getting too emotional. I shall see the bride myself and give her the jewels.'

She proceeded to remove a ring from her finger and handed it over to Nambi.

'This is yours. Your grandmother never removed this ring when she was alive. Give this at least to my granddaughter.'

'You seem to be on a giving spree. There were so many grandmothers and grandfathers it is amazing how you keep track of their inventories. Do you have any bequests to be handed over to me, by any chance?' said Kannan.

He sounded cheerful, but he was hurt. I run to him with every problem of mine and he ups and marries without even giving me a hint. I am not important enough for him.

'Well, paati, I should be going back to Tirunelveli. Congratulations, Nambi. Do show us your wife when you feel up to it.'

'Where are you going? You are going to stay here today.'

'He is coming with me paati,' said Nambi. 'I will have to check peria paati before I leave. Does she have enough medicine?'

'She has. For another ten days, unless you decide to change them,' said Radha. 'She was not very coherent today. She was asking for kallu, toddy or liquor or stone, I am not sure which.'

'You must ask thatha. He is her authorised interpreter.'

'He, too is flummoxed

Four

PONNA WAS EAGER TO KNOW THE Jiyar's decision and when she heard what Raman had to say she wept quietly. Raman came up and looked at her closely. Her beauty did not excite him any more although he still needed her. He folded his arms around her and let her weep. It must be at least ten years, Ponna thought between her tears, since he hugged me like this and I, in spite of this long hibernation, find that my longing for him remains undiminished. Her mind suddenly lurched. Is it longing for him or . . . ?

Raman tightened his arms. 'Ponna, if you lose confidence, our family will be ruined. I am not bothered about that skeleton of a Jiyar. I shall start searching for a bridegroom for Andal from tomorrow.'

Ponna said, 'I don't think that will be easy. Why can't we leave this place? We could sell our property and settle in a big town like Madras or Madurai.'

Raman realised that it was her turn to dream and he did not want to bring her back to the real world. 'Yes, yes. I shall start making the necessary arrangements. Your thatha did live in the North, miles away even from Madras. Didn't he?'

'He was a gypsy and when he had lost interest in wandering, life lost interest in him. He is not the perfect example.'

Raman was true to his word. He made many trips in search of a boy to places where the Tenkalai population was dense. There were many near-hits that kept his hope alive for a few years.

One day when he came home from a tiring trip to Srirangam, Ponna told him the news.

'She has become a woman two days ago.'

Raman's search had ended. There were families in Nanguneri that hushed up the fact that their girls had started menstruating in their desperation to marry them off. But then, they were all malnourished girls who could easily conceal their womanhood. Concealment was hardly possible in Andal's case. She looked a woman even when she was ten.

Raman's end came unheralded on a summer morning when Ponna was fast asleep. His mouth was open as usual. The pillow this time was stained with saliva and blood.

Ponna turned intensely religious for a period after Raman's death. It was not that she neglected her responsibilities. She sold a portion of their land and invested the money in a solid British bank. She asked the cook to stop serving the skeletal Jiyar and to move to her house. She saw to it that the funeral ceremonies of her husband were performed in a manner that would gladden his soul. The laddus were the size of cannon-balls and the *vadais* as big as tricycle wheels. The Brahmins after the funeral feast said in unison in Sanskrit, 'we are satisfied'. They meant it.

Poona's preparations for her prayers started in the evening. She bathed, chanting 'Narayana, Narayana, Narayana,' and changed to another sari, which was washed by her personally every day and hung up and spread out to dry on a wooden rod slung across the hall and held in place by two parallel ropes hanging from the ceiling. No one touched that sari except Ponna. She lit a big brass lamp in the Perumal room and by its light read every day exactly one hundred verses of the Tiruvaimoli. She did not recite them mechanically like the professional Iyengars of her village. She recited them slowly, enunciating every word clearly. Nammalwar's Tamil was tough, but she could understand the poet's strange longing for the Lord, who was said to be easily attainable to those on whom he chose to shower his grace.

'Lord,' she prayed, 'let me not wander. I may not be fit enough to receive your grace. At least let me not wander.'

Andal usually sat next to her, without touching her, but rarely did she recite the poems or join her mother in her prayers. Her parents-in-law came after Raman's death and offered to take her with them. Ponna told them that she would be lonely without her daughter and they agreed to let her stay.

Andal's life as a widow was not as bad as it appeared to be. The house next to theirs also belonged to the moneylender family. The family used it to lodge guests who came without notice. The houses had a sort of common garden. It remained unattended for many years and, barring the path leading to the brook and the mango tree that occupied one corner, it was overgrown with hardy weeds that survived despite the very dry soil and the sapping heat of summer. Andal took it upon herself to turn this weedy wasteland into a flower garden. Two gardeners were engaged to remove the weeds and the soil was prepared for flowering plants that she ordered from a Tirunelveli nursery. Within a year, she had chamomile, cassandra and southern wood, and varieties of jasmine, rose and oleander. There was also a champak tree; and there was Tuscan jasmine that flowered at night with its tiny white flowers filling the air with their whore's fragrance. The flowers were never picked. The garden floor was always strewn with them, fresh and wilted. Andal came every morning to the garden and spoke softly to every plant. Then she methodically tended to them which took care of much of her morning.

Her mother engaged an old pundit to teach her Sanskrit and the scriptures and her classes went on until noon. The major theological works, *Mumukshupadi, Gadyathryam* and *Sri Vachana Bhushanam* were taught to her and she memorised all of them. The Tamil *Prabandham* she read on her own, and Nammalwar who came to Nanguneri every Sunday taught her English and elementary mathematics. Her friends came in the afternoon after their hectic kitchen stints were over and they played *pallankuli*, using an elliptical wooden board with two rows, each having seven hollows to be filled with five counters. They fought, they cheated, they exulted over their hard-won victories and they wept their narrow losses. They appeared happy, Andal's widowhood not posing problems. Except when they discussed husbands and what they did to them. Except when festivals came, which they did with irritating regularity. Andal had to seek company then in other widows, warped and peculiar, who had chewed and spat out life. Ponna detested them but religion ordained otherwise. She did not want Andal to be alone and idle.

Mother and daughter visited the temple occasionally in the evenings when they knew that it would not be crowded. They did not wear white like the other widows. They did not wear silk either. They were simple and elegant widows who caused quite a few hearts to flutter.

They crossed the temple's entrance-gate over which soared the *gopuram*, bristling with a statuary medley of deities, demons, dwarves and damsels and entered a vast pillared hall, the Javanthi Mandapam. Two crouched leonine *vyalas* greeted them. Inside each vyala's mouth was a smooth rolling sphere of stone. It was a miracle of sculpting, for the vyala itself was carved from a single stone. As a child, Andal always stopped before the vyalas to roll the stones the beasts were condemned to pouch. She used to roll them vigorously, commanding the vyalas to spit them out. The vyalas were always silent, their unblinking monster eyes staring at the entrance.

The stones at least are smooth, Ponna thought, unlike the thorny porcupine of memories that rolls on in my mind, resisting expulsion. They crossed the hall and presently reached another hall leading to the Garbhagriha, the dwelling place of Vishnu. He was ceremoniously washed in six measures of sesame oil mixed with sandal oil every day – and on a special day every year with one hundred and twelve measures. The oil was carefully collected in a well and given away as a healing unction for believers with skin ailments. The Lord, sitting in the dark and mysterious Garbhagriha, is supposed to offer salve for the soul.

That day Ponna recited the ten poems of Nammalwar on the Lord Nanguneri.

I have no record of austerities; not do I possess any subtle knowledge. Still, I cannot rest even for a moment without you. Oh Lord lying on a serpent bed, I am not too much of a burden to You . . .

She looked at her daughter who, surprisingly, was praying with her eyes closed. Her brows were perfect arches. Not a single hair was out of place. Her lips, two thin and pink slashes across her face, were closed and they did not reveal her rice-pearl teeth. Her cheeks still retained the chubbiness of childhood when she used to wait for her father to bring her dosas. She had shed weight. Probably because of the gardening. Or is she not eating well? Is she a burden to the Lord? Why did he send her to us?

The priest gave them holy water and tulsi in silence – he knew that these two did not indulge in gossip – and they returned home to pray briefly again in the Perumal room.

'Do you remember him?'

'No, but appa comes in my dreams. I don't like this place, amma. Let us go to Tirunelveli. I shall miss my garden, but I don't think I could bear this Chithirai festival.'

'You have to wait, child. If the rains fail this year too, our well will go dry and we will have no other option except to move to Tirunelveli. Even otherwise, Chithirai is not the right month. Nammalwar and Pakshi will spend their vacation here and your paati wants to be here for the festival.'

Both lay awake for a long time hearing the racking cough of the cook who was getting old, and the regular creak of Krishna Iyengar's rocking-chair, which never seemed to stop.

The Chithirai festival of Nanguneri attracted both Vaishnavas and other villagers in the thousands. On nine of those ten days, the Lord regularly visited the main streets of the village in the evenings. His mount was different every day. He came mounted on Hanuman one day and Garuda on the other. He rode an elephant one day and a lion on the other. He came on a horse, he came seated in a swinging palanquin and in chariots decorated with a background of the moon one day and the sun on the other. On the tenth day he was installed in a giant wooden car especially decorated for the occasion. The car was pulled by thousands of frenzied devotees. The days were hot and the sun beat down on them relentlessly. They were bathed in sweat and perpetually thirsty. They complained loudly to their Lord for not looking after them. They went back, satisfied, to their villages.

The family skipped the festival and stayed indoors and when the Lord was in procession, the moneylender's house remained firmly shut. The old cook had to go to his tiny house to receive the Lord and offer him bananas, coconut, betel leaves and nuts.

Nanguneri was used to the games of the rains and the villagers knew that a dry spell one year was normally seconded by a very wet one the next year. That year was different. The tank went dry and its bed lay cracked like a peasant's feet. The Jiyar's spring at the centre of the tank had only a few feet of water, not enough to quench the thirst of the villagers. The well at the moneylender's house survived for a few months before its water became undrinkably clayish. The garden wilted and died slowly before the helpless eyes of Andal.

Ponna called Nammalwar and told him that she was moving to Tirunelveli with him. The cook stayed back to look after the house and Krishna Iyengar. Andal was happy. The endless discussions on water or the lack of it bored her.

Beyond the bridge on the northern side of the road connecting Tirunelveli Junction and Palayamkottai was Vannarpet, a tree-lined suburb. A few British officials lived there. Their bungalows were close to the high road, but the inner suburb had a few fine houses available to the natives. Nammalwar had rented one of these for his family.

They all liked the house. It had a guava tree in front whose fruit had blood-red flesh, seed-filled and tasteless. An ancient jungly badam was in the backyard and its nuts were very white, spongy and delicious. The house's balustrade had a fine, dignified row of stucco amphorae. The hall appeared bigger than the one at Nanguneri. It had cream-coloured tiles and a high ceiling, from which domed glasses in brilliant colours hung. The well in the backyard was thankfully full and water lay within a few pulls of the rope. Ponna could now cook for her sons who were growing and in need of good food.

Her neighbour came to Ponna the next day.

'I am happy that I now have an Iyengar neighbour. My husband is very fond of puliyodarai.'

The neighbour indeed had a happy face, smooth and unsullied by frowning lines. Bright red *kunkumam* shone on her forehead.

'We are from Kadayam. My husband is a lawyer, but he doesn't like law-courts. He is happy with his newspapers. I am your friend. Don't hesitate to ask me for anything.'

Ponna was initially hesitant but her neighbour was aggressively helpful. She ordered provisions for her and got her solid, dry faggots for the kitchen. She took her to the Vishnu temples nearby in her own covered cart drawn by two fine bullocks with sharp, shining horns. She did not mind Ponna's polite refusal to accompany her to Shiva temples. She didn't mind either when Ponna told her that she wouldn't partake of food cooked by Iyers.

Her husband was heavy-set and he sat all the time on the veranda reading the *Hindu* and the *Swadesamitran* despite his royalist leanings. He was a great admirer of Queen Victoria. When the Empress passed away, he paid his ultimate tribute to her by bathing ritually, as he would if any of his relatives had died. He told all who cared to listen to him that her demise marked the onset of the wicked age.

Ponna did not like him. She had a suspicion that this wrestler-Brahmin had the attributes of a lecher. She ignored his attempts to ingratiate himself with her and warned Andal to stay in the kitchen whenever he came into her house, which he did frequently without waiting for an invitation. She was forced to tolerate his betel-stained leer because his wife was an angel. And Ponna needed her help.

The Brahmin was a limpet. He came almost every day and sat cross-legged on the floor of the hall.

'What is the menu today?'

I do not run a hotel, Pona thought. She would however say, 'I am not as god as your wife. Why do you shame us?'

'Iyengars and bad cooking do not go together. My wife says you are an extraordinary cook.'

Ponna would not tell him the menu and he would not bother. He was happy asking futile questions and trying to draw her into chatter, a task in which he was never successful. When he ran out of his repertoire of questions he would sit silently, staring at the ceiling and admiring the domed glasses. After a while he would say, 'I am going. If you need anything, please tell me directly. I don't want my wife to mediate between us.'

Ponna first thought of telling Nammalwar, then she realised that her hot-blooded son would start a quarrel that might lead to bitterness between the neighbours. After all, the Brahmin had not misbehaved so far.

Squishy little circles of rice paste, diligently spiced and cooked, crisped on a clean white cloth in the sun. A thin white net was spread on the cloth to ward off crows. The crows did come. They cawed and circled around the cloth. The net dutifully frustrated them and they gathered in convenient pods to hold noisy, ineffectual conferences. The little circles would be delicious when dry and fried in coconut oil. They were Nammalwar's favourites. Andal kept waving her hands and shouting 'choo, choo', but her mind was not on the crows. She was sitting on the roof by a parapet wall that gave her shade. The experience was novel to her. She had never seen the roof of her house in Nanguneri. There were no steps leading to it and she was terrified of climbing up a wobbly ladder. The stucco steps in this house were steep no doubt, but they were at least permanent and they did not threaten to topple her at any moment.

The roof had a fine view. One could see the backyard of the house and behind it was a narrow mud track. Rice fields stretched beyond the track as far as the eye could see. The farmers had already begun readying the fields for the *kar* season, ploughing and sowing them. They turned up the land again so that the seeds were covered. They smoothed the surface over with a plank drawn by bullocks, brown and dutiful. The fields were now ready for water. It would arrive in a few weeks. River Tamraparni would carry it for them – water emptied by the heavy clouds of the south-west monsoon over the Potigai hills.

Andal's mind was on the fields, barren and dry. Even their ridges, which marked them out in squares and rectangles, had no suggestion of green. This would change soon, she thought, when water arrived. Within a few months the fields would be crammed with rice stalks. They would then be cut close to the ground and carried off in bundles to have the grains beaten out of them. The threshing ground away in the distance would be crowded with peasants, their women and their children. The big children would carry little loads, tend the bullocks and burst into raucous fights every now and then. The little children would run around each other in circles and urinate wherever they pleased. When they grew tired, they would sleep in the cloth-cradles effortlessly created with rope and old cloth by their mothers and hung from the branches of the neem tree at the edge of the ground.

She remembered that she had clothes to dry. She went down hurriedly, collected a bucket of clothes from the wash room and came out to the vacant plot by the side of her house. The plot was an oblong one boxed in by the side walls of the houses and two parallel walls that hid it from the street as well as the fields. It was treeless and had a long clothesline strung between two wooden poles. Andal took out the wet clothes from the bucket one by one, wrung the water out of each, shook it vigorously and spread it on the line.

She knew that Subbu was watching her.

The other side of the plot had a room opening into it and Subbu was glued to the room's window. He was the wrestler-Brahmin's son and was trying to navigate the dangerous shoals of BA. The hidden mud banks of English had already toppled him twice. He hated Shakespeare, particularly *The Tempest* and *Othello*. The grandiloquent magician-king and the stupidly suspicious moor befuddled him and threatened to condemn him to a degree-less future. Green-eyed monsters and ungrateful savages were passable but they refused to take shape in his words. English words.

His Shakespeare-scarred mind had also to contend with thoughts of his bosomy cousin, touching sixteen and waiting for him to graduate. Despite his wife's implorements, the wrestler-Brahmin had blocked Subbu's marriage and commanded him to get his BA first. Now Andal disturbed him. From where he sat he could see her lovely profile and her plump cheek framed by black tresses. He could see the knots of her bodice through the disturbed folds of her sari. He could see her breasts lifting up whenever she stood on her toes and raised her arms to spread a garment on the line. He started feverishly to fondle himself.

Andal was used to masculine stares in the streets and in the temples. The men's unhurried appraisals left her shuddering with revulsion and made her look down and carefully adjust the folds of her sari. She mentally bathed and scrubbed herself clean every time. But that was in the streets. Or in the temples where the Lord was her guard. It had never happened in her house. This time the stare remained with her and followed her to the kitchen, to the hall and to the roof, where she climbed up to collect the clothes, still sticking to little circles of rice paste. The little circles would let go of the cloth the next day, when the sun would stare at them again.

She felt moist and squishy and sticky. She did not bathe that day and was delighted to be dirty.

She continued to dry her clothes and Subbu continued to watch her. After a week he came up silently behind her and touched her shoulder. She brushed aside his hand and ran back to her house without collecting the bucket. She came back the next day and this time she allowed Subbu to keep his hand on her shoulder for some time. He came so near that she could smell his armpit-odour, which hovered around her like a cloud of mosquitoes after he had left.

When she came again the next morning he hugged her close from behind, his hands gently squeezing her breasts and his erection poking her at odd places. She turned round to face him and slapped him hard. Then she ran back to the house, tears wetting her sari and her heaving bosom.

The broken rice went up in swirls and fell on the edge of the winnowing pan and on the floor in an unfailing rhythm. Ponna's hands holding the pan wore no bangles and the only noise in the hall was caused by the rice hitting the pan and the floor. The small stones in the rice did not gain height and stayed in the pan; Ponna periodically stopped winnowing to pick them out laboriously and put them in a container. I shall take this to our village and show it to our men as proof that they are not doing their job sincerely, Ponna thought. The stones appeared to outweigh the rice. Andal came running and buried her face in her mother's lap. She was sobbing uncontrollably.

Ponna stroked her hair gently. She had watched her daughter's grief very closely and her sobbing did not worry her much. Sobs, like menstruation, will stop one day, but that day is a long way off.

'Andal, stop weeping. What is the point? It is his command that we suffer. Tears won't move him.'

'Amma, I want to go back to the village. I don't like this place.'

'Are you mad? We have spent hardly a month here. I am tired, Andal. Another shifting is beyond me. Your brothers have just started eating properly. Who will cook for your brothers?'

'You need not come, amma. I shall stay with paati.'

You are too fragile to be left under the care of that old woman, Ponna thought. She said, 'Let us ask Nammalwar tonight.'

Ponna did not broach the subject with Nammalwar that night. She thought Andal would change her mind.

When Andal refused to go to the vacant plot to dry the clothes Ponna sensed that something had gone wrong and she carried the bucket herself. She could see her neighbour's room; she could see Subbu sitting on a stool with an open book in his lap. When he saw her coming, he got up hurriedly and disappeared into the house, forgetting the book which had fallen off his lap. Ponna took her time arranging the wet clothes on the line.

That day she spoke to the wrestler-Brahmin.

'I have a request to make to you.'

'I have told you, I am at your service.'

'Your son is now ripe for marriage. You should not delay it any longer.'

'What? Has that wastrel misbehaved with you?' His nostrils flared and his right hand punched the air. 'I shall whip him today.'

'No, no, no. You are mistaken. He hasn't come anywhere near me. But people do speak to me and I thought I should tell you.'

Andal resumed her drying duties the next day. This time I will not resist him, she thought. The room however appeared dead. She stood there idly for a few minutes. Disappointment welled up from the pit of her stomach and choked her. She rushed to a corner of the plot and threw up.

The wrestler-Brahmin did not know what had happened and he did not want to take a chance. He moved his son to the other wing of his house, muttering dark threats of reducing him to pulp for being randy without being studious. Subbu did not protest. He felt debased and thought of ending his life by throwing himself in front of a train. He gave up the idea solely for the sake of his comely cousin to whom he was married within a month. His degree remained a distant dream and in the fullness of time he replaced his father on the veranda, perorating on the lasting benefits of the British Empire.

The wrestler-Brahmin and his wife brought their son and daughter-in-law to Ponna's house to seek her blessing. Subbu was distinctly uncomfortable, but the bride chattered away after her initial hesitation. She went to Andal and holding her hand said, 'You must visit our house. We could be close friends.' Andal said, 'Yes, I must, one of these days. I do need a friend like you.'

The feisty winds of *Adi* pelted everyone with a fusillade of grit. Still, the Tamil Brahmins went on their religious picnics to riversides on the eighteenth day of Adi. The rivers were full and they sat on the banks admiring the swell of water and chasing away the curious non-Brahmin children. When night was about to fall they gorged themselves on a bewildering variety of rice – spicy, nutty-brown tamarind rice; fragrant, bright-yellow lemon rice; cashew-embedded coconut rice; saffron-flavoured jaggery rice and creamy curd rice. They tasted divine, and occasionally gritty, when river-sand found its way into them.

Ponna remembered one such trip to the banks of the Tamraparni, before Andal was born and when Pakshi was at her breast. They started early in the morning in a spacious double-bullock cart and travelling beyond Palayamkottai town took the sloping road that ran along the western river bank to the lovely little Krishnan temple of Kokkirakulam. The priest of the temple was an Iyengar of their branch and he had arranged the picnic. They went down the flight of steps leading to the still hot sands of the river. They chose a clean spot and Ponna spread a cotton cloth on the sand to arrange the baskets of food. The elders gossiped and Nammalwar and the priest's children, in love with sand, turned somersaults and played vaulting horse. Soon sand dotted their oily hair like lice. They all ate heartily and sat there until the river was no longer visible. They went back to the temple groping in the dark, bumping into each other and supremely happy.

Ponna made elaborate preparations for the eighteenth of Adi this time, as all her children were with her. Nammalwar and Pakshi went to the river to join their friends, taking with them a big basket of food. For Andal, she arranged rice in colourful little palmyra-leaf baskets and took them to the roof. She waited for Andal to arrive for her private picnic. She waited watching the now verdant fields. She waited until the sun went down behind the river. She came down for her evening prayers. The rice-in-baskets stayed on the roof, turned cold in the twilight, kept well during the night and went stale in the morning.

Ponna tried all the ruses she knew to prevail upon Andal to remain in Tirunelveli. She took her to the nine sacred temples of Vishnu which dotted the banks of the Tamraparni. She called a gardener from Palayamkottai to transform the vacant plot into a garden and asked Andal to oversee his work. She requested Nammalwar to advise her. She even learnt to make superlative dosas. Andal was not persuaded. When she stopped eating one day, Ponna had to send her back to Nanguneri.

The monsoon seemed to have made a special detour for Nanguneri and all the rivulets that fed the tank were now overflowing. Ponna's well was full. One could touch its water by bending over. Andal engaged her old gardeners to resurrect her dead garden and soon it regained its beauty. The house had also gone mouldy in Ponna's absence. The lumber-room was piled high with broken chairs, stools, string cots, kitchen racks and other detritus. The last cleaning, she remembered, had been immediately after the death of her father. She was determined to clean it again and she worked on it for three days without rest. On the evening of the third day, when her task was almost complete, she was bitten by what looked like a snake. She had only a fleeting glimpse of it before it slithered away into the bowels of the earth. Snake charmers were called later to coax it out of the room but their attempts were of no avail.

There were no visible fang marks at the site of the bite though it was painful. Without losing time she called the cook and told him to fetch the local expert on snakebites. She wrapped a cloth tightly around her bitten leg and waited for help to arrive.

The expert was a broad-shouldered Iyer boy. He ran to the well, quickly poured water over his head and came fully wet to Andal. He unwrapped the cloth and surveyed the site of the bite. He made an incision with a knife he had brought and allowed the blood to ooze out. He then put his mouth on the incised spot, sucked the blood and spat it out in a bowl. After repeating this operation a few times he went out to the backyard and washed his mouth. He returned to Andal, washed her leg and applied on it the sacred ash from a pouch he carried. Sitting close to her, he chanted a few mantras in a melodious voice.

'There is no need to worry. The poison has been drawn out. She should not move for at least a week. I shall be visiting her every day. I must now return home for an elaborate puja to propitiate Nilakantha.'

Fever visited Andal that night and did not leave her for a fortnight. Her leg became swollen and it took more than a month for it to subside. In the end she recovered because she was very healthy and probably because the bite was not deep enough to cause much harm or the snake was not a poisonous one at all. Or because the mantras chanted by the broad-shouldered boy reached the Lord of the Serpents.

Ponna who had to return to Nanguneri to nurse her daughter found in her a sullenness which made conversation with her a painful exercise. Andal's replies to even routine questions were needlessly aggressive. She raked her mind for the cause of this change, but she could not come up with a plausible reason. Muteness dimmed her daughter's incandescent defiance and while nursing her, Ponna kept a palpable silence.

Ponna was not without a chatty companion, though. Krishna Iyengar must have heard the flourish announcing the arrival of death, for he became the babbler that he had been before his wife's murder. He called Ponna to his side and said, 'I am sorry, child. We have always been a bunch of wife-beaters.'

Ponna had not heard him talk for years. Earlier, even grief could not prise his mouth open. When his granddaughter lost her husband, he had his rocking chair shifted to the upper storey and he remained there until the numbing rituals were exhausted. When Raman's bier was placed at his feet, he whined like a starving puppy, but he did not speak.

'Why are you saying so, appa? My husband was always nice to me.'

'That was why he was taken away, perhaps. My father used to beat my mother with a log. I still remember her quietly applying oil on her bruises. My grandfather banged his wife's head on the wall with such force that she became cross-eyed and could not see properly till her end. And I? . . . You know what happened to your mother-in-law.'

She said, 'I know you were kind to my mother-in-law. My husband was extraordinary, appa. Let alone beating, your son hadn't even spoken harshly to me.' Her eyes were full of tears.

'You are perhaps right, but Raman's children may take after me. Or, worse, my father or grandfather. I . . . I want a promise from you.'

'Yes, appa.'

'I shall tell you where I have kept the jewels. You may sell them or do whatever you like, but if you decide to bequeath the jewels or their proceeds, they should go to your daughter and daughters-in-law and not your sons.'

He waited for a few seconds to allow his words to sink in.

'Choose good wives for your sons, as I had chosen you.'

He took from the folds of his veshti a bunch of ancient keys. He selected one of them and asked Ponna to remove it from the bunch.

He told her where he had hidden the jewels. They were, as Ponna had suspected, in the other house in a box underneath the tiles of an unused room. They were magnificent jewels, collected from generations of lecherous zamindars and litigious landlords by the moneylender and his rapacious ancestors. Ponna did not tell any one either of the hoard or of the promise she had made to her father-in-law. She scrupulously kept her promise.

Krishna Iyengar's death meant another cycle of ceremonies, and when Ponna tried to go back to her daughter, she found that Andal had travelled a long distance. She did not have the celerity to catch up with the child again.

She thought she had found solace in the *Tiruvaimoli* and in its songs of separation, sung of the soul's longing for God. She read them during the day and at night. She could now recite them without much effort which she did, while cooking, while bathing, while praying and while thinking of things that she felt should not be thought of.

She loved *'malaiyum vandadu, mayaan varaan'*, the penultimate poem in the ninth ten of the ninth hundred.[1]

> *Evening has come,*
>> *but not the dark one.*
>
> *The bulls,*
>> *their bells jingling,*
>> *have mated with their cows*
>> *and the cows are frisky.*
>
> *The flutes play cruel songs,*
>> *bees flutter in their bright*
>> *white jasmine*
>> *and the blue-black lily.*
>
> *The sea leaps into the sky*
>> *and cries aloud.*
>
> *Without him here,*
>> *what shall I say?*
>> *How shall I survive?*

Solace bilked her. The poet's earthy metaphors, instead, prickled a quiescent monkey. She started staring stealthily at men whom she came across everyday – the temple priests who were paunchy and thick-jowled and smelt of camphor and sandal paste; the tenants who exuded a horrendous aloe-smell; the palmyra climbers who were lean and sinewy and toddy-smelling and the broad-shouldered Iyer boy who was visiting Andal to chant the poison out of her system and whose smell Ponna did not go near enough to draw in. She was young. And

---

[1] *Translated by A.K. Ramanujan*

in the flush of her excitement, she forgot her daughter. Even the mother-songs of Nammalwar did not remind her of Andal.

Her name was Isakki and heavy *pambadams* once adorned her ears. She now had only dilated earlobes that lolled on her shoulders and dangled whenever she moved. She was the most faithful servant of the moneylender household and she kept guard when Andal or Ponna had to retire to the room adjoining the backyard for three days every month. Her only problem was the wonderful gift of sleep she had been bestowed with. Once she went to sleep, one had to prod her in the ribs to wake her up. Little noises did not bother her at all.

He came as promised. She could hear the faint creak of the hinges, the muted footsteps, the thuds of her heart and finally his passionate panting. His hot breath singed her cheeks and his lips moved over her neck. He had not visited the barber for days and his stubble spiked her soft flesh. One hand rapidly tried to untie the knots of her bodice and the other probed her between the thighs. She sighed and embraced him tightly. He took her hand in his and guided it to his erection.

She pulled away from him and sat up.

'Go away. I don't want it.'

He was confused. He thought it was one of those feminine ploys to make him more determined, and he grabbed her in the dark. She was strong and she fought with demonic fury; her kicks hurt him. Their scuffle was intense and in its intensity they did not first notice darkness yielding to feeble visibility.

Ponna's sleep had always been fragile. She knew it could not be thieves. There were expert house-breakers of course but house-breaking was not a very silent operation and it was rare that the same house was broken into twice. She fervently prayed for her suspicion to be proved wrong. She took a thick stick and a night lamp and went in measured steps towards the backyard.

He saw her first. He jumped up, gathering his veshti. Andal was still on the floor, her hair covering her face. He was stunning in his fright. His lips quivered and his tuft, undone, flowed over his broad shoulders that tapered gracefully. His stomach curved like a string cot about to lose its tautness and his chest filled with black curls of fire was commodious enough for two. The nipples were sleepy little corns of pepper. Raman had a hollow pigeon chest and his nipples were pimply bitter gourds.

He said in trembling voice, 'Believe me, she called me here.'

Ponna looked at Andal who was still on the floor, tying her hair.

'Yes, I called him. Don't look at me like that. Nothing has happened.'

'Believe me, she called me here,' he repeated. He waited for Ponna to respond, but she was just staring at him. He pushed her aside and ran into the night.

Ponna wanted her daughter to get up and stand in a corner demurely, guilt-bitten. She wanted to hit her, bash her head against the wall and scream at her like other distraught mothers would scream, 'You are a slut. Why don't you die?' She was afraid that her daughter was expecting such words to be spat at her. Andal would then die; her unuttered thought that her mother was no better would also die. She averted her eyes from Andal's gaze, which she feared would burn a hole in her.

'Are you really unfit to enter the house? You must be feigning.'

'I called him here. I wanted him.'

'Come inside. I think I can safely touch you.'

'No, no, don't touch me. I don't want you anywhere near me.'

'You have lost your senses. Do you realise what you have done?'

'Yes, I do. Nothing happened between us. You were sniffing around.'

Ponna burst into tears. 'Andal, you are being cruel. I shall talk to you tomorrow. Please come inside and at least sleep beside Isakki.'

'I don't want to talk to you, ever. And if you come near me, I shall jump into the well.'

Ponna placed the lamp in a corner of the room, came out and bolted it from outside. Isakki was snoring peacefully.

She crossed the hall and thought of waking up her father, sleeping in the front room. Instead she unlocked the front door and came out to the street. The night air was bracing. String cots, bowing under the loads of blanketed figures lined both sides of the street, which died a hundred yards away to the right of her house, giving way to the massive temple complex. She could clearly make out the outlines of the temple gopuram below the starlit sky and with folded hands she mumbled Nammalwar's ten on the Lord of Nanguneri.

She tried to focus her thoughts on her daughter, her dead husband and her sons in Tirunelveli. She tried to lift the terrified snake-bite boy by his ears and throw him out of her mind, but he would not let her go. His embrace was tight and stifling on that terrible night. She stayed awake till she could hear the 'sh' . . . 'sh' . . . of the broom sweeping the entrance. It must be Isakki. I haven't noticed her walking past me. She gathered herself together and walked into the backyard to start another day. She gently undid the bolt and pushing the door ajar, looked inside. She could see the crouched figure of her daughter and she stood and listened for the sound of her daughter's breath. She was relieved to hear it clearly.

Andal came into the house in the morning after a bath at the well into which she had wanted to jump. She asked Isakki to light up incense for her hair. Widows were not to indulge in such luxuries but she did not care.

Ponna called the local medicine-woman that afternoon. She had never discussed her physical problems with others until then – she had never had any major ones anyway – but this time she was frantic.

'Lately I have not been myself, Avudai. I am not able to sleep and when I do, I get dreams that a woman of my station shouldn't get. At times, they come during the days too, when I am fully awake. You must suggest some cure.'

Avudai was a seasoned village-doctor and she understood what Ponna was hinting at. She said, 'Amma, what you have with you does not die with your husband. Men have a way out; they marry again or go to other women. It is different with us. It is probably the Lord's way of punishing women for the sins of their previous births. Still, I shall suggest an effective remedy that should give you relief. Take a handful of coriander seeds. Grind them and roast them lightly in ghee. Take this powder every day in the morning before you start the day.'

Ponna followed Avudai's prescription meticulously for a long time. She had willed herself that it would work. It probably did. She was not sure.

Andal had to speak to Ponna, for, in spite of her belligerence, she needed her mother for everyday-nothings. Both made separate covenants with silence on what happened that night. Andal's sobs became rare and they eventually dried up long before her menstruation did. Ponna never had occasion again to stroke her daughter's head. Andal buried her head, when she felt the need to, privately in Isakki's lap.

Five

IT WAS DIFFICULT FOR KANNAN TO KEEP UP his injured silence and within a few minutes in the course of their trudge towards the bus-stand, he bumped into Nambi to avoid a fat buffalo which was vigorously fanning its rump and scattering tiny bits of dark green dung all over. Both burst into laughter.

'You obviously don't consider me close.'

'You daft bugger. You know it's not true. You are the only idiot-cousin I have. Well, there is Radha . . . She is a mere child. And she is bright.'

'Idiots do get invited to marriages. They provide the comic relief. Don't they?'

'Kannan, try to understand. I did not inform anybody, except of course thatha and paati. They too got just a hint. I wanted this decision to be mine alone. It was not love. Though you consider me a sort of a *praeceptor amoris*, I am not a loving man. There was no leisurely, complex swordplay with a view to eventual coupling as there seems to be between you and Uma. It was a purely utilitarian arrangement. There was nothing to celebrate. If the old man hadn't gone overboard, causing paati considerable distress, I would even have delayed it. I acted quickly because if I had waited I would have perhaps been swayed by my love for them to change my decision. Now I am glad that thatha blowing his top hurried me into doing what I have done. Our marriage has solved all our operational problems. We can now move around together without giving the villagers a chance to gossip about us.'

'Rosa, it must be Rosa.'

'You have guessed correctly. You know she is a gynaecologist. She looks after the wives and I the husbands. And they no longer drop broad hints about the unwisdom of having a virgin as your pillion rider. Well, not exactly pillion now. Yes, she is not a Brahmin. It doesn't matter though it is probably one of the causes of thatha's anger. It is somehow beyond that Gandhian that I don't aspire to the status of a good Brahmin, or even a nominal status like the one you seem to hang on to. The people whom we visit are so desperate they don't bother about these trifling matters. Now that they are sure that we don't live in sin, our rate of acceptability is bound to increase dramatically.'

'Still, I don't see the logic of your making a mystery of your marriage. Rosa is a sensible person. How did she agree to this cloak and dagger wedding?'

'She left the decision to me. Like me, she is without parents now. Her father died two months ago.'

Rosa came barely to Nambi's shoulders. Though she did not possess the lazy elegance that Kannan thought marked many Tamil upper-class women, Rosa was still the petite dynamo that she had been before the accident, and she moved around on crutches without great difficulty. She had big eyes made bigger by the thin outlines of kohl, which appeared to touch her thick, curly hair, flowing down in ringlets over her temples. Perhaps that was about the only concession she had made to beautify herself. She was wearing a dark blue sari that made her look darker than she was and a loose blouse that made limp pouches on her arms. She was genuinely happy to see Kannan.

'Kannan! This is indeed a surprise.'

'The bigger surprise, Rosa, was what you both did. You have forgotten me.'

'Nambi is the culprit, Kannan. He was in a tearing hurry. God knows why. Come in. Our story is too detailed to be discussed on the doorstep.'

The house was small with a sloping red-tiled roof. It had three small rooms, a kitchen, a bathroom and a lavatory. The front room was to receive patients – it was a rural doctor's room with a big chart indicating in Tamil the various parts of the human body, a table, a chair, two stools and a narrow bench. A wash basin and a covered bucket with water occupied one corner. A sizeable medicine chest covered one wall. A framed print of Lenin addressing the workers of St Petersburg adorned the other one. Kannan also noticed a bust of Gandhi on the table besides two fat books on medicine, a stethoscope and a sphygmomanometer. There was only one of what could be called a doctor's chair in the room. They probably took turns to see their patients. The other two rooms looked almost bare, though Nambi had put down stools at convenient corners for Rosa to relax if she should feel the need to do so. The lavatory had a western-style commode with a rail fixed just above it. There were no cots in the house except a single foldable one of striped plastic webbing. They both probably sleep on the floor, Kannan thought. The folding cot is for me who has come unannounced. Rosa has come through the grind because she had no other choice and my hero has deliberately chosen the tough path. Thatha may not think so, but they suit each other well. Still, it is unbelievable that Nambi is now married to a girl he has picked personally. I thought he was outside the wheel of life, standing apart and guiding reeling mortals like me.

'You are going to have your dinner here, Kannan,' said Nambi.

Rosa looked sharply at him and said, 'No, he is not, unless he has changed his good habits and graduated to mutton.'

'He still remains a strict vegetarian, Rosa, unlike his prodigal cousin who has descended to flesh-eating.'

'Oh, don't bother. I am full. Paati has stuffed me with idlis. Rosa, tell me honestly. I am sure you are already regretting the decision.'

'Which decision?'

'The decision to marry Nambi, of course. I haven't seen anyone in my family, except paati, who did not cry for mercy after a few minutes of his company.'

'Oh, he is the original comic genius,' said Nambi. 'Come on, I shall take you to Iyer's Hotel. He serves reasonable tiffin.'

I wouldn't discuss my problem with Nambi. Certainly not after his marriage to Rosa. Uma may be an Iyer, but she is still a Brahmin. Nambi will laugh at me if I tell him that our Iyengar-Iyer union would set the town on fire.

Ponna, escorting the young Nambi to school, used to tell him that the family did not have any doctor and she depended on him to set right this hiatus. He did not take her remarks seriously, but his teacher's gentle persuasion was different.

Isaac Devairakkam was a soft-spoken and brilliant homosexual. How he landed in Nambi's school was not known, but he was still teaching there when Nambi left, when Pakshi moved to Nanguneri. Krishna Iyer Hindu Aided Elementary School was a miserable place. Its walls, chipped and pock-marked, never saw a lick of whitewash as long as Nambi was there and when it rained, water came down effortlessly through the ceiling and gathered in convenient puddles for children to jump in. Krishna Iyer had two reasons, according to Ponna, for bestowing this gift on the unwary people of Tirunelveli. The first, the ostensible one, was to clear the mist of ignorance from young minds. The real one however was to offer gainful employment to his wife's relatives, who were otherwise unemployable. The school crawled with them. Nambi went there because it was a stone's throw away from his house, which enabled Ponna to amble in whenever she felt like and watch the academic progress of her great-grandson closely. There was not much to watch. To Krishna Iyer's relatives, who never seemed to cross the barrier of retirement, the school sessions were pleasant stretches of slumber with a blissful intermission of wakefulness during lunch. The children did pretty much what they wanted. Mr Isaac was different from the Krishna Iyer clan. He was a shy scholar. If he found a boy redeemable, he would ask him to sit close to him and, gently stroking the boy's thighs, unravel before him in language he could comprehend the secrets of science and the pleasures of both Tamil and English literature. He was a cornucopia of information that always delighted and educated the children. His forays in the thigh region usually came to nothing. A frown was enough; the wandering hand would withdraw. No child ever complained to his parents, for Isaac's homosexuality was gentle and not predatory.

Nambi usually pumped him for information about the human body. The teacher told him, 'The best way to know the inside of us is to become an anatomist.' He took Nambi to one of his doctor friends and showed him a print.

It was *The Anatomy Lesson of Doctor Tulp*, a polished work by Rembrandt that decorated the wall of the doctor's waiting room. It was not very appropriate to instill confidence in the minds of patients, depicting as it did Doctor Tulp showing his students a very dead man and his dissected left hand. Most patients sat under the painting in order to avoid seeing it and some even requested the doctor to remove it. The doctor let it hang because he felt it was a talisman that brought in patients in droves. The dead man fascinated Nambi. It was he who appeared to dominate the scene and bring life to it and not the anatomist and his curious disciples.

'Can I open up men like that?'

'You can, son. You can. But only dead persons.'

Once he had made up his mind, it was easy for him to get admission, for he had always been a brilliant student.

Rosa was the only daughter of an agricultural labourer who did not marry after his wife's death and who had the sense to understand his daughter's dreams and the courage to make them real for her. He was a remarkable man who led a dignified life in spite of his station and never allowed anybody to ill-treat him. Since there were many others available for ill-treatment and since he was an excellent farmhand, his landlord tolerated him.

Though he was an early member of the local Communist Party, Rosa remembered him as a fine singer who sang the Ballad of Nambaduvan regularly during the Karthikai festival of the great Nambi Temple. It was the story of an outcast singer, an ancestor of Rosa's father. Nambaduvan, a devotee of the Lord Nambi, was caught by a ravenous Brahmaraksha, a Brahmin demon, when the singer was on his way to worship Nambi. He promised the demon that he would come back to offer himself as dinner and the Brahmarakshas, trusting him, let him go. The singer came back as promised after worshipping the Lord – he could not enter the temple owing to his caste and the Lord had graciously shifted his flag post to one side to afford his disciple a fine view from the entrance. But the demon's hunger had disappeared miraculously and when the singer insisted that he would like to keep his promise, the demon demurred. The moral tussle between them seemed interminable until The Lord intervened. He praised the uprightness of his devotee, relieved the demon of his demon-hood and gave him back his human, Brahmin status.

Rosa was not impressed with the story so beautifully sung by her father. She asked her father, 'Why didn't the Lord invite your ancestor inside the temple, if he had loved him so much?' The moral of the story for her was that the Brahmins devoured you in any case, either in human form or the demonic one, unless the Lord chose to interfere in exceptional cases. She had a fascination for that avuncular man, Joseph Stalin, who from his framed photograph smiled at her charmingly every day, narrowing his eyes. She enthusiastically attended Communist meetings with her father and though she did not become a member of the party, she never made a secret of where her sympathies lay.

When Rosa passed her school finals, she knew she would study medicine. The village Communists who had promised to fund her education had a year's lead as she had to complete her pre-university course. Yet they could collect only a few hundred rupees, hardly sufficient to get admission in the medical college. It was finally the Catholic priest of a nearby village who ran around and arranged a scholarship for her, after eliciting a promise from her that she would not run away to a big town on getting a medical degree.

Nambi was an already famous figure in his college when Rosa joined there. He was in his final year. On a dreary day when the sun was threatening to reduce everyone to cinders she came to his room parched and soaked in sweat. Her Communist friends had told her that he was a different Brahmin with strong pro-poor sympathies.

'May I come in, sir?'

'Come on in. I don't yet deserve the honorific "sir". It will be fine if you call me Nambi. You look dehydrated. Let me make some sherbet for you.' He pushed a stool right under the ceiling fan and said, 'Make yourself comfortable. May I get a towel for you?'

It was the first time Rosa had seen a senior student without any affectations, a quality all the more rare in a highly-rated medical student. He presently brought her a glass of sherbet.

'I am sorry it is not iced . . . I haven't asked your name.'

'Rosa.'

'Roja?'

'No, it is Rosa. First year. I am from Tirukkurunkudi. I understand you are from Nanguneri.'

'Yes. Strange that your parents chose this name for you. Surely the Tamil "Roja", for rose, has become the elegant

"Rosa". The people of our region usually stumble at pronouncing "ja". Am I right?'

Rosa laughed. Her lips were dry and flaked, but she had a lovely set of teeth with bright pink gums to match.

'No, you are not right. My father took me as an infant to a district Communist leader for a suitable name and this was the one he chose. After Rosa Luxemburg.'

'You don't have a brother named after Karl Liebknecht to match you, have you?'

She giggled. 'No, no. I am a single child.'

'So am I. But I was named very traditionally, after the Lord of your village. I was born, so they say, after long years of prayer in many temples and it was your Lord who finally consented to bring me forth.'

Rosa was fascinated by Nambi. It did not take her long to understand that he was not keen on becoming a prosperous medical practitioner in a big town. Nambi told her that after his degree he wanted to work in a village near Nangueri and she told him that it was her mission in life to teach the poor women of the villages around hers safe, inexpensive prenatal and postnatal care and to treat them free, if possible, for their various afflictions.

Nambi waited for her to join him and both opened a clinic in Rosa's village. Ponna had invested fifty thousand rupees in Nambi's name and he received an interest of five hundred rupees every month. As salary, Nambi paid two hundred rupees to Rosa out of his income and they did not charge their patients. There was of course a collection box in which willing patients dropped whatever they could afford and the proceeds went to buy medicines. They spent their mornings in the clinic, visited the villages nearby after midday on Nambi's motorcycle and came back to the clinic in the evenings.

Though the villagers of the region were aggressive in many respects – the murder rate of the area was one of the highest in the Tamil country – they surrendered to diseases rather tamely. They came running to the doctor only when self-medication – learnt through grandmothers, wandering salesmen or medical shop attendants, or simply by watching the qualified doctors – had failed. They had learnt to distrust the traditional medicine man of the village, usually the village barber, but had not fully appreciated the fact that for certain illnesses, local medicines were both effective and cheap, and at hand. Service, unless it came in a religious garb, was viewed with suspicion by them. It was hardly possible for them as victims of centuries of chicanery to imagine that there could be people who would be willing to help them without any pecuniary motive. It was hard for Rosa and Nambi to win their confidence, but they won it eventually.

The accident that resulted in the amputation of Rosa's left leg from the knee was a freak one and it happened on a rainy afternoon. She and Nambi were returning from the Tirunelveli General Hospital after discussing a complicated case with its doctors when Nambi had to brake suddenly to avoid a goat which seemed to run headlong into his motorcycle. Rosa lost her balance and was catapulted heavenwards. She came down heavily in the middle of the road. Nambi was horrified to see a speeding bus bearing down on her. He ran towards her and it was a miracle that she survived, though her left leg was mangled. She went back to the hospital they were returning from and stayed there six months. Nambi knew that the accident would not deter her. He attached a sidecar to his motorcycle and took her back, crutches and all. He never took out his motorcycle again without Rosa in the sidecar.

He waited six months and one evening when there were no patients around he said, 'Rosa, why don't we marry?'

She looked up and said, 'It is a nice idea.'

'Nambi came this evening,' said Veda when Pakshi returned from the temple.

'Is he still here? I feel rather poorly today. He should be able to tell me why.'

'He has already left. He says he has married that girl.'

Pakshi said, 'I am not surprised. My brother's son has left behind an army mule.'

'Are you less obstinate? What was the need to quarrel with him? Or with Kannan? Your problem is you don't come down from your high pedestal.'

'Don't be foolish. Nambi's happiness is as important to me as it is to you. I wanted him to lead a docile, happy life like other doctors, but this fellow wants to caper about without understanding what life is. A good Iyengar girl would have pinned him down. Well, I understand this girl is more besotted than your grandson is.'

'You have no right to comment on that girl without even seeing her. I have seen Rosa. I called on her when she had that horrible accident. She is a fine girl and he will be happy with her. Let us go and meet them tomorrow.'

'I shall go only when that fellow comes and invites me,' said Pakshi.

'You are being silly. I am going to him tomorrow.'

'You have, I must say, peculiar grandsons. They have decided to be heroes – as if our family had been short of such characters. Kannan, I hear, is infatuated with an Iyer girl.'

'Oh, Kannan is not a problem. This is a temporary phase and he shall eventually find a good Iyengar girl. '

Veda's eyes were suddenly full of tears. 'You should not turn your back on your brother's grandson, even if you don't like Rosa. That is the least you could do for your brother.'

Pakshi said, 'Who said anything about giving him up? If not for anything else, I depend on him for my medicines. There is no better doctor than him.'

Six

STRANGELY, THERE WERE NO PARROTS ROOSTING IN its upper branches. The tree stood knobbly and brooding at the northern corner of the playground. The students devoured its big, luscious, parrot-proof mangoes and willingly fell ill. Nammalwar was not one of them. He didn't like its mangoes, which he thought were without character. He preferred the mangoes of his tree in Nanguneri, tiny misshapen ones, which started a small fire under his tongue and set his teeth on edge. Like him, the tree was special – it was nurtured to adulthood by his mother. It flowered once in two years and its lap turned into a delicate, soft bed for Nammalwar to lapse into his reveries. It was his personal tree. His mother and siblings knew it. The tree and the fat parrots perching on its low fruit-laden branches knew it. It bore mangoes only for him. No one else touched them. The college tree was bigger and its shade covered a larger space but it was not a personal tree and its mangoes, like a public woman, pleased everyone. He came to its shade frequently though, running away from the dazzle of Euclid radiated second-hand by the geometry teacher, Sitarama Iyer. He completed *Guy Mannering* and *The Talisman* sitting under the tree he did not prefer.

Nammalwar loved his physiology classes. On every new-moon day Sundara Sastri, his physiology teacher, bathed in the river Tamraparani early in the morning and spent two hours fervently praying in the Varadaraja Perumal Temple, which stood facing Sannidhi Street. He was a vegetarian and he shunned even onions in his food, but as part of his teaching he had to dissect a goat that day. He usually had a he-goat – its testicles a delicacy for his laboratory attendant – chloroformed, killed and skinned, and neatly laid out on the shining table. With tears streaming down his cheeks and his hand drenched in lemon-grass oil, he dissected the carcass with a precision that never ceased to amaze Nammalwar. The gory spectacle induced nausea in many students and they usually went without food. Nammalwar was not afraid of blood. Long after he had learnt the basics of physiology, he continued to attend Sastri's dissection sessions, only to watch his master's flawless performance. It is this precision we generally lack, he thought. Even Sastri is apologetic about his rare skill. Tilak. He has a precise mind. And he is not afraid of telling the British what they are worth.

But the nuggets of information I get about him are dipped in the usual cloying Tamil syrup that masks their significance. Nammalwar was upset and he was reading a proscribed book that described two important cases involving Tilak in a style that only Tamil writers could conjure up. The first was the one in which he was sentenced in 1898 to undergo eighteen months of rigorous imprisonment for writing seditious articles; the second was the more sensational case of the Chapekar Brothers who were sentenced to death for murdering Rand, a British officer, who took rigorous measures to control plague in the city of Pune and, in the bargain, injured Hindu sentiments. Tilak came out strongly in support of the brothers. Both these cases are prime examples of British savagery, Nammalwar reflected, but Tamil prose transforms them into the fantasies that one comes across in Vikramaditya stories. A few more leaders like Tilak will force the white crowd to pack up and leave our shores forever, but books like this are not likely to inspire them. It is unfortunate that we still depend on alien books for our inspiration. And an alien language. Subramania Bharathi's Tamil prose is luminous but we need more writers like him. Till then I will have to make do with English books. Well, even if the whites run away, they should leave their books behind them.

The Hindu College had a splendid library and it regularly ordered books from England. Nammalwar was friendly with the college librarian, Suryanarayana Pillai, who often allowed him to borrow new books, still in their jackets. The principal of the college, Edward Winckler, the Shakespeare wizard who had so befuddled Subbu, loved to keep books in pristine condition and he had a horror of lending new books to students whose hands, he felt, were normally grimy. He had issued strict instructions to Pillai not to lend new books to students. Pillai thought he did not violate the principal's order when he lent books to Nammalwar as his hands were spotlessly clean. He read fast and returned the books in a day or two.

One day, when the stellar arrangement in Pillai's horoscope was not very much to his advantage, Winckler chose to inspect the library.

He saw the arrivals register and exclaimed, 'Ah, *Napoleon of Notting Hill*. The new Chesterton. My wife is dying to read it. Mr Pillai, may I please borrow this book?'

Pillai very nearly wet his veshti and did not answer the principal for a few seconds. Then he said, 'Sir, I am very, very sorry, sir. The book is not available, sir.'

Winckler thought one of the teachers had borrowed the book.

'Don't worry, Mr Pillai. Tell me who has the book. I shall ask him to lend it to me. My wife will be delighted.'

'Actually, sir, the book, sir, is . . . is with a student, sir.'

Pillai expected Winckler to blow up in anger. Instead, he said calmly, 'Mr Pillai, would you please come closer? I have to talk to you in private.'

Pillai thought the worst was over. He came closer to the principal, his torso bowed in obedience. Winckler pounced upon him and what appealed to him immediately was Pillai's succulent right ear, inlaid with a lovely red stone. He sank his teeth into it in an effort to pull it off its base. Pillai's scream was heard through the entire college. The blood-letting did not satiate Winckler. He went back to his room and was pacing up and down like a caged puma when a student made the mistake of peering in at him through the window. The principal took a mouthful of water and spat it in the face of the hapless boy.

When Nammalwar heard what had happened to the librarian and to one of his fellow students, he was furious. He took a full bucket of water with him to the principal's room and emptied it on the now cool head of Winckler. Winckler did not react at all. He asked his attendant to lock his room and cycled all the way to his house in Palayamkottai to change his clothes.

Pillai was treated in the municipal hospital and he lived in mortal fear of rabies for about two months. His right ear looked ruddier. Winckler was fined fifteen rupees by the First Class Magistrate for what was termed unacceptable behaviour. He came back to the college the next day and was accepted by all, for he was a wonderful teacher of English literature. The teachers, however, ensured that their ears were fully covered by their turbans whenever they met him. Winckler invited Nammalwar to his house and presented him with a thick vellum notebook and a beautifully bound edition of *The Mayor of Casterbridge*. He never apologised to Pillai.

Arbuthnot & Co. of Madras had a reputation that was unrivalled except perhaps by the Bank of England. It was a hundred-year-old company and it was considered the epitome of British solidity. It was a people's bank. If princes and rich Chettiars deposited their money in millions with the bank, old men and widows too kept their small savings with Arbuthnot, secure in the knowledge that their money would always be safe with an Englishman. Sir George Arbuthnot, the chief partner of the firm, was an extravagant man whose resplendent phaeton was drawn by the most magnificent horses of Madras and admiring people routinely gathered on both sides of the streets to watch his passage. His bank employed 12,000 people and paid at least a million rupees every year as wages and salaries.

The bank crashed on 22 October 1906. The other partner of the bank, MacFayden, committed suicide. Sir George was made of sterner stuff. He claimed that he was innocent and that it was the London office of his company that had led him up the garden path. When the case came up for trial, Sir Arthur White, the Chief Justice, was not convinced by this logic and he sentenced Sir George to eighteen months of rigorous imprisonment. *The Hindu,* welcoming the judgment, said, 'It would have been a scandal of the gravest kind in the administration of justice if the chief partners of this firm had escaped condign punishment for their grave crime of deluding and defrauding the investing public.' That Sir George was suffering the indignity of a prison sentence was of little consolation to the investing public. According to the Official Assignee, the liabilities of the firm stood roughly at twenty-eight million rupees and its assets about seven million rupees.

Ponna had fifty thousand rupees with Arbuthnot & Co. She got back, after years of correspondence, barely one-fifth of her deposit.

Nammalwar did not have a head for figures and he did not fully understand the reason for the sinking of Arbuthnot. He was however happy that the perfidy of Albion had been exposed. That his family had probably lost a fortune was secondary to him. His friends told him that V.O. Chidambaram Pillai of Tuticorin was launching a new company, the Swadeshi Steam Navigation Company, and he was looking for investors. The next day Nammalwar set off for Tuticorin.

Tuticorin was an important port, second only to Madras in the entire Tamil country. It changed hands between the Dutch and the British a number of times before finally falling to the British in 1825. Its pearl fisheries were world-renowned but it was the railways that signalled the rapid progress of the town. It became a thriving trade centre, shipping to Ceylon the cotton and other commodities that were brought from the Tirunelveli plains by the Southern Indian Railway.

The north-east monsoon was aggressive that year and it was whipping Tuticorin in fury at the time of Nammalwar's arrival. He was drenched when he reached Chidambaram Pillai's house. Pillai, a dark dumpy man with piercing eyes, was startled to see a tall, dripping Brahmin boy knocking at his door. He invited him into the house and gave him a towel to dry himself.

'Would you mind having a cup of coffee in my house?'

Nammalwar, overawed by the presence of the great man, was speechless. He simply nodded.

'Your name? . . . Nammalwar? A nice Tamil name. Vadakalai or Tenkalai? . . . Tenkalai? . . . Must be from Alwar Tirunagari. No? Nanguneri? . . . mmmm . . . *Notra nonbilen. Nunarivum illen.* Was it not how Nammalwar felt when he saw your place?'

Pillai, an erudite man, laughed and recited the first poem of the ten sung by Nammalwar in praise of the Lord of Nanguneri.

'Are you familiar with *Prabandham*?'

'Not all the four thousand, sir. But I am familiar with Nammalwar's work.'

Pillai knew that the young man had not come to him for a discussion of Vaishnava literature.

'May I know the reason for this privilege?'

'Sir, I heard that you have started a Swadeshi company. My family would like to invest in it.'

'I am happy that young men like you are ready to plunge into a Swadeshi venture. I will however advise you to consult experts before investing. What are you doing?'

'I am in the Senior FA, sir, in Hindu College.'

'What is your father?'

'He is no more, sir. My mother will invest.'

Pillai went inside and presently returned with a sheaf of papers.

'I shall be happy if you could read them now. I don't want you to take a hasty decision.'

Nammalwar did not tell Pillai that matters of finance terrified him. He obediently pored over the papers. The prospectus of the Swadeshi Navigation Company said that its mission was 'to establish a cheap and reliable steamer service between Tuticorin and Colombo and all such ports and places and to popularise the art of navigation among the Indians, Ceylonese and other Asiatics and to make them profit by it.' The company had announced 40,000 shares priced at Rs 25 each. It also promised a dividend of 100 per cent.

'I must say the response so far has been overwhelming, especially in the wake of the Arbuthnot fiasco. Many Tamil patriots are canvassing for the company. I am fortunate that Lokamanya Tilak is supporting the venture.'

He came up and touched Nammalwar's shoulder.

'You are an eager boy and I must tell you more about this attempt. Tuticorin ships cotton, betel and other produce from the Tirunelveli plains to Ceylon. There is also considerable passenger traffic between the Tamil country and the island. The prospects of our company are excellent. Shipping has so far been the monopoly of a few European shipping companies. The foremost among them is the British Indian Steam Navigation Company. This company will be our main rival.'

'They all will disappear without a trace.'

'The reality, Nammalwar, is likely to be a little different. I suggest you consult Sankara Iyer of Tirunelveli. I am convinced that if young men are as enthusiastic as you are, I shall see Swaraj in my lifetime. When we meet next time we shall discuss Nammalwar. Mama swears by him.'

Nammalwar did not know who Mama was. He did not realise that Chidambaram Pillai was referring to Subramania

Bharathi, who was to become the greatest Tamil poet of the century.

Ponna did not like the idea of investing in the Swadeshi venture. It was not that she was against the Swadeshi movement but she was yet to recover from the Arbuthnot collapse and she dreaded another speculative foray. Sankara Iyer, a wealthy Tirunelveli lawyer, turned out to be a classmate of Raman and he had attended Ponna's marriage. He came to Nanguneri to discuss the investment with Ponna.

'I last visited Nanguneri at the time of your marriage. I still remember the potato roast and tomato rasam. The years seem to have wings.'

He was sitting in a high-backed teakwood chair right under a framed photograph of his classmate whose unblinking stare focused on the plate of fruits placed in front of Iyer. Ponna stood behind the kitchen door and only her smooth white right hand and her lovely face were visible to Sankara Iyer.

'You are indeed fortunate. My years are manacled. They limp ever so slowly. I sometimes wonder whether there is any purpose in living.'

'You do have a purpose. You have to bring up the children.'

And their children. And their children's children. And their children's children's . . . Life itself is its purpose. I am not honest enough to accept it, Ponna thought.

To Sankara Iyer she said, 'You are right. I will have to get a girl for Nammalwar. He needs to have a purpose. You are in Tirunelveli and you must be having many Iyengar friends. You should be able to find a suitable girl.'

Sankara Iyer extricated himself from this web of matrimony with alacrity.

'Yes, yes, that will be my first task when I reach Tirunelveli. Nammalwar must have told you about his proposal to invest in the Swadeshi company. He says you have to give the final approval.'

'I am a poor uneducated widow. What do I know of investment? I depend on the advice of good friends like you. I am still to recover from the swindle of that white rogue. May he be carried on his funeral bier.'

'We are not cheats like him. And ours is a noble cause.'

I don't want to lose money nobly, thought Ponna. She said, 'I fully understand, but if anything untoward happens we shall drown. I have nothing to fall back on.'

'I shall be the last person to reduce you to poverty. I am not compelling you. If you do not want to invest . . .'

'No, no. I won't send you away empty-handed. I was thinking of five thousand rupees. That is all I have now.' Nammalwar's happiness is worth more than five thousand rupees.

'I am very happy,' Iyer said. 'You shall not be disappointed.'

Ponna hesitated for a moment and said, 'I need some advice from you. You are my husband's friend and his son's welfare is equally dear to you. It is Mother Varamanga who has sent you here.'

'Please feel free to tell me anything. Your problems are mine.'

'It is about Nammalwar. He is bright, but he hardly concentrates on his studies. I am afraid he may go astray. He keeps strange company.'

Ponna came from behind the kitchen door and gave Iyer a printed sheet.

'He has a number of copies of this notice. I can't read English, but I am sure what is printed here is serious and Nammalwar may invite trouble because of it.'

Iyer was hardly concentrating. Though Ponna was without any adornments, the old nine-yard sari she was wearing accentuated wickedly her slender waist and her heavy, gracefully sloping breasts. Her unsurpassable beauty had an overpowering effect on him. Raman is a fool, he thought, to have disappeared from this world leaving his treasure behind.

He said, 'I shall discuss this with him. You don't worry at all. It is my responsibility now to bring him back to the right path, if indeed he has gone astray.'

When Sankara Iyer returned to Tirunelveli, he headed straight for the well in the backyard of his house. He had a cold bath with his clothes on and came fully wet to his prayer room and stood for a long time before the picture of that archetypal ascetic, Shiva.

The leaflet given to him by Ponna was a reprint of an article written by Tilak. The Indian National Congress was then going through a phase of ideological conflict. While the old-school politicians, 'the Moderates', were happy with the goal of self-government under British paramountcy, the new school, 'the Extremists', demanded freedom from all foreign control. It had, however, no objection to nominal, theoretical control. Both were competing for power within the party and Tilak was the undisputed leader of the Extremists. Chidambaram Pillai, a devout follower of Tilak, was the foremost leader of this school in Tamil Nadu.

The leaflet spoke about another legendary Maratha hero, Shivaji, who in the eighteenth century resisted the Mughals and killed their general, Afzal Khan:

> *It is needless to make further researches as to the killing of Afzal Khan. Let us even assume that Shivaji deliberately planned and executed the murder, was the act good or evil? The question cannot be answered from the standpoint of the Penal Code or of the laws of Manu or according to the principles of morality laid down in the systems of the West or of the East. The laws which bind society are for common folk like you or me. Great men are above the principles of morality. Did Shivaji commit a sin in killing Afzal Khan . . ? The answer to the question can be found in the Mahabharata itself. The Divine Krishna teaching in the Gita, tells us we may kill even our teachers . . . and no blame attaches, if we are not actuated by selfish desires . . . God has conferred on the* mlechhas *no grant of Hindustan*

inscribed on imperishable brass. Shivaji strove to drive them forth out of the land of his birth, but he was guiltless of the sin of covetousness. Do not circumscribe your vision like frogs in the well. Rise above the Penal Code into the rarefied atmosphere of the sacred Bhagawad Gita and consider the actions of great men.

Sankara Iyer was steeped in the tradition of the brotherhood of Madras lawyers – a tradition that held that the Indian Penal Code was as immutable as the laws of nature. He did not like what he had read.

Sankara Iyer's broad two-storied house was the first in the northern row of Sannidhi Street. Nammalwar and his brother Pakshi, who was studying in the Christian Missionary Society School, were now living a few yards away in West Car Street. Iyer sent his clerk to fetch Nammalwar.

'I understand you dabble in politics. Do you belong to the Extremist school or the Moderate school?'

Nammalwar knew that Sankara Iyer, though a Congressman, belonged to the 'wait and watch' school like most other Brahmins.

'The Moderates wait at the tables of the British, sir. They are satisfied with the leftovers. They are quite happy with the goal of local self-government.'

'So?'

I am a follower of Tilak and Chidambaram Pillai. We will be satisfied only when we get rid of the white pest.'

'I thought you were civilised. I didn't expect such words like "pest" from you. May I use a similar one? The British can be the very devils when they want to be. Wisdom lies in slowly distancing ourselves from them. Chidambaram Pillai is my dear friend but I am afraid he lacks this wisdom. By the way, I saw the leaflet you are circulating. What is the idea?'

'Sir, there is a Tamil version of Tilak's piece doing rounds among the students. We thought it distorted what he had written . . .'

'Do you think you are doing a public service printing this?'

'It was a collective effort of the Senior FA, sir.'

'The entire Senior FA is going to land in jail, then. It is one thing for Tilak to write this. He is a big leader. What are you? You are still to make a mark in life. Think of your mother.'

'Thank you for your advice, sir, but I don't think we have committed a crime.'

'That is not what the police are going to think if this leaflet reaches them. It unblushingly preaches murder. Remember, son, if you rise above the Penal Code, as this pamphlet wants you to do, you are not likely to land again on the planet earth.'

He saw that Nammalwar was crestfallen. He said gently, 'Don't mistake me. What is foremost in my mind is your welfare. Leave the Swadeshi business to experienced persons . . . . You are having your dinner with me today.'

'I have my brother with me, sir.'

'Bring him along too.'

Iyer's wife was an excellent cook and a gracious hostess, and Nammalwar and Pakshi, used to the insipid fare of their grandmother, found the food irresistible. Her fried eggplant was heavenly.

After the brothers had left, Iyer's wife said to her husband, 'It is a pity that the boy happens to be an Iyengar. We would not have found a better groom for our Sharada. He is as handsome as Lord Skanda.'

You should have seen his mother, Iyer thought. He said, 'He is hobnobbing with the Swadeshi crowd.'

'You must do what you can to steer him away from them . . .' She spoke again, on an impulse, 'I am glad he is an Iyengar. I don't think he is destined to live long. Such uncommon persons return to God rather quickly.'

'You are talking rubbish. This boy shall live to be a hundred.'

Iyer was almost right.

The Swadeshi crowd was swelling alarmingly in Tirunelveli. Though the whites were not exactly spat at, there was little doubt that the town was overtaken by a tide of militant nationalism. The stockers of prime English merchandise found to their dismay that the citizens' usual unsated appetite for things foreign had been replaced by an intense desire to be seen in Swadeshi attire. Being practical, they knew that the tide would ebb shortly. Meanwhile they did brisk business in Swadeshi clothes by the simple expedient of affixing 'Made in Bombay' stamps on bales of Lancashire cotton.

Nammalwar was exhilarated by the mood. He called a meeting of the students under the parrot-less mango tree of his college.

'The days are gone, friends, when we had to prostrate before these leucodermic riffraff. Japan has conclusively proved that the Europeans are not invincible. They have driven out the Russian from Port Arthur. Asia shall rule the world one day. We shall rule our country and throw these cow-eating mlechchas into the sea. We shall wear what out brothers have woven and not what Lancashire has dumped on us.

'Support the Swadeshi cause. Support Chidambaram Pillai. *Vande Mataram.*'

When Winckler's attendant came to fetch him, Nammalwar knew that he was betrayed. His guess was Pumpkin Srinvasan. Everyone knows that he is Winckler's spy. I shall crush that pumpkin and squeeze the pips out of him, swore Nammalwar.

Winckler was exceedingly polite to him.

'Allow me first to congratulate you, my boy. We have amidst us a young demagogue who can set the college on fire. Secondly, let me share a secret with you. I am no doubt a mlechcha, but I hate Indian beef and so does my wife. We find it too stringy. Your cows are thus reasonably safe from us. Thirdly, I hear you have already charted our navigation to the sea-bed. How fast will our seaward propulsion be?'

Nammalwar squirmed. 'There's nothing personal in what I spoke, sir. I hold you in high esteem . . .'

'Let me finish, my son. Finally, what you spoke was treasonable. I could report you to the police.'

'It is your prerogative, sir,' said Nammalwar primly.

'Don't be stupid. Now you really make me angry. Swadeshi is your business and I wish you good luck. All I ask of you is, air your adulation of Tilak or Pillai or whoever outside the campus. As an honourable academic I wouldn't like the police to set foot in our college.'

'Thank you, sir. Thank you very much. I shall never utter a word on Swadeshi inside the campus.'

'As a reward, I expect you to reserve at least a corner seat for me in the submarine adventure you are organising for the Tirunelveli Whites.'

He was now a saintly Methuselah. Many events of his life grew fluffy and were blown away from his memory. Yet the medley of events that spanned the years 1906 and 1911 miraculously withstood the gales of time and stayed with him. Sixty years later, when he was sitting crouched before a log fire in his ashram in Joshimath, a few miles south of Badrinath and a few thousand north of Nanguneri, he had a vivid recall of those events. He suddenly longed to see what he had left behind, a longing his ascetic rigour had so far been crushing underfoot.

The Congress was moving inexorably towards a split, and the popular Madras leaders were all with the extremist party of Tilak. The entire Presidency was electrified by the arrival of a fiery extremist from Bengal, Bipin Chandra Pal who delivered seven lectures, on seven separate days, to huge crowds assembled on the Marina beach of Madras. Nammalwar, leading a team of students from Tirunelveli, attended the lectures each day.

Nammalwar liked Pal's enunciation of boycott. He said:

> *Boycott strikes at the very root of the prestige of government.*
> *The determination of the people to assert themselves, within*
> *absolutely legal bounds, against the despotic authority of the*
> *government, takes away from authority the magic, the*
> *illusory thing which they call prestige, which is more potent*
> *than authority itself. We propose to do this by way of boycott.*

The crowd that came to listen to Pal had melted away and after
seeing his friends off, Nammalwar sat back on the beach to
wallow in the sea breeze and to listen to the undying roar of the
Bay of Bengal. He was new to the sea. Kanyakumari, the land's
end, was only forty miles south of Nanguneri, but he had never
been there.

He was furious with himself and he thought the sea would
soothe him. Why did I promise mother that I would marry and
raise a family?

Ponna had cornered him one day and said, 'It has become
impossible to live with your sister, Nammalwar. I need your help.'

'Should I talk to her, amma?'

'No, she will only pounce on me. I need, probably she does
too, another girl in the house. She will come between us and is
sure to soften Andal.'

'What should I do, amma?'

'Get married, son. I haven't asked you for anything so far.
Don't disappoint me.'

Should I marry like every one else, sleep with the girl,
produce children and live happily thereafter? Swaraj will surely
come without my help.

'If you say so, amma,' he had said.

He sat there for hours facing the sea. When he had had
enough, he walked slowly back to the house, exciting the stray
dogs which ran behind him barking and gave him up only
when he had crossed their territories. The house belonged to the

Matam and was used as a rest house for visitors from Nanguneri. An ancient Iyengar was in charge of it Nammalwar was ravenously hungry, but it would be idle to expect the old man to have kept food for him at three in the morning. He knocked softly not expecting any answer. He stood outside the door for a few minutes, thinking. He then gathered his towel and, holding one end, beat the veranda floor with it, scattering the dust. When the haze settled he spread the same towel on the spot that he had tried to relieve of dust, lay down on it and, using the crook of his left arm as a pillow, sank into a limbo between sleep and wakefulness.

The next day he was tired, but he sought out Pillai who was also in Madras for the Pal lectures. Pillai greeted him heartily.

'Welcome, Iyengar. Let me guess your name. . . . Mmmm . . . Yes, you are the Nanguneri man, Nammalwar.'

'Sir, I feel flattered that you consider me significant enough to remember my name. I have come here with a few students of Hindu college for the Pal lectures.'

'I am happy. Do you like them?'

'They are marvellous, sir, but we usually stop at listening to lectures.'

'You want to act, do you?'

'Yes, sir.'

'Come tomorrow. Mama will also be here. We shall find a way out.'

Mama – Subramania Bharathi – was there the next day. His eyes shone like embers of coal and he had, unusually for a Tamil Brahmin, a luxuriant moustache, its tips pointing heavenwards. He embraced Nammalwar and said, '*Paiya*, I like you. You have such a brilliant name. How can one whose name is Nammalwar think small? Young men like you should think big. Keep away the thoughts of daily things. There are millions of others to take care of salt, tamarind, chillies and rice. You are onto grand things.'

Nammalwar extricated himself and said, 'I am a regular reader of your *India*, sir.'

'You must be one of the few who are. Pillai tells me that you want to act. I have met many who want to talk. They may fit well in the Moderate camp. Have you heard of Mazzini?'

'The Italian patriot, sir?'

'Indeed, yes. You are bright. Have you read his books? Have you heard of Young Italy?'

'Yes sir, a secret society founded by Mazzini. I haven't come across any of his works.'

'Here is a copy of the oath Young Italy's members had to take. I am publishing a translation of it in India.'

Nammalwar read the first few lines.

'Each member will, upon his initiation into the association of Young Italy, pronounce the following form of Oath . . .'

'May I take it home and read it?'

'It is your copy. If young men like you are interested, we might start a similar society here. Pillai and a few others are there to guide it.' He added, 'You need not take the trouble of coming here again. We know you are eager to act and we shall get in touch with you.'

When he read the document carefully in the muted light of the rest house he felt he was really onto grand things.

It read:

In the name of God and Italy –

In the name of all martyrs of the holy Italian cause, who have fallen beneath foreign and domestic tyranny –

By the duties which bind me to the land wherein God has placed me and to the brothers whom God has given me –

By the love – innate in all men – I bear to the country that gave my mother birth, and will be the home of my children –

By the hatred – innate in all men – I bear to evil, injustice, usurpation and arbitrary rule –

. . .

By the memory of our former greatness, and the sense of our present degradation –

By the tears of Italian mothers for their sons dead on the scaffold, in prison or in exile –

I,

Believing in the mission entrusted by God to Italy . . . give my name to Young Italy, an association of men holding the same faith, and swear:

To dedicate myself wholly and forever to the endeavour with them to constitute Italy, one, free, independent and a republican nation,

To abstain from enrolling myself in any other association from this time forth,

To obey all the instructions, in conformity with the spirit of Young Italy, given me by those who represent with the Union of Italian brothers; and to keep these instructions even at the cost of my life,

To assist my brothers of the association both by action and counsel,

Now and Forever.

This I do swear, invoking upon my head the wrath of God, the abhorrence of man, and the infamy of the perjurer, if I ever betray the whole or a part of this my oath.

Mazzini's ennobling oath did not fail to stir the imagination of Nammalwar and its distinct Italian flavour delighted him. I would join Young Italy, if only to pronounce grandly this oath, he thought, but he was not sure how good its Indian version would be. Many other questions plagued him – what would be the society's name? Who would be its members? How would it get its arms, if its aim was to eject the British violently?

He waited for the call. It did not come as long as he was in Madras and he had to return to Tirunelveli disappointed.

Nammalwar met Pillai again in Tirunelveli at the residence of Sankara Iyer.

'You must be tired, sir, after this long journey from Surat.'

The Congress had finally split at the Surat session. There were ugly exchanges of both words and fists and Tilak was not only prevented from speaking but was forcefully ejected from the dais.

'No, I am not tired at all. In fact the session has breathed a new freshness into us. Now that we have broken free of the ball and chain of moderation we will present our case to the people with vigour and conviction. We are arranging a series of lectures throughout the Presidency. Mama will help me. Subramania Siva is joining me shortly.'

'Your company, my friend, the great Swadeshi Steam Navigation Company, is fast running out of steam and you are busy spitting fire at the British. You are not trained to ride two horses simultaneously, Chidambaram. Leave it to the riders of the Abel Circus,' said Sankara Iyer.

The company's rivals had money and they could wait. They reduced the fare on their ships drastically and, when that ploy did not yield the required results, they offered free trips if the passengers would travel with them. The Swadeshi Company did not have the capital to resort to such methods.

'Sankara, the passengers are still flocking to our ships.'

'They all have this fever. Swadeshi fever. When it subsides, Chidambaram, your ship will run only empty trips to Ceylon.'

Chidambaram Pillai thought for a moment and said, 'If I have to make a choice between the Swadeshi cause and the running of this shipping company I shall always choose the former.'

'Brave words. But that will not be the choice of your investors.'

The Abel Circus had pitched their tents on high ground on the Palayamkottai side of the river, confident that their shows would attract crowds from the twin towns and the neighbouring villages. The menagerie included a baby giraffe, a hippopotamus and a chimpanzee; it had an amazing troupe of acrobats, clowns, riders, jugglers, knockabout comedians and trapeze artists. But it had reckoned without the Swadeshi movement and its xenophobia. The Hindu College students passed a unanimous resolution to boycott it and went door-to-door to request parents not to take their children to the circus. That the circus was from Europe, as far removed from the British as the ordinary Indians were, and that it was positively hostile to the government because of the harassment it faced from its clerks, did not matter to them. That its artists were white-skinned was enough.

Nammalwar was called to the Tirunelveli Bridge police station and made to sit before a podgy Naidu sub-inspector whose tiruman rivalled Nammalwar's.

'Iyengar, what is the need for you and your friends to act out a circus? The Abel fellows have come here to earn their livelihood. Let them do the circus.'

'We are not stopping anyone from going to the circus. We are only telling them politely . . .'

'That you would smear them with cow dung if they visited the circus? Come on, Iyengar. You are a Brahmin. Why waste your time in catching crabs? Such rabble rousing is not for you. Your principal tells us you are a bright student. If your name is entered in our records, you won't get a government job, ever.'

'Naidu sir, are we doing anything unlawful? We don't even go in gangs . . .'

'That will be enough. If there is any trouble, you will be the first to be arrested. I hate to do it to a Srivaishnava, but you must realise I have a job to do.'

'May I go now, sir?'

'What is the hurry? The way you are acting it appears you will have to spend much of your time in police stations answering questions.' Naidu paused for a moment and said, 'Don't be upset, Iyengar. I need your help in solving two problems.'

Nammalwar sat up and said, 'Naidu sir, please tell me. I am here to help you, if I can.'

Naidu took out a few gold coins and handed them over to Nammalwar. He instantly recognised them as the Swadeshi coins in circulation. One of them had the word 'Swadeshi' surrounded by a laurel wreath and the whole encased by the words 'Chastity, our household divinity'. The reverse had 'Faith, Hope and Success' inscribed on it. The second coin said, 'God Bless, Fine Indian Neck Jewel 1907' and its reverse had a figure of Goddess Lakshmi and the words 'Lakshmi on Lotus' removed any doubt one might have had as to the identity of the Goddess. Nammalwar knew about this mad venture which he thought would achieve nothing except benefiting a few goldsmiths. He also knew who were behind it, but he decided to keep quiet.

'I am sorry, Naidu sir. I don't get to see gold coins every day. I am not sure I can help you.'

Naidu looked at him closely. 'Was there any discussion of these coins in the Swadeshi circles?'

'If there was, it was not in my presence. I am still a student, Naidu sir, such weighty matters are not discussed in my presence.'

'Fine. You can go now.'

Nammalwar hesitated. 'You said there were two problems.'

'Thank you for reminding me. When I am on duty, personal problems get the least preference. I have a son, studying in the fifth form. He is not very good at English. If I could send him to you . . .'

'By all means, Naidu sir. I shall certainly do what I can to help him. May I leave now?'

'I shall be very happy if you could also teach him the *Prabandham.*'

'I am not very proficient myself. Still I shall teach him Andal's poems and of course, the *Tiruvaimoli*.'

When the police summoned him Nammalwar had counted on spending a night or two in custody. He returned a happy man. Teaching the Inspector's son would not be a problem. He could be studious and he might not need a tutor's sustained assistance.

The Abel circus had to move out of Tirunelveli rather hurriedly when their hippo started losing weight and the baby giraffe breathed its last. The boycott was total and it was difficult for them to find even animal feed.

Winckler moved to a Madras college early that year. Before his departure he called Nammalwar and told him to finish his BA first before diving into the treacherous waters of Swadeshi.

'When you come out of it, Alwar, there won't be anyone to receive you. You will stand shivering at the edge of the pool unnoticed. Swaraj may come eventually, but we may not live to see it. Neither are your children likely to herald it. It is still in the impenetrable mists of the future.'

I respect him, but he now sounds like a platitudinous bore.

Nammalwar said, 'Maybe sir. We are only attempting to penetrate that mist to see how far away Swaraj is.'

'Oh, you are impossible. I have this for you. This may keep you away at least for a few hours from the Swadeshi mischief.' It was Water Scott's *Ivanhoe*, a book he had already read.

Winckler's replacement was Herbert Champion, a young Adonis whose passion was music. He had a lovely voice too, but Tirunelveli was as unfamiliar with the cadences of his music as he was with the wayward ways of his students.

Chidambaram Pillai was at the pinnacle of his fame on his return from the stormy Surat session. In Tuticorin he led a successful strike of workers against the British management of the local textile mill. He and Subramania Siva, another great orator in Tamil who could raise the mood of the crowd to a sudden crescendo, held a series of meetings on the Tuticorin beach, which was swamped by thousands of their admirers. The authorities thought sedition was palpable though none, at least not those in Pillai's camp, uttered a word of it.

The confrontation that every one was expecting came in March. Pillai and Siva announced their plan to celebrate the release of Pal – who had been arrested earlier on sedition charges – on 9 March by bringing out a giant procession and hoisting the flag of Swaraj. Wynch, the Collector of Tirunelveli, thought his Joint-Magistrate in Tuticorin was a weakling and asked for an immediate replacement. He told his government that there existed *'a very critical state of feeling against Europeans generally and the classes who are well disposed towards government and a corresponding state of anxiety amongst the European loyalists.'* He arrived in Tuticorin on the eighth and ordered Pillai and Siva to appear before the District Magistrate in Tirunelveli the next day.

The stars stippled across the night sky abounded with winks of light. On the road to the temple of Murugan, woebegone fireflies quavered before going into hiding behind the dark shadows of mango trees. Nammalwar did not keep pace with his teacher but walked a step behind him. Both kept silence; they preferred to watch the nictitating fireflies and listen to the screechy cicadas.

The finicky physiology teacher Sundara Sastri had been waiting for him when he returned home in the evening.

'Nammalwar, let us go for a walk,' he said.

They chose a sandy patch on the bank of the river. The temple was at a distance; two castor-oil torches were burning at its entrance.

Sundara Sastri folded his hands in supplication in the direction of the temple. He sat and motioned Nammalwar to do likewise. The sand radiated heat and it was not comfortable.

March nights were normally pleasant, but it was different on that day. Nammalwar could feel his eyes puffing up.

'Did you attend the meeting?'

'Yes, sir. Did you?'

'No, Nammalwar. I had some other work. Do you know what happened in court today?'

'No sir.'

'Wynch has asked both Pillai and Siva to appear again on the twelfth. They are sure to be arrested and remanded to police custody. We should not be helpless spectators.'

He was surprised. He only knew his teacher to be an unwilling dissection specialist. The Swadeshi streak was unknown to him.

'What should we do sir? Britannia rules not only the waves but also the law courts, lawyers and justice.'

'We could at least organise a protest rally by the students. You should take charge of our college.'

'It is difficult to unite all the students, sir. There are many who will run to their mothers if they smell trouble. There are also a few blue-blooded loyalists. Still, I shall try and gather as many students as possible. Have you informed any one else of this meeting, sir?'

'No, but I have a few more disciples like you. They don't wish to be identified.'

Wynch was prepared for trouble but he did not anticipate the fury with which the town responded to the arrest of Pillai and Siva. On that sweltering Friday, fire tongued every building of importance in the town and the sky rained pieces of granite and broken red tiles. Like the Scarlet Pimpernel, Wynch was here, there and everywhere because he felt it was his order that had caused the rioting; he wanted to show the rowdy town that British justice stood ramrod-erect in the face of such assaults and British firepower would cow it to conformity. He immediately ordered the police to fire into the crowd and his score was four dead and fifty-four injured.

Champion had had a few letters from England the previous day and he initially wanted to lounge in his easy chair and ruminate on their contents. Instead he rode his bicycle to college humming to himself. He would save the letters for the day after.

The crowd saw the cycling white figure at a distance and rubbed their hands in anticipation. Champion saw them too, but he knew that people in India flocked to flimsy attractions like crows would to a carcass. He thought they would scatter at the flick of his hand.

It was different this time.

Champion tried to glide through the crowd but the phalanx was impenetrable.

'He is the principal. Teach him Vande Mataram and he can teach his students.'

'Say Vande Mataram,' boomed the crowd.

'What rubbish! Why should I?'

'Kick him, kick him.'

'Blacken him.'

'Let us carry him on our shoulders and dump him into the river from the bridge.'

The crowd was closing in on him when Nammalwar appeared there with a group of students.

'What is going on here? He is our principal. Leave him alone.'

'He refuses to chant Vande Mataram.'

'Leave him alone, I said. He is a man of literature and he has nothing to do with the government.'

Nammalwar and his friends formed a circle around him and took him to a building nearby.

'You should feel safe here. We are sorry for what has happened, sir.'

The principal smiled to himself. He remembered his Shakespeare and the fate of Cinna the poet in the hands of citizens in *Julius Caesar*. He said, 'Thank you, Nammalwar. Thank you very much. This morning, I had no will to wander out of doors, yet something led me forth.'

Nammalwar was quick. He said, 'Then you must thank your stars that they did not tear you for your bad music. They have no ear for your type of music.'

The students were definitely not the arsonists, though a few had flung a stone or two or intimidated a recalcitrant shopkeeper into closing his shop. They too were taken aback by the town's spontaneous wrath. Wynch did not believe it was unpremeditated. He had information that a Brahmin teacher was responsible for instigating the students. He said to his Superintendent of Police, 'I understand this fellow specialises in dissections. Your officers may teach him how we dissect to obtain information.'

The news about the riots in Tirunelveli reached Nanguneri the same day and Ponna felt fear wringing her heart. Is another death in store for me? She remembered how her grandfather had died. Government bullets should not pick on the same family twice.

Nammalwar escaped arrest by a whisker. Inspector Naidu told his superintendent of police that the Iyengar boy was not one to indulge in mischief. Since the C.I.D. reports stated otherwise, the superintendent decided to check with the principal. Champion was livid when he heard that the police were contemplating the arrest of Nammalwar. He said that he probably owed his life to that Brahmin boy and if the police misbehaved he would write to the governor. He called Nammalwar and asked him to leave town for the time being.

Sundara Sastri was not that fortunate. He was arrested and the police almost peeled his skin off, but they could not get the names they wanted.

The arrests and the immense presence of police in the town caused the town to go back to its usual docility. The deaths and punitive taxes perhaps numbed its soul for it saw Pillai and Siva being handed stiff sentences with an unconcerned air. They were both charged with sedition, and after a trial that lasted four months, Siva got ten years and Pillai forty. Sastri was lucky to get away with seven. While sentencing him the judge was sanguine: *This punishment might deter the present generation of Tinnevellians at any rate from indulging in similar outbursts in future.'*

Wynch gloated in a letter, *'I think they were stunned at the heavy sentences. They begin to realise at last that the offence of preaching sedition is a grave one . . . I don't think any one would dare to speak a word against the British Raj again.*

No one dared. Swaraj and Swadeshi died in the town unsung. The heroes of Tirunelveli were gripped by a stupor from which they did not fully wake until Independence.

Nammalwar returned to Tirunelveli to write his examinations and he followed the trials of his mentors closely. The monstrous sentence angered him but he waited patiently for a call from Madras.

Cherankulam girls were supposed to be well-endowed. But he found his wife Lakshmi to be a fleshless spidery girl, prone to quick, copious tears. Nanguneri was alien territory and it scared her. Nammalwar scared her further. He was sore about his marriage, which he thought was foisted on him, and was kind to her in a superior way. During the initial days, she noticed the disdain and ignored the kindness. The three years of their married life had many unhappy days but the few happy ones were incomparable.

The happiness of Ponna and Andal was unalloyed and Lakshmi too, once she understood that they were both longing for feminine company, liked to be with them. Ponna wanted to set up Nammalwar's family in Tirunelveli but he flatly refused. He wanted to continue his Swadeshi work unhindered and this lachrymose girl would only be an impediment he could well do without. He arranged to visit Nanguneri every weekend which, initially, he rarely did.

Whenever he did come Ponna ensured that he went to bed early and that his wife took with her a pot of almond milk laced with saffron when she went up to join him.

The call came in the form of a sadhu who spoke English with a thick Bengali accent. On a Sunday when he was reading his newspaper, the sadhu arrived at his door.

'I am Buddhananda Paramahamsa. I have come here straight from the railway station.'

Nammalwar prostrated at his feet and said, 'Swami, I am honoured. You must be tired. Please be gracious enough to have lunch with us.'

'I have no time, son. I am rushing to Shenkottah. I only came here to tell you that you should go to Punalur this Saturday.'

'May I know the reason, Swami?'

'You must surely remember Mazzini's oath. Ask for Venkateswara Iyer's house in Punalur. He will escort you to where we have to go.'

Punalur was a scenic town in the lap of the Western Ghats. It was not a British territory but a part of the princely state of Travancore. There was little difficulty in finding Venkateswara Iyer's house for he happened to be a well-known lawyer there. The hall of his house crawled with clients but he greeted Nammalwar with genuine warmth. He was a pleasant man with a barrel-belly. He took Nammalwar aside and said, 'I was expecting you, Iyengar. We are holding a meeting in a friend's house tomorrow. I shall take you there. You may rest in my house today.'

The meeting was held in a ruined garden with shrubs that grew high and rank. Nammalwar did not see any familiar faces. The sadhu was nowhere to be seen. He was one of the twenty-odd present there. A young man from Madras, who introduced himself as Nilakantan, spoke.

'Pillai and Siva are now being tortured in prison. Pillai is being made to pull a heavy oil-press as a substitute for an ox. And Siva? Well, he is believed to have contracted leprosy. WE make merry while our leaders rot in custody. Should we not avenge them? Should we not teach the British a lesson? Their King George V is visiting Delhi next year. We should make up a suitable present for him.'

Someone asked, 'What sort of present?'

'That will be decided later. WE are here today for the initiation ceremony of our Association, the Bharata Mata Association.'

So this is it, Nammalwar thought. It has taken time but finally it is on.

The Bharata Mata Association first offered prayers to Kali and after distribution of sacred ash and holy water made red with vermilion, an oath was taken. The oath did not sound as grand as Mazzini's. It simply said that the taker of the oath would defend Swaraj with his life and property and he would not reveal the association's activities to any one. The finale was the bloody smearing of the thumb on a sheet.

Later Nammalwar asked Nilakantan, 'What plans do we have? The Raj is a giant of monumental proportions. Where do we get our weapons from? Are they sufficient? Have we established contact with other associations outside Madras?'

'All in good time. All in good time. You are in a tearing hurry.'

'I am, because the Raj is. If we don't act fast, we shall be annihilated in no time. Are the people gathered here reliable?'

'They are as reliable as you are. We have set out priorities and targets. We shall act according to our plan.'

Nammalwar was not satisfied. Nilakantan said, 'We have friends abroad. Madame Cama and Shyamaji Krishna Varma have promised to help us. Iyer is now in Pondicherry. If everything goes smoothly we might even procure German arms. And yes. We are in touch with other Associations. Remember it was that Bengali sadhu who directed you here.'

She looked lovely now with her contours filling out and her face aglow with expectation. Her initial resentment had vanished and she had learnt to adjust to Nammalwar's waywardness. Nammalwar began to discover in her virtues he had not noticed before and he now visited Nanguneri every weekend. His lovemaking was silent; she chattered away under him, telling him what had happened the week before. At the right moment she joined his silence, closing her eyes and tightening her thighs.

In time, the moneylender family had a happy occasion to celebrate and it made excellent arrangements for the Pumsavanam and Simantam ceremonies. The Grihya Sutras, the code books of the Brahmins, stipulated that the Pumsavanam, the male producing ceremony, be performed in the third month of pregnancy, but Ponna's astrologer said that it could be coupled with the Simantam – 'the parting of hair' ceremony – and performed in the seventh month. On the fifth month, Ponna called a bangle seller from Tirunelveli and asked him to cover her daughter-in-law's hands with beautiful glass bangles. There was a throng of *sumangalis* in her house who crowded the bangle-seller, for Ponna had ordered bangles for all of them. She asked one of them to fry sweet *appams* and nine of these were tied to the edge of the pregnant girl's black silk sari.

Nammalwar did not want to be melodramatic, but he thought his wife deserved to be told of his plan. He said, 'Lakshmi, I must tell you something. I don't propose to continue my studies.'

The family had planned that he should join the law college after his degree. Lakshmi said, 'It is your decision. So long as I am with you, I am not too worried whether you are a lawyer or a medicine man or a clerk in the taluk office. Promise me that you will not force me to stay here in Nanguneri when I come back after the delivery.'

'Why? Are you not happy to be with amma and Andal?'

'You are teasing me now. When did I tell you that I am unhappy with them? If you think that living with you is much the same as living with them, I have nothing to say.'

'Don't get angry. I am now so involved in the Swadeshi movement that I shall be away most of the time when you return here with our son or daughter.'

'Don't say daughter. I'll give you a son.'

'I . . . I may even be arrested by the police.'

'Why? What did you steal? Don't imagine things. It has become your habit to speak of stupid things during auspicious days. If this continues, I shall go down and sleep with amma and Andal.'

She started to snivel and Nammalwar spoke no more.

The Bharata Mata Association held its meetings intermittently at odd places, spleening against the government and its callous treatment of patriots in prison. Their blood-smeared thumbprints had long dried and turned black on the sheets and that seemed to be the only blood-letting they would ever do. There were no signs of German arms. Nammalwar had not yet held a firearm in his hand – he had only seen them in books and in the hands of the police – still he found the very thought of the Germans recognising their Association and agreeing to supply arms to them exhilarating.

Nilakantan appeared one day unannounced and said, 'Please come with me to Tirunelveli town.' He usually wore a coat but that day he was without one. He took Nammalwar to a small hotel and said to the person sitting at the counter, 'How much do I owe you? Iyengar will clear my debts.'

'Four annas, sir. He ate sixteen idlis and wanted to go without paying me.'

Nammalwar paid the man four annas and asked Nilakantan if they could move out of that rather seedy hotel.

'Yes, when I get my coat back. Where is my coat? He wouldn't let me go otherwise and I had to leave my coat as a surety.'

When they were in the street Nilakantan said, 'We are going to meet some promising people. Will you come with me?'

'Who are they?'

'There is a Pitchandi Thevar from Marukalkurichi.'

'Marukalkurichi? It is right next to our village, and I know Pitchandi. Come to Nanguneri, I shall send word for Pitchandi Thevar.'

Pitchandi came and met Nilakantan at the moneylender house. He said to Nilakantan, 'Swami's family is the most influential in this area. We have been their tenants for more than two hundred years, if not more.'

'That is good, Thevar. We can discuss matters frankly before Iyengar then. Do you have your three thousand persons ready?'

'Where will they go, Iyer? They are without work and they waste their time in the villages, drinking and chasing women. I could collect them within a week. But where are the guns?'

'The guns are coming Thevar, be patient.'

'We are patient, Iyer. Do we have any option?'

'Yes, please train with dummies. The arms are coming, Thevar. Coming quickly.'

After Thevar had left, Nammalwar asked Nilakantan what he would do with three thousand men.

'Not three thousand, Iyengar. Mappillai Chami, a descendant of Kattabomman, has promised another twenty thousand. They are all waiting for the German arms to arrive.'

'German arms for twenty-three thousand persons? Are they supplying free? Where will these persons be trained without attracting the attention of the British? How are you going to feed them? Where will they be billeted?'

Nilakantan sighed. 'Kali Mata is with us. She shall find a way. Money shall be arranged. The Maharaja of Baroda has promised to help us.' In his revolutionary fervour, Nilakantan had lost his sense of irony. Nammalwar had not. He wondered how the revolutionary was going to arrange the enormous sums required for training when he could not arrange for four annas.

Nammalwar did not meet Nilakantan again but there was a curious meeting of a few members in the French territory of Pondicherry. They were called up one by one by V.V.S. Iyer. He was a legendary hero to all the members of the Association. He was one of the old India House hands and had had many hair-raising escapades before arriving in Pondicherry on an arduous route from London. He was dark and bearded like a prophet and spoke a flowery Tamil that was music to the ears of Nammalwar.

'You are a fine specimen of manhood, Iyengar. You should not waste away.'

'I am at your disposal, sir.'

'Are you prepared to undergo firearm training?'

'I shall be delighted, sir.'

'Then you are prepared to kill for a cause.'

'In a battle, yes, sir.'

'Battles are years away, Iyengar.'

'I am not in a hurry to kill, sir.'

Iyer thought for a moment and said, 'You may go now. We shall fix another day for your training and call you.'

A twig from the banyan tree was carefully selected. It was pointing north when it was plucked and it had two little fruits attached to it. It was placed on a grinding stone and a little girl of five from the neighbourhood was asked to pound it. Ponna gave the girl a silk skirt and two silver rupees. The pulp was gathered in a new silk cloth and given to Nammalwar who squeezed it into the right nostril of his fasting wife, saying in Sanskrit, 'You are a male child.' Oblations were offered to the gods and ancestors marking the end of the Pumsavanam ceremony. Nammalwar picked up a porcupine quill with three blades of *darbha* grass and a twig of fig with fruits attached to it. He used it to part his wife's hair, bringing to an end the Simantam ceremony.

Several delicacies were served during the feast, but Lakshmi's favourtie was *varagarisi*, a mélange of roasted, spiced pulses and cereals. When fresh, they were delectably hard and she had to use her molars to crush them. Ponna had mounds of it prepared for the function and when she sent her daughter-in-law for her delivery, she gave her two brass containers full.

There was still a pot in the family kitchen filled almost to the brim with Lakshmi's favourite, now chewy and unappetising, when Nammalwar's son came to Nanguneri without his mother.

The last call also came from Pondicherry.

Krishna Pillai's gardens appeared too sprightly to host a secret meeting but on that fine day in June the decision to draw blood was taken before forty men of the Bharata Mata Association. The air was charged with religion, the religion of Kali, who donned a garland made of the skulls of her adversaries. Subramania Bharathi was there and he sang his splendid poem on Sakti. Nammalwar had not seen him after their Madras meeting. He did not dare go near Bharathi who was so keyed up that he was unable to recognise acquaintances. Nilakantan was nowhere to be seen. Nammalwar had heard that there were tactical differences between V.V.S. Iyer and Nilakantan.

V.V.S. Iyer was there. A callow young man from the gathering came forward and placed a gun at the feet of Iyer. Nammalwar recognised him immediately. He was Vanchi, a ranger in the Travancore Forest Department. He hardly spoke in the earlier meetings and looked overwrought whenever Nammalwar had tried to strike up a conversation with him. He is the chosen one, Nammalwar thought. He has perhaps agreed to kill in a hurry.

He was calm and collected this time. Iyer said, 'You are the lucky man chosen by Mother Kali. You have her blessings and you have a sure place at her feet, which is our Valhalla, the Viraswarga.'

The Collector of Tirunelveli was now Robert William D'Estecourt Ashe, who assisted Wynch during the episodes of 1908. He had been the Joint-Magistrate in Tuticorin, posted there at the specific request of Wynch on the eve of the

Tirunelveli riots. Tuticorin had its share of riots but they were not as ferocious as the Tirunelveli ones. Nevertheless Ashe put them down with such wanton savagery that the Governor of Madras had noted that Ashe's performance in Tuticorin had done them no good. But such remarks of dismay did not stop his progress in officialdom. He was hard working and rarely went on a holiday when he was a bachelor. But in the year 1911, he had married and his young wife was insistent that they go on a holiday to Kodaikanal. He planned his trip meticulously. He was not to know that he would never reach the famed hill station.

The train left Tirunelveli at 9:35 a.m. and reached Maniyachi junction about an hour later. Ashe boarded the Boat Mail from Tuticorin for his trip to Kodaikanal and he was in the first-class compartment with his wife, waiting for the train to start. He was surprised when he saw on the platform a tufted young man in a green coat pointing what appeared to be a revolver at him. He thought, it must be a toy, but the bloody thing looks so real. Shouldn't take chances. He flung his hat at the tufted man to divert his aim, but it was too late. The bullets pierced his heart and he died on the spot, drenching his wife with blood.

Vanchi ran to the nearby latrine and shot himself.

Fear came to dwell in him. It slept with him, waking him up at odd hours. It asked him endless questions, harassing him. It burrowed into his mind, emerging when he least expected it. Nammalwar hated the British no doubt. He wanted to do away with all of them if possible, on a far-off day, but the immediacy of Ashe's death had unnerved him. Nammalwar did not understand his murder. Though he was no angel, Ashe came very low in the order of the Association's demonology. Nammalwar had been under the impression that Vanchi's target would be either Wynch or Judge Pinhey, who pronounced the sentences of Pillai and Siva. Perhaps they were not so easily approachable. He stayed in his house in a petrified state, waiting for the police to pick him up and to peel his skin off like they did to his physiology teacher.

They did not come for him.

Fourteen people stood trial in the Ashe Murder Case and Venkateswara Iyer was not one of them. When the police came to get him he was bleeding to death from a slash across his throat. They could not get anything out of him. Strangely, Nilakantan was prime accused and V.V.S. Iyer's name was not on the list.

The telegram was waiting for him when he reached home after a long walk. Pakshi was away and his grandmother was wailing loudly: telegrams generally were harbingers of doom. He too smelt death. Whoever is near me is marked for death. The telegram read: 'Lakshmi serious. Child safe. Start immediately.'

He did not see her alive. In death she looked awful, her mouth obscenely open, betraying the tartar on her front teeth. Her elbows stick out like twigs. His father-in-law said she had developed fits and the local doctors could not rescue her. He refused to see the bundle that was his son. His grief was intense, though between bouts he had to think away the thought that Lakshmi had solved his problem by dying.

The infant counts for nothing. It does not need me. And I want to be as far away from it as possible.

After the cremation, Lakshmi's father approached Nammalwar cautiously and broached the issue that his son-in-law wanted to avoid.

'God's will has been done. At least she left this world a sumangali with flowers in her hair and kunkumam on her forehead. The child worries me.'

He paused for Nammalwar to respond. When he met with silence he continued, 'The child needs care. Your mother of course will rock him to sleep in a golden cradle but he wants a mother to nurse him.'

Nammalwar looked at the ceiling.

'I have a suggestion. My son-in-law should not misunderstand me. You know Veda is ready to be wed. If you marry her, your son will have a mother who will not ill-treat him.'

Veda was Lakshmi's younger sister. Nammalwar ripped out in fury.

'You should be ashamed of yourself. What sort of suggestion is this? You want me to warm the bed of another woman when Lakshmi's ashes are still hot? I am not going to marry again. If you think you will solve the problem of hunting for a bridegroom by getting your daughter spliced to me you will be disappointed. I don't want that child. You can keep him with you or you can bundle him off to my mother.'

Nammalwar felt as soon as he had spoken that he had been monstrously offensive. He said to his father-in-law who was on the verge of tears, 'I am sorry. I should not have spoken like this.'

His father-in-law recovered quickly. It was the rule of his community that sons-in-law should be tyrants. He said 'You need rest. Your mood does not seem to be right just now. I should not have broached the subject. I will talk to you later.'

He quietly went to his wife and told her to arrange a wet nurse immediately for his grandson.

The trial dragged on and he read every report of it in the newspapers word by word, hunting for his name. It was not there. He was not very happy that they had forgotten him. Nilakantan was sentenced to seven years' imprisonment and others were awarded sentences of lesser severity.

Nammalwar remembered Nilakantan's impossible dreams of organising an army of twenty-three thousand men. Where are they now? The use of one revolver by another has landed Nilakantan in jail for seven years. Twenty-three thousand revolves would have taken him and all of us straight to God's landing.

What should I do now? I stand shivering at the edge of the pool, as Winckler had predicted. That too without taking the plunge. I do not have it in me to fight until the end. Death scares me. That is clear. I could be with the Moderates making routine noises against imperialism while professing abiding loyalty to the British King. I don't want that.

Another marriage is beyond me. The female stench, the squelch of sex and its gluey fluids and the hideous gash and its hairy cover; I liked them all once when I was with Lakshmi. I may like them again if I am coerced into a marriage. I won't be. I shall go away.

Amma is the problem. If I am with her, she will not leave me in peace. She will expect me to rear Lakshmi's child. She will slowly domesticate me and chain me to the piffling life of a lawyer or worse, a landlord. Though she professes contempt for the way father lived she won't mind my leading a life of leisure if I so desire.

There is another pool where I can swim to my heart's content. I am not very spiritual, but religion may give me the freedom that I desire. Fortunately I can afford to experiment. My mother is there to take on my, or rather Lakshmi's, load. I could even return if I am tired of what I seek.

He met the Jiyar.

Although he had chosen sanyasa the corpulent Jiyar was a man of the world and he was not impressed by Nammalwar's problem.

'I don't understand you. You are young, good-looking, educated and moneyed. You have no problems at all.'

'I want to be free, swami.'

'Who has chained you now? It is all in the mind. Your mother is a helpless widow and it is your duty to look after her. Listen to her and get married. If you don't like Nanguneri girls, I know a fine girl from Alwar. Tirunagari and I could talk to her family.'

Ponna saw him pacing up and down the hall of the house. He was talking to himself. When he was tired of it he quietly stared at the floor. She thought the death of his wife troubled him. She also noticed that he was not eating well and he had stopped reading books. On a rainy night when water threatened darkly to flow into their house from the inundated street, Ponna talked to Nammalwar.

'Nammalwar, what is troubling you? I have been watching you for a month now and you are not yourself.'

'There is nothing, amma.'

'There must be something. You are young and you shouldn't waste time brooding. There are already two in this house to whom God has entrusted that task.' She continued, 'You have your son to think of.'

'No, amma. Let him stay there. I don't want him here.'

'How is that possible? He is our child and he should be here. Your father-in-law has written to me. His suggestion that you marry Veda is a very practical one.'

'I am not going to marry again.'

'That is what every male says,' said Ponna severely.

'I am different, amma.'

'How are you different? In what way are you different from your father? Yes, he sat in this house and ate his way to death and you have now started pacing the hall, up and down, without care. That is perhaps the difference.'

The words were meant to hurt. Ponna on that wretched night bristled with anger.

Nammalwar expected his mother to retract her words. He expected her to say she was sorry.

He thought, you have seriously misjudged me. I am different. The least you could do is to recognise it. I am rooted here because of you. If you fail me, I am free.

Ponna said again, 'You must marry. More than that, I want my grandson to live with you either here or in Tirunelveli or wherever you choose to settle. Think, Nammalwar. There is nothing for you in this village. What will you do here? Get out of here quickly. I shall stay with you till you get a wife.'

Nammalwar looked at her serenely and said, 'I don't want a wife. I don't want you to leave the village for my sake. If you insist, amma, let me leave the house. Alone. I may not come back in a hurry.'

Ponna blurted out in frustration, 'You are grown up. How can I control you?'

He picked up an umbrella and moved towards the door.

'Where are you going?'

'You have just said you can't control me.'

'At least wait till the rain stops.'

The rain dwindled in the morning and stopped finally in the evening. Nammalwar went out of the house without the umbrella.

Ponna had never expected Nammalwar to disappear without a trace. She thought he would come back once he had cooled down. She knew she had spoken hurtfully on that night, but she thought mothers had the right to hurt their sons occasionally when the sons hurt them all the time. There was something more to the cause of his disappearance than the words that were hurled at him.

When the Jiyar came to know that Nammalwar was missing he called Pakshi.

'I must tell you, Pakshi. Your brother came to me the other day and talked of freeing himself from the family. I told him he had a duty to perform and he should take care of his mother. I was sure he wanted my blessings for his becoming a sanyasi, but seeing my mood perhaps he didn't reveal his intentions.'

Pakshi told his mother that Nammalwar might have taken to sanyasa. Ponna said, 'We had every type of persons in our family. We had villains, we had lechers, we had gluttons and we had wife-beaters. If the Lord has desired that one of our men should become a sanyasi, so be it. I am sure my son will return one day.'

Pakshi received the letter a fortnight after Nammalwar had disappeared from Nanguneri.

Dear Pakshi,

I should have written this letter to amma. I haven't the heart to do so. I had always thought myself to be courageous but I now understand that it is a gift I have not been blessed with.

Renouncing worldly ways does not require much courage in our country. You always get the respect you don't always deserve. There will always be someone to feed you. You can return home if you are satiated with the life of a sanyasi.

Swaraj is a stale dream for us. The angels seem to be on the side of the Empire and it would be futile fighting it, unless you want to die a dog's death and to figure in the list of martyrs for later generations. I do not want to give in to death that easily. Or perhaps I am not up to it.

You have been living with me long enough to know that female flesh doesn't attract me the way it should. Lakshmi was briefly sent by God to define happiness for me and now that she has returned to the lap of God I have no wish to seek happiness again in the arms of another girl which is what amma wants me to do.

I have no wish either to look after what Lakshmi has left behind. Amma, I know, has the sense and courage to bring him up. She may miss me, but she has other things to do. And you are there to take care of him.

I want freedom. I want to be far away from the musty air of domesticity.

I may come back. Not immediately.

Yours,
Anna

The flamboyance of Nammalwar was missing in Pakshi. He trudged on, unnoticed, setting his sights on what was visible to him. He did not much bother, in his early years, about what was happening around him as long as it did not concern him directly. Most of the time he sat at his desk making detailed notes for his examinations. His academic record was even better than Nammalwar's, although it was not noticed.

He found the underlying cold-bloodedness of his brother's letter staggering. Amma may be tough, he thought, but the monstrous unconcern of her darling son's letter, the unconcern that its stylish veneer cannot hide, will kill her. He decided not to mention the letter to Ponna.

Though Nammalwar's disappearance upset Ponna, she was convinced that her son was preordained to be a restless wanderer. She waited for him to return and when waiting was no longer possible she called both Andal and Pakshi and said, 'There is no point in expecting Nammalwar's return. He may not return at all.'

Andal was not rude to her mother this time.

'Why are you saying so, amma? He is not the sort to take his own life. He has to return one day.'

'That may take years. I may not live to see him, though I think I will see him at least once before I pass away. I know my son. Even if he returns he is not likely to lead a normal life.'

She turned to Pakshi and said, 'His son, your nephew, belongs to this family. It will be shameful if we allow him to grow up with Lakshmi's parents.'

'I agree,' said Pakshi.

'I have a proposal for you, Pakshi. You have seen Lakshmi's younger sister. She is very good looking. I have had her horoscope compared with yours. They do match. If you marry her, your brother's child could be with you without my having to worry about your wife neglecting him.'

'He could be with me,' said Andal.

'Yes, but when he grows up he will need a father. Ask Pakshi. He had at least Nammalwar with him.'

'I have no objection amma,' said Pakshi. 'Did you consult her parents?'

'The idea came from them.'

Interlude

THERE MUST HAVE BEEN NECTAR IN THE wet-nurse's milk. The child was a cherub. He crawled the length of the house on hands and knees, chasing Andal wherever she went. When he wailed in frustration, Andal gathered him in her arms and held him tight and coddled him with the warmth of her young breasts craving to be lactescent. There was no wet-nurse in Nanguneri but the child did not wilt. Ponna bought a fine black cow and built a shed for it in the courtyard of the other house. The cow's milk sustained the child until it took to solids. The house now sparkled with the countless small pleasures of aunt and nephew at play and Ponna was happy once again. She cuddled her grandson only when her daughter was not present. The child was Andal's, though the original idea had been to leave him with Pakshi. She hinted to her daughter-in-law that the bright harmony that the house was radiating now would have to be nurtured and the child should not be the cause of its demise.

Veda was a fine example of Cherankulam beauty. Tall and full-breasted, she wore a lovely golden girdle that accentuated the slenderness of her waist. She did not want to compete with Andal. She was fond of her sister's son, but she knew she would bear her own children. She adhered to the family routine of carrying saffron-laced milk to her husband and becoming pregnant without any loss of time. And she returned safely with her child.

Nammalwar's son, Madhurakavi, soon began to toddle and tattled words that sounded Tamil and brought joy to both Ponna and Andal. He would be as good as his father, thought Ponna. Only, he should not inherit his oddities. Ponna's prayers were now tinged with hope. Her mind had stopped wandering.

He slept with Andal, hugging her and clasping the edge of her sari. Andal allowed him to wet her. She did not move for fear of disturbing his sleep and she lay silent and delectably damp. When words came to him coherently, she taught him first the Tamil *Tiruppavai* and then the Sanskrit *Vishnu Sahasranaman*. She made him recite aloud and did not scold him if he demurred. He shed his rotundity as he grew and became angular and bony like his mother, but he was unusually healthy; even the common cold stayed clear of him.

Pakshi sailed through his law course and emerged with a first class. Sankara Iyer took him as his junior and it did not take him long to establish himself as a leading member of the Tirunelveli Bar.

He became a celebrity on his success in a case that involved the poisoning of a dog.

'Sir, I admit that I hated that dog. It never stopped growling whenever I was around. It always tried to creep up between us at inappropriate moments . . . . But sir, I swear upon my son that I did not poison it. My wife does not believe me. She has gone ahead and filed this case,' said the distraught zamindar who was the accused. The zamindar loved his wife to distraction but her love for the dog was overpowering.

Pakshi made elaborate charts of the dog's dietary habits with the help of its attendant and argued that the diet suited a full-grown lion rather than a pedigree dog. He also got a few unimpeachable palace servants to testify that the dog had the disgusting habit of rummaging through refuse bins. He then had a reputed veterinary doctor from Madras give his opinion that the dog could have died of natural causes: it was after all ten years old. Pakshi asked the zamindar to build a little cenotaph over its grave and got him to buy another expensive dog for his wife. When he won an acquittal for his client he went to the zamindar's wife and said, 'an acquittal from you will please him even more.'

When the reconciliation came about, the zamindar was ecstatic. He gave Pakshi ten thousand rupees, a fee unheard of at the Tirunelveli Bar for a case of this nature. What was more, on his recommendation well-heeled clients started pouring in. They were murderers, cheats, thieves and burglars and they came to Pakshi with the hope that he would win their cases for them. They were not far wrong.

His leisure was devoted to the activities of the Home Rule League. The League demanded self-determination, but demanded it in such a manner that it did not upset the government too much. Annie Besant was, after all, a famous name and prosperous lawyers considered it reasonably safe to associate with the movement started by her. Pakshi patronised the league more as an act of expiation than as one of conviction. When Besant was interned, he quietly switched over to the Theosophical Society which dabbled in reincarnation, auras and astral bodies and believed in a mishmash of Karma and what had been said in the *Dhammapada* and by Pythogoras and Appolonius and Madame Blavatsky. Pakshi was wonderfully confused about the whole thing but soon headed the Theosophical Lodge of Tirunelveli. He honed his skills at fence-sitting and managed to please both the district officials and the Congressmen.

The politics of Gandhi soon made fence-sitting an impossible pastime and most of the lawyers of Tirunelveli hated him for it. They clung to an assortment of societies until the societies themselves disintegrated. Gandhi was hugely popular and anti-British winds again began to blow across the country. Tirunelveli responded too, but in a subdued way. It had 1908 in mind. Pakshi did not participate in the Non-Cooperation Movement and stood aloof with some Madras Iyengar leaders of the Congress who thought Gandhi was going too far. But it was impossible to resist Gandhi for long.

Madhurakavi was now a boy of twelve. Andal still pampered him and he still wetted his bed. He was sent to the village school, unlike Pakshi's son Tirumalai, who was with his father in Tirunelveli and went to the Hindu High School. Andal soaked cooked rice in water overnight and gave him a huge ball of it mixed with curd in the mornings. He ran home to lunch, a three-course meal of rice and sambar, rice and rasam and rice and curd. Heaps of vegetables – cooked, fried and spiced – and a few fried *appalams* accompanied his meal. When he came home in the evening there were snacks waiting for him. The night's meal was the same elaborate three-course routine. He was not gaining weight, but he was becoming sloppy and immobile with Andal always waiting at his elbow.

More than what Andal served him, he liked the feasts which the Matam gave to Brahmins with a satisfying regularity. The food at the Matam had a different flavour; the devout said the flavour was divine. Madhurakavi adored it. He and his friends gathered in front of the Matam at least one hour before the start of the feast so they could partake of it in the very first round. Later the delicacies were likely to disappear. When the gate opened, the boys rushed in with Madhu leading them. More often than not, they crashed blindly into the old Brahmins, who were also waiting for the feast to start, and were roundly cursed by them. The boys did not care. They kept running and came to the dining room on the floor of which were spread row after row of banana leaves that served as receptacles for the feast. The boys took their positions and reserved for their not-so-agile friends as many banana leaves as possible by the simple expedient of standing in front of them with their legs widely spread.

It was during one such feast that Madhu picked the quarrel which led to his leaving Nanguneri. He was standing with his legs apart in front of some leaves when another boy not belonging to his group quietly pulled one of the leaves towards himself and sat down in front of it. This was a blatant violation of the rules the boys had made for themselves, and Madhu warned him that he would be beaten after the feast. The boy was too hungry to care. When the feast was over, Madhu and his friends took the offending boy to the tank and forcibly kept his head under water until he thought he would die. He did not, but the fright made him throw up all that he had eaten at the feast. His father came to Ponna.

'Your grandson needs to be controlled. Today he and his friends pushed my son into the tank and it was due to the Lord's grace that he is alive.'

When she heard what had happened, Ponna felt that Raman's ghost was haunting the house. Though she loved her husband, she did not want her grandson to walk in the footsteps of his gluttonous grandfather. Then she realised that she had her daughter to contend with, who was beyond reasoning generally, and infinitely more so in matters concerning her nephew. She called Pakshi from Tirunelveli.

'Madhurakavi is becoming increasingly lazy. He rarely goes out to play and he has gluttonous friends with whom he spends most of his time. He does not miss a single feast given by the Matam.'

'Andal is spoiling him. Why don't you tell her?'

'Will she talk to me? She is raring to pick a fight with me and this will give her an opportunity.'

'What should I do, amma?'

'Take him with you.'

'He has another aunt to pamper him there. Give me some time to think.'

Pakshi returned and consulted his friends. They told him of the *Gurukulam* school recently started by V.V.S. Iyer in the village of Chermadevi.

Pakshi came back to Nanguneri and spoke to his sister.

'Andal, I am worried about Madhurakavi. He is as bright as his father, but his school record tells a different story.'

'What are you trying to imply? Am I spoiling him?' asked a bristling Andal.

'No, this school is not good enough for him. Please think. If Nammalwar comes back tomorrow and asks us about his son's progress, we must be able to give a reply that will not shame us. I have thought about this and I have a solution. V.V.S. Iyer has started a fine school in Chermadevi. It is a residential school and a nationalist one. Nammalwar, if he was here, would have surely approved of it.'

Andal had to give her reluctant consent, though she extracted a promise from her brother that the boy would visit Nanguneri at least once a month. Madhurakavi appeared to be comfortable with his languorous state. He said to Pakshi, '*Chithappa*, I don't want to go to another school. What is wrong with my present school?'

Pakshi hugged him and stroked his head.

'Everything is wrong with your school, Madhu. At your age, your father could recite the entire *Elegy written in a Country Churchyard*. Who wrote the elegy?'

'Edward Gray. I know a few lines.' He started reciting, 'Full many a gem of . . .'

Pakshi stopped him. 'It is good that you know these lines. Still you can't recite the entire poem. And it is Thomas, not Edward. Madhu, you are twelve and your English is good, but it could be better. The new school has wonderful teachers.'

'Chithappa, I have problems at night. Who will wash my sheets there every day?' said Madhu in a voice choked with shame.

Pakshi released his nephew from his embrace and made him stand a few feet away. Touching Madhu's shoulders with extended hands Pakshi said, 'Don't worry. Bed-wetting is a gift from our ancestors. I used to do it till I moved to Tirunelveli. In a new place you don't sleep well and you will be cured of this habit there. If you continue here you will keep wetting the bed and, when you get a wife, she will have to wash your linen. Do you want that to happen?'

The boy shook his head.

Though Iyer was the mastermind behind the murder of Ashe, the police were unable to prove his involvement. He later renounced anarchist methods, joined Gandhi's Non-Cooperation Movement and went to prison. On his release, the idea of starting a school modelled on the ancient Indian universities of Nalanda and Taxila came to him, and with the help of a few well-wishers and the Congress Party he was able start a school in a village near Tirunelveli.

Pakshi took Madhurakavi to Iyer and said. 'Sir, he is the son of one of your disciples.'

'I am not able to place him. Whose son is he?'

'He is the son of Nammalwar, sir. My elder brother.'

Iyer knew all the members of the now-moribund Bharata Mata Association.

'Oh, our tall and handsome Iyengar?' He smiled at Mahurakavi and said, 'you are welcome here, son. Your father is a remarkable man. He must be working somewhere, quietly, for the nation. Have you come here willingly or under compulsion from your uncle?'

Madhurakavi did not reply. Pakshi said, 'He was in Nanguneri doing things at leisure.'

Iyer laughed and said, *'so, he will not be tied to hours not 'pointed times, but learn his lesson as he pleases.* That may not be possible here, son.' He turned to Pakshi and said, 'He will still be no breeching scholar. We have no birchers in this school.'

Iyer wanted his school to be in an idyllic location that would have pleased the ancient sages of his country who spent their lifetimes educating. It was his fortune that he could find such a place. Spread on thirty acres of fertile land, with emerald green rice fields, frondy coconut groves and fruit gardens, it afforded a fine view of the Kolindiya hills of the Western Ghats and the river Tamraparni flowed just three miles away.

Madhurakavi, so used to the ministering of his aunt and the sleepy ways of his village school, griped initially about the sapping regimen. He had to wake at four o'clock in the morning for his exercises. He then marched to an allocated place with a small spade for his toilet, which meant that he had to dig a small pit, do his business and cover it with what he had earlier dug. After bathing he, along with other students, went round the village singing patriotic songs. The boys were taught ploughing, manuring, transplanting, harvesting, stacking and winnowing. They learnt carpentry, weaving, bricklaying and cooking. The academic sessions were in English and Tamil and besides the basic subjects in the arts and sciences, they were taught Sanskrit and Hindi. Their food was mild, without a hint of the chillies, tamarind and other rich seasonings of Andal's fare.

Madhurakavi's amazing transformation came about within a short time. His lassitude disappeared and his sheets were dry. He began to love the school and what he did there. Like his father, he was ravenous when it came to books and Iyer, himself a bibliophile, wanted his boys to bury their noses in books when they had done what the school had demanded of them. Madhurakavi was one of the few who came up to his expectations.

He called him one day and asked him what he was reading. Madhu said, 'Dickens, sir. *Oliver Twist*.'

'Forget the white-skinned writers. You still have time to read them. I am starting a class on the Kamban Ramayanam. Would you like to join them? You won't be disappointed. Our Kamban can bear comparison with the *Iliad*, the *Aeneid*, and *Paradise Lost*, and with the Sanskrit epics of the Mahabharata and

Ramayana. It is a pity that Iyengars who should have known better have neglected this epic. You could wash away the sins of your forefathers by mastering it and singing its glory.'

Iyer's eloquence was beyond the boy but he was proud that he was singled out and asked. He readily joined the classes.

'Is it true, Madhu, that the Brahmin boys of the Gurukulam do not eat in the presence of the non-Brahmins?' asked Pakshi. He was in his room where he received his clients, but on that day two of his friends were with him. Madhu had been visiting him during the school holidays.

'No. In fact the one who usually sits next to me is a Reddiar boy. Iyer too joins us occasionally.'

'What did I tell you? How could you expect Iyer to practise segregation?' said Pakshi to his friends.

'Madhu, are there any Brahmin boys who eat separately?'

'Yes, there are two boys from the nearby villages. Their parents insist that their children will not eat in the presence of non-Brahmin boys. Iyer has tried his best to convince them but they refuse to listen.'

'Pakshi, what a fall! Iyer who once was the most enlightened of the Brahmin leaders now listens meekly to two local bigots! He should have flatly said no to them. That he has chosen to bow to their unreasonable demands clearly shows that he has fallen a victim to orthodoxy,' said one of Pakshi's friends.

Pakshi said, 'Ramaswamy Naicker must be rubbing his hands in glee. The battle between the Brahmins and the non-Brahmins has begun. Unless the Mahatma does something, this fight is not going to end in a hurry. The Brahmins will fight hard but will be punched out eventually.'

There were arguments and counter-arguments that Iyer, who was supposed to run his school on non-sectarian, Gandhian principles, had succumbed to the wishes of the orthodoxy. Ramaswamy Naicker, now beginning to be hailed as Periyar, was furious that Congress money was being used to further caste-segregation. Others felt that Iyer was helpless and such prejudices should be allowed to wither away slowly. The episode came to its end in a way nobody had expected.

Madhu was disappointed that Iyer would not accompany the students on the picnic. They had planned a school trip to the nearby Papansam hills. They were to lunch at a spot near a spectacular cataract. A session of the Forest Book of the Kamban Ramayanam with the cataract as the backdrop would have been wonderful. I could have recited the resonant poems on the destruction of the demon twins, Kara and Dushana, at the hands of Rama, matching the drone of the forest, he thought. Iyer is not himself nowadays. He is no longer the head of the Gurukulam. The rumour has it that he has resigned because of those two boys. It is a pity they are not with us. We could have pushed them down from a precipice.

Iyer did join them after all, though a day later. His daughter Subhadra nagged him until he duly listened to her. The mood of the boys which had been sullen earlier lightened immediately and they all embarked on a climb that took them to the upper reaches of the river above the cataract. The river here was not deep or wide, but was full of boulders and devilishly swift. It was fordable, though. Madhu and his friends crossed the river stepping gingerly on the boulders. He had gone only a few steps ahead when he heard Iyer screaming, 'Subhadra!' He turned around and saw Iyer's bobbing head in the river, his left hand groping for a hold and his right clutched around his daughter's braid.

They were not sure of Subhadra, but they were confident that Iyer would emerge unscathed. He was an ace swimmer, the Tamraparani was like his mother, and mothers did not devour their children. The Tamraparani did. She spat him out after five days.

When Madhu returned to Tirunelveli he told Pakshi that he would not be going back to the Gurukulam.

Though he lost his religion, Madhu kept his affair with Kamban, even after Iyer's death. Communism did not diminish his love for the poet, and he used to puzzle his friends with quotes from the Tamil epic when they were debating ideological issues. It was his continual exhortations that finally brought Pakshi to the great work.

Andal went mad with delight at the demise of the Gurukulam.

Ponna said, 'I don't know why you are delirious. Is he going to return to Nanguneri? He has to go to Tirunelveli and complete his school finals.'

'I know, but I can be with him. Surely he is not going to stay in a hostel in Tirunelveli.'

'Andal, I will then be alone here. Let him stay with Pakshi and Veda.'

'I am going to Tirunelveli. I shall hire a small house and live with Madhu and cook for him. Why don't you go and live with your son? Why do you insist on haunting this house like a ghost? Does Veda fight with you? It is your pride. The pride of a cook's daughter who has come up to queen over what is not hers.'

'Andal, you are being unfair. Can I stop you from going to Tirunelveli? Why are you picking on me?'

'I have better things to do than quarrel with you.'

Madhu had changed. He loved his aunt but there were no physical expressions of his love as there had been when he was in Nanguneri. He knew he was the anchor of his aunt's life, but her touch repelled him and he bawled out, 'Don't touch me,' which often left her in tears and despair. 'I have been reduced to the status of a cook. His ears have been poisoned by his grandmother,' she lamented.

Years later, Pakshi told a curious Nambi how his father got involved in the freedom movement.

'Though your father studied in the Gurukulam, he was apolitical for a long time. He wanted to be a Tamil scholar. He had a friend, Vaiyapuri Pillai, with whom he used spend long hours poring over the palm-leaf manuscripts of the Kamban Ramayanam. They were to edit the Alwar Tirunagari recension.'

'How did he become political all of a sudden?'

'Like most of the youngsters of his generation, he came under the spell of Gandhi. It was in 1926, no, I think it was 1927. Gandhi came to Tirunelveli and on his way to Nagercoil he agreed to spend an hour in our village. I was the leader of the reception committee and your father was made the head of the volunteer corps. He was thrilled that he would see Gandhi at close quarters. He worked very hard. Your father had a tough constitution and he rarely fell ill, but as luck would have it, he had a raging fever on the day of Gandhi's visit. Still, he plodded on. When the Mahatma's entourage was about to arrive, somebody discovered that the milk had turned sour, and there were a number of Tamils with Gandhi who would go on a satyagraha if they were not given a milky coffee on arrival. The task of finding the errant milkman and charming a few measures of milk out of him fell on Madhu's shoulders.

'Gandhi arrived on time and was about to leave when your father came in with a can of milk. I had to divert him to the kitchen-tent without allowing him to come anywhere near Gandhi. The entourage was restive without coffee. Madhu was in tears, but he obeyed me. Luck was however with him. Gandhi was impressed with the volunteer force and he wanted to congratulate its leader personally. When he heard that the leader was still slogging in the kitchen even though he had high fever, he went straight there. Imagine Madhu's surprise when he turned to meet the person who had gently touched his shoulder, and found himself face to face with Gandhi. That gentle touch converted him and it was Madhu who was in the forefront of the agitation in our village for allowing the untouchables' entry into the temple.'

'How did he become a Communist?'

'That happened, if I am correct, after the salt satyagraha in 1930 and when Sardar Bhagat Singh was executed, though he joined the party much later. I don't want to discuss that period of your father's life, Nambi.'

Gandhi's decision to go on the salt march had come at an inopportune time for Pakshi. The busy lawyer had an unusually large number of cases to defend that year and imitating Gandhi might land him in prison, probably with his clients. On the other hand, it was inconceivable that a Congressman do nothing about his own salt when Gandhi was walking across Gujarat to manufacture his. Pakshi read and re-read the salt laws and found an ingenious way to stay out of prison.

He found that even collection of sea water by a person not licensed to do so might technically invite punishment under the law. What he did was to persuade one of his clients who owned a salt factory to sell him drums of a slushy, semi-manufactured concoction of salt which he transported to Tirunelveli. There, in the spacious courtyard of his house, he with his eager admirers performed the defiant act of heating and stirring up the slush in giant cauldrons. The resultant sediment, which was black and bore no resemblance to salt, was distributed among the jubilant onlookers. The Pakshi-salt found its way to most of the local Congressmen's houses and they all had the satisfaction of breaking the hated law, the existence of which had been unknown to many until Gandhi chose to violate it. The district officials were not sure whether or not Pakshi had violated the salt law; they wrote to the Madras Secretariat, who in turn took up the matter with the Delhi government, who did not respond at all.

Madhu did not approve of this legerdemain. He had just returned from Trichy, disappointed that he did not find a place in the team that was to march to the coastal village of Vedaranyam to manufacture salt under the leadership of Gandhi's confidant and conscience-keeper, Rajaji. He said to Pakshi, 'Chithappa, what you are doing is not Gandhian. You know the unwholesome thing you keep in those cauldrons is taxed salt-slush. Where is the violation of the law?'

'What is important is the act and not the fine points of the law. The people here feel that they have defied the law; that is sufficient for me.'

Madhu was not convinced. 'I must say Gandhi had not reckoned on such crafty interpretations of his lofty cause.'

'What is Gandhi's purpose, Madhu? He wants to spread disaffection against the British in a non-violent way, which is precisely what I am doing.'

'Without having to visit a British prison?'

'That is not for me to decide.'

Madhu did not keep quiet. He led a team to nearby Tiruchendur and performed the illegal act of manufacturing salt. The authorities promptly arrested him and sentenced him to six months' imprisonment.

The sentence meant that Madhu's value in the marriage market crashed to a level that caused Ponna to worry.

'I should blame you, Pakshi. You should have controlled him. He will be losing one year of college now. Andal wanted to see him married off this year. I don't think that is any longer possible,' said Ponna.

Pakshi said, 'It is my responsibility to see that Madhu leads a normal life. I shall persuade him to marry quickly when he comes out of prison.'

Madhu did not marry immediately on his release, which came within three months of his imprisonment because of the Gandhi-Irwin Pact. It took Ponna, Andal and Pakshi two years to persuade him. He relented only when Andal repeated her old threat of jumping into the well. It took him another eight years to produce a son. He was by then a member of the Communist Party, but he accompanied his wife, Kamala, to the mountain-temple of Nambi where she prayed for a son. It was one of her very few wishes granted by the Lord.

The Return

Seven

THE TEACHER CAME BANG ON TIME, careening in on a bicycle dented with age. Its accessories, or whatever it had once been decked with, had decayed long ago and now the riding machine had only a few basic parts that made it mobile. Its handlebars were rusted tubes, its pedals tiny rods sticking out, its wheels elliptical jumbles and its tires grey with beards of fraying rubber, but he rode it safely though narrow alleys and highways humming with fancy transport, to be with his children. His cloth bag bulging with yellowing dog-eared papers, he sat on a mat in a sunny room opposite the one where Tirumalai received his clients. His students took time to gather before him but he did not mind. He waited patiently, mumbling to himself and stroking the fluid beard that flowed all over his chest.

'I told you yesterday to learn by heart the most important events of this year. What are they?' With the words, wind whistled through his mouth, which had once been intrusively toothed, carrying with it betel-rich spittle. The students were beyond the range of the spittle shower, but the adult aroma of tobacco-laden betel was well within range. They found it disgusting. That was the only disgusting thing about their master; he was wonderful otherwise.

'Tenzing touched the peak of Everest, sir.'

'Yes. Tenjing.'

'Sir?'

'I said Tenjing. What is the other event?'

'Elizabeth became the Queen of England.'

'Yes, Elijabeth.'

'Sir?'

'Elijabeth. E-li-ja-beth. Are you deaf? I am pushing seventy and I can hear a snake slithering. You are deaf at the age of seven. It is because you eat rice and dal and I eat mutton.'

'What is mutton, sir?'

'Mutton is the flej of goat.'

'Which of goat, sir?'

'The flej of goat.'

'Do you drink its blood, sir?'

'No.'

'How can you have its flesh without blood?'

'That is different. I don't drink its blood like you drink buttermilk.'

The boys roared with laughter.

'Is it sweet or salty, sir? The flesh.'

'It is neither.'

'Is it sour?'

'No.'

'How does it taste, sir?'

He thought for a minute and said, 'Yes, it is like a tough palmyra root.'

'We don't know how it tastes, sir,' said Kannan. Brahmin houses avoided the root.

'It is . . . it is like chapatti.'

They did not like chapattis either. They pouted in disgust.

'Have you brought mutton today for lunch, sir?'

'For lunch? Do you want your parents to sack me? Kannan, Subramani and Narasimhan are Brahmins and this Ganesan is a *saiva pillai*. Can I eat mutton in front of you? In your home?

You visit my house and I will show you what mutton looks like. Or chicken. Or fij.'

'Would you kill the goat in front of us, sir?'

'I am a teacher and not a butcher. We don't even have a chicken coop.'

Tirumalai entered the room, and the teacher made an effort to get up, while Tirumalai made an effort to touch his feet.

'How are they, sir? Are they troubling you?'

'No, but they are not like you, Tirumalai. They ask too many questions.'

He was Tirumalai's teacher too, and Tirumalai knew how deliciously ineffective he was. The tuition was a charade. His teacher was short of money and he frowned at charity. The kids seemed to enjoy his session immensely and they did learn a few things at times.

The teacher's problem was that he was sincere and he felt that no question of his students should go unanswered. The students naturally asked the questions they liked and the result was that he never taught them what he had intended to teach. He sounded indescribably funny to the children without his being aware of it.

Tirumalai was also grateful to his teacher, for he was one of the few who voted for him in the municipal elections. He had assured Tirumalai eight votes from his family and relatives, which were the only votes he received from the teacher's part of the town. The contest was between him, the Congress candidate, and Bala, who was fielded by the Communist Party.

Young Kannan was thrilled when a giant vessel was placed in the backyard of his house on three stones arranged in a triangle, and a fire was lit under it. In the vessel was brewed water, rice flour, copper sulphate and some other mysterious material. He stood there, impervious to the pleading of his mother not to stand in the sun, watching the sweating workers of the Congress stirring the cauldron with long wooden ladles, bringing the brew to a thick consistency. The loathsome paste made an excellent glue for sticking posters on walls.

The posters were brilliantly coloured and had printed on them the Congress symbol of the yoked twin bullocks and the words *'Vote for Tirumalai. Vote for Congress. For prosperity and progress.'* There were handbills too in their thousands, flimsy and coloured red and green which listed what Tirumalai would achieve if he was elected.

Kannan distributed the handbills among his friends free, but there were prices for the gum and the poster. The gum he gave in coconut shells for the exchange of delicacies like slices of raw mango or coconut and curls of sweet manilla tamarind. The poster was a little more expensive; Kannan demanded in exchange, a full pencil if it was made in India, and a half one if it was from England. The posters had many uses long after the elections were over: they made fine wrappers for books; they were cut into convenient pieces and stitched into rough note books to do sums on – their obverse sides were blank, after all; they were made into paper cones to transfer provisions from Tirunelveli to Nanguneri; and they served as floor mats, though persons who sat on them were careful not to rest their bottoms on the printed side.

The contest was fierce. Tirumalai made the routine attack on the Communists, on their sneezing if the weather was bad in Moscow. He said that they betrayed the nation by joining with the imperialists in 1942 when they were shedding the blood of Congressmen. He listed the vile abuses they had hurled at Gandhi and Nehru. He could not criticise the Communist candidate personally, for he was his cousin's friend.

Bala too did not attack Tirumalai personally. He said the Congress was the party of the landlords and big businessmen and it only served their interests. He said, 'Yes we do sneeze when the weather turns inclement in Moscow and Peking, but we sneeze for the ordinary, toiling people, and it is a sight better than sneezing for the rich. And for the USA. And for Britain.'

Regarding the accusation of betrayal in 1942, he reminded Tirumalai that he, Bala, had spent the prime of his youth in British prisons. The year 1942 was different. Congress had chosen a wrong time to rise in revolt when the world was engaged in the difficult task of defeating Nazism.

The people were not interested in grand politics. Their preoccupations were immediate and related to edible rice in ration shops and good drinking water. They knew the Communist would fight for these issues more vigorously than the Congressman. They voted Bala to victory by a huge margin.

Kannan's friends ribbed him for a few days about the defeat of his father, but as the posters started peeling off from the walls and eventually fell off, the defeat was forgotten. Tirumalai remembered it for a long time however, as it signalled an end to his political ambitions, though he remained a keen follower of politics.

Narasimhan told his friends that some men were weird. They grew hair in odd places very fast and if they didn't take measures to remove it periodically, the hair would eventually cover their bodies and they would become black bears.

'You are bluffing.'

'I have seen German Iyengar going to the barber just for this. I have heard that he has grown hair inside his throat and it is a problem for the barber to remove the hair without slashing his throat.'

German Iyengar was the priest who took care of the many rituals their fathers had to perform. His original name was Ramanuja, but he was known as German because, as a young boy during the first war, he supported Imperial Germany.

'You should take us with you next time.'

The barber's hut was on the way to the bathing ghat. Kannan was usually dragged there by his father for his haircut. The clippers scared him and his father had to cajole him to keep still when the barber went about his work. This time he marched bravely with his friends. The door of the barber's hut was closed.

The boys gently pushed it and were happy to note that it was not locked. Kannan pushed it further and peeped inside.

German Iyengar was standing stark naked with his eyes closed in ecstasy, arms akimbo and legs wide apart. The barber crouching between German's legs was busy with his razor and Kannan could see clumps of hair all over the floor. Subramani, in his eagerness to see what was going on, elbowed Kannan, who went tumbling down in front of German. Subramani and the others ran away, but Kannan could not escape.

A very agitated and fully shaven Iyengar took Kannan to his father.

'Swami, listen to what your son has done. He came peeping in when I was having my *sarvanaga kshavaram*. Such curiosity at this age is not good at all. The barber laughs and says he will charge separately from the boys.'

Tirumalai gave two rupees to German Iyengar to pacify him and after he had left he gently tweaked the ear of his son and said, 'So this is what you are doing when you are supposed to study.'

Kannan said, 'Will he turn into a bear if he doesn't do this every month?'

'Rubbish. If you indulge in such mischief I shall lock you in my cupboard. Your mother will search for you everywhere and not find you at all.'

Kannan went back to Narasimhan and told him that there was no danger of German Iyengar turning into a bear and that he, Narasimhan, was a bluffer and he, Kannan, would not listen to him anymore.

Narasimhan sniggered and said, 'As you wish. But today I have learnt a secret from my great-aunt.'

'What is it?'

'Why should I tell you? You are not going to listen to me anymore. The secret is about the Tenkalais.' Narasimhan was a Vadakalai Iyengar.

'Then let the secret die with you.'

'What will you give me in exchange?'

When the negotiations came to a successful conclusion, Narasimhan told him the secret.

'My great-aunt says the Tenkalais are not Brahmins at all.'

'How could she say that? Look at me and look at you.'

Kannan was very fair and Narasimhan chocolate-skinned. The Brahmins were supposed to be fair, or rather all fair persons were supposed to be of Brahmin stock.

Narasimhan let that pass. 'She says your ancestors were all *Shudras* and were made Brahmin by . . . by . . . yes, Ramanuja.'

This, Kannan considered, was the biggest insult that could be hurled at him. He punched Narasimhan on the nose and ran back to his house.

He went straight to his mother and asked her, 'Amma, are we Brahmins?'

'Yes, we are. If we are not, there are no Brahmins in the world.'

'Narasimhan says our ancestors were all Shudras.'

'Who? That Vadakalai boy? Mischief runs in their blood. Your peria paati is here. Ask her.'

Ponna seated her great-grandson on her lap and asked him what was worrying him. When she heard him, she said, 'Don't worry. He is lying. In reality the Vadakalais are the descendants of *Rakshasis*. You know who Rakshasis were. They lived in Ravana's Lanka and had two or three human beings for lunch everyday. When the war between Rama and Ravana was over and Ravana was slain, the Lord wanted to return to Ayodhya quickly. A *Pushpaka Vimana*, a chariot that could fly, was arranged for him. Some of the Rakshasis, who had now come over to Rama's side, implored him and Sita to take them to Ayodhya. Being compassionate, the divine couple readily agreed. Hanuman did not like this decision, but he could not argue with his master. When the vimana was flying over these parts he quietly pushed a few Rakshasis, without the knowledge of Rama and Sita, out of the vimana. They, being Rakshasis, were not hurt at all when they fell down. They were rescued by some persons who had all the qualities of Ravana, but were themselves Brahmins of the North. They married these Rakshasis and the Vadakalais were born.'

Kannan loved the demon Vadakalai story. Narasimhan is indeed a demon. He is still my friend. My demon-friend. He giggled uncontrollably.

He loved Ponna paati. He loved the fragrance of camphor and saffron that she seemed to radiate, and the crinkles of her warm sari into which he routinely wiped his nose without her being aware of it, whenever she took him in her arms. He loved the hot little balls of *pongal* that she gave him, heavenly pongal that was ghee-anointed and embedded with slivers of fat cashews, stinging drops of black peppers and chewy pieces of ginger.

Those were wonderful years for the moneylender family. Pakshi had more or less retired into religion, choosing to stay at Nanguneri and coming to Tirunelveli only to appear in complicated cases. He bequeathed his practice to his son and Tirumalai prospered in no time.

Nambi was with Pakshi but he came to Tirunelveli every weekend to visit the libraries. He was only eleven and according to Renganayaki, Kannan's mother, he had read the entire *Vyasa Bharata* – in its Tamil translation – and could tell the names of all its thousands of characters. Though Kannan boasted to his friends of his cousin's prodigious memory – he himself could not tell Hidumba from Bakasura – he hated his cousin and his wonderful gifts. What was more, the prodigy kept tweaking Kannan's ears which turned red and remained so for days, causing his friends to call him a red-eared monkey.

Narasimhan gave him an idea without the least knowledge of what Kannan was up to. He said one day that a mixture of crushed tamarind seeds and myrobalan pips made one lose one's memory and only penance for two years on a mountain without water or food would bring it back.

'If you lose your memory, how will you remember about the penance?'

'Don't ask silly questions. Your mother or father will be with you, constantly reminding you.'

'Will they go without food or water too?'

'I have no idea, but I don't think that is necessary.'

When his bearded master came, Kannan asked him, 'Sir, is it true that some seeds could cause loss of memory? Narasimhan says so.'

'Maybe. I am a teacher and not a doctor. Why do you require them? You can't even remember what I have told you just a few minutes ago.' The other boys laughed and the master said, 'I was only joking. The other day Kannan recited "London Bridge is Falling Down" after reading it just twice.'

He was afraid of consulting his father and he went to his mother and asked her. She said, 'I don't know. I have to ask your Ponna paati.' She patted him on his shoulders and said 'Run, I have to cook. You should be in search of a medicine that improves your memory and not one that causes its loss. I just remembered. Why don't you ask Nambi?'

Kannan did not confide in his mother that his aim was to administer the medicine to Nambi. He thought that as Nambi has no parents, Ponna paati and Veda paati will help him during his penance. Finding the ingredients was not a problem. There were a number of tamarind and myrobalan trees in the garden opposite his house.

He made up his powder carefully and folded it neatly into a square of paper. He kept the packet in a secret alcove he had discovered under the staircase. The next day he swallowed a mosquito and his life was in great danger.

The mosquito flew into his open mouth and before he could spit it out, it got swallowed. Narasimhan said gravely 'You may not realise, but your life is in danger. Imagine, persons bitten by it just once shiver for months with fever, and you have a full mosquito inside your stomach. Your stomach probably has to be cut open.'

Kannan went screaming to his house and bumped into Nambi. 'What is the problem? Why are you screaming your head off?' 'I am going to die. My stomach is going to be cut open.' 'Who told you this?' 'I have just swallowed a mosquito. It is refusing to come out of my stomach. Narasimhan says it is difficult to save me.' 'He is pulling your leg. And you are so foolish you don't realise that the mosquito has by now been digested in your stomach. You don't believe me. Bring me ten mosquitoes, I will swallow them all.'

Kannan said shyly, 'It is God's punishment.'

'What?'

'I was going to make you lose your memory. It was wicked of me.'

He told Nambi about the medicine he had made. Nambi laughed and said, 'It must again be that Narasimhan who is filling you with these stories. Where is your medicine?' When Kannan retrieved the packet from his alcove, Nambi snatched if from his hand and unfolding the packet took a pinch and tasted it. 'Mmmm. It is bitter, that is all. It is not going to do anything to me.' Kannan gaped at him, awestruck.

There was no observable impairment to Nambi's memory, but the bearded master became dangerously ill with jaundice. Kannan wanted to call on him, and in spite of Renganayaki's protests that her son should not be taken to such a polluting place as a Muslim's house, Tirumalai took him there.

The street where the bearded master lived was at the end of the town beyond a warren of narrow lanes. It had a ridge of refuse at its centre and its edges were effluvium-soaked and littered with the putrient innards of slaughter. The bearded master had no children and his wife, now tending to her dying husband, was resigned to his death. She told Tirumalai that the doctor had given him only a few days to live. The master had turned yellow because of his perforated liver and he exuded a rank smell.

Tirumalai went up to him and said, 'Sir, I am Tirumalai. Do you recognise me? I have brought Kannan with me.'

The teacher said feebly, 'You shouldn't have. He knows a different master.'

'I am sorry sir, but he insisted.'

The master looked at Kannan and said, 'I can't show you mutton today. I don't think I shall ever eat mutton, even if I recover. Come near me.'

Kannan shrank from him. He sniffled and hid behind his father. Death had kept a distance from the children of the moneylender's family during Kannan's childhood, and he was not very familiar with it. He had imagined that his teacher would be cozily ill, tucked between warm sheets, as would happen to him if he was sick. His yellowed master was a terrifying sight and his illness repulsed him.

'He is fearful of coming near me. You should not have brought him here, Tirumalai.'

Tirumalai glared at Kannan and tried to push him towards his master, but the master said, 'Leave him alone. Let me embrace him when I get well.'

While returning home, Tirumalai said, 'Kannan, you have behaved abominably with your teacher and this is not expected of a good boy.'

Kannan said, 'But he smells, appa. Like a lavatory.'

Tirumalai said, 'Enough. If you speak one more word, I shall hit you. He is dying and every dying person has one oddity or the other. I have to die, and even you have to die. Remember that.'

'May I speak now?'

'Yes.'

'My death and yours must be a long way off. Are they not?'

'Probably they are.'

'Then why should I remember my death or yours? But appa, is sir dying? He says he will embrace me when he gets well. Are you sure he is dying?'

'We shall pray for his recovery,' said Tirumalai unconvincingly.

Renganayaki was very angry with her husband when he told her of his visit. She heated an iron ladle until it became red-hot. She immersed it in a tumbler of buttermilk and forced Kannan to drink the iron-scalded drink. 'This will cure you of the scare the wretched visit has caused you,' she said to him.

When his master died, Kannan told his friends, 'I knew he would die. He was yellow and was urinating through his skin. I visited him at his house.'

His friends did not believe him. But whenever one of them thought he was dying, he would ask his friends to see whether he was turning yellow and whether he smelt of urine.

Eight

THE DELUGE USUALLY CAME WITH DUE WARNING. Loudspeakers blared at people to move out of low-lying places and the edges of riverbeds. The poor waited, nevertheless. When the river swelled, they watched, praying that the rising waters would not touch them. They remained awake all night, through the rain, wishing that the river would subside. The river did subside sometimes; at other times, it did not. It was never furious. It brought in its water, brown and thick as gruel, slowly, and children gazed with pure joy and wonder at the river climbing its way to take over their huts. Sludge-covered snakes coiled round the poles that supported the huts. The children were familiar with snakes and were not surprised by their presence. The water also brought some buoyant baubles from places upstream which the children accepted with glee. The floating carcasses, they ignored. Their parents used long poles to push these foetid floats back into the river.

The water was inexorable and the hut-dwellers had to move out to safe places. They had already trussed their possessions in cloth bundles and cardboard cartons. They moved out without any fuss, at the right time, sad children clinging to them. The mud huts disintegrated leisurely and the roofs floated away.

The Brahmins were happy with the rain. The sweltering heat that preceded the rain had forced them to sleep outdoors and without their wives. The rain made their interiors cool and cozy. And their houses were on high ground that the river could not reach. They slept well with their wives, snuggling up under thick sheets of cotton. A few of the hut-dwellers came to disturb them and occupied the backyards of their houses, but normally the poor moved quietly into schools and other public buildings.

Tirumalai went in the morning to admire the floods and Kannan tagged along. They went first to the Sulouchana Mudaliar Bridge, which afforded a grandstand view of the river in spate. Its noble spans, modelled on the Waterloo Bridge across the Thames – so the people of Tirunelveli claimed – were now fully submerged, and the river had risen so high it threatened to overflow the bridge. The crowd on the bridge did not feel that this could be imminent, for they dawdled across, with umbrellas under their armpits, comparing the year's flood with the ones they had seen in the earlier years. They could see a few persons standing on the roof of the Thaipusa Mandapam. The bums, wanderers and vagabonds had overslept in the Mandapam, which sat almost at the centre of the riverbed, until the water woke them and pushed them up on the roof. They were not unduly worried about their plight and they waved merrily at the gawking public. They were waiting for the police boats to arrive.

Tirumalai and Kannan then walked slowly to their bathing ghat. The temple of Ganapathi had gone underwater and, excepting a lamp-post near the submerged temple, there were no visible landmarks across the river until the other bank. The water was soupy with undissolved dung and other flotsam but Kannan desperately wanted to swim. He knew his father would not allow him to enter the water. I will come later during the day with my friends, he thought, to swim till my eyes turn red. This is one field in which Nambi can't hold a candle to me. He won't go in the water for a million rupees.

Tirumalai turned to him and said, 'I know what you are thinking. Don't even dream of it. Remember your promise to Ponna paati. At least keep your promise till her death, which could be any time now.'

Kannan learnt swimming the hard way. His friends just pushed him into deep water and left him there to find his way to the shallows. His legs did not reach the river floor though they were probing frantically. He thought he would drown, but when his terror left him he flailed his arms about, and reached the side rather easily. He then sought water. He swam in the river, and when he was sated with that, he walked long distances to swim in irrigation wells and temple tanks. He invariably came back to the river at nights, if it was not in flood.

He found the Nanguneri tank irresistible when he saw it in its majesty, its waves washing the walls of the temple. Nambi was then with him. Kannan asked his cousin to keep his spectacles and shirt and entered the water with his half-pants on. The water was rough and Kannan had never swum in choppy waters. It appeared to Nambi that his cousin would be sucked in by the tank. In panic, he raised an alarm and Kannan was rescued when he did not need to be rescued.

When Ponna came to know of this episode she had a nervous breakdown. Kannan had always found her steady, but this time she was trembling all over.

'Kannan, you don't know what you have done. Ours is an accursed family and water is our enemy.'

'Paati, I am a strong swimmer. I was in no trouble at all. It was Nambi who took fright and set rescuers upon me. They could have drowned me. I would never drown on my own.'

'I don't want to listen to your brave talk. I need a promise from you. You will not swim again.'

'That is not possible, paati. Ask for promises that will not be broken.'

She took her great-grandson to the temple and got a promise from him in front of the Lord that he would never again swim in rivers and tanks when they were full and rough.

'Do you remember Andal paati?'

Kannan had a vague memory of her. She was not brought to the Tirunelveli house when she was sent back from the Madras Mental Hospital. She was too violent and obscene for the children. She went to Nanguneri to die, showering terrible curses on her mother who she said had ruined her. The children were not invited for the ceremonies of death.

'Her husband was also a good swimmer. He died swimming, at your age – no, he was a year or two older – at the very place where you swam today.' She did not talk about Andal. She felt no need to make the children unhappy, but her mind was flooded with the events that led to Andal's mind snapping beyond recovery.

Andal was in the bathroom when she heard the loud wail. She came rushing inside the house with her wet clothes and saw Pakshi clutching a telegram in his hand. Madhu's wife was lying on the floor with her hair undone. Ponna was standing with her back to the wall, holding the baby Nambi in her arms.

'Who is dead now? It is nothing new for us.'

When she heard that it was Madhu who was dead, Andal said quietly, 'I thought it was Tirumalai. Pakshi never had a personal bereavement and this was really his turn.'

'Andal, what are you saying? Please be quiet,' said Ponna.

'I won't be quiet. You must have been praying for this tragedy to occur. You are very close to God and he grants you whatever you want. Why don't you pray for our welfare for a change?'

Andal had to be put under sedation that night, but she recovered quickly and even began doting on the infant Nambi. She erupted suddenly in Tirumalai's house.

Tirumalai was then staying in the old Vannarpet house. It was the same house where Ponna had been staying with her progeny when Andal had compelled her to return to Nanguneri. The wrestler-Brahmin's son was still his neighbour, but the walled space between their houses had now been converted into spacious rooms. It was in one of these rooms that Andal started her obscene, unstoppable tirade against her mother and Tirumalai.

'It was here, right here that I saw that bitch fornicating with her neighbour. I have kept quiet all these years. I am not going to be silent any longer.'

Of Tirumalai she said, 'He has to die. If he doesn't, I'll kill him. It is he who has conspired to have Madhu killed.'

Those were the years of the war and Madras was afraid that the Japanese would flatten it with bombs. There was an evacuation on and the beds in the mental hospital were not at a premium. Andal stayed there, off and on, for nearly ten years.

Ponna tried hard to erase the memory of her daughter out of her mind, but Andal was inerasable. Ponna became morose and listless and it was her neigbours who informed Tirumalai that the old woman was sinking. The local doctors were not able to diagnose what her ailment was and she was brought to Tirunelveli. Tests revealed that she was suffering from typhoid. The attack was so severe that the fever did not come down at all and she constantly complained of severe pain in the stomach. It was perhaps the first serious illness of her life. She was then pushing ninety.

Doctor Rama Iyer was a very fat man but his movements were nimble. He often played tennis, in which he was a lob-specialist, with Tirumalai in the District Club. He treated Ponna, but he was not very hopeful.

'At this age Tirumalai, it is very difficult to treat her. She may develop peritonitis. Please check her stool constantly, and yes, send telegrams to all whom you would like her to see before her departure.'

Tirumalai knew there was one person she would like to see before her death. Still, he asked Ponna.

'Paati, doctor says he is doing his best. It is typhoid he says.' He sat by her head and gently stroked it. 'Would you like to see anybody, paati.'

Ponna said, 'Yes, call Nammalwar.'

Tirumalai said, 'We don't know where he is, paati. How can I call him?'

'Don't worry then. I am not going to die. Let him come and see me at his leisure.'

The entire village of Nanguneri came to see her. Veda's relatives, Renganayaki's relatives and even relatives of Andal's husband, they all came and saw the old woman on the verge of her final journey. A journey she did not choose to undertake. After a month, her health took a turn for better, and the fever vanished, and with it her stomach pains. She silently got up from her bed one day, entered the kitchen and made strong coffee for herself when she did not find Renganayaki there.

The obese doctor said, 'So, the old battleship refuses to sink.' He was an erudite man and quoted Ogden Nash.

> *Your hopeless patients will live,*
> *Your healthy patients will die,*
> *I have only this word to give,*
> *Wonder and find out why.*

Tirumalai said, 'You are a strange fellow. I have seen many of your healthy patients dying and you have never wondered. Now my grandmother is the first case of a hopeless patient surviving your grim forecast and you have started wondering.'

The river in summer was a king-sized brook. Huts, clumps of weed and mounds of turd in various stages of parching uglied its sides. Its sand flats, though, retained their shimmering charm even in days of feeble moonlight. Swimming was hardly possible, with the water barely reaching knee-level, but bathing was immensely pleasurable. Lord Ganapathi looked splendid from the water, his ample oily frame darker than the darkness of the sky. Kannan circumambulated him after his bath, in wet half-pants, asking his reprieve for whatever sins he had committed that day. The fat god was a friend of his. The priest who gave him a pinch of sacred ash said, 'Go home quickly. Your mother will be worried.' He was not in a hurry. He lazed on the sand for a few minutes to get his half-pants and his hair reasonably dry – he never carried a towel. His friends that day had ditched him, and except the old priest who slept in the temple, there was not a soul in sight. He lay on his back counting the stars and when he reached two hundred and fifty he jumped up, dusted away the sand sticking to his body and ran back to his house.

He stopped for breath at the entrance and peered into the house to see whether his father was in the hall. Tirumalai was in his room, busy with his case files. Kannan leaped in and reached the kitchen in a flash to demand his supper from his mother.

'You are absolutely useless where it concerns Kannan. He comes home every night at nine in wet half-pants and you don't even know about it,' said Renganayaki to her husband when she was serving him food.

'Why don't you ask him to take along a towel and dry half-pants?'

'You are impossible. I want you to stop him from visiting the river after dark. Only evil and black winds are active by the river at night and your son keeps them company. Then there is this problem.' She told him what it was.

Tirumalai caught his son the next night when he was entering the house.

'Where are you coming from?'

'From the river, appa.'

'From the river? Is this the time to bathe? Who accompanies you there? Your friends? They are equally useless. You don't have one useful friend. Your hair is wet, so I see are your half-pants. Do you know what will happen if you roam about in wet half-pants?'

'Why are you silent? I shall tell you what will happen. You now have two little marbles between your legs. They will soon be tennis balls. Then footballs. Which will knock you down every time you walk.'

When he learnt that his son's nocturnal visit to the river was the final round and the previous rounds included irrigation wells and temple tanks during the daytime when he should have been at school, he was worried. He went to his tennis partner, Rama Iyer.

'I don't understand him. He wants to be in water all the time, except when he is sleeping. Even then he probably dreams of swimming in oceans.'

The fat doctor said, 'There is no cause for alarm. He obviously has nothing to do and he is bored. He does what he loves. Create a few more loves for him.'

'What loves? I have better things to do.'

'Then let your son wallow in water.'

Tirumalai then went to another friend of his, Gopala Pillai, a Malayali lawyer settled in Kokkirakulam. He had a flowing mane of white hair which fell to his shoulders but his face was as smooth as a boy's.

'Rama Iyer is right. Bring him to me. I shall cure his hydrophilicity.'

'What?'

'Hydrophilicity. His affinity for water.'

'Then why didn't you say so? I shall bring him to you tomorrow.'

Gopala Pillai lived alone in a big house crumbling slowly into ruin. It was cleaned fitfully when his crusty maid felt like it, and while Kannan was sitting in the hall, he counted nine cobwebs slinging across the room with plump, comatose spiders at their centres.

'So you are the young swimmer. Having exhausted the drains we have here, you must surely be dreaming of the English Channel.'

'Gopal, I haven't brought him to you for words of encouragement,' said Tirumalai severely.

'Now tell me Kannan,' said Gopala Pillai, ignoring his friend, 'what would you like to do if by chance you are not able to soak in water every day and, as your father might add, every night?'

Kannan said, 'I would play cricket.'

'At night? If you play inside the house you will break things and your father will break your back. Will he not?'

Kannan warmed to him. He said, 'Yes sir. He will. I like to read at nights.'

'School books?'

'No, other books.'

Gopala Pillai immediately pulled out a book from a heap on his desk and gave it to Kannan. 'This is a book written by the greatest batsman ever.' It was Bradman's *Farewell to Cricket*. 'Have you read this book?'

'No, sir.'

'I bet you will take a year to finish this book.'

Kannan was touched to the quick. 'I shall finish within a week, sir.'

'We shall meet next Sunday and exchange notes. Your father is a busy man and we can't discuss things frankly in front of him. Let him not accompany you next time.' He added, 'Keep a dictionary by your side when you read. I don't think you will need to consult it, but it will give you confidence.'

Farewell to Cricket was a big book but Kannan struggled with it and managed to finish it within a week. He said to Gopala Pillai triumphantly, 'I have kept my word, sir.'

'Indeed you have. Let me ask you a question. Bradman has some good words for one of our batsmen. Who is he?'

'This is easy, sir. Vijay Hazare, who scored a century in each innings at Adelaide. He has spoken highly of Amarnath too.'

'Good. Now would you like another cricket book? No? Any other readable book? For me, every book that has been printed is readable. They may not be likeable. Come along, I will show you my little library.' They slowly climbed the fusty stairs to the upper storey.

The stairs let to a sunny veranda and Pillai's library was a big room opposite it. The floor of the room was a swamp of books and its walls were lined with dark brown almirahs, many open and spilling a chaotic variety of books. Dusty paperbacks perched on the windowsills.

'Don't be fooled by the numbers. I haven't even opened many of them.'

He pulled out a good-sized book from the bottom of a pile on the floor, causing the stack to topple.

'This is another great book. *The Wonderful Wizard of Oz*. The books written in English by the British are rather forbidding. You can come to them later.'

'I don't see any law books here.' His father's library housed staid law reporters and legal tomes from London and Allahabad.

'Law books are for duds like your father. I know the ways of the judge, although I may not know much law. The more law you read the more confused you get.'

'That might also be true of books, sir.'

Pillai eyed him curiously. 'You have brains, son. I see no reason why you should be confused with books.'

Though his love affair with water did not abate, he stopped bathing at odd hours, and his marbles remained marbles, to his father's relief. There was a steady stream of books from Gopala Pillai and he read them avidly, but he had other distractions. It was about this time that he developed an urge like a scratchy cow to rub himself against hard edgy objects. The edge of his writing table was the prime spot. He would hang on to the table with his elbows and with his heels touching his haunches, he would rub his centre vigorously against the edge until his tiny, erect penis spasmed without ooze. It returned to its state of peace in no time, though Kannan felt raw and uncomfortable for another hour.

He consulted his friends and they were happy with their hands. Somehow he could not get down to fondling and he persisted with the rubbing, until one day the maidservant saw him moving up and down against the writing table. She rushed laughing to his mother and said, 'Amma, the little Iyengar is ready for marriage.'

Renganayaki explained to her husband what the maid saw and he called Kannan to his room.

'I hear you are fond of edges nowadays.'

'I don't get you, appa.'

'You know very well what I am saying. One fine morning it will fall off and you won't know where to look. Listen to me. This is not the time to think of girls. You are hardly thirteen and I can't fix your marriage now.'

Kannan could have died of shame. His eyes were brimming and he turned sideways so as not to face his father. Tirumalai pulled Kannan towards him and hugged him though he struggled to get away from his father.

'Keep your room's door bolted, son. You are then free to do what you want without others barging in. But beware of edges. They could cause real harm. Ask your friends. There are other ways.'

'I can just about stand his photograph in newspapers and magazines. What gets me down is being asked to stand up and perform ovational rituals in appreciation of the old man,' said Nambi to Tirumalai.

Gopala Pillai used to say, 'Though Rajaji's politics are such as will make even conservatives wonder whether they are becoming dangerous radicals, your mulish father remains his unabashed admirer. Mahatma Gandhi said once, perhaps by mistake, that Rajaji was his conscience keeper. This was enough for the Brahmins to enthrone Rajaji as their permanent political guru. To them he is infallible and his intellect is supposed to be as gargantuan as those of Socrates and Marcus Aurelius and Sankara. Ask your father and he will add, "Even John Gunther says, and he is not given to empty praise, that Rajaji's brain is as sharp as a razor." It might have been so once upon a time, but now it is an overused razor that scratches without doing its job.'

Tirumalai was not happy with Nambi's remarks. 'I invited you because I thought you should by now be sick of Communist drivel and would jump at this opportunity of listening to a world-class statesman. It will be your loss, not mine. I am taking Kannan with me and shall ask Rajaji to bless him. I shall catch him before the public meeting.'

'Thank you, chithappa. I prefer to stay away from him. His politics is crazy.'

He was too polite to say, 'Yours too' to his uncle, but Tirumalai was the one who wrote to Anthony Eden congratulating him for his role in the Suez crisis. He received an acknowledgement from a surprised Eden – his must have been one of the very few appreciative letters the British Prime Minister received from India – and he was brandishing it for days at the Tirunelveli Bar. His hatred for Nehru was obsessive after the Avadi session of the Congress at which Nehru had announced that he would build Indian society on a socialist pattern. He regarded the Communists as plague-rats, but to his consternation his nephew whom he loved dearly was fast turning into one. Tirumalai did not possess the intellectual rigour to argue Nambi out of his affliction and he was too democratic to force his views on his wayward nephew.

His father Pakshi was philosophical. He said, 'They were both wild horses, his father and grandfather. Like them he wants to choose his own grazing ground. I shall try and tame him when he comes out of college.'

Tirumalai found Rajaji peering through his glasses, thick as marbles, at a sheaf of papers. A timorous young man was standing by radiating reverence.

'Mmmm . . . *Gandharva Ganam*. The Genie's Song. So you have set it to music?'

The barb went over the head of the shaky poet. He said, 'No sir, I have written the song.'

'How? Are you a *Gandharva?* Then you would do well to approach Kubera.' Kubera was the lord of the Gandharvas.

The poet giggled nervously and said, 'Sir, your foreword is more precious than anyone else's.'

'Your flattery is worse than your poetry. I shall send a foreword from Madras on one condition . . .' he smiled and said, 'that you transfer your considerable skills to prose.'

He turned to Tirumalai and asked, 'How is Pakshi, our defender of the Tenkalai faith?' Rajaji was a Vadakalai Iyengar.

'He is fine, sir. He no longer practices now. He is in Nanguneri. I have brought my son, sir. Please bless him.'

He commanded Kannan to prostrate before him.

'May you live to be a hundred. What are you doing?'

'I am in my sixth form, sir.'

'Good. Are you coming for the meeting, Tirumalai? I am late already.'

Rajaji chose a hall for his speech, but other less-exalted politicians preferred the riverbed, which in summer was a boon to political orators. Its sandy expanse on the northern side of the bridge became a platform for them to harangue the populace of Tirunelveli and its surroundings. The populace obliged them no doubt, but their preference – and this was the preference of the entire Tamil country – was for Tamil cinema which they loved with an ardour that had no parallel anywhere. They recognised no boundaries between the real world and the illusory one and kept gliding between them with effortless ease. Thus, the gods of cinema were the gods of the Tamil world too. These gods were jealous gods like the ones of the myths. Their mindless quarrels percolated right down to the streets – where their devotees fought furious and bloody battles to establish the hegemony of their deities. And these battles determined the celluloid hierarchy.

At the top of this hierarchy was the holy trinity of Tamil cinema. Kannan loved the first of the trinity, the ageless MGR whose primacy was challenged now and then but without success. MGR sang ebullient songs of love or despairing ones of separation as the mood demanded, wearing pantaloons that would look bizarre in a circus. Nambi loathed MGR. He used to complain in later years to Rosa, 'In the days of yore, he fenced furiously with handsome villains to rescue thick-waisted heroines who ought not to have been rescued. Now he is the beau of belles who could have been his granddaughters. Strangely, his fans think never will a hymen be ruptured, unwillingly and outside wedlock, when he is around.'

Renganayaki swore by Sivaji, the tubby, thick-jowled Sivaji who grimaced at the least expected moments, and spouted monologues like ticker tape. He was called the Brando of Tamil, but unlike the Hollywood mumbler he spoke in a voice that left no room for doubt. He was frequently caught in the shifting coils of emotion and the miracle of his extrication brought him thousands of fans.

The third was the dandified Gemini Ganesan who was stuck as routinely in the swamp of romance in real life as he was in his films. He did not have any admirers in the moneylender family, but his scrubbed looks attracted urban girls who preferred smooth Brahmin faces.

Both Veda and Renganayaki were unrepentant movie-maniacs. The trouble was, they insisted that Tirumalai accompany them to every movie, a task that he detested and tried to delegate either to his head-clerk or Nambi or even Pakshi when he could persuade one of them. But Renganayaki would succeed more often than not in dragging him, protesting, along.

Tirumalai's presence in the movie hall was always an irritant to dedicated movie-watchers. He would start with his comments when his mother and wife were watching a decisive scene in the film. 'I say, my sympathies are with the king.' It was a film in which the hero, a prince, was in danger of being disinherited by his father, the king, who did not seem to like the queen either. 'The king I must say is very patient. This terrible mother-son pair is capable of irritating Buddha the way they speak their dialogues without stopping for breath. I would have said "Off with their heads" long, long ago.'

Renganayaki would say, 'You are impossible. The king is wicked. He has sought comfort in this other woman.'

'What else do you expect him to do? He does need his stretches of silence. The other woman is not bad either. She does not roll her eyeballs like the wife.'

'The prince, you must admit, speaks excellent Tamil.'

'Maybe, but even excellence needs a pause. This is not cinema as I understand. I come to cinema primarily for its images and not for dialogue. I have had enough of these close-ups and mid-shots of this excruciating prince and his blubbering mother.'

'Shut up and watch the film,' Veda, who was happy with every film and every hero, would respond.

'I don't want to. It is because of you both that I am here.'

'Sir, I too have paid for the tickets. Let me watch the movie peacefully,' would interrupt one of the connoisseurs watching the film and Tirumalai would sink into sullen silence.

Cinema was the people's passion all right, but cinema halls were few and watching cost money. Political entertainment was free. So they came in their thousands to listen to the Congress debunking the Communists and the DMK, as traitors to the nation – one pandering to the red nations and the other plotting to balkanise India; to the Communists accusing the Congress of being servile to US imperialism and the DMK of peddling puerile dreams of separation to a gullible lumpen audience and of reducing politics to a burlesque; and to the DMK deriding both, the Congress and the Communists, in insincere Tamil studded with alliterations and assonances and delivered at the speed of a machine gun, for serving the interests of corpulent, avaricious Northerners and their language.

Politics permeated everywhere. It was impossible to be alive and ignore it. Kannan's mathematics teacher was a staunch Communist, the Tamil master would die for the DMK and the headmaster was an old Congress hand. The vegetable shop at the end of his street had an oleograph of Anna of the DMK in a mauve three-piece suit, with the caption 'Anna in UN', representing the fantasy of his disciples: Anna bewitching UN dignitaries with his pristine English. Kamaraj, the unlettered genius of the Congress, who routinely had, his admirers said, political novices for breakfast, was smug in his frame at the provision shop. The Communists carried prints of Lenin and Stalin in their purses. Gandhi and Nehru shared their honours with gods and their prints were the most ubiquitous.

Ponna's family divided along predictable lines. Nambi was electrified by the Communists; Pakshi feigned aloofness but was there at every Congress Party meeting. Kannan's friends supported the DMK and in spite of its anti-Brahmin stance, he went along with them. Tirumalai swore by Rajaji and his newly formed Swantara Party.

Gopala Pillai, the sneering Malayali stranded in this Tamil oasis, would make fun of them all but his special barbs were reserved for the DMK. 'These fellows are nebulous about everything; about God, about socialism and about their allegiance to the Indian union. Yet they are the winners by a long chalk.'

'Will they get their Dravidanadu?' Kannan would ask. Though he knew the answer, he liked to see Gopala Pillai go red in the face with anger.

'Oh, never. The people of the other regions of the south are not even aware that their freedom from the Indian union is being demanded by a bunch of nitwits from the Tamil country, but this minor matter will not deter the DMK from issuing periodic, blood-curdling threats to New Delhi.'

A few of Kannan's friends accompanied him to watch Gopala Pillai expend his fury, but they were not impressed. 'His English is no good. He must hear Anna speak English.' According to them Anna was such a peerless exponent of English that Oxford University urged him to occupy one of its prestigious chairs, but being passionately devoted to the cause of the Tamils, he declined the offer.

Kannan carried these tales to Gopala Pillai. He said, 'Yes, yes. He is their Bernard Shaw and their Ingersoll. A very original thinker. What is that famous slogan he has thought up for his *thambis*?'

'Duty, Dignity and Discipline?'

'Yes. How startlingly innovative he is!'

Though Nambi did not condescend to hear Rajaji speak, there were many who did, in rapt attention. Rajaji was of course a polished speaker and his admirers hung on every word of his oracular pronouncements, which came thick and fast.

After the meeting Tirumalai went to Gopala Pillai's house with Kannan.

'How did the old jackal perform today?'

'Rajaji? You missed him. He was as always full of wisdom.'

'You are his toady. If he is full of wisdom, I am made of gold. Let me give you a piece of advice, Kannan. Don't go anywhere near that conservative crowd. And don't get swayed by your father's eulogies of Rajaji.'

'And the Communists, sir?'

'They are traitors. The DMK fellows, I have told you a million times, are comedians who parody the Nazis and the Congress rascals are busy swindling public money. Blast them all! Well, perhaps Nehru should be spared, though your father will like to set him on fire. Stick to books, Kannan. Politics will numb your brain and make you an unquestioning fool as it has made your father.'

Tirumalai laughed. 'Strange a Malayali should speak thus.'

'That is why I left Kerala. I was sick of its politics.'

Tirumalai turned to Kannan and said, 'This fellow wants you to be a questioning fool by making you read a motley pile of books. Pack it up. Your examinations are fast approaching.'

Kannan quickly changed the subject. 'You didn't tell him about the young poet.'

'Yes, I have forgotten. This was how Rajaji ribbed him.' Tirumalai narrated Rajaji's treatment of the author of *Gandharva Ganam*.

Gopala Pillai exclaimed with his nostrils flaring, 'What? How dare he treat a young poet like this when he himself is a lousy poet?'

'I read in one of the cricket books you had lent to Kannan that one need not be a hen to criticise the quality of eggs.'

'But he is a bloody hen and he has laid rotten eggs.'

Tirumalai realised what Gopala Pillai was referring to and he started chuckling.

'Do you know why your father is neighing? This poet-basher himself wrote a poem. It was so execrable I wrote a postcard to Rajaji: "Sir, I read your poem on the atomic bomb. Personally, I prefer the bomb to your poem".'

'You are biased. You did not tell him Rajaji's reply.'

'He was graceful,' Pillai grudgingly admitted. 'He wrote back: "On second thoughts, I share your preference".'

'You shall never have that grace. I should leave now. My client will be waiting,' Tirumalai said and stopped. 'Another thing. You must advise this fellow. He listens to Hindi film ditties all the time and reads abominable books.'

'You consider the books I give him abominable?'

'I am not talking of your books. He has started reading smutty books in the lavatory. The other day I saw on the lavatory sill a book called *Lady Wrestler*. My wife can't read English books and Radha is too small to spell even the title, but this fellow denies that it was his.'

'How could one be a lady and a wrestler?'

'Very droll. This is not the time for your jokes. Ask your disciple and he may give you the reply.'

Kannan stood with his head bowed. One mistake, you are in the dock.

Gopala Pillai patted him on his shoulders. "Smut can wait, son. Everyone reads it but there is a time and place for it. The place is probably all right. The time is not. Finish your school finals and come to me. I shall open a treasure house for you.' He winked at Tirumalai who said, 'You will do no such thing.'

Kannan later asked Nambi if he liked pornography.

Nambi said, 'What is there to like? If I happen on one, I may browse through it. I wouldn't go fishing for it though.'

Kannan did not believe him. 'I am all excitement even with a glance at the cover and you claim you are indifferent to its attraction. There is another thing. Gopala Pillai considers politics to be worse than pornography. He has offered to open his smut library for me after my examinations, but his animus against politics has to be seen to be believed.'

'I am political, I am afraid. It may be possible for Gopala Pillai to be full of lofty air and mock-thunder and keep away from politics. He gets his nose out of his books only to make sorties to bookshops. Yes, and there are these who are poignantly undecided. I have just remembered a few lines from Housman.'

Nambi recited from memory.

> *To stand up straight and tread the turning mill,*
> *To lie flat and know nothing and be still,*
> *Are the two trades of man; and which is worse*
> *I know not, but I know that both are ill.*

Nambi said slowly, 'It is easy to choose finally the less taxing ill of lying flat and being still.'

Kannan liked Housman. He asked Nambi to repeat what he had said and copied it down in a notebook. When he met Gopala Pillai he rattled off the Housman piece and told him Nambi's views. He said, 'I know more about people than he will ever hope to know in his lifetime. Politics and people are not inseparable. Being him here. I shall cure him of his malady.'

Nine

GOPALA PILLAI DID NOT OPEN HIS TREASURE house as he had promised but smut was accessible. Kannan, like Nambi, soon grew indifferent to it. He did not grow tired of his father's friend and his book heaps or his cricket blather.

Cricket engulfed them. They spent hours fiddling with Gopala Pillai's Ferranti, a valved monster, to pluck the waves of Radio Australia. West Indies were then on tour to Australia. They were of course rooting for the West Indies. Memories of the unflappable Worrell and his flighty prodigies remained with Kannan and Gopala Pillai.

'Oh, for a Sobers on our side!' sighed Pillai.

'Or a Kanhai.'

England had sent a club team under Dexter, without Truman or Statham or Cowdrey, but Gopala Pillai was sure that India would lose every match.

He was wrong. Dexter's team was defeated not once but twice in India, in Calcutta and in Madras. On a warm January day, when Durrani and Borde bowled out England to earn a 2-0 victory for India, Gopala Pillai danced in the street to the embarrassment of Kannan.

'I should make something of it,' said the dancing Pillai. He was distributing toffees by the handful to the bemused urchins of his street. 'Our winning a cricket match is about as rare as your grandfather worshipping Shiva.'

When Nehru died he was inconsolable. 'It is the Chinese debacle that killed him,' said a tearful Pillai. 'He was the most intellectual and moral of politicians. With his departure the ailing politics of this country is finally dead. It will only putrefy if it is not buried quickly. Keep away Kannan, keep away.'

On summer days the river was fordable. Kannan waded across it, holding his chappals under his armpit and lifting his veshti right up to his upper thighs so that it barely covered his crotch, to reach the steps leading to the Krishnan Temple. Another flight of steps from the temple took him to a potted road which swerved and became increasingly crumbly before he could get as far as the alley in which Gopala Pillai's ramshackle house was situated. Nambi, as a rule, accompanied him whenever he was in Tirunelveli, and if he did, they stopped on the way to chat with Bala. He lived in a tiny house overlooking the Krishnan Temple and one could see a portrait of Stalin beaming at passers-by through the haze of dust and the barred window of his living room. Lenin, Marx, Engels and Mao were on the other wall, hidden from public view.

Bala was single and his visitors sat on a bench to face him sitting on a stool. He never wore a shirt inside the house and his wiry frame throbbed with conviction when he argued the finer points of his creed with Nambi. Mostly, however, Nambi drew him into conversation only with a view to digging out nuggets of information about Madhurakavi.

'He used to come here like you do now. There was a lull in the freedom movement during those days, with Gandhi going through one of his supine phases. Your father was reading Burton's translation of *The Arabian Nights* then. Somebody had lent him all the volumes. We would walk to the river after dinner – my mother knew what your father relished and she plied him with *idiappam* and coconut milk – and Madhurakavi would narrate to me the wonderful stories he had read. Your father had this capacity of bestriding both worlds, the fantastic and the real, with equal ease. He never allowed me to linger in the other world. He would stop midway, let out a stream of abuse at the Congress leaders and their elephantine ways – Gandhi and Nehru always exempted – and continue with the story from where he had left it.'

'He revered Gandhi. Didn't he?'

'He did, initially at least. During the Salt March we both travelled to Trichy to participate in the march being organised by Rajaji. But he had already selected the volunteers and we had to return disappointed. Those were the years of hope and Gandhi could do no wrong. The Gandhi-Irwin Pact was a disappointment, but the last straw was the execution of Bhagat Singh. That was the only time your father used foul words against Gandhi. We all felt that he did not do enough to rescue the young Bhagat Singh – he was hardly twenty-four when he mounted the gallows. The Mahatma was friendly with Lord Irwin, the Viceroy, and could have used his undeniable charm to save Bhagat Singh. There was no doubt your father adored the peerless Sardar. Another hero of his was Jatin Das who died in Lahore jail after a marathon fast, protesting against the treatment of political prisoners by the British.'

'Was he a Communist then?'

'No. We both were with the Congress Socialist Party for a long time. We became Communists sometime in 1937, when we felt that Nehru's support to Socialism was so much hot air.'

The relationship between Gopala Pillai and Nambi was not an easy one. Nambi borrowed freely from the lawyer's amazing collection of books on art and travel, but the lawyer was never free with him. He was excruciatingly polite when Nambi was present but in his absence he gave broad hints to Kannan that he preferred to receive him alone. Kannan never conveyed the hint to Nambi. He was sure that the Malayali lawyer needed his company desperately, with or without Nambi.

Pillai also felt that his protégé was being slowly dyed red by his commie cousin and he even discussed the matter with Tirumalai.

'Your son is undergoing home-made indoctrination. If you don't watch out, you may find him marching with a red flag behind that eccentric cousin of his.'

'Don't worry. Kannan has a broad base. He wouldn't keel over that easily.'

'He is your son. Don't tell me later that I didn't warn you.'

'He is your disciple.'

The estrangement between master and disciple came rather unexpectedly.

Kannan remembered his Hindi classes more for the hilarity they had evoked than for the knowledge he had gained. A sad Iyer, who had several rows of teeth, taught it to a few petulant students who were long past the age of learning alphabets.

'Repeat after me. *Ka. Kha. Ga. Gha.*'

A few Brahmin students who had a smattering of Sanskrit could follow their teacher, but it was impossible for the others.

'*Ka. Ka. Ka. Ka,*' they said in chorus.

'No, no,' said the teacher and called the most studious of them to come near him. 'Repeat, Ramalingam. *Ka.*'

There was no problem. '*Ka.*'

'First class. *Kha.*'

'*Ka.*'

'No, no,' cried the teacher in exasperation. 'It has to be aspirated. From the throat. *Kha.*'

Ramalingam collected himself and said, '*ikk . . . ka*' and cleared his throat for the effort. The teacher was close to tears. He said, 'I give up. It is for the sins of my previous births that I am saddled with you. You may learn the alphabets like this.

This is the first *ka.*' He wrote on the board. 'This is *Kha.* Sorry, the second *ka.* This is the third *ka* and this is the fourth *ka.*'

There was one serious student of Hindi in the Tirumalai household. It was Renganayaki. She was one of the very few who took Gandhi's advice that all Indians should learn Hindi religiously. She passed her *Praveen* examination from the Dakshin Bharat Hindi Prachar Sabha and taught Hindi, without any fees, to a number of boys and girls in the neighbourhood. The girls were studious and the boys wanted to be near the girls. The inflections of Hindi were incomprehensible to them but they plodded on nevertheless in the hope that, in the event of their migration to the famed North Indian cities, the Hindi they had learnt from Renganayaki would be of much assistance.

'This is what comes of eating too many things fried in ghee and swilling down pot after pot of buffalo curd,' Tirumalai said to his wife. 'The fat has seeped into their brains. I see no other reason why these Delhi-wallahs should have announced that Hindi will be the official language of the country from the twenty-sixth of January and English will be eased out.'

'Hindi is now a dirty word in Tamil Nadu. I have a good number of students and they will all stop coming now.'

'Yes, the students have announced that they will observe twenty-fifth January as black day. The DMK for their part have stated that twenty-sixth January will be observed as a day of mourning. The winner, mark my words, is going to be the DMK. Thanks to the stupidity of the Congress, these theatrical mountebanks are sure to emerge as serious politicians. The Congress is seriously underestimating the resentment of the students and the people. Their confounding arrogance is going to cost them the Tamil country.'

'Let the DMK emerge the winners. The Congress has been ruling all these years and they have done nothing good to us. My present worry is about the children.'

On twenty-fifth January Kannan did not attend college to stay away from trouble. That evening he was standing at a newspaper stall near his house with a few of his friends. His friends told him that the protest was a success and that the students had managed to hoist a black flag at the residence of the local Member of Parliament. It was Narasimhan who said, 'Look, a posse of police is coming this way.'

One of the heroes of the protest shrugged his shoulders and said knowingly, 'Oh, locals. They are harmless. We should only worry about the Malabar special police. This morning our policemen even offered us tea.'

To their horror the police came storming towards them, clenching their teeth and brandishing their mean lathis. They had been good to the boys in the morning no doubt – for which they were severely rebuked by their bosses. They were also irascible because of the hide-and-seek games they had been playing with the agitators throughout the day. The boys took to their heels, but Kannan tripped. He fell on his face, crushing his spectacles in the bargain. He could do nothing to escape from the police lathis raining on him. After exhausting their anger, the police left him bruised and barely conscious. The doctors later told Tirumalai that his son had suffered a simple fracture of one of the left metacarpal bones and sprained his right ankle.

Kannan had become an instant champion of the anti-Hindi cause. The DMK posters screamed, 'The agents of Hindi at work. A flower, almost felled at its bloom, cries for life.' Anna sent a telegram wishing him a speedy recovery and the local DMK chieftain sent a message in which he said: 'Brother, I salute your undaunted determination to place your head at the altar of Hindi.' When Nambi read the letter he murmured, 'He has got it wrong. He should have written foot instead of head.'

Rajaji who was the first chief minister to introduce Hindi in schools way back in 1937 and who now was a persuasive advocate of English, sent a postcard to Tirumalai. 'I understand from my Tirunelveli friends that your son has been hurt in an incident involving the local police and that he has been confined to bed. If he has nothing else to do, ask him to memorise the *Thirukkural*. On his recovery which I am sure will be soon, let him loiter less and concentrate more on his studies.'

Gopala Pillai was furious with Kannan for what had happened. 'Believe me. I had no role at all in my attaining this dubious stardom. My only fault was that I tripped when I shouldn't have,' pleaded Kannan.

Pillai appeared mollified and said, 'I thought you were in cahoots with the anti-Hindi riffraff. The nation needs an official language and it has to be Hindi. The shenanigans of the DMK and that cunning old Brahmin Rajaji will do us no good.'

Kannan nodded in approval. His world had nevertheless changed.

The agitation took a turn for the worse in February before losing its momentum. But the 'riffraff' hoisted Kannan on political platforms and he found himself liking the attention he received. There were coordination committees, student delegations and secret conclaves and Kannan was a natural choice for membership. He had to travel frequently to Madras and other towns on anti-Hindi business. He drifted slowly away from Gopala Pillai, who for a period kept sending word through Tirumalai that he would like to see his disciple until he realised that he had lost him. Tirumalai was sorry for his friend but he was helpless.

Kannan met Gopala Pillai again before he left for Madras for his postgraduation. The meeting was awkward and they exchanged only empty pleasantries.

Kannan's mofussil stardom died for want of space in Madras, which had mega-martyrs. Many had had their legs fractured and arms broken and had spent months in prison. Kannan thought his sprained ankle would only invite derision in their company. For the first time in his life he was alone and not surrounded by admiring relatives and affable friends. His metro peers at his college, in trendy trousers that were flared at the bottom, sneered at his low-hipped abominations.

His professor was yet another who sneered at him for his uncouth ways. The professor was a stubbly giant who had never learnt to shave closely.

'Are you going to gag me?'

'I beg your pardon, sir?'

'Why are you clutching your grimy, snot-spattered handkerchief in your hand? The trouser pocket is the right place for it, unless you have other secret places to shove it in.'

'I am sorry, sir.' He hurriedly inserted the kerchief into his trouser pocket.

'What is an isotone?'

'Atoms having the same number of protons in the nucleus. No, no, no. Neutrons, sir. Neutrons.'

'Make up your mind.'

'I have sir.'

'To go back to where you have come from?'

'No sir. Isotones have the same number of neutrons but different atomic numbers.'

'You do possess after all some dim knowledge of physics.'

Kannan turned hot under his collar. He said acidly, 'I don't want to parade all I possess, sir, which I assure you is considerable.'

'Don't get fired up. We shall see what you possess during the course of the next two years.' He dismissed him with a wave of his hand.

In his two years in the college that was the only long conversation he had had with his professor. The giant's classes were indescribably dull. He considered asking questions a defect not easily remediable and no student dared to interrupt him when he attempted to explain the intricacies of classical mechanics. Kannan spent these periods of tedium gazing at the sea through the bay window of his class. The other lecturers were hardly different.

His lodgings were comfortable, but his roommates had nothing to do with physics. One was a wafer-thin laboratory technician who hissed his words through the broad slits between his front teeth. He went ferreting out at nights for female company and returned well past midnight to regale Kannan with prurient dainties – 'Her cunt was like the onion *uthappam* of Sukha Niwas'; Or, 'I probed her tonsils with my dick.' Whenever he had attacks of gonorrhoea, which was frequently, he lay on his bed howling, 'It burns so fiercely I shall soon have a piece of charcoal for my tool.'

The other was a junior lawyer under the wing of a senior one whose major clients were film actresses. The senior passed on the starlets who came to him for advice to his junior. Kannan's room thus resembled a cat-house at times with erectile bachelors crowding its corridors. As the lawyer was fiercely possessive of his clients, the whoring technician had to keep away from them. This frustration provoked him to abuse his lawyer-friend in juicy expletives. It was to this dubious place that Gopala Pillai paid a visit.

He was waiting in the room when Kannan returned from the college. The junior and the technician were sitting on their beds, silent and embarrassed.

'I wanted to give you a surprise. I have come here on a case. I too have some gullible clients.'

Kannan started introducing his roommates to Gopala Pillai, but he said, 'No need, no need. We have already met. As it happens, your friend's senior was my classmate.'

The junior said, 'We have to meet a friend. Uncle should excuse us.' He dragged the obviously surprised technician out of the room.

'So these are your digs. I must say your lawyer friend has some breathtaking clientele. I had a fascinating discussion with one of them just before your arrival – I was initially confused who was whose client.'

'They don't come here often, sir.'

'I fervently hope so. I don't smell physics here. Are you still at it?'

Kannan was not sure himself. His time was mostly used up in chess and political discussions. The elections were round the corner.

'I have brought a book for you. This will tell you something about the original Nazis.' It was William Shirer's *The Rise and Fall of the Third Reich*. 'I am sure you are still pally with our own tin-pot Nazis.'

He was again right. Most of his friends were with the DMK. Kannan said, changing the subject, 'Are you coming for the Test match?'

'No, I don't think I am. My health has taken a turn for the worse.'

Kannan noticed that Gopala Pillai had aged visibly. His silvery mane had lost its sheen and his once boyish face had deep furrows now. Kannan was sorry for him.

'Have you bought your ticket? Sobers has just rubbed the English nose in the dust. He will pulverise India. I should be going now. I am glad I have been able to see you.'

Fifteen days after Gopala Pillai's visit, Tirumalai came to Madras.

'Gopal was not exaggerating this time. Is this a place for a student to live?'

'The food here is excellent, appa.'

'I don't want to listen to you any more. I shall stay here until I find a decent room for you.'

Kannan had to shift to a less disreputable place to placate his father.

The virile rays of the sun went suddenly limp. The wind, which had been gentle and susurrating, swiftly gained strength to howl and lash without restraint. The sea erupted in support. Storm clouds scudded very low to disgorge themselves. Rain came in thick pillars. Kannan was imprisoned in the corridors of his college and he cursed the rain. He was there to catch up on work he had missed, but the laboratory staff had judged the weather better. There was no one to receive him in the laboratory except an unsteady assistant who was well past the state of recognising acquaintances. He slurred his words and spewed queasy breaths of country liquor. Though there was a roof above Kannan's head, it was no protection against the wind-driven water, which chased and drenched him. He waited in a corner, shivering, for the rain to subside.

'Got trapped like us?'

Kannan, lost in his thoughts, snapped awake and realised that he was being greeted. The man was tall, with a black beard that glistened with drops of water. With him was a girl of medium height in glasses. Wetness gave substance to her protuberances.

'Yes, the rain has stunned me. I am Kannan. First year. MSc, physics.'

'I am Rajaraman and this is Mythili. We are in the second year. political science. I have seen you on buses. You must be in Mylapore.'

'That is right. How do you come to be here? You too were not expecting the rains?'

'We had a meeting today. No one turned up. We had to. We are the organisers.'

She said, 'It was to be a protest meeting against the US aggression in Vietnam. It appears our protesters are not prepared to brave the rain.'

'Now that our friend is here, we can give him our booklet.'

She took one out from her cloth bag. Its letters were red. 'Please read it at leisure.'

Kannan felt like an evangelist's victim. He knew that a bitter war was being fought in Vietnam. Nambi frequently railed against the USA, but Kannan's political knowledge was confined to what was happening in Madras and its districts. Even the Shirer that Gopala Pillai gave him remained unread. He liked Hollywood and his idea of America was shaped by it. It was the America of the usually chivalrous Second World War warriors, whose indiscretions were confined to seducing a few English and French maidens or locking Elizabeth Taylor out of the house on a snowy night in Paris and causing her to die tragically of pneumonia.

'I shall definitely read it at leisure.'

The rain did not show any sign of abating. The strong wind was now fast turning into a monstrous cyclone and it was impossible for them to stand in the corridor. Rajaraman kicked open the doors of one of the classrooms and they ran into it.

Rajaraman said, 'Please wait here with Mythili. The chemistry laboratory must be open. Let me go and check up.'

'Let the storm subside. You will probably be blown away.'

'I have seen several storms like this. If I don't go now, we shall be trapped in this classroom for another two days.'

The chemistry laboratory was open, and its attendant sober. Rajaraman was right. A few minutes after they had taken shelter in the laboratory, the cyclone hit the Madras coast with a fury rarely seen in living memory. It poured without relief for two days and the city longed for the fiery heat of its summer. Wind spelled the death of hoary trees which lay spread-eagled on roads. Drains acquired muscles of water to show off and the slums that studded their banks keeled over and were carried away. The government insisted that there were not many deaths, but the people knew better. The sea did its work too. It ran aground a Greek ship which putrefied like a beached whale long after the storm had passed. Its bleached and fish-nibbled sailors, wrapped in spume, bobbed on the waves until the sea lost patience and slapped them against the shore.

The laboratory was safer than the classroom, but they were still trapped. Fortunately the attendant had a few packets of biscuits and a big jar full of tea-leaves. They survived the two days of the cyclone on these measly victuals. Mythili was given the teachers' room. The other three huddled together in the laboratory.

The cyclone changed Kannan. He was not used to nature's fiendish undulations and those dark days were for him the forerunners of death. He knew that they had not been sent to fetch him but their very sight was enough to send him into a depression that he had never experienced before. He recovered quickly but the days he spent in the laboratory haunted him often.

He was grateful to Rajaraman and liked his unconscious warmth. They became intensely friendly in those two days and Rajaraman, despite the cyclone and the starvation diet, was full of Vietnam.

'One American general says, "I just kill people and save lives." He hasn't said whose lives he wants to save in Vietnam. Considering the rate at which he is killing the Vietnamese he is likely to save only the lives of the rats and roaches of that unlucky country.'

Why do we need a war to die by the thousand, Kannan thought. This cyclone, if commanded, can wreak more destruction than a dozen such lunatic generals. It is a harbinger of death all right. Only, it will pass me by; it hasn't been sent to fetch me.

To Rajaraman, Kannan said, 'You must lend me some books on this war.'

'I shall give you a load of books. Not only on this war but on other revolutionary wars as well.'

Kannan was in his old room with the junior and the technician when they heard loudspeakers blaring incoherently. They came hurriedly out into the corridor and saw a column of jeeps with the black-and-red flags of the DMK moving slowly. A crowd of agitated men and women were milling around them. The announcement was now decipherable:

'Puratchi Nadikar MGR is safe. He is recovering in the hospital. There is no danger to his life. Long live MGR, long live Anna, long live the DMK.'

'What is wrong with MGR? Has he suffered a heart attack?'

'If you asked the crowd they would tell you all kinds of stories. Let me ring my senior.'

The junior went out and returned in a few minutes.

'It appears that Radha has shot him in the neck.'

'Radha? Male or female?'

'Male. The actor.'

'The hero or the villain?'

'M.R. Radha, the villain. And he has shot himself. You probably don't realise, but if MGR's condition worsens there will be no cricket match in Madras. That I am sure.'

After a long time Kannan wrote a letter to Gopala Pillai.

Dear Sir,

The MGR episode had resulted in a frenzied crowd of his fans disemboguing itself onto the streets of Madras and bringing life to a standstill. They were astonished that MGR could be felled by a mere bullet. The walls here sport stunning posters of MGR in hospital, with his neck swathed in bandages. My friend's senior – your friend and classmate – seems to know Radha personally. According to him, Radha is unrepentant and has laid the blame on the revolver. He appears to have said, "My revolver is the culprit. It hasn't killed him and it has refused to finish me off." The Test match could take place only because MGR chose to recover. He happens to be an ardent fan of cricket after all.

And what a match it was! It began with an unbelievable cannonade by Engineer who smashed the first three balls of Wes Hall for fours and ended with a fairy-tale rescue by Sobers. When the West Indies were tottering at 193 for 7 at tea we all thought India had the match sewn up, but Sobers being Sobers thought otherwise and staved off certain defeat. He hit a towering six off the young Bedi in the first innings, but even more memorable was Pataudi's six. He casually flicked the ball and it sailed over mid wicket. As simple as that. If only

Pataudi bats like this in all his innings! You must have been at the radio, our dear old Ferranti, but the drama of this match was beyond the staid vocabulary of our commentators.

My physics has faded into the background because of the elections. I must confess I am working for the DMK whose victory seems certain. Even beggars in the train say on receiving alms, 'Don't forget the rising sun, the symbol of the DMK.' It amuses me to think that this is the first time that appa, Nambi and I share the same political platform. I have just received a letter from Nambi. He says the victory of the Rajaji (should I say Swatantra?)-Communist-DMK alliance is a foregone conclusion. Even my mother who has lost her Hindi horde is rooting for the DMK. This must all be galling to you, but there it is.

Take care of your health. You didn't look too good when you were here.

With love,
Kannan

A few years later, Nambi showed Kannan a clipping.
'This is so hilarious I thought I should preserve it for you.'

My name is William Calley, I am a soldier of this land,
I've vowed to do my duty and to gain the upper hand,
But they've made me out a villain, they have stamped me with a brand,
    As we go marching on.

'The record of this song has sold hundreds of thousands of copies,' said Nambi. 'This canonisation of the My Lai hero is no less ludicrous than that other canonisation, forty or fifty years ago, of Horst Wessel.'

'The hero of the Nazi anthem? Nambi, this is amazing. Only yesterday I received a letter from Rajaraman.'

'Your Madras mentor?'

'Yes, he says he has now started seeing things in the correct perspective. He adds, believe me, Calley, yes, even the Calley of My Lai has a point. The news of his recent conviction is all over the United States and it has troubled my friend. Rajaraman is now at the University of California.'

'His lady friend, the other person who charged you up?'

'Oh, she has joined one of the Midwestern universities, I don't know which.'

Kannan continued, 'You know Nambi, Rajaraman appeared then to be the only one who had come unscathed through the furnace of conviction. He was so serene and so sure. It was he who introduced me to authors whose very names thrilled me. Edgar Snow and Agnes Smedley and Anna Louise Strong. Fanon and Guevara and Giap. He had a massive collection of clippings of the Vietnam War. And this was even before the Tet offensive. He pressed them and a host of other revolutionary material on me. It was impossible to resist him.'

The Rajaraman-Mythili pair ran into him again one day after the elections. They were sipping coffee in the college canteen when Kannan came in. They hailed him to their table.

Rajaraman hugged him. 'Why are you avoiding me? This time I am not going to let you go. We have another meeting tomorrow. I shall come and pick you up from your room.'

Kannan was in no mood to resist Rajaraman. The victory of the DMK did not give Kannan the satisfaction he had expected it to give. On the other hand, disillusionment with the rulers had set in rather soon. The only change they had brought about seemed to be that the name of Madras State was changed to Tamil Nadu. The river Cooum that flows through the city of Madras was as smelly as it had been during Congress rule, but the slums by its sides now had a riot of the black-and-red DMK flags.

Kannan went to the meeting reluctantly, but the speaker was good. He said: 'It is a pity that the pelvic gyrations of this singer, Elvis Presley, who hoots like a municipal siren, send some of our friends here into a frenzy, but the agony of millions of people who are victims of American aggression in Vietnam does not evoke any response in them.' Kannan was not an admirer of Presley but he saw the speaker's point.

Vietnam had started to interest Kannan and he decided to join the protesting group. It was a pleasant affair. They trooped in front of the American consulate, shouted a few blood-curdling slogans with might and main at the closed doors and walked away, mostly in pairs, to the near-by drive-in restaurant, feeling puffed up and heroic. He wrote a letter to Gopala Pillai and told him of his activities. He received a prompt reply in which Pillai said, 'By this action, you are only atoning for your earlier sins of supporting the DMK. This is a dirty war and it has to be protested against, if not fought shoulder to shoulder with Ho's soldiers. Incidentally, I am moving out of Tirunelveli.'

Kannan did not write back. He had become a full-bodied sympathiser by then and was ashamed to inform Gopala Pillai about it. Edgar Snow and the other fellow-travelling writers were at least readable but the Marxist classics made him groggy. He was familiar with the names of most of them – Nambi's bookshelf was bulging with these tomes – but try as he did, he could not progress beyond the second page of any of these famed books except the *Communist Manifesto.* He felt low until he realised that most of his friends in the shouting brigade were even less knowledgeable than he was. They all parroted a few familiar quotations – 'Political power grows out of the barrel of the gun'; 'Antagonistic contradictions can only be resolved through force'; 'A single spark can start a prairie fire'; 'One divides into two' – and debated on wobbly ideological issues for hours. Rajaraman and Mythili were certainly better informed, but they were too polite to call the brigade's bluff. Vietnam gave them an opportunity to be angry about something in front of an admiring audience and they were content.

Kannan said to Nambi, 'Rajaraman was no doubt my pathfinder but having led me down the path this far he has taken wing to nest in faraway California.'

Ten

THE POSTBOX STOOD BRIGHTLY IN FRONT OF her house, a red fat cylinder with a wide brim above its cavernous mouth. The broad latticed house looked forlorn. A wooden screen, ancient, spliced and placed right in the middle of the huge veranda covered the entrance to the living room and beyond, muffling the patter of existence. Kannan, his elbow resting on the brim of the post-box was talking to his old friend Narasimhan, but his eyes were on the house. Politics provided the fodder for dialogue and Narasimhan, who looked as insubstantial as a shadow, had the voice of a giant which he was exercising to the full.

'We are orphans here. Our boys don't get admission in colleges. There are no jobs, no money, no future. Do we have any other option than to leave this place? Even our girls are in danger. Hitler was better. His men butchered the Jews all right but they were never after Jewish girls.'

This piece of Nazi history was new to Kannan but he kept quiet.

Narasimhan prattled on, 'These DMK fellows, the scoundrels, they are after our girls and they want to seduce them.'

'Our girls? Are they worth seducing? The seducers surely have better material available. Calm down Narasimhan. Don't be febrile.'

'This is the problem with our community. We are not united. Follow the Jews, if you ask me. They are united and they have their homeland, which keeps getting bigger and bigger.'

'This is a new trail you are blazing. I am sure not even the most rabid Brahmin fanatic has come up with this idea so far.'

'The time has come Kannan, for us to act decisively and quickly. We have got to save our girls.'

From you, Kannan wanted to say. This moron would not stir out of his bed if his neighbour's house were on fire. He was rapidly losing patience with Narasimhan, but he had to keep the conversation going.

'Where have you located the promised land? Here in Sannidhi Street?'

'You are not serious. This is the problem with you. If Brahmin boys are not supporting the Brahmin cause what can we expect from a government that is avowedly anti-Brahmin?'

'Tell me. What about Brahmin boys seducing non-Brahmin girls?'

It was common knowledge that Narasimhan was carrying on with a Naidu girl and he was being tolerated by her parents only because they were not likely to find a better groom for the girl.

'Let us not be personal,' said Narasimhan primly. 'We are not talking of individuals here.'

Uma appeared from behind the wooden screen, her long hair plaited and tasselled, swaying gracefully to the jingle of her silver anklets. Her forehead had a *pottu*, a shining black exclamation mark that wrinkled when her densely-lashed eyes narrowed in a smile. Her nose, reluctant to emerge from its base, seemed to have given up its prominence to her full, arched, slightly parted lips which revealed a hint of fine teeth. She saw Kannan and he was sure she greeted him with a flutter of her eyes. In her left hand were a few banana leaves crumpled together with the remnants of evening tiffin. She walked briskly to the end of the street only a few yards ahead, flung the mess at a family of gamboling pigs and went back to disappear behind the screen, the jingle swiftly passing by.

Kannan was happy. He hurriedly took leave of his homeland-seeking-friend and walked back to his house. I have a theme for my dream today. The jingle is new. Had she worn the anklets to announce her arrival to me? She knew I would be waiting for her.

Kannan timed her to perfection and stalked her everywhere. When she came to buy her toiletries he was there in the shop carefully selecting toothpaste. He sat a few rows behind her in the local cinema concentrating on her flower-laden nape. He chased her rickety college bus, a green-and-yellow affair, on a bicycle, unmindful of the giggles his unequal chase evoked among the girls. He followed her to the local Shiva temple and circumambulated in her steps the God he did not believe in. He stood in front of her house enduring that lunatic Narasimhan for hours. Feigning illness, he even sat in the waiting room of a doctor she had gone consult for a minor ailment. He found her maddeningly attractive. She was different from the rest of the girls of his town in an elegant, unobtrusive way. She never came out scruffily attired, even on routine outings. She never hastened. She never ran to catch her bus. Her charm was such that the elderly driver waited for her to board his bus, a concession he rarely made to others. She never laughed openly. She put her handkerchief to her mouth and laughed into it.

Uma liked his presence around her. He was handsome in a Brahmin way, fair, thin, and with spectacles that shrank his big eyes to human proportions. His face was classical and his nose, unlike hers, was prominent and dominated the scenery despite the spectacles. He spoke quietly, never to her but to anyone within earshot of her, in sentences peppered with English which was usually beyond the person listening to him. When there was no one to speak to, he simply tucked his embryo paunch in and stretched his chest to its limits in a desperate effort to look muscled and masculine before her. He was seldom without a book, which he would hold at a convenient angle for Uma to read its title and author. Usually it was Wodehouse or Richard Gordon or Henry Cecil. Never Chase or Christie. Once it was *The Golden Treasury*. He was loveable. Uma was not sure she had started loving him.

In spite of his Marxist anointment, Kannan led a comfortable life of leisure in Tirunelvli junction. His exertions in the D.D.T. College did not amount to much – he was sincere no doubt – as the college had its annual quota of vacations, holidays and strikes, which meant that he had to teach only for about four months in a year. He read, visited cinema halls and ate his tiffin in the company of Narasimhan and a few other Brahmin friends in any of the many vegetarian eating places that the town was infested with. They usually discussed cricket and girls and hardly any politics. Narasimhan was a rabid Brahminist and his other Brahmin friends were dreaming of immigrating to the US; it was thus difficult for Kannan to be indignant in front of them about the appalling condition of the poor in the country, and the necessity of a revolution to alleviate their suffering. He had another set of friends for that purpose.

Muthu came from Tirunelveli town every weekend and he usually brought along a different fellow-traveller every time. They moved on to quiet 'military' hotels – usually run by Muslims and which served non-vegetarian food – to discuss the main currents of Marxism and important international issues. Kannan sipped hot tea, burnt his tongue and blazed against the US aggression in Vietnam or the anti-people attitude of the Tamil Nadu government. They returned home supremely satisfied that they had done their bit for the suffering masses. When there was a lull in the Vietnam War and when the local newspapers had nothing sensational to report, they were disappointed, for their tea-sessions became listless affairs.

The first time he spoke to her was when the thief came to Sannidhi Street.

Though they were not uniform, the houses of the street were terraced and had flat roofs; once a person managed to climb up on the roof of one house he could, without difficulty, conduct a survey of all the houses in that row at leisure. All he had to do was to hide in a cosy unfrequented alcove – there were many available – until night fell. The thief was spotted by Uma's aunt, a quiet, pocket-sized lady suffering from insomnia ever since her lawyer-husband had gone mad. The thief peered through the skylight and looked straight in at the horrified lady. She let out a shriek that almost brought the roof down and woke up every one in the house, and eventually, the street.

The elders of the street hurriedly organised a meeting and Sankararaman, a rancid middle-aged correspondent of a local Tamil daily, the *Dina Mottu*, was asked to form a surveillance group. Sankararaman had been cashiered from the Indian army, which made him an expert on planning. He said in a grave voice, 'The threat is real and he may even be armed. Now that he has found out we are vulnerable he is likely to strike again. The counter-measures require careful planning.'

Kannan could hardly believe his luck. Although the aromatic correspondent was a dolt, he was a tenant in Uma's house and joining his brigade meant he would be close to her.

For the next ten nights, a string cot placed on the veranda of her house served as the meeting place of Sankararman's men who climbed up and down the roofs to ferret out the thief. The correspondent, as usual, was effusive in giving senseless directions. A few phantom thieves emerged to frighten those who ventured out alone, a few more skylights were peered through in expectation of steamy scenes and a few ankles were sprained. The real thief however never showed up again. As the novelty of staying awake for long hours began to wear off, the group began to disintegrate fast.

Kannan persisted. He could watch Uma's world from his cot. The subtle nocturnal smells of her household, the hushed female voices, the subdued light from her table lamp, the swish of her sari and finally the quietude of sleep heightened by the drone of the ceiling fan all combined to make him tremble with desire. The desire was barely sexual. It was corrosive and peculiar.

She appeared before him one day when he was alone and when he was least expecting it. Normally it was her aunt who ministered to the volunteers' needs.

'Do you require anything?'

He had never seen her so close. She was freshly bathed. There was a tang of sandalwood in the air and he thought he saw tiny little soap bubbles clinging to her earlobes. Lacquered bangles, dark red and thick, covered her wrists and her damp braids rested on her swelling breasts, sensuously outlining them. Her face gleamed softly with health and contentment. She looked directly into his eyes and smiled.

'Do you require anything please? Shall I bring up a glass of buttermilk?' Her voice had an alluring hint of masculinity.

'I am okay, thank you.'

'No, you really should have a glass.' She went inside and came out presently with a glass of buttermilk.

'Here you are. You must all be very tired trying to catch the thief,' she said without a tinge of sarcasm.

'Yes. We are calling it off tomorrow.'

'Oh, it is a pity. That means I won't get to see you often.'

This is it! Kannan was brimming over with happiness.

'Oh, yes, you will. If you really want to.'

She broke into a peal of laughter. There was no handkerchief to hide it now.

'We shall see.' She disappeared into the house.

Uma was there the next night too. She brought him a glass of water this time and expected him to start a dialogue.

'May I borrow a book from you?' asked Kannan, his mind almost stunned by her presence.

'I know you love books. I have never seen you without them. I shall bring a few of mine.'

She brought a stack of books and he chose the fattest.

'Ah, Trevelyan! Like it?' Kannan looked at the spine. It was Trevelyan's *English Social History*. He had never heard of the book.

'Yes, very much. It would take months for me to finish it, though.'

'I won't be needing that book. Take your time.'

He wanted to hold her hands, talk to her about how she had come to pervade his life and ask her whether he occupied her thoughts. He did nothing. She stood there for a while smiling and looking marvellous in a blue sari. Then she turned away and disappeared into the house.

Kannan must have written at least a hundred imaginary letters to Uma, all masterpieces, billets-doux that would withstand the march of time. Writing a real letter was the problem. It would be foolish to bamboozle her with literary Tamil, Kannan decided. She, being Bombay-bred, was doubtful in her Tamil and a letter in that language would only put her off. Kannan was very defensive about his English and he had a horror of the phrasal verbs and prepositions with which the language seemed to be densely strewn. He thought of Nambi.

'Why are you so juvenile? Why don't you talk to her straight?' said Nambi.

'It is not that simple. She does like me but it may not be love.'

'Why bother her, then?' Realising that he had hurt Kannan, Nambi added, 'Come on, I was only joking. A practicing lover can't afford to be too sensitive.'

'A letter, a dignified one, might do the trick. It gives her time to reflect. If she loves me she may respond.'

'On the other hand she may choose to keep quiet, driving you mad.'

'I am prepared to take that chance.'

'She may complain to her relatives here. They may go to your father. They may even arrange to get you beaten to a pulp. The possibilities are endless.'

'I am prepared for everything, though I am sure I will get a reply.'

'Say it with a poem, Kannan, to begin with.'

'It will then remain unsaid for ever. Poem? I can't write a sentence without feeling faint and you talk of poetry.'

'No you idiot. I don't want you to compose a poem. Choose a good one from the many already written.'

'And claim authorship?'

'No, no,' said Nambi in exasperation. 'Is she that thick to mistake you for a major poet? Choose a solid, known one. Touch her heart, or whatever you want to touch.'

'You have to select one for me.'

After rummaging through reams of poetry, Nambi came up with a dense sonnet.

'This is from the big Willy himself. "The Marriage of True Minds". She is bound to be impressed.'

'I can't make head or tail of it.'

'Neither will she. That is not important. But if she has a taste for poetry, she will fall for its music and marvel at your choice.'

The sonnet sank without a ripple.

At Nambi's suggestion, Kannan tried his luck with Tennyson's 'Now Sleeps the Crimson Petal' and then with Rosseti's 'Sudden Light'.

The response, which came after two months, was succinct.

Dear Mr Kannan,

I want to call a stop to this game before you graduate to Thomas Ford or some such lovelorn poet. The bombardment should cease. I have enough of poetry in college. Why don't you write a simple letter for a change?

Uma

PS: Where is my Trevelyan?

Dear Uma,

Thank you. I thought the response would never arrive. I am not very articulate and hence I had no other way than to express my feelings towards you through borrowed poetry. Why don't we meet? I haven't spoken to you since the thieves' hunt and that was the only time I spoke to you. I don't propose to wait till the next hunt, which may never materialise, since the thieves appear to have deserted us.

With much love,
Kannan

PS: I haven't progressed beyond the first page of English Social History. *To tell you the truth, I heard Trevelyan's name for the first time at your house.*

Dear Kannan,

I agree we cannot await the thieves' arrival. The problem is, our meeting in the vicinity of Sannidhi Street would set tongues wagging and your prop, Narasimhan, will have an endless series of field days. My aunt has a load of problems already and I don't want to add to them.

I suggest the High Grounds bus stand. This Saturday. At 1500 hours.

With love,
Uma

PS: I hate Trevelyan. I scored very low marks in social history.

She came in a flower-strewn half-sari and a parrot-green full skirt, heavily brocaded at the hem.

'Hello.'

'Hello.'

'Where shall we go?'

'Maria canteen?' He immediately regretted his suggestion. The canteen was a meeting place of vagabond students unwilling to attend classes. It was located between two men's colleges and was rarely graced by women.

'No, I don't want to be the cynosure of those rogues' eyes.'

'I can't think of anywhere else.'

'It is funny, isn't it?' she laughed. 'We can't find a quiet place in this stupid city to sit and talk. Shall we walk down to the next bus stand?'

'Yes, that is a nice idea.'

She was not tall and came to just above his shoulder. She walked very briskly and close to Kannan. Her fragrance swirled around, sending him into a panic about the stale smell of his sweat reaching her. He eyed her and was happy that she was not sniffing.

'If it be love indeed, tell me how much,' she said softly.

'What?'

'Never mind. What are your plans? Are you going to rot here in Tirunelevli?'

'What options do I have? Moreover I am very happy with teaching and with physics.'

'I am not sure I could live here,' said Uma with a sigh.

Kannan walked silently. He was sad that he could not come up with an answer that would brighten her. In the end, it was she who cheered him up. 'Let the future wait. I adore Manna Dey. Do you?'

'Yes, very much. Though my Hindi is zero.'

They waxed enthusiastic about Hindi film music till they reached the bus stand.

It was difficult for him to contrive another meeting with Uma. He kept seeing her in the temple, at the shops and bus stops, and behind the vertical bars of her house, watching the tight-rope walkers or the snake charmers, but it was impossible to snatch a conversation from her, surrounded as she was by cousins, friends and aunts. She was also ceaselessly watched by Sankararaman, the self-appointed secret agent of her father. The High Grounds meet nevertheless sustained Kannan for months. It hoisted him on a cumulus of his own and left him there, making him cocky and causing him to look down upon his friends who had not been able to notch up a score with the girls of their dreams. The badinage between them was now less risque and rarely on girls and never on Uma. Even Marxism took a backseat for a while.

Uma's Trevelyan went back to her through Kannan's sister, Radha. Inside it was a gushing letter from Kannan that he had painfully patch-worked from the passages of authors known and unknown to her. Uma laughed and said, 'Ask Kannan not to waste time composing literary letters.'

Radha said, 'I am not much of a go-between, but I think he will be offended if I tell him what you have just told me. He sits on a pedestal nowadays and it will be a pity if this message of yours dislodges him.'

'I shall write to him. It will then be personal between us.'

Dear Kannan,

Language is a fun-mirror; it either dwarfs one or makes one a giant. It does not reflect the truth about oneself. I love you not for your language, which in any case is not fully yours. I want to be near you and feel you and I do not want to imagine you through your letters, especially since I am so near I could hear you if you speak loudly in your house. I am arranging two tickets for one of the evening shows at the Central Theatre, when it screens one of those unwatchable

movies, which must happen fairly quickly as they far
outnumber the watchable.

Love,
Uma

The movie was not an unwatchable one but it was old, a black-and-white comedy starring Gemini and Vyjayanthimala. In spite of his fancy clothes Gemini looked the staid Brahmin that he was. Vyjayanthimala was tall and vivacious.

Kannan had seen it with his grandmother at a 'touring talkies' in Nanguneri when it first appeared. There were intervals after every reel and the audience shouted derisively whenever Gemini Ganesan appeared on the screen. It was an outlandish romance set in fabulous Kashmir and the protagonists looked insufferably posh. The sand he had squatted on warmed his bottom to an uncomfortable degree. He had had to keep his hands away from the sand, for if they had wandered, they would have been pasted with tobacco-spittle or something more obnoxious.

This time he was in an air-conditioned cubicle and Kashmir seemed possible as he had Uma nestling close to him. The cubicle had four seats and the other two seats were vacant. Only lovers looking for dark and private space would waste five rupees on a seat for an old black-and-white movie. Uma knew that the probability of two pairs of lovers in Tirunelveli looking for such space on the same day, for the same show, at the Central Theatre's air-conditioned cubicle was rather remote, but she was relieved to see the vacant seats.

She was wearing a black blouse and a pale yellow sari. The blouse was tight and he had to undo a few buttons to reach the soft fabric of her brassiere. He stroked her softly, filling the cubicle with a flowery scent. He kissed her and his tongue darted in without meeting much resistance. His hand was bashful and it took a detour to reach her nipple. She pulled his hand out of her blouse.

'Don't wander farther afield. I am not going to be seduced in a cubicle with Gemini and Vyjayanthi watching.'

'They are busy with their romance.'

'Still, I need a better setting. A nuptial bed for example.'

'I am not in a hurry to marry, Uma.'

'I am not in a hurry to be seduced either. These things can wait, Kannan. I want you to get out of this hole – not this cubicle, I mean this town – quickly. One escape route is through the civil services examination. Why don't you sit for it?'

'I have a horror of examinations, Uma. And the civil service is the biggest monster of them all.'

'I was sure you would sit for it, at least for my sake.'

Kannan hugged her but his hands were now quiet.

He met Uma again in his house when she came to see Radha. The lights went off and Radha vanished inside the house and they stood on the staircase leading to his room on the upper storey, holding hands.

'Uma, I have been made permanent.'

'What does that mean?'

'It means even a team of horses cannot separate me from the position I hold in the college, unless of course I decide to resign.'

Uma this time took pity on him and did not say a word about what he dreaded. She was touching his nose with the tip of her tongue when the lights came on.

Uma loathed Bombay though she grew up in it. She had then had a child's idea of Tirunelveli, which she visited every vacation. It was almost pastoral after the lunatic bustle of Bombay, where they lived in a grim, narrow tenement that had not seen a lick of whitewash for years, and to which her father clung with a monstrous tenacity that greed had bred. He was paying a rent of five rupees a month that had remained unchanged from the days of the Second World War. He was now an officer with Air India and had acquired an airy flat in Juhu, but the tenement was too inexpensive to let go. Uma's elder sister was married to a mousy little man from the village of Brahmadesam, a few miles west of Tirunelveli, who clerked for a heavyweight Gujarati and earned much more than others thought. He was given the keys of the Juhu flat on the understanding that he would move out when his father-in-law wanted to move in, which Uma thought was not going to happen in her lifetime. He also paid his father-in-law a goodly rent, which they did not show in their tax returns. She would have moved in with her sister but for her brother-in-law who, in her sister's absence, stared unblinkingly at her breasts.

Electric trains, onto which her father clambered every day to reach his office and return home, roared past the tenement every few minutes during the day, sending it into a tremor. They also mangled at least one human being every week, splashing the wall that separated the shaking tenement from the tracks with flesh and brain matter. The tenants routinely climbed the roof to have an aerial view of the gory litter and commiserate on it. Uma had never seen any one cut decently by the electric train.

When she had completed her school finals, she told her father that she wanted to move on to Tirunelveli for her degree. He shammed reluctance but he was happy with his daughter's decision. His son had married recently and the living room was too cramped to accommodate Uma, her father and her mother. He also thought the creaking of the bed and the other love noises at night, which the thin walls that partitioned the house could not fully muffle, would put ideas into the mind of his adolescent daughter.

The Tirunelveli household was run by women. Uma's uncle – her father's elder brother – was a choleric lawyer named Ramaswamy. He lost his mind while arguing a case vehemently before a doughty judge and threw a stout law book at the clerk of the court. The act almost pulled his arm out of its socket, but the book missed its aim and the lawyer was sent to an asylum. His wife was a courageous woman and though she had two daughters of her own look after, she welcomed Uma into her fold. The lawyer went in and out of asylums so frequently that his disappearances from the household were hardly noticed by the residents of Sannidhi Street. They watched him going up and down the street, waving his hands, spouting law points before a non-existent judge and scoring imaginary legal victories. All the houses of the street allowed ingress to him either for a cup of coffee or snacks or both. He hardly ever refused an offer and consequently had violent belly-aches at nights. The other problem was that at times he started his courtroom drama without a scrap of clothing on. His wife took great care to lock him inside the house on such occasions. Once or twice he slipped out but the neighbours promptly tied a veshti around his waist and brought him back. The children of the street did not torment him at all. They admired the torrent of English that came from him with effortless ease. They protected him from the children of other streets.

He would visit Kannan's house regularly for a pinch of snuff, which he borrowed without a word from his one-time lawyer colleague. He would stand in front of him, his hand extended and the tip of his forefinger touching that of the thumb. Tirumalai would open his silver snuffbox and offer it to his friend. He would take a liberal pinch, snuffle it in and close his eyes in pleasure. He would then say, 'Thank you, Tirumalai, thank you, thank you,' and walk out resuming his arguments. At times, when he saw Kannan playing chess with his friend, he would stand behind him and observe the moves. He played with Kannan when the mood took him and beat him every time. Afterwards he would pat Kannan on the shoulders and resume his walkabout, playing chess in the air.

Her cousins and aunt were wonderful, but Uma began to dislike the sidling ways of the people around her who were always eager to know every business of hers, but would not ask her. She particularly detested her neighbour, Sankararaman, the reporter for the *Dina Mottu*, who lived in the partitioned other half of her house. He had a massive hydrocele that he seemed to drag along with pride. His deriders commented cruelly that he had no need for a table, since he had the rare convenience of sitting at his balls and writing his reports. He was also skunky and the house exuded his aroma even in his absence. He had taken it upon himself to protect the virginity of Uma, the helpless Bombay girl, and wrote regularly to her father about her actitivites. He was a die-hand Smartha and had nothing but contempt for the uppish Iyengars. He eyed Kannan with extreme suspicion because he sensed that the wily Iyengar was leading a poor Smartha girl up the track of seduction.

Initially Uma's father had not been unduly alarmed, but as Sankararaman's letters in purple Tamil continued to bring him news about the scandal his daughter was likely to be at the centre of, he decided to make a trip to Tirunelveli.

Uma's father's rosier dreams had an IAS boy as a marionette, flailing his arms and beckoning Uma. Kannan, he thought, could be that puppet of his dreams. He had heard that the boy, though an Iyengar, was bright, and had a good chance of clearing the examinations and decided that he would not lose sleep over such minor issues as the boy's sub-sect. He did not chide his daughter. He mildly told her that she was in Tirunelveli to get her degree and not to moon over boys.

Uma was not afraid of her father. She said, 'This is the problem here. I just had to speak to a boy and the whole street gossips about it. Who am I mooning over?'

'There is an Iyengar boy, they say.'

'Oh, Kannan. He is just a friend, appa. He is very good and I like him, but it does not mean I am going to elope with him, which is perhaps what your sneaking Bond has suggested to you and which has made you come all the way here.'

'No, I just wanted to see you,' said Uma's father defensively. He added, 'Sankararaman tells me – what is his name? –

Kannan, he is close to the local Communists. He roams around with Bala, he says. Bala was my classmate and even then he was a rank Communist. He had a friend, Madhurakavi. He was also a red, but he died young. Friendship with Communists could be dangerous.'

'Appa, I can't take any more. I don't want to say this, but Sankararaman uncle is so used to distorting information for his tattling rag, he can never speak or write straight. And his word is gospel for you.'

Uma's onslaught gagged her father.

When she met Radha again she asked her, 'I hear Kannan has some strange friends. Is it true?'

'He always hobnobs with oddballs. Which one are you talking about?'

'His Communist friends.'

'Oh, don't worry about that. It has been a fad since he went to Madras for his postgraduation. He gave me an article from the *Indian Express* to read the other day. "Behind the Bamboo Curtain" or some such title. I told him we had enough curtains around here to look behind, and bamboo and other curtains abroad could wait. He felt deflated and hasn't spoken to me properly after that.'

'Is he with the dangerous variety? The Naxalites?'

'I don't think so. Even if he becomes friendly with them, he has a fine survival instinct. He will extricate himself at the right time. Yes, my other cousin, Nambi, is a serious person. So is Bala uncle. They haven't yet made him a serious Communist. Not to my knowledge. If I were you, I wouldn't lose sleep over Kannan's friends.'

Eleven

THE RAILWAY STATION LOOKED DESERTED EXCEPT for a vendor brooding over his tepid vadais. Kannan sat on a bench near him hoping to strike up a conversation. Uma's train would take a few minutes to arrive. She was going to Bombay on vacation and she had asked Kannan to meet her on the way. It was her idea that they could travel together for a few hours.

'Vadai, sir, hot vadai.'

'I am full, friend. Just returning from a marriage feast. How is business?'

'Why are you making fun of me, sir? You are the only customer around and you are full. Koilpatti is a wretched place. Why don't you carry some vadais home?'

'No, friend. I am not going home. I am going to Madurai. Tell me, is your family big?'

'It is not, sir. But selling vadais is not enough to fill one stomach and I have three to fill.'

'Which party do you support?' said Kannan, changing gear. He wanted to make common cause with the underclass for whom his heart at that moment was overflowing with the warm milk of kndness.

The vadai-man wanted Kannan to shut up and mind his business, but politics was always engrossing and here was a target close at hand to exercise his expletives on.

'Don't talk to me about politics or politicians. They are all pricks. Syphilitic pricks even a two-anna whore wouldn't touch.'

Kannan did not expect this explosion. 'You sound bitter. Not all of them are bad. The Communists are doing their best to help persons like you.'

'Then you don't know the Communists. They are the smelliest and the most pustulous pricks of them all. There I was, happy with my job in the spinning mill. These booming farts came there, made our life miserable and ensured that the mill was closed for ever. I am now rotting here in this shithouse. Sir, do I look like a professional vadai-seller?'

The whistle of the approaching train rescued Kannan from continuing what he had started with hope and empathy. He hurriedly bought a dozen vadais for three rupees to douse the fire burning within that ex-member of the proletariat.

It was not difficult to locate Uma. She was standing at the entrance of the compartment looking eager. Her long braid gently lashed her broad back in a bewitching rhythm when she vigorously waved her hand at Kannan.

'I thought you might not be here. I am glad you could make it.'

'I don't get a chance every day to spend two hours with you,' said Kannan.

She was in a pink sari and a matching blouse. Its twin sweat-spots under her arms, damp, dark and circular, were causing a mild tumescence in him. She came to him and dragging him by his wrist, took him to her berth.

'This is my friend,' said Uma to the old couple who were sitting on the opposite berth. They simply nodded. Kannan was squirming. It did not happen every day that a Tamil girl introduced her boyfriend to strangers on a train. 'I don't want them to get curious,' she whispered in his ear. 'We can move on to the entrance once the train picks up speed.'

The landscape rushing away from the train was unrelievedly dry and the trees looked stunted, gasping for life. Children, naked and savouring their snot, stood dangerously close to the running train and blew kisses at the passengers.

'How was the marriage?'

'Oh, it was wonderful. The food was fantastic and I made a pig of myself at the feast. I bought some vadais for you here, at the railway station. Here you are.'

'Forget vadais, Kannan. What about your friend? Is he going to spend some time with his wife? When is he joining the academy?'

Kannan knew that Uma would broach the issue and that he had no satisfactory answers for her.

'Must be this June.'

'Is he joining the police service or the revenue service?'

'The police service. Uma, I have not come here to discuss Subramaniam's bright career. I am here to talk to you about our plans.'

'I want you to do precisely that. When are you writing your civil service examinations? Are you really serious about it?'

'I am, Uma, I am.'

'Don't lie to me. I know you are not serious. Look Kannan, it will be impossible for us to live in Tirunelveli once we are married. I don't want to be pointed out at the bazaar as the brave Iyer girl who got hitched to an Iyengar boy. I want to lead a quiet life with you, which you know is not possible in our wretched town. I talked to Radha and she agrees with me. She says you are just too lazy to do anything worthwhile.'

'Uma, life does not begin or end with the civil services. There are other honourable professions too. Mine is one such profession though you seem to think otherwise. Radha . . . well, she is a precise girl and the world is neatly laid out for her to take measured steps in the direction she chooses. She does not like anybody sauntering by, which is what I like to do.'

'Don't get angry, Kannan. You know I have nothing against teaching. These are practical problems . . .'

'Uma, I shall surely find a way. Let us talk of something pleasant.'

Both knew that it was difficult for them to talk further. They held hands for a few minutes and quietly returned to her berth.

The temple town of Madurai was in a permanent state of insomnolence. The food stalls on both sides of its arterial roads never closed their doors and they sold round the clock idlis, vadais, dosais, rice plates, rotis, *parottas*, omelettes, boiled eggs, aphrodisiac halwas, coffee, tea and countless other Tamil sweets and savouries. Lottery-kiosks illuminated by powerful mercury vapour lamps briskly sold tickets to prospective millionairedom (K.A. Sekhar! The man who has the golden touch! K.A. Sekhar! The man who makes millionaires by the dozen!). Behind these buzzing hives were small, stinking hotels that doubled as budget lodging establishments and economy brothels.

His room on the third floor had the luxury of two windows – one opening into the drainage shaft and the other, the smaller one, overlooking the street. One of its betel-juice-spotted walls displayed a framed photograph of a podgy film hero in an attitude of acute constipation. Its wobbly wooden cot had a threadbare bedcover on it. Kannan was thankful for the absence of pillows which were usually bug-ridden and black with the noxious stains of myriad hair-oils. There was no table in the room, but it had a stool occupied by a stainless steel water jug and two rimless tumblers. A folding chair leaned against the wall. The bathroom had two giant taps that were hot to the touch and wheezed when turned on. It had, thankfully, two iron buckets brimming with water and two large mugs with wide, single ears. The hole in the floor was reasonably clean – there were no visible faecal remnants.

Kannan sat on the cot expecting it to creak. It was disappointingly silent and he could feel melancholy creeping in and enveloping him. Though Uma did not exactly say I was a never-do-well that must surely have been how she felt . . . All our meetings so far have ended in us both nursing silence. If this is love, life is likely to be one long stretch of stillness. It may suit me, but she loves incessant chatter. My Marxist pretensions are not even known to her. It is a surprise Radha has so far refrained from informing Uma of my affliction. If she comes to know of it . . . .

He needed to go down for air as his thoughts were suffocating him. There was a knock at the door.

'Who is it?'

'May I come in sir?' The person entered without waiting for a reply.

'Are you expecting anyone, sir?'

'No, but how does it concern you?'

'If you are not, I could arrange some colourful company for you. Good Kerala stuff, sir. They carry their coconuts on their chests.'

'Will you please get out?'

'I also have nice Brahmin girls. College educated. Very cooperative. Only twenty rupees. They are fresh, sir, no VD.'

The man was comically short – he was hardly four feet – and he smelt of sweat and sour curd. His emetic leer never left his pitted face.

'I am going out now. We shall see later.'

Kannan locked his room, hurried down the flight of narrow stairs and came out to the street. Its irregular throb and the human detritus that lay scattered along it made him feel disoriented. 'God, fuck the pimp. It's all his doing. I was happy in my room.' Red posters decorating the lamp posts announced a grand sale of Marxist classics in the New Century Book House.

The book house was not crowded, though the prices were unbelievably low. There was a slip of a girl standing guard over the Soviet books. She had a likeable face and a bosom a couple of sizes too big for her frame.

'Do you have *The History of the CPSU(B)*?' Kannan knew that the bookstall did not stock Stalinist material, yet he wanted to hear it from her.

'It is out of print, sir.'

'What about *On Practice*?'

Now the girl was frank. 'We don't stock Chinese material, sir.'

'Are the Chinese books banned?'

'No, no. We just don't stock them.'

He knew his Marxism all right but its parading did not seem to rouse her. She stood there ignoring him, looking at the floor, her chest heaving dangerously. Kannan went up to the stacks of Lenin. He picked up the three-volume edition of Lenin's selected works, available for just fifteen rupees.

Her dugs are diverting. Will she sleep with me? His tumidity started to hurt and he half-ran back to his room, though Lenin's tomes weighed like stones.

The lady did not have any coconuts. Hers were shrunken bottle-gourds touching the sides of her waist. It was difficult for her to close her mouth. Her large sulphur-coloured front teeth, suggestive of halitosis, pressed on her ashy lower lip, making indents on it.

'How much did you pay for me?' Her lisp was affected and pathetic.

'Twenty rupees.'

'He told me fifteen. Greedy bandicoot. You must give me five rupees more. Why don't you come to me directly? It's much cheaper. I live opposite Nagapattinam sweet stall. Should I remove my petticoat?'

She removed the rag around her waist and lay down on the cot with her knees bent and her ankles brushing her haunches. Kannan sheathed himself and lay next to her, gently kneading her flappy breasts.

'Are you trying to make rotis? Take them in your mouth.'

Strands of unsightly hair sprouted from her right nipple. The divine Kannan drew life out of Putana's poisoned breast. Will I die drinking poison from this shrivelled-up thing? I ought to be ashamed. Are working-class breasts purveyors of poison? He reluctantly closed his mouth on the sleeping left one, which was dry and rough on his tongue.

'Are you a Brahmin? You look fair and thin. Where is your sacred thread?'

'No, I am a Mudaliar. What is your name?'

'Saroja Devi.' It was the name of a famous film actress. And of a best-selling pornographer.

She weighed his scrotum in her palm and gently scraped it with her fingernails for a minute. She then moved up and rolled his covered member between her thumb and middle finger like an expert smoker making a personal cigarette, while whispering into his ear all the time the Tamil word for penis. This is perhaps her idea of sex-talk, to make me shake with desire.

He smiled to himself and she asked, 'Are you happy?' He did not reply. He vaguely nodded and attempted to lie on her.

'There is no pillow in this room. I need a support for my bottom.'

She looked around and saw Lenin. Placing two volumes on the cot she touched them reverentially with her calloused palms. After praying for a minute – she mumbled what sounded to Kannan like a popular Tamil devotional poem – she brought the sacrament to an end by touching her closed eyes with her fingertips. She covered the books with her discarded blouse and carefully lowered her bottom on to them. Having achieved the desired elevation after making a few minor adjustments, she motioned to Kannan to begin.

Kannan made few desultory attempts at penetration.

'Mine is like a virgin's. You have to work hard.'

He looked down. It was a burnt pink mess surrounded by a wiry profusion. He again jabbed at her without much success.

He kept missing and hitting instead the covered Lenin. She did nothing to help him.

After a while she asked, 'Should I take you in the mouth? That will be five rupees extra.' Kannan, fearing her sulphury frontage, shook his head.

'I shall use my hand then.' She did for him what he could have done without her company. When it was over, she flung the rubber out of the window and left without speaking a word. She did not demand any extra money.

There was no damage to Lenin except that the dark blue jacket of Volume Two looked slightly crumpled.

Bala came an hour before the appointed time. He was as usual in khadi; it had stuck with him though he now had no good word for Gandhi. He had on his patented brown shirt with its cavernous pocket stuffed with papers and a fat orange pen peeping out. He must be at least sixty-five, Kannan thought. He was after all my uncle's classmate. It has been long since *periappa* left the British-ridden world – he was one of the sacrificial offerings of 1942 – and here is his friend still nurturing his boyhood dreams, dreams at the peripheries of possibility, dreams of a different world. Surely even his world will have its share of Saroja Devis. And pimping lilliputians.

'Where are the others?'

His voice was soft and slightly feminine. No wonder he was not much of a success as a Tamil orator. Kannan tucked in his stomach envying Bala's wiry fleshless frame.

'They have to come from Tirunelveli, sir. They said they would catch the morning bus. They will be here any moment.'

'I see you have the Lenin. Have you managed to read "Left Wing Communism"?'

'I bought them only yesterday. Lenin, I need not tell you, sir, is indigestible in these surroundings.'

'I see your point.' He picked up Volume Three and started turning the pages, his forehead crinkling, mouth slightly open in admiration. Kannan remembered the adoration of Saroja Devi the day before.

'This is what he says,' he said reading out a passage. '"The Communists must exert every effort to direct the working class movement and social development in general along the straightest and shortest road to the victory of Soviet power and the dictatorship of the proletariat on a worldwide scale. This is an incontestable truth. But it is enough to take one little step farther – a step that might seem to be in the same direction – and truth turns to error".'

Bala paused for breath. 'We have taken so many steps farther, truth has probably been left far behind and is following us panting for breath. Where is that straight, short magical road? And what is truth? We keep asking like the procurator of Judaea and unlike him, we wait indefinitely, and all we keep getting is laughable unsatisfactory answers.'

'Why ask the question, then?'

'That is up to you,' Bala smiled. 'As for me, I am condemned to ask this question, though I may not get an answer during my lifetime.'

Kannan remembered Nambi's words. He had said, 'Bala is Edward Lear's tumultuous tom-tommy tortoise.

'"The Tumultuous Tom-tommy Tortoise, / who beat the drum all day long in the / middle of the wilderness." He wants us to replace him in the wilderness when he is gone.'

Nambi's judgment of Bala is perhaps harsh. He may be beating his drum, but he is not on the lookout for inheritors. He has never imposed his will or his party's on us. Even today, he hasn't come on his own. It is we who have invited him.

They could hear the sound of footsteps and presently Nambi and Muthu entered the room. Muthu's bandit moustache, salt-and-pepper and nicotine-stained, glistened in the harsh light thrown by the naked bulb. It did not become his cherubic face or his dumpy frame. Kannan had told him many times to shave it off but Muthu's reply had always been that his wife loved it. He moved about briskly, twirling his moustache all the time.

'We must thank Comrade Bala for coming here to advise us. We must also thank Nambi, who will help us design posters.'

'There is no need for these preliminaries,' said Kannan impatiently. 'Let us not detain Bala sir. He has a million things to do.'

'We hear that the chief minister is visiting Tirunelveli sometime next month. We, that is Kannan and I, want to use this opportunity to bring together teachers, students, workers and peasants. We propose to organise a massive rally and present to the chief minister our charter of demands.'

'The DMK teachers may not join the rally. We could organise others who are sizeable in number,' said Kannan.

'This sounds an excellent idea, but I have to ask the party high command. Our workers and peasants will of course march under the party's banner. Will the teachers join them? The students might. You may approach other like-minded parties too. Or if you permit, I shall contact them.'

'We leave it to you to contact the other parties, sir,' said Muthu.

'Teachers get their salaries neither in time nor fully. They are chattels under corrupt managements everywhere.'

'What are the students' problems?'

'Oh, they have many. I can't list them all,' said Kannan airily. 'You can list a few,' murmured Nambi, but he did not probe further. He came at them from another angle.

'What is common between you, the workers and the peasants? Their problems are different from yours. Are you going to include their problems too in your charter?'

Bala came to the rescue of Kannan and Muthu.

'The workers and peasants shall have many other opportunities to present their demands. They are veterans of many struggles. They will join the teachers and students merely to express their solidarity with them. I think this is the best time to rally the teachers and students under one banner and we should not miss the chance.'

Nambi was not convinced. 'What is the use of this rally now? Do you really think the chief minister will be impressed? For him, the left parties are empty vessels making noise without causing any harm whatsoever to his political power. He knows that when the elections come, they will go running to him to win a few seats in the assembly and the parliament. The teachers? They are despicable. They will run away at the swish of police batons. The students are the sacrificial lambs. And what about expenses? I have just built a small clinic in my village and I know what it costs. With the money spent on such rallies, I could build a hospital, if not two.'

Kannan and Muthu wilted under the barrage, but Bala was cool.

'Nambi, this is petty-bourgeois delusion. Money does not go out smoothly from one channel into another like water. Who will give you, or anyone, money for hospitals to be built in god-forsaken places? This rally is important and, what is more, it is possible. As regards your remarks on our alliance with the party of the chief minister, this is the language of our enemies and I am sorry a sympathiser makes a similar charge. In any case, this is not the time for ideological debate.'

'I am sorry to be misunderstood. I mentioned hospitals only to highlight the expenses. I know we have no money for such drab things as hospitals. I too am hungry for action that will benefit the ordinary people. We hold rallies, disperse and do nothing till the next one comes our way,' said Nambi.

'What do you want us to do? Throw bombs at the chief minister? Nambi, please try to understand. These rallies are our oxygen cylinders. They resuscitate the suffocating people. They are very much needed. I have been organising them for more than thirty years now.' He paused for a moment and said,

'Well, I have to rush. I think this rally is a fine idea. We follow the principle of democratic centralism, don't we? How do you vote, Muthu?'

'I agree with you sir.'

'Kannan?'

Kannan was confused, but would go with his flock.

'I vote for you, sir.'

Bala said in a conciliatory voice, 'Don't worry, Nambi. I shall see your hospital before I die. We will name it after my friend, your father.'

'My father is a forgotten man, sir. Let him stay forgotten. Let us get on with the living. I will do what I can to make this rally a success.'

Twelve

EVEN TIRUMALAI TOOK THE NEWS STOICALLY, but Narasimhan was insanely indignant. He said it was deliberately arranged to treat the Sannidhi Street Brahmins to an earful of the most vicious calumnies against their community. Kannan said even if it was, it would be interesting to listen to Periyar, and the only people who were eager for a session of his Brahmin-bashing were the Brahmins themselves. Periyar was to come at seven in the evening and men gathered in groups at a distance from where the meeting was to be held to discuss among themselves their commiserable condition. Brahmin women finished their cooking early and gathered in convenient groups on verandas of the houses near the river-end of the street to listen to the nonagenarian bleater.

'This man is a turncoat. Till yesterday he was abusing the DMK. They are now in power and he has patched up with them,' said Narasimhan.

Kannan said, 'He also keeps telling them some unpalatable things. Abuse or no abuse, the DMK adore him, don't they? He remains the father of their movement and their loyalty towards him is nothing short of amazing. Narasimhan, you could accuse him of anything, but his atheism and his hatred of religion, especially our religion, and of superstition have been consistent. His tirades against the Brahmins are really amusing. I am sure he will have us in stitches. He rarely attacks the Brahmins personally.'

'Which is small consolation when you consider that his minor apostles more than take care of that aspect. I understand a particularly abhorrent specimen is going to speak today.'

As Narasimhan had predicted, one of Periyar's ideological minions, a person with blood-red eyes and a pitch-black shirt, arrived at the microphone to spit fire and brimstone at the Brahmins. According to him, they came to the Tamil land from the Central Asian wilderness through the Khyber Pass and took advantage of the innocence of the Tamils to teach them horrendous things. Originally Tamil literature was pure and the Tamil woman virtue personified. While the women had managed to remain unsullied in spite of repeated assaults on their chastity, the literature had now been hopelessly contaminated by Sanskrit, the so-called divine language. Sanskrit was full of filthy things. Why, even the Brahminical religious texts were sex-manuals.

'I shall quote from the Sukla Yajur Veda. It says: "A woman's thing makes a funny noise when she walks fast and when she sleeps with a man." This, I must tell you, is the least explicit of the many sex-slokas in the text.'

Narasimhan made a mental note of the Sukla Yajur Veda. It sounds interesting. I must read it someday.

The apostle went on in similar vein before he was rudely pushed aside to make way for Periyar. The old man's face was a ripe pumpkin with a prophet's beard. His voice trembled, but it was clear. Unlike his minions who spoke in affected alliterative Tamil with the modulation of a rice-grinder, he spoke in well-modulated natural Tamil.

'Once I met Mahatma Gandhi. I told him that I had met many Brahmins in public life but I was unable to find even one Brahmin who had set aside narrow caste considerations and placed public welfare before the interests of his community. Gandhi said I was wrong and he knew many selfless Brahmins. I asked him to name one. He said he was thinking of Rajaji. Rajaji, as you all know, is a very close friend of mine, but I told Gandhi that he was good only to Brahmins. Gandhi thought for a few minutes and came up with another name. "What about Gokhale? You can't find a purer soul than him." I said humbly to Gandhi, "Sir you are universally recognised as a Mahatma and even you had to search hard for a good Brahmin. I am a commoner, a great sinner. How do you expect me to locate such rare persons?"

'I am not saying that a good Brahmin is a dead Brahmin. The Brahmins are here in our land and we must live in peace with them. My complaint is against the Tamils who have lost their capacity to think. Religion has addled their brains. The West has put men on the moon. Here we still give raw bananas and coconuts to Brahmins to ward off the evils of a lunar eclipse. They exploit you because, I repeat, you don't think. Take the case of the temple I see at the opposite end of this street. No Brahmin woman would have carried bricks to construct it. No male Brahmin would have come anywhere near it to work as a labourer. After it had been built they must have gone in, chanted some unintelligible mantras and installed a stone idol. Now you can't get in without their permission. What do you do? Do you protest? No. You construct a car – which I see over there – weighing a few tonnes and sit a half-a-ton priest and his toys of weird gods in it and drag it round the streets. Why are you blaming the Brahmins when you are senseless?'

Narasimhan was boiling. 'These are gross distortions. Has he worked as a labourer? He has no business to talk like this. Will he dare use such epithets against the Christians? Or the Muslims? If he does, he is sure to find his head missing in no time.'

Kannan said, 'He has been speaking like this for more than fifty years now. Has anything happened? The rituals he inveighs against, they only seem to increase. Have a good laugh, friend.'

Narasimhan did not want a good laugh. He arranged an emergency meeting of the Brahmins' Association, which was presided over by a frothing-at-the mouth orator.

'The Brahmins never got justice. They were treated badly before and now they are being treated worse. I shall narrate a story from the *Kathasaritsagara* that goes like this. Once, a pregnant Brahmin lady chased a donkey out of her kitchen garden. The foolish donkey stumbled and broke its hoof. The washer-man whose donkey it was came to the woman to remonstrate with her and it was her turn to run. She fell down and had a miscarriage. Her husband went to a magistrate for justice. The magistrate heard the case and his judgment was that the woman's husband had to do the work of the donkey for the washer-man till his animal's hoof healed, and that the washer-man had to do the work of the Brahmin and impregnate the woman since he had caused the miscarriage. If this was the justice in ancient times when things were not too bad for the Brahmins, what do you expect today when we are ruled by avowed anti-Brahmins? These DMK fellows came to power with our support, and now they kick us, for they no longer require our help. What Periyar says is of no concern to them. It is they who egg him on to hurl filthy abuses at us. Unless we act decisively, unless we make our presence felt, not even a dog will bother about us.'

Opinions varied from flinging Molotov cocktails at Periyar meetings to staging relay fasts before the municipality. Finally the meeting passed an acidulous resolution roundly condemning Periyar and all he had said. The first copy of the resolution was sent to the President of India, the last one – there were eighteen in between – to the municipal councillor who happened to be a Brahmin, and who had attended the association meeting on the sly.

Narasimhan's father was a stamp-vendor and though he made enough money to feed his family of five – himself, his wife and three sons – there was never enough money for extravagances. Narasimhan was the eldest and had had delusions of clerkship in an air-conditioned bank when he emerged from his college with a third class degree in mathematics. He could also peck at the typewriter, which he thought would be an additional point in his favour in the job bazaar. The bazaar punctured his hopes in no time. He found that he had nothing much to do, except to gossip with Kannan in the evenings and to work gratis for the Brahmins' Association. He forgot that mediocrity gets ruthlessly exposed in unjust societies, unless the mediocre stumble upon fame or fortune. He laid the blame of his joblessness at the door of the Brahmin-hating government and sulked openly.

He also had a secret sulk. He passionately wanted to see a woman at close quarters without clothes on, but there was little chance of that. He had fleeting glimpses of what he sought in the bathing ghats, when the wind helped him or when the woman herself was careless. Such glimpses only whetted his desire. Even a quick five-minute encounter with a woman would do, he thought, and my eyes would have their fill. It was not that he had had no sexual experiences. He visited the Mada Street brothels occasionally when he could manage five rupees, but the brothels operated at night and he had to grope silently to perform the act for which he had paid. The women there detested the light. They demanded a huge extra, and he never had enough to pay to see them with lights on. He was in no position to marry because of his status, and the Naidu girl he was in love with was now beyond his reach, as her parents were able to find her an employed bridegroom.

He first tried his chances with a schoolteacher who lived alone with her mother. She had a pockmarked face and no boy gave her a second look. Ingress to her house was not a problem, for every Brahmin house was generally open to every other Brahmin in the street, on religious pretexts. The teacher contemptuously rejected his amorous advances when he told her, while her mother was away, what he thought she must surely be pining for. When he persisted, she brandished a broom and he had to run out of her house. He expected her to complain to his father, but the teacher chose to keep quiet.

His second choice was the shit-collector.

There was no flushing system in some of the houses of Sannidhi Street and human refuse was manually cleared every morning. The shit-collectors were, for the Brahmins, a strange community. They lived in feculent colonies outside the town amidst fat, shit-eating pigs and rusting bins of faeces. They spoke among themselves a language which was not Tamil. Their women, at least when they were young, were maddeningly attractive for some Brahmin boys. They were the succubi of their dreams.

She came through the door at the back of his house and did her revolting job without any fuss. She needed only water from the household. Narasimhan sat on the washing-stone beside the well and waited breathlessly for her arrival. They said she flourished on porcine flesh, but flourish she did. She was a lascivious woman who did not bother much to hide her charms, and as he poured water in her container, he ogled at her huge endowments. She was the only other female he could approach overtly for sexual purposes. He thought, we pay her a laughable sum of three rupees a month, and I shall offer her eight rupees for five minutes. The smell may be shitty, but at least I will be able to see what she has. He was tragically wrong.

The pencil-like Brahmin had initially amused her but later his bold stares became increasingly irritating. She said to him one day, 'Ai, Iyer, you have a wandering eye. If my husband sees you staring at me like this, he will gouge your eyes out.'

'Why should he know?'

That day she left without replying, but he was there every day without fail to pour water for her and make lewd remarks. One day to his delight she appeared pliant. Narasimhan said they could go to a lumber-room in the backyard of his house and she readily agreed. When he came close to her she kneed him in the groin, slammed a handful of turd on his face and howled for help, though it was he who now needed helping. Narasimhan's father came running and saw the state his son was in. He begged the shit-collector to keep quiet, promising to pay her fifty rupees for her silence. Even in his agony, Narasimhan could not help thinking that the Mada Street whores had demanded just fifteen rupees to strip in the light. She went back without accepting the money the old man offered, but returned at the front door with her husband and a few others to abuse Narasimhan in a string of raw expletives which scandalised the neighbourhood women who had come to gawk. The entire street had a very good idea of what had happened within minutes.

When Narasimhan's father recovered from the shock, he told his son to say that he was trapped by the woman. Though it was true in a way, Narasimhan refused to say anything. His father's taunts had no apparent effect on him. After eating a good lunch served by his snivelling mother, he went to his room on the upper storey.

The posters, pink, red and green, appeared on the walls of the town that afternoon. They were the handiwork of the Periyar camp and they dwelt in some detail on the lustful nature of even wispy Brahmin boys. They rubbed salt in the Brahmin wounds by highlighting the fact that the boy in question was a prominent member of the Brahmins' Association. The district administration was alarmed. It was still discussing whether or not to arrest Narasimhan when the news came that he had committed suicide by hanging himself.

The shit-collector had not expected Narasimhan to kill himself and she followed his funeral bier, wailing loudly. The Brahmin Association was so ashamed that it did not even pass a resolution condoling its member's death.

Kannan was shattered by the news of his friend's death. He had made fun of him many times, for he was sure that Narasimhan would not take the banter seriously. That Narasimhan had hidden deep within him a sensitive core that drove him to suicide surprised him and he cursed himself for not being of any help to his friend. He knew about Narasimhan's forays into Mada Street. What he did not know was that his friend died because he obsessively wished to see a woman naked. Uma, who was Narasimhan's neighbour, had only a warped version of the incident and she was told that both were caught *in flagrante delicto* and that the shit-collector spread the canard of Narasimhan trying to seduce her to extract money. She detested Narasimhan but not to the extent of wishing him dead. She felt sorry for him but his death troubled her for the wrong reasons. He was Kannan's good friend and it was possible, just possible, that they were doing such things together, though not necessarily with the same woman.

Thirteen

Dear Kannan,

My mistake was that I thought that, for the purpose of passing away, the place where I was born would be better than the ramshackle Kokkirakulam house. This place I find now is too spruce to die in. My son Achutan does not agree and I am in no position to make another move without help, my sugar count having shot moonward. Will I be asking too much, if I ask you to come here at your leisure so that I could summon up in your company my booksy auld lang syne? Bring your commie cousin along, if he is still a commie.

Tirumalai, I am sure must be very fit. Conservatives usually have long lives. God having sent them down is probably in no great hurry to call them back.

He, I am afraid, is in a tearing hurry in my case.

With affection,
Gopala Pillai

Kannan gave the letter to his father, who said, 'The rogue hasn't changed at all. But you must go and meet him before his departure.'

'How do you like this place?'

'It is like you. Tidy and spartan.'

'Come on Kannan, I have no use for honeyed words. Try them on Uma,' said Rosa. Her face was glowing with pride. It was difficult for her to move – she was heavy with the child – still, she insisted on showing Kannan round the new clinic they had opened near their house. Nambi was away on his rounds. There was about her a tranquility that pleased Kannan. Expectant mothers, even Marxist mothers, are essentially the same, he thought.

'How is she?'

'How is who?'

'You know who I am referring to. She came here the other day with Radha. She is a radiant girl and I must say you are lucky.'

'It is your turn now for honeyed words. I hardly meet her nowadays. She is unhappy with me for being so lazy, and what is worse, for being non-IAS material. This fellow Nambi is taking his time.'

'Should be here any moment. Anything special?'

'Yes, I am taking him to Kayamkulam.'

They could hear the roar of his motorbike and presently Nambi appeared at the door, his clothes covered in mud. He brightened when he saw Kannan.

'I was in fact thinking of you. There has been no news from Bala after our Madurai meeting. Muthu and you are irritatingly silent.'

'I have come here for another purpose, Nambi. Our Gopala Pillai is dying and he wants to see us.' He gave him Gopala Pillai's letter.

Nambi read the letter twice.

'I wish I had a mentor like him. You were a fool, Kannan. You shouldn't have deserted him. Rosa, read this letter.'

Nambi said, 'I don't mind coming with you, if Rosa does not have any objection.'

'I have already asked Radha to come and stay with Rosa till your return. She will come here straight from college.'

They took a circuitous route to Kayamkulam by Trivandrum as Nambi wanted to purchase some medical equipment for his clinic. The heat made everybody in the bus thirsty and crabbed, and mothers whacked howling children, causing them to howl louder.

'The driver must be a superman to drive this behemoth under these frying conditions. I am used to heat, but this is hell-fire,' said Kannan vigorously fanning himself with a magazine.

'The driver travels through hell-fire everyday. You have become soft, Kannan, which is perhaps what you are supposed to be.'

'If you equate being tough with being a quiet, uncomplaining flagellant, I prefer to be soft.'

'Let us not quarrel. We have a long way to go,' smilingly conceded Nambi.

As the bus journeyed southward, the sea-breeze made short work of the heat and the passengers snored in relief. Kannan felt drowsy, but Nambi nudged him in the ribs. 'Don't snooze. Read this.' It was Maurice Dobb's *Soviet Economic Development Since 1917*.

Kannan said in disgust, 'You're doing it intentionally. You thrust this soporiferous book under my nose and ask me not to snooze. How do you keep reading these books with such fervour?'

Nambi laughed. He said, 'As a neophyte Communist, you should learn about the road traversed by the pioneers. No, I was joking. Rosa has been asking me to read this book for days now. It was she who thrust it under my nose. She said it cleared many of her doubts. Rosa is now certain in her belief. I am Caravaggio's Thomas. I poke my finger deep into the wound to ascertain its genuineness.'

'Will you ever be cleared of your doubts?'

'I don't think I will. I admire thatha. He is firm in his faith. So is peria paati, even after drudging through the endless labyrinth of life. And Rosa. I am condemned to be a neuter. Once during an argument, Pakshi thatha came up with a wonderful quotation by Bishop Blongram or some such name. "All we have gained then by our unbelief / Is a life of doubt diversified by faith / For one of faith diversified by doubt." I think I have inherited this trait from my father and, maybe, my grandfather.'

'Your father was steady in his faith.'

'I am amazed you should say that. He was no doubt a member of the Communist Party for some time. He left the party at the right time to die – during the Quit India movement. Comrade Bala tells me that he knew that the movement would be crushed in no time, but his hatred for the British was so overpowering, he quarrelled with his comrades for not supporting Gandhi and resigned from the party.'

Kannan had heard that his uncle's hand was suspected in a case of arson in 1942 when an airport was set on fire near Coimbatore.

'Was he really involved in the Sulur incident?'

'I don't know. What is certain is that he was there when the airport was burning. His was one of the charred bodies found when the fire was doused. There was no doubt he was one of the leaders, but it is not clear how he could have been involved in such an insane act. Comrade Bala says he could have gone there to persuade the arsonists, but that sounds far-fetched. Those were tense years and one could have temporarily lost one's capacity to think logically.'

'I don't remember *periamma.*'

'I can't remember her either. She was a timid woman. There is a photograph of her standing next to my father. You must have seen it in Nanguneri. It was taken when she was very young. To me, she looks seedy in that rather smudgy photograph and I am not prepared to believe that she could be my mother. After the Sulur incident, she willed her death and simply faded away. Peria paati, I understand, tried to be very supportive, but she had to tackle Andal paati too, who went berserk when she came to know of my father's death.'

'I know the story of Andal paati. Veda paati has told me. Your thatha was another mysterious person.'

'I don't want to discuss him at all. I rarely feel bitter about anyone but he is an exception. He was, maybe he is, a heartless, selfish wanderer. How anyone could run away from Ponna paati is beyond me, but he did exactly that, deserting his infant son. If anything charitable could be said of him it is that he took our religious mumbo-jumbo a bit too seriously and went on a voyage to discover his soul. Perhaps he is still discovering it. Let us wish him success in his pursuit, if he is still alive, though I doubt it.'

Nambi continued, 'Ponna paati was the convenient repository my progenitors used to deposit their earthly loads on, when they chose to die or desert. She was of course a rare woman and I don't say this lightly. I have never heard her blaming anybody. If religion sustains such persons, religion has much to commend it. Rosa does not agree. She quotes the opium bit of Marx. Marx may be right, but his world too, if it comes about, will do well to have such women. Ponna paati told me, when I was a believing boy, that a curse was hovering over our family. I should say my side of the family. Though I don't believe in curses, I am sure there is something genetically wrong with that side.'

'Nonsense. It is your distress speaking, not your common sense. We both have come from the same genetic soup.'

'You mean there is nothing odd about you?'

'Now you are the old Nambi.' The harsh brown of the Tamil country was swiftly giving way to soothing green. The bus was entering Kerala.

'I have been wanting to ask you another thing. The present infatuation. How did it come about? You were surely not a godless goon to begin with.'

'Atheism comes first only in dictionaries. Everybody, at least here in our country, begins his thinking life with God.

Someone said we must believe before we can doubt. I did not attend a theological seminiary like Stalin did when he was young, but I was a pious boy. Hearing from Ponna paati the story of Dhruva, the little prince who undertook fierce penance that made Lord Narayana grant him the boon that he would shine permanently in the firmament as the pole star, I wanted to run away to a forest to do a similar penance. Paati had to use all her persuasive skills to stop me. I was that religious. Why, you used to make fun of my thick tiruman.'

'Yes,' Kannan said. 'We used to call you the temple elephant for the broad streaks on your forehead.'

'The change came so imperceptibly, it even surprised me. I used to go to Tirupati every year with Pakshi thatha for the ritual tonsure. Suddenly when I was fourteen or fifteen, I refused to accompany him. By that time I was perhaps intelligent enough to discern, or filled with arrogance, to presume that the talk of God granting your wish for offering him what you consider valuable is just waffle. I told thatha to his irritation, that I would very much like to keep my long hair and I was not interested in offering it to God.'

'You haven't still told me about how you got to be a red.'

'Probably I again sort of inherited it. When I learnt that my father was in the Communist Party, I wanted to know what it was that was worth dying for. His name, I need not tell you, is rarely mentioned in our family circles. Nobody told me then that he didn't die a Communist. By the time I came to know of it, it was too late. As your father would say, the poison had already spread.'

'And as he would again say, you have managed to spread some of it to me.'

Achutan was dry and distant. He was even reluctant to receive them.

'He wrote me a letter asking us to visit him. We are not fortunate,' said Kannan politely.

'That was his favourite pastime during his last days. He wrote reams of letters to all he could think of. You must be one of them.'

You are lying, Kannan thought. You don't want me to preserve my dignity intact. I am not one of 'all.' At least not to Gopala Pillai.

Kannan and Nambi stood silently, leaning against the wrought-iron gate of Gopala Pillai's neat house for a few minutes. Women bustled about inside on obsequial errands and the cold Achutan stood opposite the duo, his hands folded across his bare chest, unspeaking and resenting their presence. Nambi said, 'We have to return immediately. Accept our condolences.' Achutan was in no mood to speak at all. He simply nodded and walked away from them.

Kannan quivering with fury exclaimed, 'What an asshole! I can't understand the cause of his hostility. We haven't come here to demand a share of his father's property.'

'Perhaps he resents that you once shared his father's affection.'

'This is curious. He must be at least twenty years older than I am and this is the first time I have seen his face. He is a top man in one of those business machine companies. The least he could be is correct and civilised in his behaviour.'

'I have met him once earlier.'

'What? How is that possible?'

'Your father asked me once, when you were in Madras, to accompany Narasimhan to Gopala Pillai's house. Perhaps your father had been promised by him that he would find a position for your friend. When we went there, this fellow was with Gopala Pillai and it seemed that Pillai was to recommend Narasimhan to Achutan for a job in his company. He was even more hostile then than he has been today and he did not make any effort to conceal his contempt for the circus his father has managed to collect around him.'

'How interesting! Narasimhan didn't say a word about it.'

'Nothing came of it except that your friend was made to feel like a gnat being trampled upon by an elephant. Achutan asked him first, in a bizarre accent probably put on to intimidate Narasimhan, to name the language spoken in Brazil. Your friend said, in all innocence, "Spanish". He snorted in disgust and asked, "What is loyalty?" to which Narasihman replied, "It is faithfulness". This fellow then delivered a lecture on the difference between loyalty and faithfulness and how he, the great corporate man, could not be expected to take a dimwit under his wings who did not know even that simple difference and could not name Brazil's language. That was the end of Narasihman's ambition to be a clerk in a foreign company.'

'Poor Narasimhan. Did you speak to Achutan?'

'He would not recognise escorts.'

'He was probably the reason Gopala Pillai hid himself in Tirunelveli as long as he could.'

'I wonder what Achutan will do with his father's books.'

'I am sure he is not going to ask us to take them away. What is the use of talking about them? I know them so well, the very thought is depressing,' said Kannan.

Suddenly they heard crackers going off and he remembered. That was the first time since his childhood that he had forgotten a cricket match. He dragged Nambi along and almost ran to the nearest shop.

'Do you have a radio?'

'This is a medical shop.'

'I mean, what is the score?'

'I am a football fan and I don't follow cricket. Try the fruit shop round the corner.'

The fruit shop had a jubilant crowd clustering around a radio.

'What is the score?'

'Don't you know? India has won. Abid Ali has just hit the winning stroke.'

Kannan's eyes filled with tears. Ten years ago he was with Gopala Pillai when India won its first game against the MCC. But that was in India and against a weak team; this was in England and against the best team England could field.

'He died a day too early.'

'Maybe his spirit made a stopover at the Oval. The god of death could be cricket-crazy.'

Fourteen

THE BIG RALLY SO GRANDLY PLANNED BY Muthu and Kannan did not come off. The chief minister had changed his mind and decided to postpone his visit to Tirunelveli. In any case, the duo found it hard to persuade their colleagues of the necessity of such unity between the teachers and the students. The D.D.T. College Teachers' Association had only a few short, intermittent sessions of wakefulness after its success in the jacket-struggle. It had to be nudged awake every time by Muthu and Kannan. The other teachers were not interested, just as they were not much interested in teaching. They were busy commuting the dues they would receive from the government or were dreaming about the hefty profits they could make through their numerous real-estate deals. Their implacable hostility towards the students was barely concealed when they were in their common rooms, though they sang a different tune in the classes and at student gatherings. What they intensely wanted to conceal was their inability to teach. The good students, however, weighed their teachers accurately and rejected many of them as derisory. It was thus difficult for Muthu and Kannan to bring them together on a common platform.

Though the students could still be plastic and were persuaded to speak for their teachers in spite of their contempt for many of them, the teachers were rigid and full of themselves and they did not deign to speak for their students.

Indira Gandhi solved the problem for them. The Indian army's advance into East Pakistan was too momentous even for the cynical teachers of the D.D.T. College to ignore. Even Chandran attended the joint meeting organised by the teachers and the student leaders.

Muthu began by promising to trample Pakistan underfoot and went on to condemn the US for ordering her Seventh Fleet to the Bay of Bengal. He thundered, 'Down with US imperialism and their lackeys in the West, the butchers of Vietnam, the bedfellows of dictators.'

Chandran said, 'Don't go overboard. Our war is against Pakistan and not the United States.'

'We don't want war, but if the US desires war, we are ready.'

'In Tirunelveli?' murmured Chandran.

The draft resolution read: 'We the teachers and students of the Dhanapakkiamammal, Draupatiammal and Tayammal College, Tirunelveli, Tamil Nadu, strongly condemn the genocide committed by the barbarians of Pakistan in Bangladesh and welcome the Indian army's march of liberation. We also strongly condemn the nefarious designs of the imperialist forces headed by the US in unashamedly supporting dictators and for their act of aggression in sending the Seventh Fleet to the Bay of Bengal. We are prepared to shed our last drop of blood in defence of our Motherland.'

Chandran said, 'I suggest a change. We must not use the word "condemn" against the US. WE are not at war with them. We could say "deplore" instead. We could also do without any reference to "imperialist forces".'

Somebody asked the English teacher, 'Are "condemn" and "deplore" not identical?' The teacher was nebulous himself and he promised to look them up in the dictionary.

Muthu said, 'I see no reason why we should be solicitous towards the US when they don't respect us, the biggest democracy in the world. Let us put the resolution to vote.' Muthu's resolution received overwhelming support and it was promptly telegraphed to the president and the prime minister.

The balloon of patriotic fervour came down quickly once the war was over, but the students and teachers came together for another cause.

Professor Rengarajan looked forward to his retirement. He had been teaching chemistry in a Palayamkottai college for more than thirty-five years and was now disgusted with it. His wife had left him years ago and although nobody was sure why, it was rumoured that the Professor went limp at untimely moments, vexing his wife. After her desertion he lived with his brother, who was a postal clerk, and his wife who was a very presentable woman. He was quite successful at teaching physical chemistry and he followed a system which he did not change at all in the thirty-five years of his service. He made lists of the Madras University questions on physical chemistry every year for the preceding ten years of the degree examinations, and dictated the answers to his students. He asked them to memorise these and reproduce them when the old questions were repeated, which usually meant all the questions in the paper. His logic, which was unassailable, was that no person who had been chosen by the university to set the question paper for physical chemistry was likely to be original, and further he was unlikely to be curious enough to look back beyond ten years of question papers. He was never proved wrong, except once when the university chose someone who was disappointingly original. Even then Rengarajan bullied the chief examiner into giving grace marks to the students on the ground that the questions were tough. He was naturally very popular with the students who were sorry that he was retiring.

Inspector Sudalai was also retiring and he was not sorry. He had stashed away a tidy sum from what he had received as bribes and through extortion. With that money he wanted to build a nice little temple for Ganapathi in his village. He had a very happy and prosperous family. His mountainous wife wore an unusually long gold chain that brushed the ground when she sat on a chair. His daughter was married to a deputy collector, who had got as dowry at least five kilograms of gold, and his elder son was a quiet civil engineer with sources of income other than his salary. His younger son was studying in Madurai for his commerce degree. It was this son who was responsible for his father being sent to prison.

He was a personable young man who liked to dress well. Every evening, whenever he was in Palayamkottai on holidays, he preened himself before a full-length mirror for an hour. He pomaded his hair, combed it and adjusted it carefully so that a quiff bounced stylishly on his forehead. He and his friends then promenaded the street adjacent to the Ramaswamy temple to assess the Brahmin girls, who gathered in groups to giggle at and comment on the passers-by. The girls themselves were secretly pleased that they attracted the attention of the youthful gang but their mothers were alarmed. They told their husbands that the strolling boys must be checked.

When Sudalai's son came to the street the next evening with his friends, one of the indignant parents approached him.

'Excuse me, I would like to have a word with you. There is a big ground just a few yards away. Please shift your operations there.'

The boy was rattled, but being the son of a police official he tried bluster. 'This is a public road and I have every right to walk on it and you have no right to stop us.'

'Don't talk too much. It is not good for your health. We all know why you come here in the evening. Our girls are not display pieces for you to admire.'

'Lock them inside your houses then. I am not going to change my route and I shall bring a few more friends tomorrow.'

'If you set foot on this street again we shall call the police. You can stroll inside the prison cell. No, that may not be possible, for they would break your legs.'

Sudalai's son went straight to his father who was enjoying his sundowner with a few of his friends at the police station and said, 'Appa, I have been threatened that my legs will be broken.'

'Who said that?'

'A few Brahmin priests at Ramaswamy street. They also told me that I would be put behind bars.'

'I will fuck their sisters. We shall see who goes behind bars.' He called four of his constables and ordered them to go with his son and bring the offending priests to the police station. One of the qualification requirements for constables in India is that they should not exactly brim over with intelligence, but the four chosen by Sudalai were dim-witted even by police standards. Working themselves into an ersatz fury, they rushed to the street with Sudalai's son.

Professor Rengarajan and his brother usually visited the temple for the evening puja in their ritual attire of veshti and *angavastram*. They were returning from the temple when they saw a few policemen pummelling their neighbour. The professor rushed to his neighbour's rescue and shouted, 'You can't do this. What right do you have to beat up an innocent man? I shall complain to the DIG of police.'

The constables did not know that the Brahmin in veshti and angavastram was a college teacher. They said, 'We will bugger you in front of your wife. Are you trying to teach us the law? We will take you to a better place where you can resume your teaching.'

The professor and his brother, who had not spoken a word, were not able to ward off the blows that fell on them. The constables tied their hands with their angavastrams and dragged them to the police station, beating them all the way.

Sudalai was in a drunken rage when his faithful constables brought in his unintended quarry.

'Ai, you lickers of bucket-cunts, you wanted my son to be put behind bars, didn't you? I will make you all eat shit in the lock-up tonight.'

The professor's lips were lacerated and bleeding profusely. He still managed to say, 'You are making a mistake. You don't know who I am.'

'Who are you? You might have come straight out of God's arse but this is my station. You have to lend your arse to my command here. If you want your girls to remain virgins, don't ask them to go on a parade. If they strut about in the streets, the boys will naturally sniff their scent.' His rage reached a crescendo. 'Is the street owned by your mother? Did she acquire it by peddling her cunt? Tell me, TELL ME,' he kicked the professor with his heavy boots. 'Shove them in the lock-up. I'll come back after dinner.'

The Deputy Inspector General of police was a student of Rengarajan. When Father Anthony Raj, the principal of his college, rang him up say that the professor was in the lock-up, he knew there could be trouble. Big trouble. He rang up his inspector at his house, but Sudalai was in his paramour's house. The DIG and his superintendent rushed to the police station and released the professor and his brother immediately.

'I am sorry, sir. There has been a terrible mistake,' said the DIG to his teacher.

Sudalai returned very late to his house and when he heard that his DIG had called him, he too smelt something wrong. He rang his police station and to his surprise found that his superior officers were waiting for him.

'I know you have reinforced concrete inside your head instead of brains but I never thought you would descend to this level and assault a professor. The students are only waiting for an opportunity like this,' said the DIG when he saw Sudalai trying unsteadily to salute him.

'I am sorry, sir. I shall touch his feet and seek his forgiveness.'

'His feet are swathed in thick bandages. You idiots have broken his legs. He is in no position to listen, even if you take your wife to wail in front of him. He must be under heavy sedation. Why did you pick him up? The fools here give me some stupid story.'

Sudalai said, 'They were engaged in a drunken brawl, sir. I had to arrest them and bring them here.'

'You are a shameless liar. You smell like a pot of toddy and you accuse that poor man of being drunk. Professor Rengarajan was my teacher and I know he doesn't even drink tea. You didn't know he was a professor, did you?'

'No, sir, I didn't. They looked like local priests, he and his brother.'

'You think priests can be assaulted without compunction? It is difficult to defend your action.'

His words were hollow. The unwritten covenant of the police was that the First Information Report filed in the police station was to be treated as God's truth. That report stated without mincing words that the Professor was drunk and he had to be arrested to maintain public order and that he injured himself while falling down the steps of the police station.

Uma was relieved that her green college bus came dot on time. She had her Shakespeare paper that day and she had been fully prepared for it. The bus did not cross the bridge. It was stopped by a mass of students.

'What has happened?'

'Our professor has been beaten up by the police. His injuries are serious and he may die any moment. We should all protest. It is the professor today and it may be you tomorrow.'

Some girls wanted to join the procession and some wanted to return home. No one was keen to go to the college. Uma decided to join the students. She was outraged that this could happen to a college teacher. She was also vaguely conscious that she might be able to meet Kannan during the day.

The affair between Kannan and Uma was going through a trough because of Kannan's disinclination to sit for the civil services. Uma had stopped pleading with him, but it distressed her that Kannan could be so asinine when it came to moving out of Tirunelveli. He was tethered to the place and made no attempt to free himself. Though she had fobbed her father off on the subject of her love, she was aware that he would not give his consent to her marrying a lowly college teacher in the backwaters of Tirunelveli. Sankaraman was still writing to her father and updating him on the increasing worthlessness of the Iyengar boy Uma had so unwisely chosen. She loved him dearly but her love for him had not reached the apogee which would impel her to give up everything and go with him. Radha, as always, was practical in her advice.

'I don't think this fellow has it in him to succeed in a competition. If you really love him, love him for what he is and not for what you want him to be. I think you started with that intention. Remember the letter that you gave me first? You forced me to read it. You gave the impression in that letter that you would love him for what he was. It was convenient for him to be under that impression. Now he is sulking that you have changed.'

'What would you have done if you had been me?'

'Honestly, I would not have chosen Kannan. Even if I had chosen him by mistake, I would not linger on like you. I would decide quickly.'

Kannan had no thoughts of Uma on that day. He was beside himself with fury when he heard about the assault. He and Muthu set about organising the teachers and students and they decided in consultation with the teachers and students of other colleges to converge on the collectorate.

Their basic demands were that the inspector be arrested on charges of criminal assault and that the government apologise publicly for the brutal treatment of the professor. For their part, the police issued a statement that the professor was arrested for drunken behaviour and his injuries were due to his tumbling down the steps of the police station, that the police had been exercising restraint in spite of grave provocation and that the inspector was being transferred temporarily in order to respect the sentiments of the students and teachers.

The district collector had himself been a teacher before he joined the civil services. He did not believe the police version, but he had also seen some very sozzled professors. When he met the students and teachers he was trying to be impartial, which did not satisfy the agitators.

'How do you say that the police version is a lie? It may be, but we can't jump to conclusions. I have ordered a magisterial enquiry and the report will be available in fifteen days. Be patient.'

Muthu was furious. 'We know your methods. You will defend your tribe, though they are criminals in uniform. The professor is a saintly person and it is monstrous to accuse him of rowdy behaviour under the influence of alcohol. There are at least two thousand students here who will swear on the names of their mothers that their professor does not even consume tea. On the other hand, the inspector who had brutally manhandled the professor is a confirmed alcoholic. We want his arrest. Otherwise the consequences will be serious.'

The collector said, 'Don't threaten me. I have seen many rabble-rousers like you. We can't dance to your tune.'

'We know. You will gladly dance however to the tune of your corrupt police. Let us move out. We won't get justice from such an anti-people administration.'

Events took a swift turn after the failure of negotiations. The students surrounded the collectorate and the police had to resort to firing to break the students' siege. Their tally was one killed and ten injured. The dead boy was not even a college student. He was a rag-picker who stood on a vantage point to see what was going on. Being a rag-picker he did not count and his death went almost unnoticed.

The collector understood that the inspector had to be arrested eventually as there was overwhelming evidence that the professor was as far away from alcohol as the police were from truth. As a blue-blooded administrator, trained by the ICS war-horses, he decided to teach the rebel teachers, who ought to have known better, a lesson they would not forget in a hurry. This time he called the local politicians for negotiations.

The Communists and the Congressmen were with the agitators. Bala was their spokesman and he said, 'The administration should bow to the inevitable. They should arrest the inspector for assault immediately. Any delay may lead to a further deterioration of law.'

'The arrest of a police officer is not that easy. It may lead to the revolt of the police. I have to tread cautiously. If the police are at fault so are the teachers who misguided the students. They too deserve punishment.'

The DMK who rode on the backs of students and teachers to power was now reluctant to antagonise the police and they jumped at the offer. 'Yes, the collector is correct. As Anna said, the teachers are like lighthouses. If lighthouses misguide, ships will run aground.'

'Arresting the teachers will trigger off another agitation. It is no solution at all and the teachers have every right to agitate if the police go on a mad rampage,' said Bala.

The collector said, 'I am not thinking in terms of arresting them. I will request the college management to suspend them for a few months. It will then be a local decision and local agitations could be handled firmly.'

'We shall never be a party to such a decision,' said Bala, but the collector had clinched the issue.

The news of his and Muthu's suspension came as a shock to Kannan. Tirumalai said, 'Chandran met me at the District Club. He was sorry about you, but he says you keep bad company.'

'He is a vengeful person, this friend of yours. Muthu is much better company than that rodent can ever hope to be.'

'Well, there is no accounting for taste. But if you keep calling your principal a rodent in public, I don't think you will ever enter the portals of your college.'

'I don't think I will ever want to, again.'

Kannan thought of Nambi. *He would have given me sound advice.* Uma did not get an opportunity to speak to Kannan at all on the day of the agitation. She saw him from a distance, leading a group of slogan-shouting teachers and even if she had gone closer, he would not have had time for a personal chat. It was Radha who told her the news of Kannan's suspension.

'Things look bad. It appears that the collector has taken the agitation as a personal insult and it is he who is behind this act.'

'I want to meet Kannan. Would you please tell him? There is no need for any camouflage now. If he agrees, I shall come to your house. You are right. I can't postpone things any longer. I am going back to Bombay next week.'

Fortunately for her, there was nobody in the house. Renganayaki and Tirumalai had gone to Nanguneri. Uma climbed up the stairs hurriedly and came crashing into Kannan's arms. She was in a flaming red sari and the ascent had left her cheeks flushed. She was still panting when Kannan kissed her full on the lips. She did not resist when his tongue dallied inside her mouth, searching and slowly picking up her tang and when his hands ran all over her, holding her breasts and exploring her. That was the day he saw her fully.

'May I?'

'You may not.'

Kannan did not want to force her. She was his and he was not in a hurry. He did not feel stymied and his excitement ebbed deliciously as Uma disengaged from him.

'I have nothing to give in return for your love, Uma,' said Kannan. He looked different without his glasses. His eyes were bulging orbs of permanent wonder. There were two red ridges under his eyes, the marks left by the glasses. She softly touched his eyelashes with her tongue which then travelled down to moisten the angry streaks.

'You are being silly. I wouldn't barter my love for you for anything you could give.'

'I am happy that you haven't changed. I will get my job back quickly. That is for certain. But I am not sure I want to go back to the college after what has happened.'

'You have decided to sit for the civil services, after all. Haven't you?'

'Should I Uma? Should I? I have a few other plans too.'

Uma's anger welled up along with her distress that he could be so impractical. She did not even ask him what his plans were. His unconcern for her feelings was now beyond tolerance.

'Who do you think you are? Are you under any illusion that the world is waiting with bated breath for your next intrepid act? You have been lucky so far. Had you been without a vocation like Narasimhan was, your ideas would have shrunk to nothing long ago. In any case, I am not prepared to wait.'

Her change of mood unnerved him. Why did I lie to her? I have no plans whatever and I am too lazy to sit for an examination. He persisted with his charade. 'Uma, listen to me. I haven't told you what my plans are.'

'Damn your plans. You are worthless, that is what you are. I don't want to see you again.' It was difficult for Uma to control her tears.

'Uma, please listen to me. You haven't heard me out.'

'What is the use?'

'I just wanted to tell you that I have applied for physics jobs elsewhere. If I get one, there is no need for me to write this examination.' His lies were contemptible even to him.

'You don't realise that you are unemployable. Your physics has rusted and there are hundreds of freshers in competition. Who are you trying to fool? You can't cloak your laziness from me by such ruses. I have had enough of you, Kannan. I am going back to Bombay. Goodbye.'

Radha too was angry with Kannan. She told him, 'You haven't an idea what you have lost. She would have been a fine influence in your life. The other influences are all unreal. When you start your search again – that will happen sooner than you imagine – you will realise how difficult it is to get a companion like Uma.'

She is right. It is difficult for me to get anybody as vivacious as Uma.

'I don't think I have lost her. Her anger is temporary and she will come back to me. Or if it satisfies you, I shall go back to her. Please tell her I have decided to sit for the civil services, if that will ease her anger.'

Radha said, 'She is not going to believe you. She knows you are a lost cause. Dream your red dreams now till reality wakes you up.'

Radha told Uma when she met her to bid her farewell, 'He was beastly, you deserved better. It is my loss, Uma. I would have been very happy to have you as my sister-in-law.'

'You have spoken too soon, Radha. You may still have me. I don't think I have given up Kannan. He will come to me. If I am available, I'll accept him.' She would have accepted him if he had come to the railway station to see her off. Even after the whistle had blown and the goodbyes had been said her eyes searched for him. He was nowhere to be seen.

Fifteen

THE POSTMARK WAS SMUDGY BUT THE handwriting was strangely familiar. It was addressed to Pakshi.

Dear Pakshi,

As I am alive, I address this letter to you in the hope that you are also alive. I broke the link sixty years ago and I know it will be a miracle if I am able to find the segment I had wantonly flung away and reforge it with what I have. My state is such that I have to believe in miracles. I am not going to ask about amma; she must have passed away long ago. She has remained with me all these years as I must have remained with her as long as she was alive. My son should be more than sixty now. Andal will be nearly eighty. I do not know who are now in the family. My blessings to them all. There is nothing much to write except that my wanderings ended long ago and I have been in Joshimath for the last thirty years.

I would have come without writing to you. I haven't because I want to be sure there is at least one person in the family who has known me, albeit years ago.

With my blessings once again,
Nammalwar

If Pakshi has passed away, this letter may be handed over to his progeny or mine, his brother's.

Nambi read the letter and returned it to Pakshi.

'Why has he surfaced after so many years?'

'You will have to ask him that, Nambi. I am happy that my brother has been found. He has made many wrong assumptions but fortunately for him at least one assumption, that I must be alive, has turned out to be right.'

'Have you informed peria paati?'

'No, I am not certain that Nammalwar will be able to come here. He must be eighty-five now. He may not be fit to undertake the journey. Amma may not believe us unless she is able to see him with whatever sight she possesses.'

'Have you written to your regained brother?'

'No, I am waiting for you. After all he is your thatha. You should write to him.'

'Why should I? He was a dead person to me a moment ago. He was the only dead person in the family whose very name repelled me. That it turns out he is alive hasn't made any difference.'

Pakshi touched his shoulders affectionately. 'For my sake Nambi, don't talk like this. It is unlike you. I have another idea. Why don't you visit him?'

'Thatha, I have just told you I can't even stand his name and you ask me to visit him. No, I am not going to visit him. You don't write to him either. He has made you wait for sixty years. Let him not imagine that the people he has left behind are eager to resume contact.'

Pakshi still had Nammalwar's letter announcing his renouncement. He was thinking of showing it to Nambi, but seeing his anger, changed his mind. He said, 'I won't do anything without consulting you.'

Rosa's reaction was similar to Pakshi's. 'I agree with your grandfather. It is unlike you. The old man obviously feels lonely. You must visit him.'

'Lonelier than my mother? Yet he deserted her, without any qualms. My father was an infant just like our Indu when that man ran away.'

'That does not make his loneliness less depressing. Are you an avenging angel handing out retribution? Where is your famous objectivity? He is old and he needs your help.'

'Rosa, he caused agony to four generations of our family. There is no indication even in this letter that he is sorry. I think of him as a monster without any emotion . . . still, as you say, I am no avenging angel. Well, I won't write him a letter then. I shall go and see him first. If I don't like what I see, I shall return quietly.'

It was his first trip north of Rishikesh. As a child he had come with Ponna, Pakshi and Veda to Haridwar and Rishikesh. Their original plan had been to visit the holy shrine of Badrinath, but news of massive landslides on the way deterred them. There were no buses to Badrinath in those days. Pilgrims went up to Badrinath on foot or on horseback, along a narrow bridle path. Had we climbed north, braving the landslides, we might have run into him, he thought.

The pilgrims were absent, probably scared off by the remnants of winter and the war with Pakistan. The shrine of Badrinath was not yet open for the summer. Joshimath was serene and glowing in the spring sun, and the soaring, white-capped mountains surrounding the village were awesome. Snowscape was new to Nambi. It made him think of the voyage after death. Hindu souls travel south when they shed their human frames and I don't know why, he thought. Our mountains in the south are human, and their heavy foliage entwines us with life. If I am given a choice after death I would travel north. To these mountains. They are inhumanely divine. Or devil-driven. It is no wonder he is ensconced in this place.

Everyone seemed to know the Vaishnav Baba in Joshimath. 'He writes all our petitions,' said an old man who gave Nambi directions to the Baba's ashram.

The Baba had a clean-shaven head and his face, unravaged by age, glinted with health. Thick streaks of tiruman covered his forehead. He saw Nambi coming and greeted him with a vigorous tremor-free voice, 'You must be Madhurakavi's son. How is he? Haven't you brought him?'

Nambi had rehearsed a number of times what he would do when he met his grandfather. He was determined not to reveal his identity in a hurry. He wanted to weigh him up and then tell him who he was. He was also expecting an infirm old man, already on his way uphill. This old man was still strolling in the plains of life. Nambi was disappointed. I forgot that he could easily see himself in me.

'My father died thirty years ago, probably when you were travelling to this place. I never saw him. I have no mother either. You still have one.'

Baba's eyes clouded. 'Narayana, Narayana,' he said in a low voice. 'Is Pakshi there?'

'Yes, but Andal is not. You haven't left yesterday and I can't compress sixty years in a few bits of news.'

'I agree. It was foolish of me to imagine that the others would still be drudging as I am drudging.'

'Why this sudden recovery from amnesia? Ageing ascetics are supposed to move away from their earthly vestiges. Here you are, coming back to them.'

'I don't know. For the last five years, I have been driven by this urge. I thought my spiritual rigour would be proof against it. The urge has finally won. Today is *amavasya*. I shall make arrangements for *tarpanam*. This is a very sacred place and your father and mother will be pleased that their son offers his libations here.'

Nambi looked at him coldly. 'I am a non-believer. I don't perform tarpanam. Tirumalai chithappa, your brother's son, performs it for my sake, though he has his parents living. If I am not mistaken he offers libations to you too.'

The old man asked him, 'Are you married?'

'Yes. My wife has given me a daughter just a few months ago. I have no intention of leaving them.'

His barbs did not bother him. He laughed and said, 'I am not asking you to leave them. On the other hand, I would like to spend some time with them. I am sure you will be with me for at least a few days.'

'It was primarily fear,' said Nammalwar to his grandson, when they were sitting before the log fire after a frugal dinner. 'Yes, it was fear that drove me away. I was gripped by it, though the trial was over and there was not much chance of anyone telling the police of my involvement. I knew it was irrational, but I felt a branded man. Strangely, I was also angry that I had not been given due recognition by the British when I was not named as one of the accused. Amma came to my rescue. She wanted me to marry again. I had no intention of sleeping with another woman after the death of Lakshmi – your paati. I could have explained it to amma coolly and she would have understood. She has always been a sensible woman. But I didn't want to. She gave me an opportunity to run away and I took it.'

'Even though you saddled the poor woman with the responsibility of bringing up what you had brought forth.'

'I stamped Laskhmi's child out of my memory. Even now, I have no love for him.'

'Why? Is he responsible for your cowardice?'

'No I am fundamentally irresponsible, I think. Like all irresponsible persons, I had no scruples about transferring my burden to other shoulders.'

'I am the offspring of that poor, transferred burden. What are your feelings for me?'

'You are not a burden any more. I can love you without feeling responsible for you. No, that is not true. Grandsons are in a separate league. I would have loved you as an infant and as a snotty boy and I love you now.'

'And I must thank you for that,' said Nambi bitterly. 'What about your spiritual quest? I always had a suspicion that was only a sham.'

'No, it may have been induced by fear, but that does not make it a sham. Come on Nambi, I have spent sixty years on this path. One can't keep up a hoax for that long.'

Nambi did not speak. In spite of his hatred, he could not help thinking that his grandfather had suffered too. He is no fake. He could have led a dissipated existence as a lazy landlord. That he chose not to is sufficient proof. I am getting sentimental, he thought. Thatha might be genuine, but that did not make the sufferings he has caused to others any less severe. My father would not have died had this man been there to influence him. No, that is incorrect. I am not thinking like a Marxist.

Nammalwar said, 'Sex had never been a major problem for me. That yearning I lost when your grandmother died. The other normal human cravings bedevilled me for some time. Like the craving for my family and the craving for my roots. I thought I would return to the family after a few years of wandering, but asceticism, like smoking, is an addiction. After a short initial period of dubiety I became one of those natural ascetics – at least that was how I assessed myself. The shackles that impeded my progress along the path I had chosen were not problems at all. I could discard them without much effort.'

'How am I here, then?'

'Perhaps I am now on the path of de-addiction. I do not know, but I did not give up that easily. I have been fighting these feelings for more than ten years. There were a few people who came to Badrinath from Tirunelveli. I could have enquired about our family with them. I didn't. Finally, when it was no longer possible to stamp out the imperishable, I had to concede defeat and write to Pakshi.'

'We had been happy without the knowledge of your existence.'

'Does amma know?' Nammalwar asked, without looking at Nambi.

'She now lives in a different world where such knowledge has no relevance. You are perhaps always there with her in that world. There was a time – I was young then – when not a day went by without her talking about you. I used to tell her that I did not want any more of her Nammalwar stories, but no, she wouldn't stop.'

Nambi continued, 'I am curious to know. You once thought you were fighting for the liberation of our country. You lost that craving too. Didn't you?'

'Yes. I did. I was busy liberating my inner space. No, I am being too grandiose. I had learnt to take British rule as one of the acts of God, beyond justice, immutable. You might say it was a very convenient attitude to assume and you might be right.'

'Even Gandhi passed you by?'

'I read somewhere Gandhi quoting from the First Epistle of Paul the Apostle to the Corinthians: "And now abideth faith, hope, charity, these three; but the greatest of these is charity." I can say with humility that all these sixty years I have been working among the exploited and the poor, in the regency hills of Andhra, in Orissa, in Chittagong, in Manipur and here. I thought god had commanded that I was best suited for this rather than for revolutionary acts. Don't forget, Gandhi spent most of his years in India on what he called constructive activities.'

'It was ironic that your charity did not extend to your family.'

'I never thought they were in need of my charity. Indeed, I am in need of your charity now.'

Nammalwar did not accompany Nambi. He wanted to visit the holy places in the western part of India – Pushkar, Nathdwara, Dwaraka, Pandaripur and Udupi.

'I should be in Nanguneri within six months. Amma, I am sure, will still be there to recognise me.'

'She will be. Only, you must not change your mind. If you do, please write to us and spare us the agony of suspense.'

Ponna felt the familiar hand of her great-grandson on her head. He had been missing for a number of days.

'Peria paati, I have some news for you. I met your elder son, my thatha.'

Am I alive? Where did he meet him?

After much effort, she said, 'Andal. Did you meet Andal too?'

Nambi touched her cheek. His hands were warm and comfortable. 'I don't lie, peria paati. I did meet him.'

She did not have the energy to reply. She held his hand lightly until she fell asleep. Pakshi said, 'Till a few days ago, we had problems convincing her that Nammalwar was dead. Now we will have problems convincing her that he is alive. I don't think his presence is going to make a difference.'

Pakshi and Veda came with Nambi to his village to see little Indu. Pakshi's anger had evaporated long ago and he spent his moments in Nambi's house playing with the child.

He said, 'Radha is eighteen and this is the first child in the family after her. She is the fifth in the link that started with my mother. You should show her to Ponna paati. She may even recognise her great-great-grandchild.'

After they had left, Rosa said, 'Your grandfather is a captivating gentleman.'

'Yes, I wish I could say the same about the other grandfather who is about to make his re-appearance.'

'You are incorrigibly prejudiced, Nambi. This grandfather apparently worships the other one. He has to be good.'

'I realise now that he had not asked me anything about my dead father.'

'He doesn't know him at all. What do you expect him to ask you?'

'He should have asked at the very least how he died.'

'It will be too painful even for an ascetic to learn the details of his son's death, thirty years after it has happened, from his grandson whom he meets for the first time. In any case, he is going to be with you again.'

'That is what worries me. I don't think I can live under the same roof as him without losing my sanity. I will suggest that he lives with his brother.'

'You are getting paranoid. These things can be smoothed out in no time. I can hardly wait to see him.'

She was about to enter the kitchen but turned back and said, 'Oh, I have forgotten. Muthu and Kannan are bringing a Malayali comrade, Mukundan Menon, for a discussion tomorrow. He is from the M-L group.'

'I am not keen on any discussion. Come on Rosa, I have just returned from Joshimath filled with philosophy up to my nose, and I can do without another heavy dose of the bilge we are familiar with. Why is he coming? Is he on a proselytising mission? Or a fund-raising one?'

'I really don't know, Nambi. I would like to hear him.'

'You have heard him one hundred times. There will be nothing new.'

'Let me hear that from him,' said Rosa and disappeared into the kitchen.

Sixteen

MUTHU HAD A BIG FAMILY TO PROVIDE FOR and the suspension meant that his income would be halved. Though Nambi and Kannan promised financial help, it came as a shock to him that the collector could thwack them with contemptuous ease, just because he found them talking beyond their station. The political party Muthu supported made conventional noises about the suppression of academics, but beyond that they did nothing. They told him privately that the suspensions would be revoked when the college reopened after the vacations. Bala had a party congress coming in Madurai and he was not easily approachable.

Mukundan Menon brushed aside the problems of Muthu as of no consequence. He said that it was Muthu's petty-bourgeois milieu that made him expect that the ruling classes would treat him with kid gloves. 'You must write a letter of thanks to the collector for not deigning to order your dismissal. It is his fiefdom. You are one of his appointive minions, he can dispose of you with a wave of his hand.'

'I am not his appointive minion. Even if I am, it does not mean that I should stop fighting.'

'There are better things to fight for,' said Mukundan.

'This doctor couple we are meeting, are they serious or just curious?' asked Mukundan after a pause.

'They are serious. Nambi is the most clear-headed person I have come across. Rosa is the daughter of an old Communist and though she is not a member she subscribes to the views of our party. In any case they are bound to offer financial help.'

The intelligence report which was sent to the police headquarters in Madras stated:

Mukundan Menon, a member of the CPI(M-L), who entered Tamilnadu through Punalur for the purpose of recruiting cadres for his party and to collect funds for party activities in Kerala, had many secret meetings with his party cadres and its sympathisers in Tirunelveli District.

It went on to give at length the descriptions of persons who attended the meetings. Of the Nambi family, Muthu and Kannan, it said:

Mukundan had an important meeting at the clinic of a doctor couple in Tirukurunkudi. Our source says that the couple, who are popular with the rural people for treating them freely or at a nominal fee, are known reds. The husband, Nambi, who belongs to a well-known landlord family of Nanguneri, is a Brahmin. His father was a well-known Communist of the pre-independence days. His wife, Rosa, is a lame Harijan and her father too was a member of the undivided Communist Party. It is understood that Nambi recently visited Delhi (or Calcutta—our source is not certain) probably to receive orders from the party high command. The couple may join the CPI(M-L) soon. Muthu and Kannan, the other two who attended the meeting, are suspended college lecturers. Muthu is from a poor family of weavers from Ambasamudram and Kannan, who is

Dr Nambi's cousin, is the son of a rich lawyer of Tirunelveli who supports Rajaji's Swatantra Party. They do not appear to be as ideologically committed as the doctor couple and their flirtations with the M-L elements might be because they are sore about their suspensions.

It is suggested that the movements of the doctor couple be closely watched and the Kerala police informed, if the need arises.

Nambi was disgusted with what he had read. He was reading a magazine given to him by Mukundan Menon. 'Listen to this: "Beginning from the Champaran peasant struggle, the Gandhian leadership representing the upper stratum of the bourgeoisie and the feudal class, with its ideology of ahimsa, satyagraha, passive resistance and *charkha*, sought to tailor the national movement to serve the interests of the British imperialist rule and its feudal lackeys." If this is their assessment of Gandhi's contribution to our national liberation struggle, I don't want to have any truck with them.'

Rosa said, 'I agree, but this was more or less the Communists' assessment of Gandhi until as late as 1951. It was only in the late fifties that the Communists started singing a different tune. I don't blame them. Gandhi is unique. It is impossible to assess him with Marxist tools.'

'Their idea of armed struggle sounds very amateurish. I was talking to thatha about his role in the 1911 incident. He said that the Bharata Mata Association's plans to sabotage the might of British imperialism were puerile and they didn't stand a ghost of a chance. It is uncanny that I return and read this. These fellows have even less chance of success against the Indian army. They have grossly underestimated the power of the state.'

'They are desperate, Nambi. They have lost patience.'

'That does not mean that they should ask thousands of young men to commit suicide. Their other slogan is "China's chairman is our chairman." How do they expect the Indian people to shout such slogans? It is like "God save the King" of the British days.'

Rosa said, 'Enough of politics. Switch off the light, I am sleepy.'

It was a schoolboy's dream. The famous falls of Courtallam took alluring female forms and jiggled their chalk-white foamy breasts before him. Nambi could not comprehend it. Though he had not visited the place for years, he loved Courtallam and its falls were sacred to him. In his dream they were strumpets, slowly lifting their saris and inviting him to see what they had between their legs.

'This is crazy, Rosa. I always had a dreamless sleep in the past. I have no recollections of wet dreams either.'

'That was probably because you had your dreams during the day. Now you have become staid and practical and have lost your capacity to daydream. No wonder your nights have been taken over.'

'I still dream during the day and they have hardly anything to do with sex. These have audacious craving women. Come on, Rosa, there must be something wrong with you.'

Rosa laughed. Her breasts were now swollen with milk. 'It must be something to do with your recent visit to the Himalayas. Your system is out of balance. If I were you I would visit Courtallam and see for myself the strumpets of my dreams.'

'That is a good idea. We could return in a day.'

'I can't come with you. I am still feeding Indu. Your freedom will be restricted by our presence.'

It was the gentle Isaac who had taken Nambi and four other boys on an unforgettable excursion to Courtallam. He had told them how the river-irrigated system of Tirunelveli was dependent on a continuous flow of water from the hills, and how the forests that formerly clothed the hill had protected the heads of many streams. The destruction of much of the forest to make way for coffee plantations had almost stopped the flow. He had told them how Dr Wight, a maverick botanist, collected as many as 1,200 species of flowering plants from a small stretch in the Courtallam hills. They had visited the five falls and climbed up a steep hill to bathe under the Shenbaga falls. These memories remained with Nambi, who was Isaac's favourite. His teacher's longing looks were ignored by him and his diffident advances rudely brushed aside, but Isaac never felt insulted. He always had special morsels of information for Nambi, which he kept feeding to his student until Nambi left the school.

The Courtallam of his childhood had disappeared. Now it was a tinsel touristy sham. Buses disgorged frenzied tourists in thousands, who scurried towards the falls to stand under the thundering water and display their ugliness. The lovely Shiva temple which was at least twelve hundred years old was smothered under gargantuan hoardings promoting soaps, condoms and undergarments. The hill was defaced with lurid advertisements. As a child I never noticed human intrusion, Nambi thought. The intrusion now, of everyone trampling on everyone else's privacy, is unbearable. In the silhouette of cascading water even the female forms are disappointing. The sirens of my dreams are ragged now.

His decision to visit Punalur was impulsive. He felt let down by Courtallam and its falls and he thought of Punalur, where the floundering friends of his grandfather gathered sixty years ago to hold grandiose discussions on armed insurrection. The house of Venkateswara Iyer who had committed suicide to escape police torture must surely be there. I must find someone who can direct me to that house. He took a bus from Courtallam to Shenkottah and another one to Punalur from there.

The intelligence men of the Tamil Nadu police were normally languorous. They often missed their quarry and ended up filing fake reports. It was Nambi's bad luck that the man assigned to him was a conscientious official who followed him faithfully and fully awake. When he had reached Punalur in the same bus Nambi had boarded, he rushed to the police station and made a few telephone calls to Trivandrum after arguing for forty minutes with the inspector of the station who needed a great deal of persuasion before he was convinced that a dangerous Communist of the M-L variety had entered his town.

Nobody knew who Venkateswara Iyer was, let alone the location of his house. They had no idea of what had happened in that town in the early years of the century. Nambi felt frustrated. The amateur conspirators deserved better from the people for whose independence they had worked. That they had been swatted by the British with ridiculous ease was not in doubt but this was no reason to forget them. He walked slowly to the bus stand.

The police crowded around his seat and began beating him with sticks. They did not allow him to speak and they dragged him out of the bus.

'He appears to be an educated man. Why is he being beaten up by the police?' a passenger asked his neighbour.

'Do the police need a cause to beat you up? They say this person is a hard-core Naxalite.'

'That is possible. He looks intelligent and only such people end up as Naxalites. Will he be let off alive?'

'That depends on the strength of his wife's prayer, or his mother's, if he is not married. The present CPI chief minister, though a Communist himself, has declared war on the Naxalites. He has given the police a free hand to deal with them.'

The interrogation centre had been in a rented house in a suburb of Trivandrum before it was shifted to an upper-class residential area, Shashthamangalam, to lend dignity to its interrogators. If the subject of interrogation was in possession of his senses when he arrived there, which happened only in rare cases, he would be lulled into a sense of security by the verdant surroundings and by the display-board in front, which said in bold letters, 'Police Research Centre, Trivandrum'. Nambi was hardly conscious when he arrived there.

The heavy boot came down on his face knocking off two of his teeth. The pain was excruciating but even more unbearable was the stomach-churning smell of stale dung sticking to the boot. Nambi retched up a ruddy gunk, spattering the trousers of the deputy superintendent with blood and saliva.

'Are you spitting at me, you cunt-licking bastard? I shall cut off your cute little Brahmin cock and feed it to the dogs.' The DSP lifted him by his hair and a constable pushed with vehemence a thick stick up between Nambi's legs.

'You are spitting at me? Take this.' A vile cud of betel leaves, nuts and tobacco landed on his face and started dribbling down his swollen cheeks. He was again pushed down and a burly constable sat on him, banging Nambi's head against the floor.

'Stop. Do you want to kill him today? I am sure Brahma has written a few more days for him. Hey, you diseased son of a whore's cunt, why were you roaming in Punalur?'

'I keep telling you I came there to look at a patriot's house who was known to my grandfather but you don't believe me,' said Nambi with difficulty.

'Who do you try to fool? You have a hundred girls to fuck in your place but you come alone to Punalur, looking for fresh cunts. Tell this to your grandfather. I am a police officer with years of experience and I have broken bastards one hundred times tougher than you. Tell me the truth, you son of a eunuch, if you want your life. Is there any hideout there?'

'Hideout? What hideout? I don't know any hideout. I am a doctor and I was on vacation. You have picked me up illegally and brought me here. You are going to pay for . . .'

This time the kick almost decapitated him.

'Don't teach me the law, you cock-sucking son of a bitch. You may be a doctor but no doctor is going to set the bones we are going to break. Cooperate with us, we will let you live. Otherwise tomorrow shall be the second day of your death.'

'I am cooperating with you. How can I tell you what I do not know?'

'Do you know Mukundan Menon?'

'I don't know him personally. He came to my village about a month ago and we had a political discussion. I haven't seen him again.'

'What instructions did he give you during your fucking discussions? Did he ask you to spread your lame wife's thighs for him?'

'There were no instructions. He is not my master.'

'Did he not speak about arms? I am sure you came to Punalur for clinching an arms deal. Come clean, you will return safe to your wife who must be getting randy now for your rotten cock.'

'I have nothing more to say. I don't know anything about arms.'

'He thinks he is MGR. You are a dog and your death will be worse than that of a dog.'

A constable smeared a thin round ruler with red chilli powder and another pulled down Nambi's trousers and underwear and shoved the ruler up his rectum. He screamed till he came to terms with pain. It enveloped him slowly and finally blessed him with a welcome loss of consciousness.

Rosa thought initially that her husband was so taken with the charms of the resort that he had decided to spend a few more days there. Anxiety took four days to overpower her; she rushed to Nanguneri to consult Pakshi.

'He wouldn't disappear without notice. Perhaps he has fallen ill. I will ask Tirumalai to send someone to Courtallam to locate him.'

His unsaid thought was, 'Have I made a mistake by sending Nambi to his grandfather? Has he been bitten by the bug that bit my brother long ago? No, his world is here. His dreams are here. He is not one to run away. Something else has happened. Something terribly wrong. The moneylender family is not destined to make its truce with death.'

'You are not going back to your village, my child. Please stay here till the return of Nambi.'

'Thank you, thatha, but I have patients there to look after. I will have to return tomorrow morning.'

'I shall then ask Veda to come with you.'

How will she eat, thought Rosa. Will she eat in my house? Pakshi said, 'I know why you hesitate. She will cook for you. That will solve her problem.'

I need company, but I would not like that old lady to deviate from the path she has unswervingly followed all these years. Using my cookware and cooking in the kitchen where I have cooked meat would be too polluting for her to endure.

Rosa said, 'Thank you once again, thatha. On second thoughts, I will spend a few days with you. By then, Nambi should come back from his mysterious mission.'

Kannan and Muthu meticulously sieved the resort; they even enquired in the 'screw and scoot' joints, for which the resort was famous, as to whether anyone answering to Nambi's description had visited them a few days ago. They searched in the hospital and mortuaries of Courtallam and the nearby town of Tenkasi. They did not go as far as Punalur because it did not occur to them that Nambi might have gone there.

The pot overflowed with urine and excrement and the drain outside the cell was thick with black pestilential muck. The mosquitoes were fat and they wobbled above him, dizzy with blood. Still the cell was a relief. Torture had ceased temporarily. Probably the police had other less pleasant duties to perform. Nambi remembered Norman Bethune. Mao's *In Memory of Norman Bethune* was his favourite piece and he knew every word of it. He murmured to himself the last lines.

We must learn the spirit of absolute selflessness from him. With this spirit everyone can be very useful to the people. A

man's ability may be great or small but if he has the spirit,
he is already noble-minded and pure, a man of moral
integrity and above vulgar interests, a man who is of value to
the people.

Bethune's nobility remained unsullied because he was allowed to do what he wanted to do. His death was doubtless heroic, but he did not have to face the Kuomintang police. They could teach even our villains a trick or two. Where is my nobility? How can I feel noble when that fat constable pisses in my mouth? He would laugh if I tell him that I have so far been serving his class sincerely. He has become an animal drained of all humanity. Did Marx speak of such animals?

Am I weak? I don't know. I have so far resisted these brutes with dignity and with all the courage in my possession, but there must be some limit to human endurance, even a Communist's endurance. I have also been truthful but truth often wears the garb of lies and these idiots, so used to lies, do not recognise truth even when it comes in its own garb.

Had some spectators been watching this drama, had someone been here to tell the world later what I have gone through, my pride would at least have been salvaged. My heroism is now wasted. It is being enacted amidst mindless players and without any audience. Bethune was lucky. He had audience in abundance. What about Che, who died a rat's death in Bolivia? He was different. He crashed into his death willingly. His heroism was noticed after all. I am not willing, even if there were audience here.

Is this not a petty-bourgeois lamentation? These monsters have scratched me and I have been shown up for what I am. Hundreds of young persons have died in similar or even worse circumstances. What is so special about me?

Every person is special to himself. That one hundred others have suffered probably more horribly than I does not make any difference to what I am undergoing. Why should I suffer? Why did I embark on this journey, emulating Quixote? I never thought my experiences would be comical, but I never expected them to be brutal either. The result is the same. I am a brutalised Quixote. But my fireworks have no spectators. They ricochet between the walls of this cell before crashing to the ground.

The magistrate rubbed his unshaven chin, which screeched like a cicada. Human suffering did not appear to stir any emotion within him and he eyed Nambi's vandalised frame with bored indifference. Nambi's left eye was a blackened mess and he could open his right eye only with difficulty. His mouth was swollen and there was a wide gash across his cheek.

The prosecution lawyer began the case. 'Your honour, we have reason to believe that this person is a hard-core Naxalite. He came to Kerala to strike a massive arms deal. He has close connections with the Naxalites of Kerala. Earlier he had a meeting in Tamil Nadu with one of the absconding Naxalites, one Mukundan Menon.'

'Sir, these are lies. They arrested me when I was in Punalur on a sightseeing trip. I readily acknowledge my Communist sympathies, but I have nothing whatever to do with the Naxalites. I am a practising doctor in Tamil Nadu. What about my injuries, sir? Even if I am a Naxalite, which I am not, they have no right to treat me the way they did. I can hardly walk now. I demand a medical examination. I also demand a lawyer for my defence.'

'My child, you are in no position to demand anything,' said the magistrate softly. Turning to the prosecution lawyer, he asked, 'Do you want to interrogate him further?' The lawyer was all teeth and said, 'Yes, your honour. This person is a treasure house of information. He seems to know . . .'

'Two weeks in police remand,' snapped the magistrate.

'These fellows will finish me off,' shouted Nambi. 'Is this your justice?'

'It is, my son. Unfortunately, it is,' said the magistrate sadly. 'And it has just begun.'

The intellectual horizon of the Indian police generally remained dark, but Balachandran was one of the very few stars sparkling there and hence had easy recognition. Later, the great Jawaharlal Nehru University honoured him with a doctorate for his monumental, and some said dispassionate, thesis, 'Naxalism – the Kerala Experience'. In the seventies, he was a high-brow interrogation officer who specialised in suspected Naxalites.

'Please sit down, Dr Nambi.'

Nambi sat on the edge of the chair. It was impossible for him to sit properly. For the first time he was being addressed by a policeman without any reference to his ancestry or to his wife's private parts.

'I am Balachandran. I am sorry you had to undergo this, but our men were only doing their duty.'

'I never realised that the duty of a policeman extended to shoving a chilli smeared stick up his guest's rectum.'

'These fellows are apes, Dr Nambi. Evolution has passed them by.'

'Do the police specialise in recruiting apes? In any case apes are not torture artists, which your fellows are.'

'I understand your anger. I am here only to smoothen things out. I shall ask you some questions. Not personal ones. Intellectual, if you like. I would be grateful if you could reply to them truthfully, which I am sure you will.'

Nambi did not reply.

'Have you ever been to Calcutta?'

'Calcutta? No.'

'Did you visit any North Indian town recently?'

'Yes. I was in Joshimath recently. My grandfather's ashram is there.'

Balachandran changed tack. 'Have you read any of the periodicals of the Communist Party of India (Marxist-Leninist)?'

'Yes, many.'

'Can you name them?'

'Yes. *Mass Line. Liberation.*'

'Is there any other pro-Naxalite periodical you read regularly?'

'Yes, *Frontier.*'

'How do you get copies of them?'

'They are freely available in Tamil Nadu. It must be the same here in Kerala too.'

'Do you subscribe to their views? The views of the CPI (M-L).'

'No.'

'Why?'

'This is a funny question. Do you subscribe to their views? If no, why?'

'Dr Nambi, try to understand. I am not a Communist. You are supposed to be one. Your ideological duels are legendary. I am only trying to help you.'

'There are several reasons why I don't subscribe to their views. The foremost among them is their policy of annihilation of class enemies. They think this is linked to their other two grand tasks – those of liberating the Indian people and of ending imperialism. They are tragically wrong. They shall end up by annihilating themselves and a number of selfless young men in the bargain.'

'You are no doubt sympathetic to the Communist cause.'

'Yes, I am. You have said a moment ago that I am a Communist. I am.'

'What, according to you, is the character of the state?'

'The Indian state represents the interests of the bourgeoisie and landlord and is led by the big bourgeoisie.'

'This appears to the line of the CPI (M).'

'Maybe, but I am not a member of any organised Communist party. I have my differences with them on their assessment of Gandhi and on their antagonism towards the spiritual traditions of our civilisation.'

'Do you know Mukundan Menon?'

'I saw him for the first time when he came to Tamil Nadu. He came quite openly and we, my wife and I, had a few hours of political discussions with him. I told him clearly my views and he left my house accusing me of having a strong petty-bourgeois bias.'

'Did he tell you of his whereabouts in Kerala?'

'You know how secretive they are. Do you expect them to tell me, just an acquaintance, his whereabouts?'

'Who brought him to you?'

Nambi hesitated for a moment and said 'I have a cousin. His friend, a college teacher, a CPM member, brought him to me. As I said, Mukundan was moving freely in Tamil Nadu and we were not aware that the police were after him.'

Balachandran realised that Nambi was telling him the truth. There was no arrest warrant out for Mukundan when he visited Tamil Nadu.

The interrogation continued for three hours.

Balachandran said as a concluding remark in his long note to his superiors: *'The subject, Dr Nambi, has nothing whatsoever to do with the violent activities of the Naxalites. He appears to be a freelance Communist – one of the many cloth-headed ones our country is blessed with – who is full of hazy ideas and whose idea of revolution must be positively encouraged, primarily because it is never realisable. We ought not to disturb such persons, who live in a world of their own.'*

When he took his note to his superior, he said, 'Sir, we have a problem in hand. That brute Shanmuganathan has gone too far.'

'These scoundrels deserve Shanmuganathans.'

'Dr Nambi is not a scoundrel. He was working quietly among the poor of southern Tamil Nadu. He is only half-alive, thanks to the depredations of Shanmuganathan. His father, it appears, died in 1942 fighting the British. His appears to be an influential family of Tamil Nadu. When his story is out, the press is going to hound us.'

Balachandran's superior thought for a while.

'Well, Shanmuganathan started it. Let me allow him to finish it. We will have to support our officers, Balachandran. Even in the great Mahabharata war many innocent lives had to be sacrificed for the cause. We are all helpless victims.'

'We are not victims. Neither are we helpless,' Balachandran wanted to say, but the great traditions of the Indian police service which enjoined him never to contradict his superiors held him back. His conscience quivered for a few years before subsiding. No mention of this little episode can be found in his celebrated treatise on Naxalism. He probably forgot.

Balachandran elicited a promise from Nambi that he would not mention anything that had happened in the police station before the magistrate. Nambi readily agreed; he remembered only too vividly his earlier experience of the magistrate and his release went without a hitch. The magistrate even muttered, 'God bless you'.

It was Kannan who received the call from Nambi.

'Hello.'

'Hello, Nambi? Where are you speaking from? We are all so worried. Where have you disappeared? Rosa is shattered.'

'Relax, Kannan. I am unable to get through to Nanguneri. I will be leaving this place tomorrow morning, early morning, and should reach the village by noon. Would you please inform Rosa?'

'I shall be there to receive you. What has happened to you?'

'Not on the telephone, Kannan. I will tell you in person tomorrow.'

Kannan took a taxi to Tirukkurunkudi and informed Rosa of the news. Rosa accompanied him to Nanguneri to receive

Nambi. His grandparents were overjoyed to receive the news of Nambi's arrival and Pakshi even spoke to his grandson on that happy night.

Nambi's bus to Nagarkoil was scheduled to leave the bus stand early in the morning. He reached the place when the city was not fully awake. He had a glass of tea in a filthy tea stall at the bus stand and the attendant who served him later testified before the commission appointed to investigate Nambi's death that he did not see anyone following Nambi. His death was one of the many unsolved murders of the seventies. His body was found in an overflowing public lavatory with a single stab wound on the left side of his chest.

The police took five days to inform Nambi's family of his death. His post-mortem was performed by an experienced but inebriated mortuary attendant. The report was signed by the municipal doctor who was located, after a long search, in a marriage hall where he had gone to attend the wedding of his nephew. The doctor was annoyed that he was being asked to endorse a death certificate at an auspicious hour, and he was pacified only after the police told him that they had brought along a gold ring as a wedding present. The report did not speak of the wounds caused by Shanmuganathan simply because they did not cause Nambi's death. He quietly rotted on the cold floor of the mortuary, the wounds inflicted on him melting unrecognisably. He was handed over to the family – Kannan accompanied Rosa to Kerala – roughly packaged in palmyra leaves. The seeping gelatinous package could have been one of sweetened tobacco but for the smell, which made Kannan and Rosa change their initial decision of taking Nambi back to Nanguneri. He turned to ashes in an unknown cremation ground overgrown with prickly, dirty green weed.

Seventeen

AT NIGHT, HIS WAKEFULNESS WAS CRISP, dexedrine-induced and uncontaminated by sleep. The days were often groggy and coma-filled. He had just sixty nights. He would then know whether or not he would have to spend his life in Tirunelveli. Success in the examination would mean that he had burrowed an escape route from a place he had so dearly loved and which he had never wanted to leave. I gave up Uma in return for this place, he thought. Now every day here is hell for me.

The police came to him after Nambi's death. An old inspector and a constable saluted Tirumalai respectfully and said they would ask Kannan a few questions, and there was no need for him to go to the police station. Their questions on the meeting he had with Mukundan Menon in Nambi's house were cursory, but they were alert when they were on to the *Selected Works of Mao-tse-tung*. It was Mukundan who said all one had to do was to write a postcard to the Chinese embassy and they would send within ten days, in sturdy cardboard boxes, the four-volume edition of Mao's works. The books came when Kannan was away in Trivandrum for Nambi's cremation. He had not even opened them.

'Do you have the works of Mao with you?'

'Yes. A four-volume edition came when I was away in Trivandrum.'

'Did you order the books?'

Tirumalai intervened. 'Are Mao's books proscribed?'

'No, sir.'

'Then is it a crime to order the books?'

Kannan said, 'In any case, I did not order them. Perhaps my late cousin might have given my address for receiving the books. He was living in a village and he might have thought he would get them quickly here in Tirunelveli.' Nambi had never spoken a lie as far as I know. I am degrading him by using his name for a lie.

The inspector said, 'It is our duty to verify, sir.'

Tirumalai said coldly, 'Do you want to confiscate the books? I don't think they have even been opened.'

'No, sir. The books are yours.'

Tirumalai told Kannan after the police had left, 'If you had to lie, you could have used someone else's name. This was not expected of you.'

Immediately after the visit of the police, the Maos, the Lenins and the Marxes of Kannan ended up in Lakshmi Vilas. Though they made excellent paper-cones and wrappers for their delectable savouries and halwa, they were only worth eight annas a kilo after the cardboard covers were torn off. 'I thought they would fetch me at least ten rupees,' said the disappointed servant to Renganayaki. 'Without covers, the books were very light. The halwa-man gave me only three rupees for the entire lot.'

It was Tirumalai who tried vigorously to solve the Nambi mystery. He strongly suspected the hand of the Kerala police and it was due to his efforts that the Kerala government appointed a commission to inquire into the episode. Tirumalai did not miss a single day of the inquiry and when the commission returned a dud report he wrote angry letters to both the Tamil Nadu and Kerala governments. He filed a petition in the Kerala High Court against the commission's report which was promptly dismissed. Tirumalai would have had a heart attack if he had known that the Shanmuganathan who was awarded the President's Police Medal that year for distinguished service had had a role in Nambi's death. All governments keep such secrets well.

As expected, Kannan and Muthu were reinstated when the college opened after the vacations, but Kannan did not go back. He applied for leave and sat at home. Radha said, 'You could have done this last year and Uma would have been happy. You were not serious about her at all. Were you?'

Kannan said, 'I am not here to answer your questions. Yes, I was not very serious about her if that answer satisfies you.'

The ever-alert Radha could not fail but notice that his anger was feigned. 'You have to answer me, Kannan. I am meeting her in Bombay. She may still have some affection for you.' She was to leave for Bombay in a few days on her way to Ahmedabad where she was joining a management institute.

'I was serious about her, Radha. I don't think I am now. I have other ideas.'

She snorted, 'You and your ideas! You really are the prince of indecision. I am going to meet Rosa. Are you coming?'

'No. Convey my regards to her.'

Pakshi and Veda invited Rosa to stay with them, but she wanted to continue with her practice. Veda was able to find a good maidservant for her, to look after Indu when Rosa was in her clinic. The villagers remembered Nambi. They erected an ugly cement memorial to him which eventually became a convenient spot for buffaloes to rub their backs on.

Ponna was told of Nambi's departure, but she did not understand. 'Nammalwar's grandson? He is a child. He will surely come back. He is not like his grandfather.'

They were all waiting for the grandfather.

Kannan's examinations were at the Maharaja's College, Trivandrum. Its quadrangle screamed 'Viva la Vietnam'. He remembered that it was on a stormy day in Madras that Vietnam and the creed it stood for came into his life in a big way. They have made their exits with Nambi's death. I am now drained of the fervour I once possessed. The bombing of Hanoi and the mining of Haiphong are bits of information to be remembered for answering questions in the examination. They no longer invoke indignation.

Dexedrine had the last laugh. He was a zombie and he could not remember what he wrote. He had resigned himself to a lifeless routine at his college when Pakshi told him that his number had appeared among those who had been called up for interview.

That was the first time he had worn a lounge suit. The tailor had sewn needles into the seams at the crotch and they pricked him whenever he closed his thighs. The interviewers were in a foul mood.

'What are the main sources of energy?'

'What is Curie temperature?'

'What was Lord North's policy towards the American colonies?'

'Who was the second wife of Henry VIII of England?'

One Iyengar on the board asked him, 'Do you read books?'

'Yes.'

'Perry Mason?'

'No. I am now onto serious books.'

'Like?'

'I am now reading Sartre. His *Iron in the Soul*.' There are needles in my balls now, he thought.

'You couldn't find a better book to read? I don't know why godless literature appeals to our younger generation.'

He knew the interview was a disaster.

Nammalwar took more than six months to come to Tirunelveli. He spent a month in Pushkar and another in Brindavan. He was taken ill in Nathadwara, and it took him about two months to regain his health. He had long ago lost the habit of letter-writing – his one letter informing Pakshi of his existence was an aberration – and it did not occur to him to write to his grandson and inform him of his whereabouts.

He expected the Tirunelveli landscape to have changed beyond recognition, but he could still identify certain landmarks. An ugly over-bridge dwarfed the once majestic road connecting the Tirunelveli junction and town, but the road was very much there; so was the railway crossing. Lakshmi Vilas, whose halwa was his father's favourite, was still doing roaring business.

Tirumalai recognised him from a distance. The tall ascetic whose sprightly walk belied his great age must be my periappa, the periappa I have never seen. He went halfway to receive him and fell at his feet.

'I am Tirumalai, swami. Pakshi's son.'

'May you live to be a hundred. You could identify me easily. Yes, you have my grandson as a mark of my identity.'

Tirumalai started weeping quietly. Nammalwar said, 'What has happened? Have I said anything wrong?'

'Let us go to my house, swami. My father has come down from Nanguneri by chance.'

Pakshi has not lost much of his dense hair, Nammalwar thought, though it has greyed here and there. He has shrunk but has no loose flesh. God, we are indeed tough. Age hasn't yet won its battle against us. I want my grandson to follow in our footsteps.

Pakshi said, 'Come, anna. You have taken some time to return home.'

'Pakshi, I must thank you first. I saw my grandson. He is wonderful and it is because of you.'

Pakshi laughed bitterly. 'What is the use, anna? I brought him up only to gift him away to death.'

Years of ascetic practice were not proof against the shock of his brother's words. He was the only one for whom I would have sacrificed my self-absorption. Nammalwar sat quietly in a corner. Should I go back? This place has nothing left for me.

Pakshi said, 'His wife is anxious to see you. She has a beautiful child. You should visit them as soon as you can.'

'Who is performing the obsequies for Nambi?'

Pakshi now broke down. He said, 'It has become our tradition, anna. It was Tirumalai who performed the last rites of your son. It is again he who is taking care of your grandson's rites . . . We should not waste time. You must be eager to see amma.'

'Am I? To tell you the truth Pakshi, I was eager to see Nambi.'

He might have been a sanyasi all these years, but he has not shed his selfishness, thought Pakshi. 'I can read your mind,' said Nammalwar. 'You must surely be thinking what a self-centred fellow my brother still is. You are right. The shock of Nambi's departure is such that I am now filled with him. There is no space for anyone else. Not even amma.' He held his brother's hand. 'Give me a few days, Pakshi. I shall come around. I am not going to run away this time. I will see what he has left behind. I will of course see amma. She was the one with me before my grandson came along.'

The ascetic did not stay in Tirumalai's house. He chose a corner in the Varadaraja Temple to sit and meditate. He did not get the quietude he wanted in the temple. The entire town came to see him and receive his blessings. 'What a radiant soul!' they said. 'Only a man who has conquered all emotions could have attained such radiance.' They brought him fruits, flowers, milk and cashew nuts and there were many who wanted him to visit their house and purify them. There were invitations for lectures from the local Rotary and Lion's clubs and the colleges. They all came to know that he was a great scholar. Rosa did not come.

The gnarled mango tree of his childhood now covered a goodly portion of the garden. 'Is it the same tree? Or is it its child?'

asked Nammalwar. Pakshi said, 'It must be the same tree. I don't have any recollection of the mango tree being cut.'

The other house where my father's guests stayed has disappeared. It has become part of the house where I grew up. Amma is only a few yards away. Why am I dawdling?

Pakshi said, 'Let us go inside to her room.'

His mother was different. She must be lurking inside this wrinkled figure with a bristly head.

'Amma, amma. I am Nammalwar here.'

Ponna did not open her eyes. The touch was familiar. Nammalwar's grandson must have returned. She spoke slowly in a barely audible voice. 'Nambi, where have you been all these days?'

'Amma, I am Nammalwar.'

This time she did not speak, but rested her hand on his. After minutes of silence she said, 'I don't want your medicines. They are bitter. Please change them. Come to me often. I don't have many days.'

She refuses to recognise me. She feels my presence but she is angry. I shall keep coming to her until she finds me.

Pakshi was disappointed. I expected the pent-up emotions of sixty years to explode and envelop Nammalwar. This fellow walks away as he would if he had been calling on a convalescing acquaintance. It was just as well that she did not recognise him. She would have been heartbroken to see this unemotional apparition.

'Do you have any photographs of my son?' asked Nammalwar as he was coming out of his mother's room.

'Yes, anna. Veda has a big album of photographs that date back to your days. Madhu's photos are not many, but we do have a few of them.'

Even in this, Madhu was unable to find the middle-ground. In the few earlier photographs in which Pakshi was able to locate him, he was clinging to the edges, perilously close to being pushed out of the frame. The exception was the one taken on Ponna's sixtieth birthday; in that photo he was somewhat nearer the centre. He was the only one with a blank forehead, without the mandatory tiruman of an Iyengar.

'When did he lose his religion?'

'About the time when this photograph was taken.'

Nammalwar turned the leaves and spotted the one in which Madhu was with his wife.

'Was this mousy woman Madhu's wife?'

'Yes, anna. This is the only photograph we have of both Madhu and Kamala. She was not as bad as she looks in this photograph. She was a fine girl. Our family has always been fortunate in that respect. We all married exemplary women. Including your grandson Nambi.'

'Did Madhu feel my absence any time?'

'No, anna. Even as a boy he never felt your absence. He had stamped you out of his mind though amma was always trying to make you a living person for him. He did things in his own way and we never had the courage to stop him. Your presence would surely have steadied him . . . and Nambi.' Pakshi broke down and could not speak for a while. He steadied himself and said, 'It was not that they went astray. Both took straight paths that led them to their premature deaths. Madhu too, anna, was uncommon. I remember, it was 1940. The police made out a Communist conspiracy case here in Tirunelveli and rounded up the ringleaders. Madhu was to have been one of them. Kamala if I recall rightly was pregnant with Nambi. Fortunately the then superintendent, a white man, was known to me and I was able to convince him that Madhu was not rebel material, and eventually his name was dropped from the list. This, I later came to know, caused a few problems for Madhu in the party. He did not make an issue of it but he simply stopped discussing politics with me. He never did tell me what he was going to do when he went on that doomed venture to Sulur in 1942. In a way I feel I was responsible for his death. Had I not prevented his arrest in 1940 he would have discussed his plans with me in 1942, and maybe I could have stopped him. That was one of those rare occasions when Rajaji and the Communists were speaking the same language. Both were supporting the cause of the allies. Madhu chose that moment to break from the Communists and join the Quit India movement.'

The ascetic asked Paskhi in a soft tone, 'Do you still have with you my letter? The first one.'

Pakshi went inside his room and presently came back with an envelope.

"This is the letter you wrote to me when you left this place."

Nammalwar read the letter slowly, mulling over every word he wrote sixty years ago.

'Was I this cruel?' he asked Pakshi, who did not reply.

'Tell me Pakshi, did you show this letter to Nambi?'

'No, I did not show it to anybody. I didn't even tell amma.'

The ascetic held Pakshi's hands and said, 'I would have never seen my grandson if he had read this letter. You were alone, Pakshi. Alone all these years. Alone and helpless. But as Kamban says the helpless have everything. You still have everything.'

Pakshi did not look at his brother.

Nammalwar continued, 'I understand Madhu was a master of Kamban.'

'Yes, anna. He knew by heart at least five thousand poems. He liked the Pi.Na.Chi. edition. His Kamban volumes are still with me. He would underline the poems he had liked and write his comments on the margin.'

Nammalwar continued, 'I was reading one of Madhu's books. It was *Ainkurunuru*.'

'Your son was a fine scholar of Tamil.'

'Do you remember the ten poems on the tigerclaw tree?'

'The tigerclaw tree? Those *neytal* poems? I vaguely remember.'

Nammalwar recited in a low voice one of the poems on the tigerclaw tree. 'Pakshi, I distinctly remember I read these poems in the first Swaminatha Iyer edition under the shade of our mango tree. Those days . . . mm . . . those were the happiest days for me. I had just returned from Tuticorin after meeting

Chidambaram Pillai and I was under the illusion that Swaraj was knocking at the doors. Still, even then, these sad, forlorn, neytal poems of *Ainkurunuru*, these little jewels, which glisten like teardrops in the evening sunlight, were my favourite ones. The moods they evoked, the moods of anxious waiting, separation and grief, were so real to me. And this poem? This is the most exquisite of them all. And it appears it was Madhu's favourite too. He had underlined the poem and written on the margin "Our Story." Do you know this poem's meaning?'

'The *Ainkurunuru* Tamil is pretty tough, anna. It is difficult to unravel this poem.'

Nammalwar recited the poem again. 'Let me make a rough translation for you. Though it is like trying to make carbon out of diamonds.'

> *Friend, listen.*
> *I'll not think any more*
> *of that man on whose sandy shore*
>   *birds occupy the tigerclaw tree*
>   *and play havoc*
>   *with the low flowering branches,*
> *and my eyes will get some sleep.*

'Have you ever seen this tree?'

'Never. Even if I had, I would not have recognised it. But I have my own image of it. An image of a brooding, lonely tree whose branches are often plagued by birds. Unwanted birds.'

The ascetic continued. 'They say it is a love poem. To me it is a poem about our family. Our family is that tree, Pakshi. Mother must have been complaining to the Lord all these years about the birds playing havoc with its branches. When her husband died. When Madhu died. When Andal went berserk . . . Well, now I am sure she is not thinking any more of God, or the tree. Her eyes may have got the sleep they have been searching for.'

You are wrong Pakshi thought. When Madhu wrote 'Our Story', he must have meant his and his father's story, Pakshi thought. It is not surprising that my ascetic brother hasn't fully grasped what his son meant.

The tigerclaw tree. Is there only one tree? Nammalwar has his, I mine, and amma hers. The birds on my tree. Are they as raucous as the ones on Nammalwar's? Or the ones on amma's? I have been with her all these years. She is not the complaining type. She knows all such trees attract birds and it is the birds' business to cause havoc.

Pakshi said, 'I think we all have our personal trees, anna. Birds flock to some and ignore the others. That is what the Lord ordains. Amma surely knows this. Do you really think amma will complain? That too, for her personal happiness? Is there no difference between communicating with the Lord and complaining to him? I don't think she will ever regain her sleep.'

Nammalwar did not speak for a moment. Finally he said, 'You are right, Pakshi. You know her. I have lost her.'

The postman was ecstatic that Kannan had received a registered letter from the central government. He shouted Kannan's name when he reached Tirumalai's house, and demanded ten rupees for handing over the letter. Though his name was among the successful candidates it was so low on the merit list that Kannan had doubts about his getting a job with the government. He was wrong. There was some delay but he had won his freedom from Tirunelveli. He had been inducted into one of the many obscure services of the Government of India.

Nammalwar was playing with Indu when Kannan greeted him. 'Thatha, I have brought some good news. I now have a job with the central government. I am leaving for Delhi in a few days. I have come here to say goodbye to you and Rosa.'

Nammalwar touched Kannan's head and blessed him. 'I am sure you will do well. May you live long. May you be prosperous. Rosa is in her clinic.' The old man was still in his saffron attire. Like Yayati, he has usurped the years of his son and grandson, Kannan thought. Yayati spent his years seeking pleasure. This man, after robbing his progeny of their lives, has spilled them in the searing desert of asceticism. I hate him. He is responsible for Nambi's death.

Nammalwar did not stay with Pakshi. He came to Rosa and asked her if he could stay with her and his great-grandchild. Rosa was happy to have him in her house. She made him a request. 'Whenever you decide to leave us, please inform me. I must prepare myself for the loss. You are Nambi's past. I would like to keep you with me as long as I can.'

Nammalwar said, 'I don't think I shall ever leave this little girl, but one never knows. I promise you I won't disappear suddenly.'

When Kannan reached Rosa's clinic, she was consoling a dishevelled mother. She was wailing and telling Rosa incoherently that her child was dying.

'Touch the soft spot on his head, doctor amma. It sinks inward. My child is going to die. I trust in you like I trust in God. There is nobody who can save him but you.'

The mother was substantially right, Rosa thought. The child, already a victim of malnutrition, was severely dehydrated. Its eyes were sunken and lifeless, and its mouth dry. Rosa lifted the skin of the child's forearm between her fingers. She noticed that the skin-fold did not fall right back into its normal position.

'Do you have milk?' asked Rosa, though she knew the answer.

'No, I fed him only for a month and now I am completely dried up.'

Rosa told the mother what she should do almost mechanically. 'Take four soda-bottles of water and put eight spoons of sugar and a pinch of salt in it. If you have a tender coconut, add its water too. Keep feeding him this liquid two glasses every four to six hours. Even if he vomits, don't stop the feeding.'

From her blank look Rosa understood that what she had told the distraught mother was incomprehensible to her. She had the rehydration drink ready for such emergencies, and she handed over a bottle to the mother after extracting a promise that she would return the empty bottle the next day.

The mother did not leave. 'Don't worry. Your child will get well soon.'

'Amma, if you could give him an injection he will be cured immediately.'

Rosa did not lose patience with her. 'Listen, an injection will do him no good now. Bring him back tomorrow if he does not get well. We will think about an injection then.'

Rosa had not changed much after Nambi's death, except that her eyes were now kohl-free. She smiled and said, 'Everybody wants injections here. They think the needle is miraculous and a poke would make a dead man walk.'

Kannan said, 'This must be your routine. Were Nambi's patients different?'

'Oh, yes, he had tubercular patients, incipient lepers, drunkards with cirrhosis of the liver and VD-afflicted local heroes to contend with. I am at least easy with medicines. He never prescribed medicines unless it was absolutely essential. For minor illnesses he always suggested grandmother's remedies. He was very popular with the local medicine men because he told his patients with stomach aches and heartburns to get their medicines from them.'

'Where do they go now, his patients?'

'They have nowhere to go. It is difficult for me to treat male patients. They don't come with the truth before a woman. I can't cope alone Kannan, I can't.' She turned her face away from him.

Kannan said, 'It is tough for me too, Rosa. I hate to desert this place, but I feel incomplete without Nambi. I think it is far better to be incomplete elsewhere than where you were complete once.'

Rosa smiled. 'I have a choice, Kannan. When I was about fifteen, my father shifted our household; it was nothing much, just a transference from one murky shack to another, a few hundred yards away. My days then were short on thrills and seeing a place emptied of what once filled it and bestowed it with a distinct identity gave me a rare thrill. After my father loaded our belongings in the handcart, I went back in and I realised that a lived-in house could never be completely empty. My own odds-and-ends, scattered all over the shack, said many things about me. Even today a house or a room that has just been vacated excites me. It always has a bit here and a piece there of its earlier occupant and it is a nice little game to construct him or her in your mind from the debris. I routinely played this game in the hostel; my friends used to wait for a room to be vacated – a room in which a person unknown to me had been living – and they would come running to me and I would inspect the room minutely like a colonel on his rounds and come out with my opinion. I did that when I moved into our house with Nambi, and it greatly amused him to hear my rubbish-reading, as he happened to know the earlier occupant rather well. Nambi . . . he has shifted house now, God knows where. I construct him anew everyday in my mind. For a change, I have treasures to construct a person from.'

Her crutch, which she had stood up against the arm of her chair, slipped and fell with a thud. Kannan rushed to pick it up. It was not as heavy as he thought. 'Well, my problems have no end. What is the news from your side? Has it come, your entry-permit into the bureaucratic jungle?'

'It has, Rosa. At long last it has. I am leaving for Delhi in a few days.'

'Congratulations, Kannan. This is excellent news. Come on, I will make a special sweet to celebrate. I haven't made anything special so far for thatha either. He will also be happy.'

'Does he eat in your house? Amazing. You still cook meat in the house I am sure.'

'Yes. I do. He eats vegetarian food and he doesn't mind my cooking non-vegetarian food in the kitchen. I keep separate vessels. You must remember Kannan, that he has spent years in Bengal and the Northeast, where the Brahmins relish meat. Shouldn't we go? The old man must be hungry.'

'What is the hurry, Rosa? Does he like what you give him? He has been in the north all these years.'

She could sense that Kannan had not come to her to discuss the dietary preferences of Nambi's grandfather. He wanted to tell her something but was afraid. I am not afraid to ask him.

'What is it Kannan? Out with it.'

'What is what?'

'You want to tell me something. Don't linger. Get it out.'

'Yes, Rosa. I have something to tell you if you promise you won't mistake me.'

'Why should I mistake you? Come on, Kannan. Don't be bashful.'

'I don't know how to begin. I have been thinking about it since Nambi's death. I thought I would discuss it with you once my results were out. I can't postpone the discussion any longer. I want your decision quickly.'

Rosa waited for him to continue. He was abashed. She said, 'I know what is coming. You are going to ask me to marry you. Am I right?'

'Was I that transparent?'

Rosa sighed. She stood up and slowly walked to the window. Its curtains fluttered and she drew in the evening breeze savouring it for a moment. She came back and stood so close to Kannan he noticed that her elbow was dry and scaly. The redolence of her sweat was wholesome, like the fumes of earth after the first drops of rain. She said, 'Today I have cooked a special dish. It was my father's favourite. Smoked rabbit. We keep the meat for three days to soften it and then gently turn it over a wood fire till it acquires a delicious, smoky flavour. Nambi acquired a taste for it.'

Kannan said, 'You haven't answered me.'

'I guessed the question. It is your turn to guess the answer.'

Kannan was silent. Rosa ran her fingers through his shock of hair and said, 'I was joking, Kannan. Give me a few days to think over your unsaid proposal. Let us go home now and let me make some nice gulab jamuns for you.'

Eighteen

THE ASTROLOGER PEERED INTO HIS COWRIES for more than thirty minutes. He did not accept money, a factor that lent respectability to his pronouncements. One had to sit in front of him, bored and silent and suffocating in the incense-filled air of his minuscule windowless room. While gazing at his cowries, which leered like the teeth of a skull, he recited in an eerie and undulating whisper the names of gods, many of whom crowded the blackened walls of the room. His favourite was Bhagavati who he said regularly visited him in his dreams and bestowed on him prescient power. Everybody said he read the past accurately. On that premise, they presumed that he would be unerring on the future too.

'Your family had a history of violent deaths. Am I right?'

'You are right swami. The last one took place very recently,' said Tirumalai. Kannan received a sidelong glance from his father that suggested that Kannan's doubts about the predictive powers of the astrologer should now be laid to rest. One need not be an astrologer to say what he has said, Kannan thought. Our family is well known, so must be the broad outlines of its history.

'I have been informed so by Bhagavati. Years ago, one of your ancestors had committed an act of betrayal. It is the harvest of that betrayal you are reaping, generation after generation. The deaths will continue unless you propitiate the gods.' He suggested a series of sacrifices to be performed by the male members of the family.

'Are you serious appa? Surely you are not going to do what he has suggested, are you?' Kannan asked Tirumalai when they were returning home.

'Yes, I am going to do exactly what he has suggested. He certainly has powers. Otherwise, how was it he could speak of an unknown chapter of our family's past?'

'Come on, appa. Though he is now given over to Kerala ways, he is a Tenkalai Iyengar from our part of the district. The story of Dalavai Pillai's supposed betrayal must be known to everyone in our community. It was fairly popular even when I was a child, and my friends in Nanguneri frequently used it to blackmail me into submission.'

'You are impertinent. The sooner you get rid of your Communist mantle, the better it will be for you,' said Tirumalai angrily.

It was Pakshi who suggested that Tirumalai consult an astrologer because he was convinced that the family was accursed and the chances of its youngsters meeting with violent or unnatural ends were high. He said, 'I thought Madhurakavi's was the last of these deaths, but the evil spirits, it appears, have a long memory. Our Kurukkuturai Iyengar is a Bhagavati *upasaka* and you will do well to consult him. Don't stare at me like that, Kannan,' he continued. 'I am not sure, but I don't want to take chances with the unknown hangman. If there is some way of scaring him away from you till you come to your natural end, I am going to find it.'

'You are taking chances, thatha. The hangman is the scarer. He is not going to be scared by others.'

'The Iyengar may find a way. Bhagavati is powerful.'

The hall's floor was of fine mosaic with exquisite floral patterns, but its centre now had a deep sacrificial pit uglying it.

The pit, filled with sacred sticks, dried cow-dung cakes and rice-husk, was blazing with fire and the chanter-in-chief was stoking it through a blowpipe. The other priests sitting cross-legged around the fire were pouring ladles of ghee into it. They were chanting resoundingly and in unison the *yam kalpayanti* mantra from the *Rig Veda* to propitiate Pratyangira, an aspect of Durga, and to stir her up sufficiently to destroy the evil spirits that were buzzing around the moneylender family. They were also offering oblations to the departed members of the family, requesting them to protect the living. The heat was almost searing and Kannan found it impossible to stand near the pit. Streams of sweat flowed down his bare chest and drenched his veshti. His sacred thread was fresh and very white in contrast to the dark, dirt-encrusted ones of the other Brahmins in the hall. He had finally put on a sacred thread, symbolising his return to the Brahmin fold.

On the walls of the hall there were rows of framed photographs and portraits of his ancestors and relatives, both living and dead, looking uniformly ghostly through the shifting smoke. Krishna Iyengar and his murdered wife; the fat Raman and Ponna; Nammalwar and Lakshmi; Pakshi and Veda; Andal and her boy husband; Madhurakavi and Kamala; Tirumalai and Renganayaki; and Nambi and Rosa. Kannan was not familiar with any of the dead, except Nambi who he felt was still around. Is Nambi floating over the sacrificial fire, rubbing his eyes? Has his Marxist soul condescended to accept the oblations offered to it?

Rosa had politely refused to attend the function. She told Kannan, who went to invite her, that living in memories should not be confused with leading an ethereal life. She said, 'As far as I am concerned he is very much with us. But he is within me, within my mind. And within yours and his grandfather's. Don't reduce him to a wandering wraith needing frequent sustenance through sacrifices. He tried all along to veer you away from these spectacular and, if I may say, mindless rituals. It is ironic that his death drove you back to them. Anyway, your grandfather must be happy. His happiness is important and if you do all these to make him happy, I don't mind.'

Nammalwar too did not attend. He said, 'A soul like Nambi's will not hover around here, in the air. It will have reached the Lord's feet, never to be trapped again in the circle of births and deaths. That he did not believe in the Lord does not matter at all. What matters is the Lord's grace. I am sure the Lord has bestowed his grace on him. But I am surprised that Pakshi has come off his Tenkalai path and chosen the Vedic one.'

Pakshi had not deserted his Tenkalai faith, as Nammalwar thought. It was simply that he did not want to take any chances. In fact he even persuaded Kannan to undergo the *Panchasmaskara* ceremony, heralding his grandson's entry into the Srivaishnava community. The ceremony was performed by the Jiyar who before his sanyasa had taught literature in a Madras college. He was young and full of Srivaishnava fire.

'They all come back, Pakshi Iyengar, they all come back,' the Jiyar said when he was branding the shoulders of Kannan with the marks of Vishnu – the right shoulder with the *chakra* mark and the left with the conch mark. The branding marks attached to a long silver rod were also made of silver and were heated in a sacrificial fire kindled specially for the occasion. 'No human being can endure desolation for long. The creed that has kept Kannan ensnared so far is perhaps the most desolate of all the false credos that torment humankind. Only the Advaita Vedanta of Sankara reaches anywhere near it in its barrenness. I am happy that he has come back to the fold.'

'Don't be too sure. I am standing at the entrance. I may run away any time,' Kannan wanted to say as the sacred marks singed him, but he kept quiet. My scorched shoulders will heal in no time, he thought; the impressions of the marks will however remain. They may prompt me to come back, even if I run away.

Kannan's eyes were smarting and he came out of the hall to the backyard. Why have I become a reborn Brahmin? Am I afraid of dying prematurely? These rituals are for my long life and when it comes to my life, I don't want to take chances with forces of whose existence I am unsure. Am I selfish? Or conveniently undecided? If it gives me solace and if I am not using it to feather my nest, what is wrong if I turn to religion?

Kannan remembered the discussion Nambi had had with Mukundan Menon. Nambi said, 'We just don't take into account the cultural and spiritual longing of the people. Especially the longing of the exploited, in whose name we have hoisted the standard of revolt. The impression we give is that we are for a monoculture, and what is more, an imported monoculture. Our people are unlikely to accept such a culture, even if it brings benefits to them . . .'

'This is slander, Dr Nambi. We have never stated that we are for a monoculture. On the contrary, in the areas where we are strong, we speak the language of the local people and follow their customs.'

'I am not speaking of the areas where you are strong, which are not many. Take for example this place. Nobody will understand what we are talking about, because our idiom is so alien. We keep telling them to change without convincing them that we have a credible alternative. Ordinary people encounter injustice every day and they have evolved, over the years, their battle plans against it. Thousands of such mini-battles, unglamorous, dreary battles, are being fought here and everywhere. They communicate to God, personally and collectively, through the channels of their religion, the successes and failures of these battles. They do not expect an answer; their telling is enough. These channels are no doubt full of muck and a walk along their edges may at times be nauseating to us, but the stink does not bother the religious. We want to close these channels just because we feel we have found a better, superior channel. It may well be superior, but the people should first be convinced of its superiority. I know, it may sound shocking to you, but if people are happy with these channels, why should we shy away from them? We could use them for what we want to achieve. The diversions could be at the very end. We could also help the people to de-muck these channels. Take for example, Rosa's father. He was a member of the local Communist party, but he was also a regular singer in the local religious festivals. In his day, he had won many friends for us with his soulful songs.'

'Nambi, you are romanticising my father. He was not very happy about what he was doing and he did what he did for money,' said Rosa.

'You are missing my point, Rosa. He is known today to many of our villagers, and our comrades, first as a singer and only then as a Communist. If he had sung only for money, they would not have remembered him at all. He was unhappy because we had never told him that there was no dichotomy between what he was doing for money and what he wanted to do for his class. Religion in this country is a reality and it can't be wished away. If it could be used for our purpose in our fight against injustice, we must go ahead and shake hands with religion. This was perhaps what Gandhi attempted in an imperfect way.'

'Gandhi was a charlatan. Don't bring him into this,' said Mukundan in disgust.

'Perhaps he was. That is not what many ordinary people of this country think of him today and that is what counts.'

'I know scores of suffering people who reach for their knives when they hear the name of Gandhi,' said Muthu.

'No, Muthu, Nambi is substantially right. Gandhi's name is magic still. That we will have to concede,' said Rosa.

Menon said impatiently, 'The Gandhi conundrum will lead us nowhere and may finally render us inactive. Let us not waste our time on him. The problem, Dr Nambi, is that the religious embrace is usually fatal. You may begin well, but in the end your personal salvation may take primacy over other major issues, and you may find yourself far away from the ordinary people and their mundane problems.'

'That danger will always be there, but that is true of any movement, including the Communist movement.'

'Dr Nambi, my friends here say that your strong point is your clarity. I must say I find you hopelessly confused. You are nebulous about religion because of your own confused and chaotic social relationships. I am clear as to what religion stands for. It has always been an enslaving machine and there are no indications that it will ever change. Ordinary people are still its helots. It is the duty of every Communist to liberate them from this base, insentient state and to make them conscious human beings, who are able to live life without the support of what Bertrand Russell calls "comforting fairy tales". Your confusion is also because you have no first-hand experience of what struggle is all about. You have never worked beside the struggling workers and peasants. Don't stand outside and preach. Join a Communist party, Dr Nambi. Not necessarily my party. You may then be cured.'

'Thank you for your prescription, Mr Menon, but I still think religion has a progressive role to play in the onward march of humanity. Comforting fairy tales are necessary during the period of transition and religion provides them in abundance. Our loathing of religion and our refusal to recognise its positive aspects will only alienate us from the people. As for my joining a party, I don't think I ever will. You do require sympathetic preachers outside the flock. Well, it is impossible to exhaust scholarly arguments on this theme. Good luck to you, Mr Menon.'

Nambi spoke of the religion of the deprived people. Surely propitiating Pratyangira was not in his scheme of things? Would he have shaken hands with Brahminical religion? Would he have approved of its ghee-guzzling rituals? Are they not the muck he was talking about?

Tirumalai shouted that the sacrifice was nearing its end and Kannan went back to suffocate in the heat.

Bala was happy that Kannan was leaving Tirunelveli. He said, 'Our boys must move out. You have taken a correct decision.'

Kannan asked him, 'Sir, are you sorry that your path appears less crowded now?'

Bala did not reply immediately. He pulled out a book from his compact bookshelf. 'This is Edgar Snow interviewing Mao. Listen to Mao. "There are two possibilities. There could be continued development of the revolution towards Communism, the other possibility is that youth could negate revolution . . . But future events would be decided by future generations, and in accordance with conditions we cannot foresee. From the long-range view, future generations ought to be more knowledgeable than we are . . . Their judgment would prevail, not ours and they would assess the work of revolution in accordance with values of their own. In a thousand years from now all of us, even Marx, Engels and Lenin would possibly appear rather ridiculous".'

Bala continued, 'I would naturally not like you to forget what we and your cousin Nambi dinned into you, but if you do, I won't lose sleep over it.'

'Are you sleepless over Nambi's loss?'

'Who wouldn't be? But I had a sort of premonition that something like this would happen to him. I know I am not talking like a Marxist but that was how I felt. His father had around him a similar ring of death.'

His grandfather is immortal, Kannan wanted to say.

He touched his right ankle gingerly. It was swollen, but the pain was not severe. The mishap at the railway station had upset Renganayaki so much that he had to promise her that he would visit the Parthasarathy Temple in Madras before boarding the train to Delhi. He usually tripped on inconsequential things, but this time he stumbled on a huge iron girder lying on the platform. One moment he was waving to his friend Muthu whom he had recognised from a distance and the next he lay sprawled face down on the platform. His spectacles did not crack this time. Rosa was there and it was she who fished out a crepe bandage from her handbag to dress his ankle with. While ministering to him, she quietly slipped a letter into his shirt pocket.

This was the first time he was travelling first class and his cubicle was empty. Other passengers would board at Madurai, the ticket examiner assured him. He was happy that he could stretch his leg out. He had two letters to read.

Dear Kannan,

I must apologise to you for communicating through a letter, when a simple 'yes' or 'no' to your face would have been perfectly all right with you. But I thought I should give you written reasons for my decision, first because your decency deserves respect and secondly because, as a hidebound Marxist, I revel in debates and my letter may start a juicy one.

My answer is no. It is not due to Nambi. Of all his friends – he hadn't many – you were the closest and he must have told you many things that he hadn't told me. We could have lived together feasting on his memory. That was probably why you had offered to marry me in the first place.

Marrying you will mean my leaving this village and the closure of my clinic. The very purpose of my taking up medicine was to make a beginning in cheap and good health care in these parts and I don't want to forgo it for the pleasure of marrying you. Nambi would not have liked it.

The second reason is personal. I am older than you at least by ten years. I was older even than Nambi, though he was my senior in the college. I first went to school at the ripe age of ten. As a youngster, your needs are likely to be different from mine and, though I know you will be accommodating enough not to advertise them in my presence, I want you to

*lead a healthy, happy and yes, uncomplicated life. Your
tagging along with me may make things terribly complicated.
Radha has written to me that Uma still remembers you. She
will be the ideal choice.*

*These are my first thoughts. If I change my mind and
if you are still available, it will be I who will take
the initiative.*

*My saying 'no' now does not mean that we should stop
corresponding.*

With love,
Rosa

Rosa's no is welcome. She is too cold-bloodedly logical to
make a good, lifelong companion.

He received the other letter six months ago. The handwriting
on the cover was not familiar but inside the cover was a letter in
a familiar hand. It was written in pencil, obviously a blunt one,
which coarsened Nambi's usually fine hand.

Dear Kannan,

*I haven't written to Rosa. Though she has a courageous
visage, she is quick to take fright and my condition is
frightful. I have one good person among the monsters who
take turns to torment me and it is he who has given me this
sheet of paper and a pencil. He will wait for some time
before posting it. He has to save his skin.*

*I have been thinking about the life I have led so far.
Others might say it has been a worthy one. One's worthiness
is always measured by others. But I suddenly realise it has
never been worthwhile to me or to Rosa personally. What is
the use of this self-flagellating existence? What is the use of
living for an idea that will never be realisable or of serving
people who have an idiot's memory? As the dark shadow of
death blocks the sunshine from me, I remember what thatha*

told me when I asked him about his lack of courage in the face of oppression. He said, 'Your courage grows bonny on victories. Defeats make it a horrid skeleton and its rattles induce such disgust in you that you discard it at the first available chance. It is given to rare personalities to live in harmony with defeats in the hope of possible victories in future. That I am not one of those rare persons is not a cause of shame. The Lord shaped me this way and I have no complaints.' I have been under the illusion so far that I am one of those rare personalities. I have no such illusions now, but my crazy existentialist mind does not accept anyone as my potter.

Potters, if they exist, have always been capricious. No, not capricious. They have been consistent. I think it is in King Lear that one of the characters – Edmund, if my memory serves me right – says 'Now, gods, stand up for bastards.' They have always stood up for bastards. Only bastards.

What I have written above is probably nonsense. It is certainly agony-induced. After a good bath and a hearty lunch, it might read intolerably mushy even to me. If I am lucky, we may get a chance to read it together and assess its contents dispassionately. This letter is only for you and not for circulation. Rosa need not know that I have developed a soft underbelly. The light of life may steel it again.

With love,
Nambi

Kannan debated endlessly when he received the letter whether or not to show it at least to Tirumalai who was desperate for clues relating to Nambi's murder. Kannan finally decided against showing it to his father, for though the letter suggested his detention it did not provide any positive clue as to the identity of his tormentors. On the other hand, he thought, the clues it gives about Nambi himself should remain unrevealed.

The train had reached Koilpatti. There was bluster in the air and it gave purpose to the scampering passengers. The distant trees shivered in the wind. The glass of his window gathered fat, fickle pearls of water. Once, I waited for Uma on this station. I shall write to her when I reach Delhi. She may respond. I have finally done what she wanted.

He felt his ankle. There was no pain and the swelling appeared to have drained away. Should I remove the bandage? Or should it remain?

Gods may also stand up for the undecided.

Glossary

Adhyabaka padi: Chanter's fee.
Adi: The fourth month of the Tamil calendar, usually falling between 15 July and 14 August.
Adiyen: 'I am your foot', meaning 'I am your humble servant'. A form of address between male Vaishanavas.
Ainkurunuru: 'The Little Five Hundred'; this is a collection of short poems in the Sangam corpus of Tamil literature, written between the second century BC and the second century CE.
Amavasya: New moon.
Angavastram: Cloth used by South Indian males to cover the upper part of the body.
Anna: Older brother.
Appa: Father.
Appalam: Rice and lentil paste made into rounds and dried in the sun, then roasted or fried to make an excellent, crisp snack.

Appam: Hopper.
Avial: Vegetables cooked in curd.
Chakra: A disc-shaped weapon often depicted in Vishnu's hand.
Charkha: Spinning wheel.
Chithappa: Refers to either father's younger brother or mother's younger sister's husband.
Chithirai: The first month of the Tamil calendar.
Darbha: A grass belonging to the *Borage* family used by Brahmins for religious rites.
Dhammapada: Loosely translates as 'The Path of Eternal Truth' and refers to versified Buddhist scripture ascribed to Buddha himself.
Gadyathryam: 'The Three Works of Prose'; a religious work written in the eleventh century CE by Sri Ramanuja, the foremost of the Vaishnava acharyas (teachers).
Gandharva: Genie.

Gandharva Ganam: The Song of the Genie.

Gopuram: An ornate tapering tower usually at the entrance of a South Indian temple.

Gurukulam: 'The extended family of the teacher'. An ancient model of schooling in which students stay with their teachers for years, often in the same house, in order to learn the Vedas and other religious texts.

Idiappam: String hoppers.

Jiyar: The religious head of the Vaishnavas.

Kallu: Can mean stone, precious stone, toddy, or liquor.

Kamban Ramayana: The version of the Ramayana written by Kamba.

Kanakku pillai: Accountant.

Kar: Rainy season.

Kathasaritsagara: 'An Ocean of the Streams of Stories'; it is a collection of stories written by Somadeva in the eleventh century CE.

Keerai: Spinach.

Kolam: Floral, geometrical or pictorial patterns drawn, usually with rice powder, at the entrance of a house by any female member of the house.

Kumara Sambhava: 'The Birth of Kumara'. A book of verses in Sanskrit written by Kalidasa in the fifth century CE.

Kunkumam: Vermillion powder applied by Hindu women at the parting of the hair or at the centre of the forehead.

Kuravas: A nomadic tribe, whose members used to scrounge through refuse bins for leftovers.

Maravas: A warrior community from southern Tamil Nadu.

Marudu: *Terminalia Arjuna*; the Arjuna tree.

Matam: The residence of the religious head of the Vaishnavas (the Jiyar).

Mlechhas: Non-Vedic people, foreigners, barbarians.

Mumukshupadi: 'The book for one who desires Moksha' this is a didactic work written in the thirteenth century CE by Pillai Lokacharaya, one of the great Vaishnava teachers of the Tenkalai school.

Neytal poems: Poems on the sea, the shore and the people who live on shore.

Paati: Grandmother.

Padmasana: The Lotus Posture. A yoga posture.

Paiya: A boy.

Palla: One of the largest Dalit communities of Tamil Nadu.

Pallandu: 'Many Years' (a shorter version of 'may you live for many years'). Twelve poems in praise of Vishnu written by Periyalwar, one of the twelve Alwars (poet saints).

Pallankuli: A traditional Mancala game played in South India; a wooden board with fourteen pits has to be filled with counters that can be cowries, seeds or pebbles.

Pambadams: Heavy ear ornaments worn by women

of certain communities of Tamil Nadu.

Panchasmaskara: Five purification rituals that signify initiation into a Vaishnava clan. They are:

1. Thapa – scalding the forearms with the emblems of Vishnu (the conch shell and the disc).
2. Pundram – wearing the tiruman at twelve places on the upper part of the body.
3. Namam – being named *Ramanuja Dasan* (a servant of Ramanuja).
4. Mantram – initiation into the recital of three secret texts.
5. Ijyai –learning the rituals for daily worship of Narayana.

Panguni: The last month of the Tamil calendar.

Parottas: A layered South Indian flat bread.

Paruppu: Cooked tuar lentils.

Peria paati: Great-grandmother.

Peria thatha: Great-grandfather.

Peria Tirumoli: 'The Big Sacred Word'. A work by Tirumangai Alwar, one of the twelve Alwars.

Periamma: Mother's elder sister or father's elder brother's wife

Periappa: Father's elder brother or mother's younger sister's husband.

Poligar: a corruption of Palayakkarar, which means a chieftain of a Palayam (locality).

Pongal: A Tamil harvest festival that takes place in January.

Pottu: The dot at the centre of the forehead.

Prabandham, (Naalaayira Divya Prabandham): A collection of four thousand sacred hymns, written by twelve Vaishnava saints, collectively known as the Alwars, before the eighth century CE.

Prasadam: Food first offered to the Lord and then to the devotees.

Praveen: The final examination in Hindi proficiency conducted by the Hindi Prachara Sabha, an association which aims to propagate Hindi.

Puliyodarai: Tamarind rice.

Pushpaka vimana: Flying chariot.

Rakshasis: Female demons.

Saiva pillai: A member of one of the Siva-worshipping upper castes of Tamil Nadu.

Sakkarai pongal: Rice mixed with jaggery.

Salagram: A black fossil-stone considered to represent Vishnu.

Sanyasi: One who has renounced.

Sarvanaga kshavaram: Shaving of all parts of the body.

Shudras: Those belonging to the fourth and lowest caste – the ones who toil.

Sisupalavadha: 'Slaying of Sisupala'; the title of a Sanskrit book of poems written by Magha in the eighth century CE.

Sri Vachana Bhushanam – 'The Holy Ornament of Utterances', a religious text written in the thirteenth century CE by Pillai lokacharya, a great acharya of the Tenkalai sect.

Sumangalis: Married women with living husbands.

Swadesamitran: Translates as 'Friend of my Nationalist' – a nationalist Tamil daily.

Taluk: An administrative division of a district.

Tarpanam: Religious offering to the dead.

Teri: An arid region known for its red sands.

Thambi: Younger brother.

Thatha: Grandfather.

Thirukkural: 'The Beautiful Couplet'. A famous book of couplets in Tamil written by Tiruvalluvar, around the fourth century CE.

Thivatti Kollaikarars: Robbers who carry burning torches.

Tiruman: The sacred marks worn by male Vaishnavas on the forehead and upper part of the body.

Tiruppavai: 'The Sacred Doll'. A collection of thirty poems written by Andal – the only woman among the twelve Alwars.

Tiruvaimoli: 'The Sacred Word of the Mouth'. Collection of theological poems illuminating the glory of Narayana, written by Nammalwar, one of the twelve Alwars. It is considered the essence of the Sama Veda by Vaishnavas.

Tomato satramudu: Tomato rasam.

Upasaka: An attendant.

Uppuchchar: A stew of tamarind, lentil, gingili, and vegetables.

Uthappam: A thick savoury pancake.

Vadais: Spicy doughnut-like fritters made of lentils.

Vaithiyar: Local doctor.

Vande mataram: 'Salutations to the mother' – a mode of greeting amongst Indian nationalists, since mother here alludes to the motherland.

Varagarisi: A mélange of roasted pulses and cereals.

Vazhaikkai karatamudu: Plantain curry.

Venum: I need.

Veshti: South Indian dhoti

Vishnu Sahasranamam: 'The Thousand Names of Vishnu' a well-known hymn found in the Mahabharata.

Vyalas: A composite leonine sculpture in Indian art; could be a lion with the head of an elephant, a bird or any other mythical creature.

Vyasa Bharata: The version of the Mahabharata written by Vyasa.

Yam Kalpayanti: A mantra from Rig Veda.